浙江省2005年新世纪高等教育教学改革项目
浙江省高校人文社科重点研究基地
（外国语言文化）大学英语教材丛书

中国媒体英语阅读

主　编　杨新亮　段汉武

副主编　杜小红　张　琳　韩俊平

编　写　邬蔚群　柳　旦　周玉顺

U0105707

国防工业出版社

内 容 简 介

　　全书共 24 单元,每单元包括导读、重点提示和语篇阅读三个部分。导读部分旨在从心理学和语言学的不同角度引导读者如何阅读语篇,如何习得语境词汇知识和新闻语篇的交际功能;重点提示部分以黑体形式提醒读者从哪些方面预测和掌握语篇信息和语言知识;所选语篇涉及与中国的政治、经济改革与发展、对外贸易、旅游、体育等相关的新闻语篇,按同域主题进行编排。

　　本书涵盖了反映中国及当今国际社会不同领域的 16 个主题,教师在教学过程中,可依据不同的社会现实背景按每周两个课时安排一个主题的教学。英语爱好者以本书为读本,可在语境中提高阅读能力。

图书在版编目(CIP)数据

　　中国媒体英语阅读/杨新亮,段汉武主编.—北京:
国防工业出版社,2007.1
　　ISBN 7-118-04900-X

　　Ⅰ.中… Ⅱ.①杨…②段… Ⅲ.英语－阅读教学－自学参考资料 Ⅳ.H319.4

　　中国版本图书馆 CIP 数据核字(2006)第 146348 号

※

国防工业出版社出版发行

(北京市海淀区紫竹院南路 23 号　邮政编码 100044)
京南印刷厂印刷
新华书店经售

*

开本 850×1168　1/32　印张 10¼　字数 285 千字
2007 年 1 月第 1 版第 1 次印刷　印数 1—4000 册　定价 21.00 元

(本书如有印装错误,我社负责调换)

国防书店:(010)68428422　　　　发行邮购:(010)68414474
发行传真:(010)68411535　　　　发行业务:(010)68472764

序

随着现代信息技术的不断发展,英语报刊媒体的传播趋向国际化,传播渠道也日益多样化、快捷化。中国作为正在崛起的政治、经济、文化大国,对外开放程度不断提高,对外宣传和交流日益扩大,从而形成了反映中国特有文化背景的媒体传播渠道,其中英文报刊、杂志和网络已初具规模,构成了对外宣传和交流的庞大媒体系统。同时,也为中国的外语教学提供了丰富翔实的新闻语篇资料。目前,报刊英语已成为众多高校英语专业和非英语专业的必修课和选修课,对外语教学起到了重要的促进作用。然而,多以英美报刊资料为教学内容,对于英语专业而言问题不大,而对于非英语专业的学生就显得太难了。因此,国内日益成熟的英文媒体受到了外语教育界的关注,并在一定程度上进行了可行的、有益的尝试,取得了可喜的成就。为满足越来越多的英语学习者的需要,笔者依据近几年的教学经验和所积累的丰富英文媒体资料,系统地编著了《中国媒体英语阅读》一书。

本书充分依据现代认知心理学、认知语言学和心理学的研究理论,系统地编排阅读语篇,科学地引导读者阅读和学习中国新闻英语,从而提高语言知识和技能。全书共24单元,每单元包括导读、重点提示和语篇阅读三个部分。导读部分旨在从心理学和语言学的不同角度引导读者如何阅读语篇,如何掌握语篇系统,如何习得语境词汇知识和新闻语篇的交际功能;重点提示部分提醒读者从哪些方面预测和掌握语篇信息和语言知识;丰富的新闻语篇主题的一致性、编排的系统性、语料的充裕性和黑体衔接词汇的网络性加强了语篇语料的输入和输出。

语篇内容的选取和编排具有较强的系统性和科学性。所选内容涉及与中国的政治、经济改革与发展、对外贸易、国际交流、社会焦点、旅游、体育等相关的新闻语篇,按同域主题进行编排。对反映语篇连贯和衔接的词汇项进行黑体形式的强调处理,以此提醒读者新闻语篇和词汇网络性的关系,加强读者词与篇的有机结构意识,提高阅读和学习效率。

全书涵盖了反映中国及当今国际社会不同领域的 16 个主题,教师教学过程中,可依据不同的社会现实背景按每周两个课时安排一个主题的教学。教师可要求学生课外浏览相关的英汉媒体,了解和掌握丰富的背景资料,课内充分利用多媒体教室和网络的优势,以现实的新闻媒体视频资料,如新闻、对话、今日亚洲等 Mp3 视频资料做问题导入,激活学生的心理背景知识。结合中国新闻媒体英语的篇章结构,培养学生以事实为依据思考现实问题的习惯,从而养成关注现实、思考问题、正确面对现实并树立科学的人生观和价值观。

本书属浙江省教育厅编号为 yb05034 的 2005 年新世纪高等教育教学改革项目"大学英语课堂教学与网络自主学习"整合的成果,由宁波大学外语学院杨新亮、段汉武老师总体策划和审校。在编著过程中,得到了宁波大学外语学院大学外语部及郑州大学诸多同事的指导和帮助,在此向他们表示由衷的感谢。

由于该书内容丰富,信息含量大,语料领域广泛,编著过程中难免有不足之处,敬请读者批评指正。

段汉武

前　言

随着中国对外改革开放的不断深入与国际交流空间的扩展，中国媒体的对外宣传也在不断加强。随之产生的具有中国特色的多媒体英语，如 *China Today*，*China Daily*，*Beijing Review*，*Chinese Literature*，*The 21st Century* 等报刊杂志以及中央电视台第九频道和第四频道的英语新闻节目，从不同方面宣传中国的政治、经济、社会发展、民族风情等，展示中国悠久的历史文化和改革所取得的成就。中国媒体英语在加强对外宣传、促进世界了解中国的同时，也为中国的英语教学提供了丰富的语言素材。本书拟从语言教学的角度探讨中国媒体英语教学的可行性及其教学效益。

中国媒体英语的特征

首先，中国媒体英语除报道国际新闻、海外风情之外，主要是反映中国的社会文化、政治经济、风土人情、秀丽河山、历史遗产等。而且不同的媒体具有不同的偏重，*Beijing Review* 以中国的政治、经济政策和发展动态为主；*China Today* 则以中国民族风情、自然景观、历史文化为主；*The 21st Century* 以世界热点、中国商情、语言教学、高教与就业为主，面向中国数百万高校学生。以中国社会为背景的媒体英语，在内容和形式上都具有较强的"中国文化"特色。

其次，媒体英语的专栏性特征也同样反映在中国的英文报刊杂志中。同国外期刊一样，定期发行与社会的发展同步，及时反映社会变化，适应信息时代的要求。各媒体以相对固定的栏目，从不同的社会视角追踪报道中国社会的各个方面，所以，其语言风格、词汇选择的倾向性也就相对一致，即某一语域的词汇同现频率就比较高，有利于语言词汇的认知与巩固。如 *Beijing Review* 自然景观类栏目,固定刊登对中国黄山、武夷山、长江两岸旅游、黄河文化巡、丝绸之路风情、美丽的热带雨林西双版纳、道教名胜武当山等的描述。这里不仅可以同现描述山河壮丽、秀美的语言词汇,而且具有许多反映中国历史文化传统底蕴的"特有"的语言表达,如beauty spots, scenery, scene, scenic spot, attractions, landscape, beautiful, charming, spectacular, attract, charm, the Silk Road, Taoist, Taoism 等。

再次,中国媒体英语与汉语媒体在内容上具有一定的同步性和协调性。由于中国媒体英语的目的在于对外宣传中国,因此其内容与汉语媒体保持着一定的一致性。尤其是在政治、经济、外交事务、国际形势等领域,英汉媒体以不同的语言形式,传播同样内容的事实信息。同时,现代电子技术的应用,融声像为一体,更富有真实性和形象性。随着现代科技的发展,中央电视台电影频道、英语频道和国际频道充分利用现代媒体技术,形象、生动、真实地传播和宣传发展中的中国,向世界展示中国源远流长的历史文化、自然景观,让世界了解中国的过去、今天和未来。同时也为现代多媒体教学提供了方便快捷的声像资料。

媒体英语与英语教学

中国媒体英语以中国社会文化为背景,符合阅读过程中的"图式理论"。背景知识是影响阅读理解的十分重要的因素,它是指一个人已有的整体知识,即各种经验的学习与积累,以及有关某一专题的专有知识,即理解某一主题所必需的专门知识。先验图式论认为,语篇只是为读者或听者提供一个引导,指示他应如何根据自己已有的知识去获取或理解意义。只有当读者把自己已有的"经验图式"与语篇提供的语言文字信息联系起来,理解才能实现。这种背景知识以特定结构储存在大脑中,构成相互联系的"先验图式"。在阅读过程中,读者的先验图式与阅读语篇越吻合,阅读理解就越容易,反之则越难。中国媒体英语与中国读者的先验图式在很大程度上是吻合的,这不仅取决于他们生长于这个社会,而且汉语媒体不断强化了他们的各种知识图式。因此,中国媒体英语具有较高的可读性和预测性。

由于中国学生已有的背景文化知识，在学习目的语、阅读目的语文化语篇的过程中，往往存在"文化盲点"。中国学习者在交际过程中，其交际内容往往具有中国文化的渊源，目的语表达潜意识中就需要一个转换的过程。在此转换过程中，经常会遇到"文化或语言上的冲突"。这不仅造成了理解上的障碍，更重要的是不利于语言思维能力的培养。再者，如果语篇主题读者不感兴趣，那么就很难实现教学目的。中国媒体英语则消除了这种语言"文化盲点"，便于学生的阅读理解。而且，在语言的应用过程当中，也避免了"潜意识"翻译的过程。媒体英语广泛的题材范围，都与学习者关注的"热门话题"相关，符合读者交际"动机"的需要，易于调动读者的学习兴趣和积极性。

媒体英语专栏性的编排，符合语义关联的语言特征。语言词汇的"语域"理论和"板块式"结构认为，同一语域的词汇倾向于出现在同一主题的语篇中。现代语言学家利用电脑数据统计分析发现，英语的语言交际并不是仅仅通过单词或固定短语的使用来实现的，而自然话语中的 90% 是由处于两者之间的半固定"板块"结构来实现的。语言学家 Becker 认为："我们根据自己想要表达的信息，从大脑的词汇库中调出那些'预制'(prefabricated) 短语，经过细微的加工，就可组合成比较符合语法的句子，并使它们变成流利的语言来填充我们概念上的某些空白。即语言的记忆与储存和输出或使用并不是以单个的词为单位，而那些固定和半固定的模式化了的'板块'结构才是人类语言交际的最小单位。"而媒体英语的"主题块式"专栏结构，不仅有利于"块式"语言词汇的学习和记忆，而且有利于"块式"词汇的调用和激活。

媒体英语的教与学

中国媒体英语独特的社会背景特征和目的语风格，符合现代语言学习的认知理论及教学需求。这一点在我们长期的教学实践中已得到充分的证实。传统的教学以目的语语言材料为主，从而忽略了日益普遍的反映中国社会的媒体英语。当然我们并不否认目的语教学,重要的是探讨如何充分利用中国媒体英语解决教学中一些困扰学习者的"文化盲点"和"交际转换"中存在的问题,提高教学效益。

媒体英语教学应以"主题"和"时事焦点"阅读为主,这是由中国学生的背景知识来决定的。在当今信息社会,媒体传播形式日益多样化,信息的重复和出现频率不断提高。市场经济对人才的选择强化了学生关注社会的意识,他们从不同的渠道了解社会信息,增强背景知识图式。以此为依据选择学生关注的媒体英语资料,既增加了可读性,又符合学生了解社会的需要。同时在语言学习的渴望中,交际的需要得到满足,学习兴趣得以培养,能动性得到充分发挥。主题教学应"追踪事实焦点",以课堂阅读和课外学习相结合,要求学生课下结合课堂教学,从不同媒体大量阅读同一主题的语篇,掌握反映主题的不同角度和观点。按主题分类收集相关词汇,做到主题与表达的统一。如"人大"与"政协"两会"热点",暑假前的"旅游专线"阅读,毕业在即的"就业报道"等。

媒体英语辅助相关的课堂教学,如口语、大学英语、泛读等以目的语文化为主的教学。在现代交际教学为主的课堂上,学生交际存在的问题之一是语言知识与内容表达在文化上的不协调,以及大脑所储存的词汇缺乏"文化主题性"。学生往往能够理解课堂上所学习的语篇,而在做同一主题的交际练习时,语言编码转换的过程因受到语言及社会文化差异等因素的影响,而导致"交际的失败"。为解决这一难题,本书作者尝试比较目的语文化语篇教学与中国媒体英语教学的过程及结果,发现学生利用媒体英语交际的流利程度、语篇长度和语感能力远胜于教材中的目的语文化语篇。因此,结合目的语文化主题教学,充分发挥中国媒体英语的相关作用,可有效地提高整体语篇及口语教学效果。

媒体英语教学以交流和讨论为主,在语言应用的交际过程中巩固语篇结构概念和语言词汇知识,培养学生的交际能力。由于学生对媒体英语的背景知识比较熟悉,阅读理解没有太多的问题。因此,老师的任务在于引导学生如何组织主题与词汇的系统性,把词汇形成"块结构"进行记忆,即以主题→分主题→领属同义、近义、反义等相关词汇为整体教学模式,完成主题→词汇结构建构教学。以此为基础开展指导式和自由式的口语交流与讨论,对建构结构进行巩固与强化,形成牢固的"主题图式"和"块式词汇"知识。例如:

主题 沙尘暴 Sandstorm

↓

袭击北京及中国北方和西北←→原因→attribute to, cold fronts, expanding deserts→due to economic activities, logging, strip mining, blind expansion of crop lands

↓

shroud, sweep down, swirl, strike, engulf

sudden, violent, yellow, arid

sand, grit, dust

以此为主题要求学生课下阅读和收集相关媒体资料,引导他们联系环保主题展开讨论,找出更多的原因、危害及解决的办法,从而形成更大的主题图式和语言知识结构。

Contents

Unit One
Holidays and Celebrations (I)

导　读

　　语言交际既是语言能力的体现又是文化背景知识的反映。英语学习者依靠阅读反映英语民族文化的语篇习得英语，既要习得语言知识系统，又要构建英民族语言的文化背景系统，同时又要在本民族文化的环境交流中找到两种语言文化的共项，通过语码转换实现语言交流的目的。而学生的交流需要是把自己熟悉的具有本民族文化特征的社会、政治、经济、思想、兴趣、生活等知识系统转换成目的语。这种在本民族语境中，对具有本民族文化背景的知识系统进行目的语语码转换交际的语言学习，可谓是费尽周折。真正的交际需要在目的语没有内化之前，就只有靠潜意识的"翻译"来应付，这正是学生交际失误的困难和问题所在。而反映中国文化背景的"直通式"媒体英语，是交际背景与目的语的统一体，迎合了学生交际的需要。通过大量"现实情景式"的交际型阅读，既习得了目的语，又掌握了交际技能，具有一举两得的效果。

　　本单元与第二单元以具有中国文化特征的"春节"、"灯节"以及西方的"情人节"、"圣诞节"和其他民族的不同节日为背景语篇，通过篇章的对比阅读，可以使阅读者掌握"节日"篇章的语言风格。系列化的阅读有助于篇章和语言知识的强化和内化。

　　本单元的篇章和词汇块知识结构为 Holidays —its features — activities or celebrations involved — reflections or impacts and emotional description.

1

Key Points

1. Holidays across the globe.
2. Description of festive atmosphere.
3. Celebrations during the holidays.
4. Word *Cluster* concerned with holidays and celebrations.

Since its 1983 debut, CCTV's **Spring Festival gala** has never failed to attract large audiences across China. It has become **an integral part of celebrations** on the eve of the Lunar New Year. On Wednesday night, the curtain went up again on the long-awaited gala.

Songs, dances, acrobatics, magic, comic dialogues and short sketches. There was really something for everyone. Celebration, jubilation, good will and festivity. The gala offered everything you could want to see in the Lunar New Year in style. The lucky audience inside the CCTV studio and the millions of those sitting in front of their TVs at home were treated to **a four-and-a-half-hour** feast of a super variety show.

Comic dialogues and short sketches, which lend drama and humor to social issues, have proven to be a perennial/permanent favorite of the gala. This year, almost half of the time was dedicated to these two art forms. Many of the sketches and dialogues were inspired by the monumental events that took place in China in 2003. Familiar scenes from last year were replayed on the stage, including the fight against SARS and **the tribute** to China's first astronaut.

One audience member said,"Watching these performances gave me a chance to experience the exciting moments of 2003 all over again. I enjoyed them greatly."

For the first time this year, **exotic touches** were added to the traditional Chinese event. Troupes from Argentina and Ireland brought magic and dance to the Chinese audience. *The Spirit of the Dance* proved especially popular, **immersing** the audience **in** the mysterious soul of

Ireland.

The Spring Festival gala included nearly 40 performances put together over four months of hard work by over 1,000 staff members. But whether all this hard work was worth the effort is up to the audience to decide. Audience members are encouraged to go to CCTV.com, where they can tell us which part of the gala they liked the most. This will help the directors make next year's production even better.

The Spring Festival is the most important of China's traditional festivals. The gala offers audiences **a respite from the strain and stress** of a year's hard work and gives them lots to think about for the next few days as they enjoy the week-long national holiday.

In China, no Spring Festival would be complete without **the traditional temple fair.** Beijing alone has over twenty fairs, with a variety of themes.

The temple fair at Baiyun Guan, the White Cloud Taoist Monastery, **favors a particular mode** of transportation—the donkey. Nowadays it's kids who make up most of the passengers over the short distance leading to the main gate.

Like other temple fairs, Baiyun Guan also has its lion dance and **high stilts performance**, both of which are traditional events at such gatherings. One look at the crowd is enough to tell there must be something special. They've gathered in the freezing cold to look for the **mascot** of the coming year, the monkey.

Touching the stone monkey here is a must when you come to the Baiyun Guan Temple Fair. People believe it will bring good luck in the coming year, and especially when it is the year of the monkey.

This is one of the monastery's three stone monkeys, which are rather difficult for new comers to find. But today's long queue helps locate the **auspicious** animal, believed to **bring blessings**, wealth and longevity. A visitor said, "I waited quite a while to touch the monkey. I hope this will **bless** my family. And I did it for good luck. It makes me feel better at the

New Year."

A third attraction here is the "money eye". The **carnival atmosphere** has transformed the usually staid temple, enticing a handsome number of **hopefuls** to try their luck and aim. As one of China's most famous Taoist monasteries, Baiyun Guan gives its temple fair a religious touch.

To experience a more worldly gathering, we go to Ditan Park. It just might be the busiest place in the city at the Chinese New Year. Once the Altar to the Earth, Ditan still holds a simple worshipping ceremony. But now the park is **a vendor's paradise**. On offer is everything from snacks to traditional toys, from straw figures to hanging monkeys. Visitors come in search of fun, and find it in plenty.

A Ditan visitor said, "It's the first time for us to come to Beijing, to a temple fair. I like it. It's really **festive**." "It's good. But I wish it could be more like the temple fair I went to when I was a kid, with more folk performing arts, like **story-telling and cross-talk**," said another one.

Going to a temple fair was once a major activity for local people during the Chinese Lunar New Year. Although Beijing now has **an array of festive activities** to choose from, the tradition still thrives as a symbol of the Old Beijing.

———————◦◦◦———————

Located in Southeast China's Fujian Province, the port city of Quanzhou is known for its early involvement in the country's foreign trade. This week, the city will launch its third annual Culture Festival, which will **feature** thousands of ingeniously-designed lanterns.

This year, the Quanzhou Culture Festival is to be held around **the traditional Lantern Festival** on the 15th day of the first lunar month. With this holiday, which marks the end of the Spring Festival, just around the corner, the major streets in downtown Quanzhou are decorated with hundreds of original lanterns.

Besides traditional themes, many lanterns **depict** contemporary life in the port city. The city's 1,000 year involvement in international trade is the dominant subject matter of the lantern pictures. All the lanterns on display were designed and created by local folk artists. Quanzhou lanterns are known for their attention to detail in design.

――――――§――◄◄◄●●►►►――§――――――

People in China have hardly had a chance to finish digesting their **feasts** from the Spring Festival holidays, but already they're tucking into more **festive** snacks on Feb. 5, **sweet dumplings** for the Lantern Festival, which is celebrated on the 15th day of the first lunar month. But eating isn't the only thing people do at this time, enjoying lanterns at night is another tradition on the night of the New Year's first full-moon.

With this year's first full-moon hanging in the dark sky, the lanterns are lit up **to echo its light**. The tradition of lighting lanterns started in the Han Dynasty some 2,000 years ago, and at night people walk through the streets enjoying the lanterns to **wish happiness** for the whole year.

In the Tang and Song dynasties, lantern celebrations were held on a very large scale. As time went on, more and more celebrations were added to the festival, like **letting off firecrackers**, **cracking lantern riddles** and performing dragon and lion dances.

The lanterns on show this year are from Tianjin, which is famous for the mellowness of its folk art. The exquisitely designed and decorated lanterns tell the fairy tales, and culture and history of China, attracting young and old alike.

Following the ancient tradition, a group of old people put on festive clothes and dance yangko on the square. Everyone's face reflects the **celebrated** colors of the lanterns, and the deafening sound of gongs and drums seems to want to spread the enthusiasm across the whole country.

――――――§――◄◄◄●●►►►――§――――――

Although the tragedy in Saudi Arabia has **overshadowed the climax** of the Hajj/pilgrim to Mecca, Muslims worldwide on Sunday began celebrating the Kurban Bayami. It's also called the **Festival of Sacrifice** and goes for the next three days. Muslims in China celebrated at a feast organized by China's Islamic Association in the capital Beijing.

The Kurban Bayami began on Sunday. Over a billion Muslims worldwide will **celebrate** over the next three days. Diplomats from 30 Arab and Muslim countries **gather** at a hotel in Beijing. The feast is the biggest celebration on the Islamic calendar.

The feast begins with a prayer. They call for peace and goodwill amongst all people, and for an end to war, especially in Islamic countries affected by conflict.

Chairman of China Islamic Association said, "This festival honors Allah. We **pray for peace** throughout the world, and among all people. And we **pray for happiness** for all mankind." Ambassador of Embassy of the Islamic Republic of Iran said, "We are as Muslim want from Allah and **pray for** freedom and peace and security for all people inside Palestine and Islam countries. We hope to have peaceful relation and peaceful life for them."

According to tradition, Kurban is celebrated 70 days after the end of the Moslem **fast** in the holy month of Ramadan. Kurban takes place on the 10th day of the 12th month in the Islamic calendar. It **coincides with** the pilgrimage to Islam's holiest shrines, and the end of the Hajj in Saudi Arabia. This year, the China Islamic Association arranged for over 4,000 **pilgrims** to make the trip to Mecca.

The Arab name of the holiday has some connection with **the legend** about Abraham's offering. Abraham, whom Moslems consider to be the first monotheism preacher, was ready to offer his son Ismail in sacrifice. However, at the last moment the angel replaced Ismail by **a sacrificial animal**, and the holiday was thus established to **commemorate** this.

According to tradition, the festival begins with prayer, and the slaughter of an animal in memory of Abraham's sacrifice. After this, Muslims worldwide enjoy a day of eating and entertainment. Dance, song and traditional sports are all part of the celebration.

The western tradition of Valentine's Day has caught on big in China.

Cupid's arrows are finding their mark as people in love are using flowers and chocolates to **light the flames of romance**.

Throughout the streets, there's lots of roses, lots of chocolates and lots of love. And there's lots of love in the air, especially inside the greenhouse. Roses — the symbol of love — are **blossoming** everywhere. And even senior sweethearts are celebrating their golden jubilee.

———❦———

Valentine's Day, the annual tribute to **romantic love**, is here. Florists, card shops, and chocolate vendors are all doing raging business as lovers rush to purchase **tokens** of their **affection.**

Unheard of until the late 1990s, the event has **caught on** in a big way in China's biggest cities. Chinese, known as conservative in body language and shy in showing their feelings publicly, are showing more of an appetite than ever for displays of **affection**, especially Westernized romance.

That is not to say that China's lovers in the past lacked romance. "There are many differences between the past and present in romance," said a sociologist in the People's University of China. "But there is no denying the fact that human beings look forward to **true love** no matter where and when."

What is romance? It is an individual thing, an answer that changes from person to person, and within any one person, it changes over time.

———❦———

China's **embrace of St. Valentine's Day** was infused with a shot of double happiness this year as the celebration coincided with this weekend's traditional Lunar Lantern Festival. The dual holiday was a boon/blessing to shopping centers around the country as flowers and chocolates were snapped up along with the traditional Lantern Festival delicacy of boiled **glutinous rice dumplings** filled with sweet stuffings.

Rose sellers were seen lining the posh/busy Jianguomen business district Friday evening charging up to 40 yuan (4.80 dollars) a stem, while shoppers were also lining up at stores around the city to buy the sweet dumplings.

Although the Lantern Festival falls on Saturday, many Chinese hung their lights and ate the dumplings known as "yuan xiao" on the festival eve in order to celebrate the two holidays together. China has **increasingly embraced** Valentine's Day, which is known as "Lover's Day" in Chinese, since it opened up to the outside world 20 years ago.

The holiday has also spread deep into China's interior where **an enterprising** shopping center in remote Nanchang city, Jiangxi Province held **a marathon kissing contest** that began early Friday and garnered/amassed national attention.

The winning couple won a pair of diamond rings worth 9,999 yuan (1,200 dollars). In Beijing, roses and condoms were handed out free at some shopping centers, while in the evening restaurants were packed with couples who were **treated to intimate dinners** served with the Lantern Festival delicacy.

The two holidays do not always coincide so closely, as the celebration of the Lantern Festival is marked in accordance with the Lunar calendar, China's traditional calendar for **marking** the months and years.

———————————— ❧◆❧ ————————————

People across China are **celebrating** Valentine's Day in their own ways, and many of them, including university students, do not hesitate to spend much more than usual on roses, chocolates, meals, entertainment and even a night at a hotel to express their feelings for their **beloved.**

It is undoubted that businessmen **capitalized on** the festival. Supply of flowers, sold at prices several times higher than usual, even **fell short of demand**, a situation beyond expectation and better than that during the Spring Festival, China's traditional new year, said an owner of a flower store in the capital city of central China's Hubei Province.

To make their lovers happy, some people spent 1,000 yuan (some 120 dollars) for 99 roses, and others even much more for 999 roses, which was rare in the past, said the owner. Cosmetics, jewelry, and other **luxury**

8

goods are finding **growing favor** among Chinese buyers to show their deep love for their other half. Some queued more than one hour for a meal at Pizza Hut and other Western restaurants to spend **an exotic day**.

Some older traditional Chinese are gradually accepting the Western festival and also bought roses and chocolates, and dined with their **spouses** in restaurants with romantic **ambiance/atmosphere**. A 71-year-old had a meal with his wife in **a candle-lit restaurant** in Xi'an, capital of northwest Shaanxi Province, to celebrate the 50th anniversary of their marriage that day.

Not just a romantic festival for two, Valentine's Day has **taken on** its own meaning among many people in China, becoming a special day for **family reunions** and parties. Some families in Guangzhou, capital of south Guangdong Province, regard the special day as an opportunity for **family gatherings**. Some pairs even took part in sports contests to display their devotion to love and cooperation in overcoming difficulties. In a skyscraper in Urumqi, capital of northwest Xinjiang Uygur Autonomous Region, 19 couples were competing for a pair of diamond rings worth 4,888 yuan (588 dollars) by rushing up the 38th stories with their partners.

It is Valentine's Day afternoon on the Wangfujing **pedestrian street**, the capital's most bustling commercial street, and the most **frequently-met scene** is girls carrying a bundle of roses, happily walking with their lovers.

One stem of red roses was sold for 25 yuan here. "But red roses seem a little bit **out-dated**, I prefer the blue ones," said a girl with dyed-yellow curly hair and **trendy make-up**, while her boyfriend was buying a 180-yuan blue rose for her. "The blue-colored roses seem the most popular gift for this Valentine's Day," a flower seller on the street said, adding that "I sold more than 20 flowers within one hour, at the price of 180 for each."

Some young people preferred practical **gifts**. The outlet of "Swatch", a Swiss brand watch, was **flocked** by many young lovers. Its special set for this Valentine's Day — a black watch for him, and a red one for her, cost altogether 996 yuan and had almost sold out. "Our daily sales increased by about 10 percent, compared with the normal weekend," the manager of an outlet of "Only" — an Europe-based women's clothes brand, told the News Agency, adding that many boys preferred to buy clothes for their girlfriends as Valentine's Day gift.

Besides shops, cinemas also **enjoy good business** on Valentine's Day. A ticket seller at the cinema attached to the State-owned Central Motion Movie Cooperation said "all cinema halls are full today and almost all **the audience** are young lovers." She also claimed that the new Chinese movie " *Baby in Love"* was the most popular film in her cinema on Valentine's Day. "I think that Valentine's Day is a good time for me to express my **affection**. I don't worry too much about the cost. This Valentine's day, I bought **a box of chocolate** worth 209 yuan and 99 roses for my girlfriend," said a man at the door of the cinema.

But middle-aged Chinese still **lack the enthusiasm** of young people toward the romantic festival. A middle-aged doctor held that today's young Chinese **pursue material love** too much and "Valentine's Day is created just for commercial reasons." "I think that we have our own traditional and modest way to express love. I seldom say I 'love you' to my wife and never bought roses for her but our affection **permeates** our daily life."

"Compared with our generation, today's young people prefer **exaggerated ways** to show their love. In my eyes, they are somewhat Westernized,"said a lady, around 40. She also acknowledged that she even did not know which day was Valentine's Day before her 18-year-old son told her some days before.

Although some middle-aged people retained doubts about **the exotic festival,** the truth is China has increasingly embraced Valentine's Day, which is known as "Lover's Day" in Chinese, since it opened up to the outside world more than 20 years ago.

The holiday has also spread deep into China's interior. Last year, an enterprising shopping center in an inner city held **a marathon kissing**

contest that **garnered/amassed** national attention.

Notes

1. Read the passages carefully and associate them with what you've learned about these holidays and festivals.
2. Group the words and expressions: festivals; activities; descriptive techniques or festive atmosphere.

Unit Two
Holidays and Celebrations (II)

Key Points

1. Read more passages on V-Day in China, and note the change of thought the Day has brought us.

2. Continue the journey to Christmas Day and New Year's Day in China.

3. Familiarize yourselves with words and expressions related to holidays and celebrations.

Love Is in the Air and the Flowers Are on Their Way

February has long been a month of **romance**. With the sweet smell of roses in the air, romantic films hit cinemas and love stories fill newspapers and magazines.

On the 14th day, it is **customary** for a boy to take his girlfriend out to dinner, buy her flowers and chocolates, write poems, sing to her or even spell out her name with rose petals! This is the scene that greets you on Valentine's Day, named after Valentine who was a priest in third century Rome. When the emperor decided that single men made better soldiers than those with wives, he banned marriage.

But Valentine continued **to perform marriage ceremonies** for young lovers in secret. When his actions were discovered, the emperor had him put to death. While in prison, it is said that Valentine fell in love with the daughter of his prison guard. Before his death, he wrote her a letter, which he signed "From your Valentine", an expression that is still in use today.

Valentine died for what he believed in and so was made a Saint, as well as becoming one of history's most romantic figures.

Nowadays, Valentine's Day **wins the same** popularity among Chinese young people. It is a time when students "don't want to be alone" according to a student reporter for *21st Century Teens* in Jinling High School, Nanjing. Some of her classmates are planning to make Valentine's cards for parents, teachers and friends. Others want to hold parties at which they will exchange small gifts and eat heart-shaped cakes. The idea is to have fun and encourage people to share in the spirit of St. Valentine.

A young man, dressed elegantly, waits in the chilly night wind. He is shivering, yet excitement warms him. Bouquet in hand, he looks at the passing crowd, searching for that special someone who will be his **Cinderella** at the ball.

This will be a typical scene tonight, multiplied thousands of times across the nation's big cities. Love will be in the air, and **the aura** of romance will thicken to such an extent that cold weather can only serve to enhance **the atmosphere**.

Valentine's Day is for lovers. Yet it has not been always so as it is a relatively new holiday for Chinese — gaining ground quickly in the last decade. And it is mostly the young and the trendy that are propelling it into **mainstream acceptance**.

Imported Holiday

Beneath the surface of a brand-new imported holiday are the cross-currents of **cultural fusion** and the power of commercial interests. Love can be pure and simple, but celebrating love takes a whole mechanism of sociological evolution and the support of myriad/numerous businesses.

Roses, chocolates, candlelight dinners. These are **the images** of Valentine's Day and these are what appeal to people in China, especially the young generation. The popularity of this holiday has confounded/

confused many an old-timer/seniors. However, citing Westernization as the sole driving force is somewhat simplistic.

The fact that it comes from the West certainly has a lot to do with its fast acceptance. Chinese tend to have the **mentality** that "**outside monks chant the better prayers.**" It carries mystique, which is essential to the build-up of romantic ambience.

In their attempt to explain the origin of Valentine's Day, scholars have offered three vastly **distinct versions** that cover all bases. One comes from England and has something to do with birds mating. The other two trace the beginning all the way to the Roman empire. The more popular one of the two, according to experts, is about a priest in the third century who secretly held weddings for **lovebirds** when the tyrant of the day, in an attempt to conscript/recruit all men of a certain age, banned all weddings. When he learned of the priest's act of defiance, he did not hesitate to arrest and execute the holy man. That was on February 14 and the priest's name was Valentine. The day was later canonized/worshipped by lovers to commemorate the great **sympathizer of love.**

Just Another Occasion

Whether this is history or **myth** or a combination of both, most Valentine's Day celebrants in China do not seem to know or care. Like Christmas, Valentine's Day has descended on the Middle Kingdom **stripped of its historical implications.** As a matter of fact, many lovers treat Christmas as another occasion to be together and have fun, in other words, something in the same vein as Valentine's Day. They may not be aware of its religious origin and certainly do not know the lyrics of the carols/hymns. But the **pagoda-shaped** tree with a lot of baubles/toy is no doubt a big attraction.

The **irresistible** lure of Valentine's Day lies in its components that are compatible with middle-class lifestyle newly prevalent in urban China. Take **candlelight dinners**, for example. Thirty years ago it would never have been seen as romantic because power outages/loss, and the resultant candlelight **meals,** were commonplace.

Almost everything about Valentine's Day, including sending roses, is not part of the traditional Chinese **dating ritual.** Therefore, it is still **devoid of** ennui/boredom and nonchalance/cold that is often associated with native customs. Since it's Western in source, it carries an **exotic quality and upward mobility.**

In an online survey, more than three quarters of respondents disagreed that Valentine's Day is "vulgar" or "should be ignored." If anything, it is perceived by most people as "**in vogue.**"

Tradition Forgotten

While Valentine's Day is being embraced by more and more people, China's own day for lovers is **on the decline** in terms of popularity.

To begin with, many people don't even know that such a holiday exists; and then there are two days competing for this honour.

Lantern Festival, the 15th day of the first month on the lunar calendar, is considered by some as China's Valentine's Day. But it is in dispute. Some say it is **a fallacy** and attribute it to its proximity to Valentine's Day because it usually falls in early or mid-February.

The other **contender** is half a year away, in August. Qixi, denotes the seventh day of the seventh month on the lunar calendar. It is the day when a pair of mythological lovers, Niulang and Zhinv, have their annual meeting across the heavenly river of the Milky Way.

Over the centuries, Qixi was **observed** by lovers and everyone else. Customs evolved, but the theme of love conquering all has remained to this day. However, in modern days, Qixi is **commemorated** mostly in China's Taiwan Island. It may be an overstatement to say it is in decline because it has never **caught fire** with the current generation in most parts of the country.

Experts attribute the growing indifference towards the **home-born holiday** to its cultural inferences. In the legend, the two lovers are forcibly separated by her father, the celestial emperor, who later yields a little by allowing them to meet once a year. Yet nobody dares to challenge the emperor's authority because in feudal times, one's **obedience** to parents took precedence over loyalty to the spouse.

Qixi Tale

The Qixi tale embodies several layers of **rebelliousness:** The daughter's free will to love someone without the consent of her parents, an "upper-class" girl overcoming the **social barrier** to marry a poor farmer, and a fairy princess giving up her **eternal life** to bond with a mere mortal. However, it is essentially a tragedy because they have to pine/long or await for each other on 364 days of a year.

Qixi **immortalizes** one moment that is ephemeral and fast-fleeting. As the poem Magpie Bridge (Que Qiao Xian) comments, "When love is ever-lasting, why should we care about all the mornings and all the nights?" But Valentine's Day, to those blissfully ignorant of the old, equally sad source story, represents **a "seize-the-day-while-you-can" spirit**. It gives vent/burst to affection and passion, which Qixi and hundreds of other Chinese love stories from the ancient times have couched in euphemism and restrained expressions.

Valentine's Day, in the eyes of the young, is not so much a substitute for Qixi, but rather an extension of the love theme as well as a more accurate reflection of their more candid/blunt or frank ways of **emotional display**.

Push of Commercialism

The happiest people about the rise of Valentine's Day in China are not lovers, but merchants. From the very beginning in the 1990s, this has been the day **trumpeted by commercial interests** to the degree that it is not much of an exaggeration to say the whole thing was masterminded/ planned by a giant empire of salesmanship.

If you take a look at a newsstand, you'll find that pages and pages of Valentine's Day coverage read like product releases. Not just florists and chocolate retailers, but everything conceivable.

An **upscale** hotel in Shanghai is promoting a "**rose suite**" for tonight, replete/loaded with all kinds of heart-shaped goodies. The price: 88,888 yuan (US$10,750). No wonder people say love is priceless.

For most merchants, sales and profits, while **intoxicatingly extravagant**, can be measured or predicted. A single rose may fetch up to 300 yuan. One wholesaler in Beijing reveals that he is making about 20,000 yuan a day, hands down/easily. Guangzhou-based China Southern Airlines ships about 20 tons of flowers a day. The highest daily **turnover volume** at the city's Baiyun Airport is 50 tons of flowers.

Many delivery companies, including online stores, have been turning customers away. Our capacity was stretched by the first two days of orders, and we cannot handle a single more request, says the executive of a Beijing express service.

An online survey at sina.com reveals that 50 per cent of respondents choose to send flowers to their lover, and 35 percent **opt for** other gift items. Only 15 percent are uncertain. On the spending scale, the mostly young online crowd plan **to shell out** an average of 250 yuan each.

Not only is holiday news coverage turned into consumer guides, but even entertainment-section gossip has been made into self-promotional media exposure. A star is shooting a movie on location; a star is taking a day off and relaxing at home; a star is partying at a posh venue. Every routine is hyped/advertised **under the pretext of** Valentine's Day activities even if that star has no romantic appeal and has never appeared in a filmed romance.

What's Christmas without a Christmas tree? A 60-member team of the US Santa Goodwill Tour has been sent out to Asia on their annual mission to spread love and happiness. Now they have landed in Hong Kong, the first stop on their Asian tour, to bring the **festive spirit** to the children of the city.

It is as **shining** as usual but this Christmas there is something more in the air. That is: The spirit of a traditional Christmas passed on by the Santas.

Executive Director of HK Tourism Board said, "And in the Christmas time where is the warm feast of season, it's time for sharing love and joy and friendship. And there is no better way to invite 60 Santas from the US to serve as **goodwill ambassadors** and to share the love and joy."

For the kids, it is a moment for a wish to come true. Most of them are from the "Make A Wish Foundation of Hong Kong", an organization set up to grant one special wish to local children who are suffering from a serious illness.

A gigantic Christmas tree provided the backdrop for the team to create **a magical, festive atmosphere.** Erected in a shopping mall, a sparkling 21-meter Christmas tree was decorated with 100,000 crystals. It is being considered for a Guinness World Record for the tallest Christmas tree with the most decorative crystal items.

Christmas, one of the most important Western festivals, is being celebrated by an increasing number of Chinese. And the festivities have **injected fresh vitality to** local markets.

A stall holder in a big retail market in Beijing has seen her business prosper **in the run up to** Christmas. "Last year I only sold a few Christmas gifts on my stall. This year I've created a special stand for them. Since offering such a large variety of goods, business has been very good."

Christmas used to be a festival enjoyed mainly by young people. But now many **senior citizens** like me also celebrate it. It gives us an opportunity to throw parties and learn about the culture and lifestyle in the West.

Christmas shopping is just one part of the **festive economy**. Christmas Eve dinners, concerts, cards, not to mention all the promotions held in the name of the festival, all boost the local economy. For many Chinese, Christmas has also become a welcome break from the **hustle**

and bustle of life — an occasion to enjoy.

Christmas is one of the most **celebrated holidays** in the world. It has also become **a festive occasion** for an increasing number of Chinese. They can afford the luxury of flowers, Christmas trees and a night out in bars. But rather than a religious event, "Xmas" has become a time to shop and have fun for the Chinese middle class.

Similar to many other western things already common to Chinese, the Christian festival is now **in vogue** in the populous Asian country as well. In the biggest gift shopping mall in Beijing, throngs of people flood in to get their best buys for Christmas.

A shop manager of Shangpin Floral House said, "The Christmas sale season began late in October. Almost all of the items related to 'Xmas' have become hot. And most of the buyers are the upper middle classes who care more about **quality of life** than their budget."

She said daily sales could total as much as 10,000 yuan in her shop, one of the more than 15 "Xmas" shops in the mall. But two busy Christmas shoppers weren't doing it to decorate a house — rather for their bar's Christmas Eve celebration. From Christmas trees to tiny decorations, they searched shops far and wide to find just the right **inspirations** for their holiday fanfare/expense. In the end, they spent almost 2,000 yuan for 4 full bags of goods.

Their bar is located on Houhai Lake, one of the hottest night life venues in Beijing. Like all the bars in the area, they are now busy adding the **final touches** to their decorations. Christmas has become **an excellent occasion** for business. And they plan to **capitalize on** the opportunity.

A bar owner said, "We want to play western music in harmony with the atmosphere in the bar. People can have a cosy place to themselves to have **a serene and romantic Xmas eve**."

Of course, all of this "romance" does not come cheaply. The bill for such a dinner costs about 40 US dollars. It's not surprising that most of those taking advantage of Christmas dinners like this come from the upper middle class. They can afford to have an evening such as this. In a sense, Christmas has become an excuse for the busy metropolitan people to **slow down and celebrate their life.**

In Beijing, as well as in many other big cities throughout China, Christmas has become much more than just a "foreign" word. **A commercialized version of the idea**, if not the spirit, of Christmas —has caught on, leaving a joyful and crowded trail of **Chinese celebrations** — in its merry wake.

Though it is not on the traditional Chinese Festival calendar, Christmas has become a popular event for an increasing number of Chinese **to celebrate.** There is a variety of **Christmas celebration** options to choose from, including the conventional midnight Mass/celebration.

It is a silent night and a holy night. Like many religious people around the world, the **devout** in China gathered on Christmas Eve to honor the birth of Jesus Christ. As in previous years, hundreds gathered for the traditional midnight mass at the 300-year-old Catholic South Cathedral, which was packed full with people standing in the aisles.

A choir of both young and old **ushered** the worshippers into **a solemn and holy atmosphere**. The people at this Christmas Eve mass pray for the all best things, for people in China, and everywhere across the world.

We will pray for world peace, for our government, for the unemployed, and for our parish/community. In April this year, we prayed for the elimination of SARS. We will also pray for those living in areas that have suffered recent disaster. To love everybody is the responsibility of us and of the church.

Christmas Eve in Beijing was frosty minus-10 degrees Celsius, but many people who don't regularly **attend church** stood patiently outside the church, waiting for permission to get into the sanctuary. Some were just curious to see what was going on. Local residents, especially the youngsters, seemed to be **enjoying this "foreign" holiday** just as much or even more than the foreigners themselves.

Young generation are gradually **westernized but commercialized.** But frankly speaking, they should regard Christmas as a religious day. Because ... we regard Christmas as birthday of Jesus Christ... Personal salvation...

No matter how and why people here celebrate Christmas miracle, one thing is for sure. Christmas brings them a sense of happiness. It stands as a symbol for **a promise of love** and goodwill to all mankind.

Previously seen as a typically Western festival, Christmas was once rejected by most Chinese. But as China changes, it has become a popular holiday that many people celebrate. For most Chinese here, Christmas, just like Spring Festival, **embodies family reunion**, and is a time to **pray for peace and goodwill** in the 12 months ahead.

Nearly a hundred university students **celebrated** the beginning of the New Year in their own way in Beijing. Gathering at Peking University to mark the Youth Cultural Heritage Day, they hope to enlist support for the ancient folk art of **paper-cutting** to be given UNESCO **intangible heritage listing status.**

Students from a number of universities in Beijing as well as fine arts institutes in other parts of China signed a banner, on which graduate students from the Central Academy of Fine Arts, or CAFA, **embroidered** traditional paper-cut patterns. Also present were experts in the field of cultural **heritage preservation.** They gathered here on the first day of the year to show their concern for China's endangered folk arts.

Director of Heritage Research Center of CAFA said, "We set up this festival to make young people more aware of traditional culture **in a time of globalization.** Last year we held an event promoting China's intangible heritage in Wangfujing street. This year we want to focus more on paper-cutting."

The idea of the **Youth Cultural Heritage Day** was put forward by the Intangible Heritage Research Center of CAFA in 2002 and soon won support from Peking and Tsinghua universities and the University of Nationalities. Now many universities across the country have set up similar research institutions to join in the efforts.

A graduate student from Hubei Fine Arts Institute said,"The **intangible heritage** research center at our school is the second of its kind in the country. We'll focus on the local art forms of Hubei Province, such as wood-carving, embroidering and knitting."

The participants were also able to see a 37-minute documentary on paper-cutting by **ethnic minorities** in West China. The film, the Vanishing Mother River, was the result of the director's lengthy research and is part of his preparation to present the ancient folk art to UNESCO.

A staff member from China Radio International Italian service said, "I visited many villages in West China, where paper-cutting is still very popular among **the minority ethnic groups**. When I saw the colorful rooms decorated with paper-cuts, I really felt these were worthy of a UNESCO listing." Organizers say that with Chinese culture in a stage of transition, keeping old traditions alive in a modern society will help preserve **the continuity of the Chinese civilization.**

———————

Thursday was the traditional Chinese **Mid-Autumn Festival,** an occasion of **thanks-giving and family reunion**. Across the country, and overseas, Chinese people celebrated the event in many and varied ways under the full moon.

Fireworks and pleasure boats are just some of the newer items on the holiday menu. But some traditions still **prevail** around the country. The people of Chengdu make paper lanterns and float them down the river, praying for safety and harmony for their families.

In Nanjing, people climb Lion Mountain to **watch the full moon** and city lights. In Shanghai, poetry lovers gather amongst the flowers at Guilin

Park to **recite poems about the moon** and enjoy green tea. In less fortunate areas, nobody has been forgotten. Government officials in Inner Mongolia, Shaanxi and Anhui have been visiting the homes of victims of recent tragedies, bringing them **mooncakes**, the traditional delicacy of the festival.

In the Hong Kong Special Administrative Region, hundreds of thousands of Hong Kong residents walked in parks, and along the seaside and streets to **soak up the festival atmosphere.** At Hong Kong's Victoria Park, a large-scale lantern show attracted at least 150,000 Hong Kong residents.

Celebrations were also held in Britain, where the Chinese Embassy in London **held a banquet** in honor of teaching staff for the promotion of simplified Chinese characters. Officials with the embassy said China would increase support to their work.

Notes

1. Brainstorm a story of your own festive experience where you enjoy a special holiday.
2. Frequently links the words and expressions in a holiday-specific context, and you'll easily learn English rather than "study" it only.

Unit Three
State Visits and China's Diplomacy (I)

导　读

　　图式理论是认知心理学、心理语言学和人工智能共同研究的理论成果，是由心理学家 Frederic Bartlett 根据格式塔心理学提出的。在他《记忆》一书中写道：图式是对过去经验的反映或对过去经验的积极组织。即知识在大脑中的储存单位，包括各种各样的知识块，如有关鸟的知识，有关学校、城市、交通、银行、文学、体育、篮球等概括的或具体的系统知识。现代心理学不仅发展了 Bartlett 的理论观点，而且进一步研究了这些图式知识在语篇理解和记忆中的应用，从而发展了合适图式的激活和特定图式细节的重建理论。前者主要揭示对图式的熟悉程度在阅读过程中所产生的影响。研究发现当人们缺乏一个与正在展开的故事相适应的图式时，理解和记忆都会很困难，因为他们无法了解所描述的事件的含义。而后者则是依据 Bartlett 的另一个概念即激活的图式可以作为提取计划，而且由于图式的中心作用，帮助人们归纳某些重要细节。Kozminsky， Pichert & Anderson (1977)的研究也充分证明了这一点。在语篇信息的处理过程中，熟悉的图式往往可以引导读者对中心信息的理解和记忆。

　　图式在阅读加工中最重要的作用之一是它的预期作用，在阅读过程中，读者正是依靠图式的这种预期作用进行推理，以填补篇章信息本身的某些空白，达到对篇章的理解。因此，选取读者比较熟悉的英文语篇，有利于创造特定的语言环境，既符合读者交际的需要，又可以把语言与交际相结合。虚拟的"环境"，加强了输入的内化和创造性的语言输出。

本单元选取阅读者熟悉的与中国外交活动相关的新闻报道，通过阅读，掌握以 state visit(访问)→exchange activities(交流活动)，如: bilateral talks, statement issuance, consensus; international issues, domestic or internal affairs, world focus such as anti-terrorism → its consequences(访问的作用)，即 enhance, expand, consolidate, promote... all-round cooperation, friendship, understanding and trust, stability, prosperity...等为主题的语篇图式知识结构块和相关的词汇表达项。

Key Points

1. 熟悉"外事活动"语篇的图式知识结构，即事件 → 交流 → 影响或意义。

2. 相关的词汇项：who → president, premier, minister, chancellor from Germany, secretary from the United States 等；

    where → Japan, Vietnam, Singapore, Germany, France, Ethiopia, Brazil, and names of countries and regions, even cities' or capitals' names of countries to be visited.

    what →exchange views upon global issues, international affairs, bilateral cooperation, anti-terrorism; hold talks, issue joint statement, meet one's counterpart 等；

    Consequences → consolidate, enhance, boost, strengthen, reiterate, stress, conducive to, promote, improve, deepen, increase, expand → mutual, bilateral, reciprocal, multilateral; friendship, trust, understanding, cooperation, stability, prosperity, in the interests of both sides 等。

Chinese President left Beijing Monday morning to begin **state visits** to France, Egypt, Gabon and Algeria.

His **entourage** included his wife, State Councilor, Foreign Minister, Director of the Policy Research Office of the Central Committee of the Communist Party of China (CPC), Deputy Director of the General Office of the CPC Central Committee, Vice-Minister in charge of the State

Development and Reform Commission and Vice-Minister of Commerce.

The President was invited by French President, Egyptian President, Gabonese President, and Algerian President. The visits will last until Feb. 4.

———————————————⁂———————————————

Chinese President has arrived in France, **on a three-day visit**, which China hopes will **help improve** its relations with the European Union. The French also have high expectations, hoping that the visit of the President will **strengthen ties** with the world's fastest growing economy and Asia's rising power.

The two leaders **exchanged views** on strengthening bilateral economic and trade cooperation during Monday's talks.

French President said France was willing to **work with** China **in such areas as** nuclear energy, aviation and railway transport. In addition, he said France was ready to introduce key technologies to China to **help advance** localized production.

China would **consolidate** the gains already made in ties between the two countries and work to **broaden** areas of cooperation.

The talks also touched on the Taiwan issue. The Chinese briefed his French counterpart on China's **stance** on the Taiwan authorities' moves towards independence **under the guise of** the upcoming referendum.

Chirac said his government remained firmly behind the one-China policy, and that maintaining **stability** across the Taiwan Straits was in the interests of all sides. The French leader said that he hoped the Chinese people were able to **resolve** the Taiwan issue peacefully and in keeping with the principle of one China.

Chinese President is **scheduled** to address the French parliament Tuesday, a rare privilege for a world leader. He is expected to talk about China's economic growth as well as foreign policy.

———————————————⁂———————————————

On the second day of his **state visit** to France, the President has **underlined** China's **strategic ties** with the European country. The

Chinese president and his French counterpart explored key issues at a joint press conference in Paris on Tuesday.

The two presidents met the media after China and France signed a joint declaration. The document defines the strategic **partnership** between China and France, and will guide the two countries' future cooperation.

The newly signed joint document reviewed the development of Sino-French relations since 1997. It puts forward guidelines for **promoting** the strategic partnership of China and France. The document **sets directions** for strengthening cooperation in politics, economics, the military, culture and science, as well as for **coordinating** dialogue between the two countries in international affairs.

The two heads of state clarified their positions on diverse issues. French President Chirac says both countries **advocate a multilateral approach** to deal with international affairs. He praised China's efforts to help solve the DPRK nuclear crisis and **stressed** that France would continue to **abide by** the "one-China policy."

"We oppose any action to change the status of cross-Straits relations, including the Taiwan referendum. The issue should be resolved through dialogue instead of confrontation."

The Chinese president also used the occasion to once again state China's policy towards Taiwan.

"China's **position** on Taiwan is very clear. Peaceful unification and the one China two systems policy is our guide. We will do all we can to solve the Taiwan **issue** through peaceful means. But we firmly oppose Taiwan independence. And we will not allow anyone to use any method to separate Taiwan from China."

As to the European Union's 15-year **arms embargo on** China, the French president says it's time to **lift the ban**. At an EU meeting held in Brussels yesterday, France has asked the EU to lift its ban on arms sales to China. The embargo is out of date now.

The Chinese president arrived in Paris on Monday, the 40th anniversary of the establishment of formal ties between China and France. Both countries hope to take the opportunity to **cement** the bilateral ties.

———————————

French President and Chinese President have taken time out from talks to pose for photographs by the specially lit Eiffel Tower.

The best-known landmark in Paris is **bathed with red light** in honor of the Chinese leader's three-day visit. It also **marks** the French and Chinese governmental initiative to promote bilateral cultural exchanges. Red in China stands for happiness, joyous **festivities** and prosperity, and we are told that the French also associate it with good times.

———————————

The visiting Chinese President has held talks with his Egyptian **counterpart**, Hosni Mubarak. The two leaders agree to promote bilateral cooperation and **further** the friendship between the two countries.

The Chinese president arrived in the Egyptian capital from Paris on Thursday, on the second **leg** of a four-nation **tour**. The two leaders held a joint press conference in Cairo, during which President spoke of the warm relations China enjoys with Arab nations.

Chinese President said, "The relations between China and the **Arab nations** are very strong and have become stronger in recent years. The evidence is the increasing level of bilateral trade and expansion of economic and trade cooperation between China and **Arab states** over the past ten years."

The volume of trade between China and the **Arab League**'s 22 member states reached 25 billion US dollars last year. The visit is expected to **further promote** the economic ties between the two sides. With documents on economic and technological cooperation, China's **preferential loans** to Egypt, and investment memorandum on a special economic zone are expected to be signed.

China is also planning to send a business delegation to Egypt to **forge relations** with local firms. An agreement on further cooperation in the oil and gas industry is likely to be signed during the President's visit. Currently, there are two Sino-Egyptian joint firms in Egypt's oil industry.

Chinese President has put forward **a four-point proposal** for developing closer partnerships with Arab countries. The suggestion came during a meeting with the Secretary General of the League of Arab States. The President also met with senior Egyptian officials to **push forward** bilateral ties.

While meeting with Moussa, the Chinese president expressed China's willingness to develop ties with the Arab countries. He put forward a four-point proposal for a closer partnership: promoting political relations on the basis of mutual respect, forging closer trade and economic links, expanding cultural exchanges, and strengthening cooperation in international affairs.

Earlier on Friday, a China-Arab states forum for cooperation was established. Chinese Foreign Minister says the forum marks a milestone in the history of relations between China and Arab nations. It will be a platform for China and Arab countries to **enhance** their economic and political links.

The Chinese president also met with the speaker of the Egyptian People's Assembly and the speaker of the Egyptian Advisory Council. He says as both countries now face **a historic mission** — developing their economies. China is willing to work with Egypt to promote strategic cooperation between the two countries. The Egyptian officials praised China's economic achievements and its positive role in international affairs. They agreed that **boosting** Sino-Egyptian ties serves the interests of both nations.

The president arrived in the Egyptian capital from France on Thursday for a four-day state visit. Egypt is the second **leg** of the president's four-nation tour, which will also take him to Gabon and Algeria.

Continuing his four-nation state visits, Chinese President has arrived in Libreville, the capital of Gabon. He was **welcomed** at the airport by his Gabonese counterpart.

In a speech **delivered** at the airport, the Chinese president said relations between the two countries have been proceeding healthily, and noted that this year **marks** the 30th anniversary of diplomatic ties between their two countries. He expressed his intention to strengthen Sino-Gabonese cooperation.

During his visit to Egypt, he held talks with his Egyptian counterpart on a range of bilateral, regional and international issues. The Chinese leader also met Arab League leaders and called for a new partnership and deeper cooperation between China and Arab countries. During the president's visit, the China-Arab Cooperation Forum was formally established. Before leaving Egypt, the president and his wife visited the temples of Karnak and Luxor.

Chinese President is in the capital of Gabon for a three-day visit — the first by a Chinese head of state to the West African nation since the two countries **forged formal links** 30 years ago. Hu Jintao is expected to address the Gabonese parliament later today to outline China's policy towards the African continent.

After traveling to France and Egypt, the President arrived in Libreville late Sunday with the aim of boosting ties with the sub-Saharan nation.

His Gabonese counterpart has been on familiar terms with Beijing for thirty years. Since coming to power in 1967, Bongo has visited China eight times. Economic cooperation is expected to **come high on the agenda** of the talks between the two leaders.

Only a day before, Gabon signed a contract with Sinopec —China's largest oil refiner — under which Gabonese crude will be sold to the huge Asian market for the first time. Although it **lags well behind** oil giants Nigeria and Angola, Gabon is still a significant crude producer in West Africa.

Gabonese officials say a further oil exploration deal will be **inked** on

Monday, which will also see **a keynote speech** by the Chinese president at the National Assembly. The parliamentary complex itself is a symbol of close Sino-Gabonese ties. It is among a number of projects financed and built by China over the past three decades.

———————※————————

Chinese President arrived in Algeria Tuesday, aiming at securing further economic co-operation and exploring energy **pacts** as well as **bolstering** diplomatic ties with the influential African nation. Algerian President welcomed the Chinese leader at Algiers airport yesterday afternoon local time.

This important visit, taking place following the State visit paid by President Bouteflika to China in October 2000, will contribute to "**reinforcing** friendship and co-operative ties between Algeria and China to help the countries realize their potential **in this regard**," an official source of Algeria stressed on the eve of the president's visit.

In his written statement **released** upon his arrival, the president said that to **consolidate** the friendly ties and mutual partnership in all fields between the two countries is in conformity with the **fundamental interests** of the two peoples.

In Algeria, the last leg of the president's current visit abroad which also has taken the leader to France, Egypt and Gabon, several cooperative agreements in different fields will be signed during this visit, according to the Chinese embassy here. The agreements include **a framework document** on mineral resources exploration, economic and technological partnership, China's preferential loans to Algeria and a memoranda on **an economic pact** between small- and medium-sized enterprises.

The key part of the two-day trip will be the president's talks with his counterpart, which are scheduled to be held early this morning Beijing time.

Earlier in Gabon, Chinese President and his Gabonese counterpart **pledged** to push China-Gabon relations *to* a new high. In a communique signed there on Tuesday, the two leaders expressed satisfaction over the healthy and steady development of bilateral ties since the two countries forged diplomatic relations three decades ago.

They **vowed** to maintain the exchange of high-level visits between China and Gabon, step up teamwork in various fields and increase consultations on African and international affairs. Gabon voiced support for China's reunification. It **reiterated** that there is only one China in the world, with the government of the People's Republic of China being **the sole legitimate government** representing China as a whole and Taiwan being an **inalienable** part of China.

Both sides said that they will boost trade and investment, continue to support alliances between enterprises and implementation of signed co-operative agreements.

They said partnerships will be focused on agriculture, infrastructure construction, exploitation of resources and personnel training. China **reaffirmed** its willingness to lend support toward Gabon's economic and social development.

During Chinese President's state visit to Algeria, the two countries signed a joint communique. It **highly values** the development of friendly and cooperative bilateral ties since the countries forged diplomatic relations 45 years ago.

The communique says the two countries will **consolidate** their strategic cooperative relations, continue the exchange of high-level visits, and **strengthen** cooperation in various fields, to push China-Algeria cooperation and friendship to a new high.

It notes Algeria **adheres to** the stance that there is only one China in the world, and that the government of the People's Republic of China is the sole legitimate government representing China as a whole and Taiwan is an inalienable part of China.

Algeria opposes any move by the Taiwan authorities, including the so-called referendum, that aims to change the status, or **aggravate**

tension across the Taiwan Straits, or would lead to "Taiwan independence".

It also **emphasizes** that China and Algeria are resolutely opposed to terrorism in all manifestations. And both countries champion/support comprehensive measures that address both the symptoms and root causes of terrorism.

The two sides are also against linking terrorism to any specific nation or religion.

The two countries **pledge** to further promote the friendly relations between China and Arab and African countries. The two sides also discussed the Middle East conflicts and the situations in post-war Iraq. And they called for an early realization of "Iraqi people governing Iraq" as well as active participation by the international community in rebuilding post-war Iraq.

Chinese President's 4-nation tour has taken him from Europe to Africa. The 10 days of state visits included both developed and developing countries, **cementing** cooperation in a variety of sectors. CCTV international traces China's diplomatic marks left by the trip, **deemed** productive by many international affairs observers.

Paris was **celebrating** the Chinese New Year as the president began his 4-country state visit. The Chinese president received a rare personal welcome at the airport by his French counterpart. His first state visit to a western European country as China's head of state **coincided with** the 40th anniversary of the diplomatic ties between the two countries.

It was not just the Eiffel Tower's unprecedented holiday look that conveyed France's **goodwill.** Jacques Chirac's clear-cut opposition towards Taiwan independence reassured Beijing. The Taiwan issue has long been a criterion to measure its relationship with other countries. Despite international speculation on France's business motives, Chinese analysts say to some extent, France's stance on Taiwan represents that of the European Union.

A professor with School of Int'l Studies, Peking Univ., gave his opinion: "I believe the background is much more than the trade relations between China and France. The recent **deteriorating** cross-straits relations caused by Taiwan leader have **aroused international concerns**. **Unilateral action** will damage the peace and stability of the Asia-Pacific region. Many countries have expressed their dissatisfaction and condemnation. Chirac's stance has not gone beyond that of the European Union. He's just more direct."

His third international visit since taking office last March, the president's trip to Egypt was a milestone in the close ties between China and Arab States. A Cooperation Forum was launched between China and the 22-member Arab League. Chinese Foreign Minister has noted some unfair factors in the world political order that **hinder** the economic progress of developing countries, like China and Arab League members. The Forum was set up to address problems of **common concern**.

An Associate Professor with Institute of World History, CASS/China Academy of Social Science, commented:"The Arab League is an important regional organization of the Middle-East and North Africa. It's also a force not to be ignored by the international world. To strengthen its cooperation with international organizations is part of China's comprehensive strategy to expand its diplomatic space. For Arab countries, they want to benefit from China's booming economy as well as China's political support as a UN Security Council permanent member."

Many international observers also regard the Chinese president's trip as a quest for energy. Chinese oil demand in 2003 surged at a record pace. It has replaced Japan to become the world's second largest petroleum consumer, after the United States. Quite a few contracts signed during the trip **cover** crude oil, gas, and other energy sources. But Chinese experts say the trip is not just about **diversifying** China's oil sources.

A Professor of West Asian and Africa Studies, CASS, said:"Of course, there are petroleum considerations for China to strengthen contacts with the Middle East and Africa. But petroleum just explains part of the story. North Africa, like Algeria, has a long-term friendship with China. The Sino-Egyptian relationship is China's diplomatic **emphasis** in the Arab world and the Middle East. And it was also China's African friends like Gabon who helped China become a UN permanent member. So to **cement** and expand Sino-African friendship in the globalization process is crucial to China's diplomacy."

Many analysts say that the new Chinese leadership has demonstrated a more pragmatic **diplomatic style** than ever before. Their aim is to create a favorable environment for China's economic development. China is using active **diplomacy** as it takes its place in a diversified world.

Unit Four
State Visits and China's Diplomacy (II)

Key Points

1. This unit concerns China's senior officials' visit and Chinese diplomacy as demonstrated in Unit Three.
2. Read the passages provided and recognize the words and expressions that you need to report the state visits.

Chinese Premier has met US Secretary of State Colin Powell in Washington. The meeting is part of the premier's first **official trip** to the United States as the Chinese premier.

Earlier in the day, he toured the New York office of one of the world's biggest companies, General Electric. The Chinese Premier attended a dinner with Powell shortly after he reached Washington. At the end of his toast, Powell showed his **hospitality** to his Chinese guest. The premier then said the US and China should not let disagreement tear the strong bonds of their friendship.

He also said he was **looking forward to** his meeting with US President George W. Bush.

"I'm looking forward very much to my meeting tomorrow with President Bush and my sense tells me that the discussion tomorrow will be very successful. Like him, I'm a candid and sincere man. So the spirit that will guide my discussion with President Bush tomorrow will also be **candid, cooperative and constructive**."

Taiwan and trade issues are expected to **dominate** the Chinese premier's talks with the US President on Tuesday. On Monday, the Bush administration strongly criticized Taiwan's moves to hold a referendum that could be interpreted as **a separatist move**.

The premier is also expected to meet US Vice President and Congressional leaders during his stay in the US capital.

Before he left for Washington, the Chinese premier and a delegation of Chinese business executives and trade officials had a look at General Electric's offices in New York. The Chinese premier hailed GE's growing business as an example of a successful **partnership** with China.

Chinese Premier has begun his official visit to Ethiopia in the capital Addis Ababa. He's to **attend the opening ceremony** of the Second Ministerial Conference of the China-Africa Cooperation Forum.

In **a written statement** at the airport, the premier said it was the common desire of Chinese and African people to **enhance** friendly contact and establish a new partnership based on long-term stability and cooperation. The premier will hold talks with Ethiopian Prime Minister and other African leaders on Sino-African relations, plus regional and international **issues of common concern.**

Chinese Defense Minister met his Russian counterpart, on Tuesday, and told him that **deepening** the Sino-Russian strategic partnership in the spirit of good-neighborliness, mutual benefit and cooperation will be a diplomatic priority for both sides.

The minister arrived in Moscow on Monday night for a week-long official **goodwill visit** at the invitation of his Russian counterpart.

According to the Chinese Defense Minister, the development of friendly cooperation between the Chinese and Russian armies, is a key component of **the bilateral strategic partnership** that has also maintained a high level. The minister added that **strengthening** military cooperation will significantly **contribute to** deepening the Sino-Russian relationship.

He also expressed the hope that both sides should **reinforce** their cooperation within the framework of the Shanghai Cooperation Organization to safeguard regional security and stability.

The smooth development of a strategic partnership between China and Russia has yielded fruitful results, **bolstered** by the highly mutual trust and the bilateral treaty on good-neighborly friendship and cooperation.

He **reaffirmed** that Russia will unswervingly adhere to the principles of the "one China" policy and resolutely oppose the so-called referendum in Taiwan.

The Secretariat of the Shanghai Cooperation Organization has opened in Beijing. It is the result of **joint efforts** by the SCO member countries, namely, China, Russia, Kazakhstan, Kyrgyzstan, Tajikistan and Uzbekistan.

Chinese State Councilor, foreign ministers from the six member countries and representatives from other international organizations **attended the opening ceremony**.

Addressing the ceremony, Chinese Foreign Minister **pledged** the Chinese government support to the Secretariat. He believes that the Secretariat will help improve the cooperation among its member countries and **enhance** its role in regional security and development. A UN official delivered **a message of congratulations** from UN Secretary-General, in which he praised the SCO's role in fighting terrorism and its efforts to maintain peace and development in the region.

The Secretariat will provide organizational and technical support for SCO activities, including the study and implementation of SCO documents and suggestions for SCO **budget allocations**. Officials from the six member states will take turns to serve as the head of the secretariat.

At the request of the United Nations, China will send a police officer to Afghanistan to join peacekeeping forces there. This is the fourth UN **peacekeeping mission** undertaken by China after previously sending personnel to East Timor, Bosnia and Liberia. The United Nations has been carrying out peacekeeping efforts in Afghanistan since March 2002.

The first Chinese peacekeeping officer in Afghanistan will act as a senior police counselor. He is **currently** serving as the deputy director of the Anti-Drug Office of the Hainan Public Security Bureau. He served in East Timor on a peacekeeping mission and has been decorated by the UN.

Presently, there are over 21 Chinese police officers working for peacekeeping missions in East Timor and Liberia.

The Sino-African Cooperation Forum was launched in 2000 out of the joint wishes to strengthen **consultation and coordination**. China and Africa alternate hosting the ministerial-level meeting every three years.

China and 44 African countries attended the first meeting in October 2000 in Beijing. The two sides worked out **a framework** for their future cooperation. Chinese experts say the forum is a significant attempt to conduct a collective dialogue and **seek common development.**

"China is the largest developing country in the world, and Africa is the continent with the largest number of developing countries. We share lots of common views on international affairs, such as human rights, developing rights, and sovereignty. The forum gives China and Africa a chance to **strengthen** South-South cooperation," said director of African Research Dept. of China Institute of Int'l Studies.

Practical progress has been achieved since that first meeting. Politically, there've been more **senior-level visits**. Economically, the trade volume has **set new records** every year. It surpassed 10 billion US dollars in 2000 and will easily top 15 billion this year. By the end of 2002, China had **written off** 1.3 billion US dollars in loans to African countries. And over the last 3 years, more than 100 Chinese companies have invested in the African continent.

The Chinese government has outlined the main tasks for the second meeting. They are reviewing the implementation of the documents passed at the first meeting, and exploring new areas and measures to deepen cooperation in key fields such as human resources development, agriculture, infrastructure construction, investment and trade. There will also be **an action plan**.

"The ministerial meeting will issue an Addis Ababa Action Plan. On the one hand, it will reflect the two parties' consensus on political issues and other important international **issues of common concern.** On the other, it will lay down the concrete ideas about the two sides' cooperation in various fields in the next three years," said assistant foreign minister.

This will be the forum's first ministerial meeting in Africa. Chinese analysts say the mechanism serves the interests of both sides.

"China is one of the permanent members of the United Nations. For a big country, **to strengthen** political contacts with others is helpful to **enhance** international status and **expand** influence. And Africa has learnt a lot from the experience of China since it began its opening up policy two decades ago," said director of African Research Dept. of China Institute of Int'l Studies.

Such is the importance of the forum. And there will be more than 100 Chinese entrepreneurs seeking business opportunities this year.

Chinese President has told his Russian **counterpart** that their strategic military cooperation has helped to **foster** international and regional peace and stability. The two leaders spoke by telephone on Friday evening.

The president also **stressed** the great importance the Chinese government attaches to Sino-Russian relations. He said it was China's established policy to **strengthen** the strategic cooperative partnership between the two countries. Russian President Putin agreed, praising the development of Russia-China ties and achievements.

He **briefed** the Chinese leader on Russia's plan for high-level bilateral meetings next year. Both leaders said that a recent bilateral meeting on military technological cooperation in Moscow was a success. Both leaders expressed **their hope** that the two countries would build upon the mutual trust, economic and trade cooperation and international cooperation so far achieved in future high-level meetings.

The two presidents also **exchanged views on** the Iraq situation, the Korean nuclear issue and other issues of common concern.

———————————

China and Europe plan to strengthen their cultural links. Chinese Minister for Culture and European Commissioner for Education and Culture announced this Friday afternoon in Beijing. Both sides wish to **increase their cooperation** in the fields of culture, audiovisual, education, training, youth and sport.

The two sides met at China's Ministry of Culture. Relations between China and the European Union are now better than ever before. But cooperation is not complete with only economic and political exchange. They should now **encourage cooperation** between the two continents in the arts, music, literature and museums.

The development of the economic and political relationship between China and EU has been strong and healthy. And cultural cooperation has also grown rapidly in recent years. Sino-EU relations have now **entered a new level.** And we believe with more and closer cultural cooperation, political and economic relations will be further improved as well. The friendly relationship between China and EU is now developing in all areas.

Both Commissioner and Chinese Minister agreed that **furthering** cooperation between EU and China is important, notably in order to improve mutual understanding and strengthen their respective positions **in a global economy and a global society**. And it will also bring a great impact on the young people of the two continents.

The commissioner said, "Understanding. I believe in curiosity and all of our young people have curiosity. No matter European or Chinese, **curiosity** is a fact for young people and we have to **nourish this curiosity** and show them how diverse the world is, how wonderful it is, how rich it is...I wish a lot of friendship to come with the agreement we have signed today."

The meeting **concluded a three-day official visit** by Commissioner Reding in China.

China has promised to send another 10 million yuan worth of **emergency supplies** to Iran. Chinese Foreign Minister announced the decision Tuesday in a meeting with Iranian Ambassador in Beijing.

The minister expressed the Chinese leadership's deep concern about the **humanitarian disaster** in Iran. He said many Chinese businesses and individuals were also making **donations** of money and supplies. He expressed the belief that the government and people of Iran would overcome their difficulties and rebuild the city. The ambassador said that Iran greatly **appreciates** China's help.

The new supplies are expected to reach Iran in a matter of days. China's aid team currently in Iran has been divided into two groups and they have worked very efficiently.

Today some field hospitals donated by the international community arrived in Iran. Sites have been chosen for them and they will be built within 24 hours. A senior UN officer came to the Chinese camp and asked for two earthquake experts to **aid** his work. He has given high praise for China's **aid work** both in Iran and in the stricken North African nation, Algeria.

China values the commitment of the government of the United States, and hopes the US will continue its constructive role in the peaceful settlement of the Taiwan issue, said a Chinese military leader Thursday. "We **adhere to** 'peaceful reunification, and one country, two systems', and will make all efforts to **achieve reunification** with Taiwan by peaceful means, but will not allow Taiwan's independence."

Chairman of the Central Military Commission met in Beijing with chairman of the Joint Chiefs of Staff of the US armed forces, and stressed that the Taiwan issue is the most important and **sensitive issue** in Sino-US relations. Sino-US relations had developed although **ups and downs** still existed since the two countries forged diplomatic ties 25 years ago.

Both China and the US are major powers of the world, and with different domestic situations, the two countries have **differences** on some issues, but they also **shared common interests.** The development of Sino-US constructive and cooperative relations **conforms to** the fundamental interest of the two peoples, and is **conducive to** world peace and stability as well.

Sino-US relations have maintained good **momentum**, and the two sides should deal with the relationship from the strategic and long-term viewpoint, **expand consensus**, reduce differences, and solve problems, to **push forward** a healthy and stable bilateral relationship.

During the visit, he has good talks with Chinese military leaders on US-China military relations and the international and regional security situation, and the two sides had reached consensus.

The US is satisfied with the military relationship, and is ready to work with China to continue the existing **momentum**. The US chairman arrived in Beijing Monday on **an official visit** to China. Vice-chairman of the CMC, and CMC vice-chairman, state councilor and minister of defense of China, met with Myers on Wednesday.

———————————

Chinese President arrived in the German capital Berlin on Monday afternoon, **kicking off** his six-day **state visit** to the country. **Consolidating** political relations with deals for educational and cultural cooperation is likely to be the focus of his visit.

It's the president's second state visit to Germany since his first in July 1995. In an arrival statement issued at the airport, the President said he hoped his visit would **strengthen** the mutual understanding and trust between the two nations, **boost reciprocal** cooperation and bring Sino-German ties **to a new high**. The president also stressed that all-round cooperation was not only in the fundamental interests of both nations and peoples, but also **conducive to** world peace, stability and development. He will exchange views with President and German Chancellor. Germany is **the first leg** of Jiang's two-week five-nation trip, which will also take him to Libya, Nigeria, Tunisia and Iran.

Chinese President's two-week five-nation tour is a "complete" success. Iran is the last **stop** of his five-nation tour which also included Germany, Libya, Nigeria, Tunisia. During the visit, the president met with leaders of these countries and exchanged views with them on the development of **bilateral ties**, and China's **principled stance** on major international and regional issues.

Occurring against a complicated international background following the September 11 terror attacks on New York and Washington, the president's visit has met the expected goal of increasing friendship, deepening understanding, expanding consensus and promoting cooperation between China and the five countries.

The exchange of high-level visits has been maintained and the **mutual understanding and trust** have continuously been strengthened between China and the five nations. New areas of cooperation between China and the five countries have been **explored** during the visit to promote the overall relationship in an indepth way. A total of 23 cooperation documents were signed **in the fields of** economy, trade, agriculture, science, technology, education, oil and gas, telecommunications and transportation.

This visit is **conducive to** further promoting China's cooperation with other developing nations in Africa and Asia, as four out of the five nations are developing ones. China's viewpoint on major international issues have been made clear and leaders of both sides have discussed ways to **safeguard** world peace and stability. Leaders of the five nations have regarded China as a force for peace and stability, and hoped it play an even greater role in **international affairs**.

44

The president **reiterated** China, as one of permanent members of the UN Security Council, will continue to work for the peace process and **the easing of tension** in the Middle East. The five nations attached great importance to Jiang's visit and warmly received him, which indicated that they treasure China's increasingly important **international status** and are ready to develop the friendly cooperative ties with China on a long-term, stable, equal basis.

Wrapping up his four-nation African tour, Chinese Premier left Johannesburg in South Africa on Friday and **headed home.** His trip to Algeria, Morocco, Cameroon and South Africa is believed to have **opened a new page** of friendly relations between China and the four African states. The premier's tour from August 25 to September 6 featured official visits to Algeria, Morocco and Cameroon as well as **a working visit** to South Africa.

During his visits, the premier **held in-depth talks** with the African leaders and reached **consensus** on important issues. He witnessed the signing of a series of documents with the African leaders on cooperation in the areas of economics, trade, technology, culture and medicine.

While attending **the World Summit** on Sustainable Development in Johannesburg, South Africa, the Premier announced that China has approved **the Kyoto Protocol** to the United Nations Framework Convention on Climatic Change. The approval shows China's **positive stance** on international environmental cooperation.

The Chinese premier also called on developed countries to **assist** developing countries in **capacity building**, particularly in areas such as technical consulting, personnel training and mechanism building. He stressed that **the international community** needs to take immediate action to help developing countries improve their level of education.

His tour is one of China's most important diplomatic events this year, and is believed to have **created new momentum** for friendly exchanges between China and the four African countries.

Chairman of the Standing Committee of the National People's Congress (NPC)met in Beijing Monday with Macedonian President. The president's visit had a great impact on strengthening Sino-Macedonian friendship and cooperation of **mutual benefit**.

China was satisfied with the growing bilateral cooperative relations, and **furthering** such cooperation with Macedonia was **in the fundamental interests** of the two peoples and should be based on **the five principles of** mutual respect of sovereignty and territorial integrity, non-aggression, non-interference in each other's internal affairs, equality and mutual benefit, and peaceful co-existence.

China thanked Macedonia for its **commitment** to the one-China policy. He noted that the NPC wanted to cooperate with the parliament of Macedonia to promote friendship and understanding between the two peoples.

The foreign affairs committee of the Macedonian parliament visited China shortly/ soon after the two countries **normalized diplomatic ties,** he said, adding that a delegation of the NPC foreign affairs committee would visit Macedonia some time this year.

Chairman of the Standing Committee of the National People's Congress （NPC） of China, **concluding** his four-nation tour of Thailand, Indonesia, Philippines and Australia, left this coastal city of Australia Sunday morning for Beijing.

"The Chairman's meetings with more than 70 presidents, prime ministers, parliamentary speakers, **celebrated politicians** and other **dignitaries** in the past 20 days have further boosted China's ties with the four countries," said deputy secretary-general of the NPC Standing Committee. "The official **goodwill visit** has achieved its **preset purposes** and is a great success," he said, who highlighted the following key aspects of the visit:

—— During the meetings, the top legislator stressed China's long-standing determination to expand cooperation and exchanges, especially in the economic field, with the four Asia-Pacific nations, and China's progress will **conduce to** their well-being rather than threaten their development. He also stressed that some major deals awarded to the four countries demonstrate China's sincere willingness for mutual beneficial cooperation with the neighboring countries. Leaders of the host countries responded that the China policy is one of the most important foreign policies of their governance, and they are eager to **further advance** relations with China.

—— The chairman **elaborated on** China's people's congress system during meetings with his counterparts. Consensus has been reached that **parliamentary contacts** can serve the purpose of promoting economic development. They agreed to increase such contacts and exchanges to various levels, including the sub-committees of **the legislatures**.

—— There are a large number of overseas Chinese living in Thailand, Indonesia and Philippines, and the new immigrants to Australia are also on the rise. On the issue of overseas Chinese, the chairman pointed out that their motherland is no longer China, but the country they have been living in for generations; China is just their **ancestral home,** and they are China's relatives. He expressed his hope that the overseas Chinese can serve as **bridges for bilateral ties** and friendship between China and the countries they live in. His remarks were warmly welcomed by leadership of the four countries, as well as overseas Chinese residing there.

—— The chairman explained China's **stance** on the Taiwan issue, and the leadership of the four countries all **reiterated** their adherence to the principle of one China and **pledged** not to engage in official contact with the island authority.

The chairman's visit has strengthened mutual trust, expanded common ground, promoted friendship and deepened cooperation between China and the four Asia-Pacific countries.

Unit Five
China's Economic Reform and Development (I)

导　读

Kintsch 在吸收当代认知科学和认知心理学研究成果的基础上，提出了篇章阅读理解的建构—整合模型。该模型明确地将读者阅读时的表征分为三种水平：篇章字词本身的文本水平(text)；由命题及其关系构成的篇章语义结构水平，即课文基面(textbase)，或课文主题及其相关方面构成的篇章语义框架结构；以及与读者先期存储知识整合而成的、更深层理解的篇章表征——情景模型(situational model)。

Kintsch 将篇章理解的加工过程分为建构和整合两个阶段。建构阶段的任务是形成课文基面，它包括形成命题表征、形成微观命题、形成宏观命题和分配联结强度四个步骤，即创建课文命题网络的过程。而整合阶段的主要任务是产生新的激活向量，使网络中与节点有关的重要信息有较高的激活性，无关信息失去活性，从而突出表征中的有用节点，剔除无用信息，形成一个高度整合的篇章表征，即情景模型。如在阅读第一篇新闻语篇的过程中，读者首先要建立如下的命题框架：

The trade fair is China's first; it aims to …; the goals of this fair are to …; enterprises are exhibiting …; a delegation from Taiwan is also attending …; through the fair …; China is a country…; another two-day hi-rank meeting is held in parallel…

然后，读者从此命题网络中形成更深层的情景模型，即 the trade fair, its aims and goals; its attendants and their purpose and the event

48

involved。

本单元选取了与中国经济改革与发展相关的不同方面的语篇，包括农业、工业、金融、商业及不同区域的经济发展现状和热点。

Key Points

1. In this unit you will be informed of China's reform and development of industry, agriculture, finance, and regional economy.
2. Words and expressions chiefly concern concepts and propositions of economy and aspects involved.

The International Agricultural Trade Fair at the Beijing-based Agricultural Exhibition Center is China's first. Unlike previous agricultural **expos,** this fair aims to promote trade by providing an interactive platform for those taking part.

Chinese Vice Premier **announced the opening** of the trade fair. The goals of this fair are to improve the competitiveness of Chinese products, **showcase** the country's recent agricultural achievements, as well as promote exports.

More than 300 enterprises are **exhibiting** their products, covering goods ranging from farm produce to aquatic and animal by-products. Purchasers from more than 20 countries and a number of large domestic super markets came **to make the most of the opportunity.**

A delegation from Taiwan is also attending the trade fair to **exhibit** their agricultural goods. Composed of representatives from nine counties, the delegation is promoting more than 40 kinds of products, including fruit, tea and grain.

Head of the Taiwan delegation said, "Through this fair, we can learn more about the mainland's agricultural products, and at the same time show ours to you. We hope the relationship between our farmers will be one of interaction instead of vicious competition."

China is a country with more than 800 million farmers, a number that accounts for 60 percent of its total population. The country has been **making continuous efforts** to improve farmers' incomes, and increase the competitiveness of their products. There are **high hopes** that this year's trade fair will promote Chinese agricultural products in the international market.

"We want to make this trade fair an annual one, and also an internationally recognized one. This will also help improve our farmers' incomes," said a Vice Minister of Agriculture.

Running **in parallel with** the five-day trade fair will be a two-day Asia-Europe Hi-Rank Meeting on Agriculture, which also opened today in Beijing. More than 200 senior officials from 25 countries will **exchange views on** current achievements and challenges. The event is seen as an important **multilateral** agricultural meeting following the **stalled** Cancun talks in September.

China's central government has **wound up** a three-day annual conference on the economy, saying it's in a healthy condition. But it's also warning against complacency and says **a host of** problems have to be solved, **chief among them**, unemployment, and farmers' incomes.

The annual economic conference is the most important event on the government's calendar when it comes to **mapping out** economic strategy for the coming year. Saturday was the last of three days of intense discussion. And six major tasks emerged as the focus for 2004.

The government says it will continue with **proactive fiscal and prudent monetary policies**, while moving to expand domestic demand. State financing will focus on **stimulating** the rural economy, China's western region and the old industrial base in the northeast.

Conference participants pointed out that the threat to the nation's food supply from **declining rural incomes** was a threat to the nation's security. To ensure adequate grain supplies, the government said every effort had to be made to **reduce the burden** on farmers, by increasing their incomes and improving their living standards.

Meanwhile, **economic restructuring** will continue to **top the government agenda**. The stress will be on new and hi-tech industries based on the latest technologies. The revival of the industrial base in the northeast will be a key target for the strategy.

The central government will also **strengthen supervision of state assets** and accelerate banking reforms. At the same time, it will further open China's markets to **private capital**.

The opening up policy will continue, with an emphasis on importing advanced technologies. Greater efforts will also be made to improve the competitiveness of China's exports.

The central government says another important task is creating more jobs to reduce unemployment. To this end, it wants every level of the administration to take **a proactive role** in improving **employment opportunities**, while protecting the rights and living standards of China's jobless.

————————

Raising the income of Chinese farmers has become **a top priority** for China's central government in the new year. In a policy document issued on Sunday, a series of new measures have been **highlighted** to step up the development of China's rural economy.

During a press conference this morning in Beijing, officials **briefed the press** on the current economic situation in rural areas and explained what they are going to do to make the best of the new agricultural policies. Most important of all, officials said, how to turn these **policy readjustments** into the real benefits for hundreds of millions of people in China's vast rural areas remains **a major challenge.**

————————

The document calls for continued efforts to push forward **the readjustment of the structure** of agriculture to **tap its full potential** in yielding profits for farmers, and to develop **secondary and tertiary industries** in the countryside to open up more money-earning opportunities for farmers.

A good environment should be created in cities so that farmers can find jobs for more income, and the role of the market mechanism should be **brought into full play** to improve the market circulation of agricultural products.

According to the document, construction of **infrastructure facilities** in the countryside should be strengthened to lay a foundation for farmers to earn more, and the rural reform should be deepened to provide a guarantee for farmers to increase income and **reduce financial burden.**

The document also calls for continued efforts to carry out the task of **poverty reduction** and development in the rural areas and help the **poverty-stricken** people and victims of natural disasters **overcome difficulties** in production and daily life.

The leadership of the Party should be strengthened to ensure that all the policies to help farmers increase their income are implemented to the letter, the document says.

Despite steady economic development in the rural areas, **numerous problems** still exist in the countryside, it says. The most salient/prominent of these problems is that it is difficult for farmers to increase their income.

The document points out that if farmers' income **remains stagnant** for long, their living standards will be affected; moreover, grain production and the supply of agricultural products will be **impaired**.

It will also **constrain** the growth of the rural economy and the national economy as a whole, and **hamper** social progress in the countryside and the realization of the goal of building a relatively **affluent society** in an all-round way.

The income growth of China's 900 million farmers has lagged behind that of urban residents. The **disposable per-capita income** of urban residents grew by 9.3 percent in 2003, five percentage points higher than that of rural residents, according to the National Bureau of Statistics.

The *People's Daily* publishes an editorial Monday **highlighting** the importance of helping the country's 900 million farmers raise incomes.

In the editorial, the newspaper speaks highly of the importance of the document issued by the Communist Party of China Central Committee and the Chinese government on policies to **boost** the growth in the incomes of farmers, describing it as **guiding document** for the Party and the government in **handling issues** of agriculture and rural work.

The average income of Chinese farmers has been growing slowly in recent years and some farmers reported zero and even negative growth in incomes, causing **widening income gaps** between rural and urban residents, according to the editorial.

Such a situation, if not **reversed** as soon as possible, would not only affect the improvement of farmers' standards of living, grain production and supplies of farm produce, and rural social and economic development, but also **restrict** the development of the national economy, it says.

The editorial describes the document as the first of its kind **formulated** by CPC in cooperation with the central government on ways to **lift farmers' incomes** since New China was created in 1949, highlighting the importance the authorities attached to the issue.

The document **urged stronger support** for grain production in major grain-producing areas to help raise the incomes of grain farmers. Resources would be concentrated on the construction of state-class high-quality special grain production bases beginning this year.

In order to **reduce the financial burden** on farmers, the general level of agricultural tax rates will be cut by one percentage point this year and **tax levies** on special farm produce, except tobacco leaf, would be **annulled**.

China's **tax revenue** hit 2 trillion yuan or about 250 billion US dollars in 2003, an increase of 20 percent over 2002. At a press conference this morning, senior tax officials said China's rapid economic growth has **boosted the surge in tax revenue**. Real estate and telecommunications sectors were major **contributors**.

The officials say the country's tax revenue **hit a record high** last year, increasing by 300 billion yuan or about 37 billion US dollars, **accounting for** 17.5 percent of the country's GDP.

Director of State Administration of Taxation said: "Asset investment increased by 35 to 36 percent over the past year. This has **boosted business tax** in the real estate industry and the telecommunications sectors. And personal income tax and car purchase tax also contributed to the rise."

Meanwhile, **tax enforcement departments** intensified their efforts to **crack down on** various forms of **tax evasion and fraud.** Tax authorities pledged to continue reforms to improve the tax levying in social welfare, the projects relating to western China development and the efforts to **revive** the northeast rust belt.

Rejuvenating northeast China is **among the top priorities** for the Chinese government in 2004. That's a message from a three-day meeting on China's economic work called by the central authorities and ended Saturday. Discussions focused on formulating key policies for China's economic development next year. The northeast region was once the heavy industry base and economic engine for China. Lagging behind since the country introduced the reform and opening-up policy, northeast China is aiming to **rejuvenate** itself as China's **economic engine**.

Northeast China once **boasted** the richest natural resources in the country. In the past 50 years, the region has produced one tenth of the country's total coal output and nearly half of its crude oil. Many cities in the region's provinces have proudly called themselves coal cities or oil cities. However, the rich natural resources in northeast China have gradually been **depleted** due to **over-exploitation.** Cities that once heavily depended on natural resources have now been forced to explore new **business options** to make a living. It's become an urgent, but difficult task, for the region to **recover** from years of stagnation.

It's been three years since the government **launched its ambitious plan** to develop China's west. Since then, local authorities have been taking up the cause and trying to **capitalize on** their regional assets. Apart from taking advantage of **traditional strengths** in natural resources, some areas are encouraging the growth of high-tech sectors.

Tucked away in the mountains of the southwest, Guizhou, like many other western provinces, suggests an area with **a backward economy**. Not the place you would expect to find leading-edge technology.

But the province is now **the home to** China's first micro hard disk drive manufacturer with its own **intellectual property**. This is the result of **a partnership** between the GS Magicstor Corporation and **a top-notch** R&D team from US. The company now produces one-inch micro hard disk with 2.4G memories. The disks are used in everything from computers to **global positioning systems**. The company has broken Japan's monopoly on micro HDD technology and even enjoys **a slight technical edge.**

But how can a company from a remote Chinese region lead the international pack in a highly competitive industry?

Chairman of GS Magicstor said, "The board sees this as a technology with great **market potential** and believes China will become the largest market for HDD consumption. We therefore are quite resolute in acquiring this technology. Support of the local government also played a key role."

In a rare move, the local government **allocated** a good 1.2 million US dollars to **aid technology transfer** and to provide **quality accommodation** for the IT engineers from around the world. But the move was not without risk.

Mayor of Baiyun District of Guiyang City said, "We are investing in an area that requires **concentration of high-technology,** capital, and personnel, plus a **sophisticated** marketing network, none of which put Guizhou at an advantage. But we believe in the technology, the R&D team is excellent and we have **strong backing** from the provincial government.

So we decided to go for it."

And the team has **won out in the first round.** The market potential for the micro disk drives is promising. Global demand is expected to reach 600 million by 2005. The company is expected to command 5 percent of the **global market share** by then.

But the market continues to pose new challenges. The newborn business in Guizhou faces stiff challenges from the more established players in the industry. They have to be able to compete in terms of capital, human resources, **brand name and marketing network.** Can the firm survive the competition five or ten years from now?

We must concentrate our resources to make the HDD sector stronger. At the same time we must partner with **upstream and downstream businesses** to realize a mutually dependent environment. It's also important to race with time to keep up our **technical competitive edge.**

All going well, the region will see the birth of several businesses with annual sales revenue exceeding 10 billion yuan or over 120 million US dollars. And Guizhou Province will become the base for micro-HDD production in China.

The local government calls their practice the "**leaping strategy**", one that could provide a new way for the west to catch up with the more prosperous east. Essential to the strategy is not merely relying on a region's geographical advantages, but to try to establish their competitiveness in a few key technologies. Only time will tell whether this is an effective mode of development for the west.

━━━━━━━◆◆◆◆◆◆◆◆◆◆◆━━━━━━━

Chinese authorities have **slated** a hundred new industrial projects for the country's three northeastern provinces in the next few years. The State Development and Reform Commission says these projects are the first step in the central government's moves to **revitalise** these traditionally heavy-industry based provinces.

The commission has confirmed 61 billion yuan, or about 7.5 billion US dollars will be spent on the 100 projects. More than half of these projects will go to Liaoning Province. The rest will be shared by Heilongjiang and Jilin.

Officials say these projects will **cover a range of sectors**, including equipment manufacturing, resources and agricultural processing. **Efficiency and competitiveness criteria** for selecting the best operators in the northeastern region to do the job. The government will play a lead role in **financing the projects** but the backing will also come from bank loans and overseas investment.

The Northeast of China was once **deemed** the engine of China's heavy industry. But in recent years, the region has lagged behind coastal areas in economic growth. The unemployment caused by workplace restructuring as well as the difficulty of life in the area have **prompted** the government to take **remedial action.** Some analysts say the traditional heavy industry zones in the northeastern already have an edge in today's competitive environment. The region is **unrivalled** in its capacity produce in nearly all kinds of products and much of the workforce is highly experienced. The central government hopes to help businesses there improve their productivity and the region raise its standard of living.

The International Agriculture Fair ended Sunday with contracts **worth** 15 billion yuan, or nearly 2 billion US dollars. Chinese products are very popular for their competitive prices, high quality and attractive packaging.

Over 200 thousand buyers from 44 countries and regions visited the fair for business talks or purchases. Bargaining and **deal-making** dominated the five-day Fair.

Director of Marketing and Information Department from Agriculture Ministry said, "Purchases from overseas **account for** 20 percent of the total contracts worth 15 billion yuan. Many overseas businessmen have expressed hope for more cooperation with their Chinese **counterparts**."

A Filipino businessman said, "We signed contracts worth over 1 million

US dollars. The products include seeds and fruits. Chinese products are globally competitive because of their packages and quality."

More than 400 Chinese agricultural companies **displayed** their products including cereals, meat, aquatics, fruit and flowers. Green food and **environmentally friendly** products are among the most popular. Chinese Agriculture Ministry provides technical testing services to help Chinese agriculture businesses create some international brands.

––––––⫸⫷––––––

China's agriculture futures industry is **going global** by forging links with overseas counterparts. China's Dalian Commodities Exchange has signed **a joint memorandum** in Beijing with the Chicago Board of Trade.

The Dalian organisation also **signed a similar deal** with the Tokyo Grain Exchange. Both agreements **commit** the parties **to** sharing information on markets and supervision.

China's Dalian Commodities Exchange features trade in soybean products and is the world's third leading agricultural and financial futures exchange after Chicago and Tokyo. The deal between the three giants is expected to help the Chinese organisation expand and raise its profile overseas.

––––––⫸⫷––––––

China began a new round of surveys Monday into its oil and natural gas resources to determine the best **estimates of extractable energy reserves.** For the first time, the survey process will be conducted using international modals.

China has already **conducted two surveys** into its energy reserves, and put the figure at about 107 billion tons. However, neither survey gave a clear answer that how much of those oil and natural gas reserves is actually **extractable.** Given the importance of the issue to the country's future **energy security,** authorities decide to conduct a third survey using internationally accepted procedures.

Vice Minister of Ministry of Land and Resources said: "It seems that we have plenty of energy reserves which can be used for hundreds of years. However, part of these reserves are not extractable. The figures we have are misleading."

China imported 70 million tons of crude oil and oil products last year, and the figure is rising. Imports this year are expected to **exceed** last year's. The Vice-Minister says **an accurate estimation** of energy resources will help senior officials plan future import policies balanced against the potential for **extraction**. He said this is necessary to ensure the country's energy security and market stability. The survey team is expected to **release its final figure** by June 2006.

————————

Improving the income and general living standards of China's rural population has been given **a high priority** by the Chinese government. This was the message expressed by officials at a recent central economic conference. A reporter takes a closer look at some of the opportunities and challenges in **bringing prosperity** to the countryside.

Nestling in the mountains 50 kilometers away from downtown Beijing, a small village with only a total of 60 **households** used to be one of the poorest villages in the area. Today the village has made a name for itself as **a tourist resort**, and has **shaken off poverty**. Accounting for 90 percent of the village's total income, tourism has become the **pillar industry** for the village.

Head of the Village said, "In 1997, our village's annual per capita income was only 798 yuan, or about 91 US dollars. However, by the end of 2002, the income exceeded 8,000 yuan, or about 967 US dollars. That's **a ten-fold** increase. Tourism helped our village **out of poverty**."

The story of the remote village has set a good example for farmers in exploring ways to get prosperous through **non-farm income**. It is also one of the measures the central government has been advocating in its effort to raise farmers' income. However, for those villages that do not have particularly **favorable natural surroundings**, and are still **trapped in**

poverty, further policy support will play a critical role.

President of *China Reform Magazine* said, "There is **little possibility** for farmers to increase earnings solely through agricultural production. They will mainly rely on **non-agricultural income**. This requires a series of policies which **conform to** the situation in our country, and support the development of rural enterprises, **urbanization**, and expansion of economy at county level."

Statistics show over 40 percent of increment of farmers' income comes from **proceeds of migrant work**. To help farmers benefit more from the process of **urbanization**, experts say certain **discriminatory policies** must be eliminated. They say **rural migrants** should have equal footing for employment as city dwellers. Meanwhile, the government has pledged to continue the reform of rural tax system to reduce burdens on farmers.

The premier is calling for **every possible effort** to increase farmers' incomes and guarantee **ample grain production** for the state. The appeal comes at a time when China's grain prices have hit a six-year high, the result of **tight supply** in the world grain market.

Addressing officials and experts at a working conference on agriculture Tuesday, the Chinese Premier gave directions for more **vigorous measures** to increase farmers' income to encourage grain production.

He stressed the importance of **exercising the strictest arable land protection system**, beefing up construction of rural infrastructure facilities, and promoting scientific and technological advances in agriculture.

The premier says a better crop next year will lay a solid foundation for the sustained, steady development of the national economy.

China's railway authorities have warned that the **cost of train tickets** will rise on average between 15 to 20 percent during next year's Spring Festival holiday season.

They say the routes that will be most affected will be those **departing** from Beijing, Shanghai and Guangzhou. Prices will go up from January the 14th, 8 days before the festival. Ticket prices on some trains departing from Zhengzhou, Shanghai, Nanchang and Chengdu will first fall about 10 percent from January the 21st to the 23rd, and then **go up** after the 24th. Railway officials say ticket prices on the busiest routes are allowed to **float** higher during **peak travel periods**. The **price hikes** will remain in place for no more than 15 days from January the 24th. During the festival, charges applying to ticket return will be the same as usual. Tickets can be returned for a refund up to 6 hours before departure.

Unit Six
China's Economic Reform and Development (II)

Key Points

1. Passages hereafter refer to China's achievements and reform in domestic economy, especially in finance and insurance.
2. Try to group words and expressions in the context of these aspects.
3. Before your reading, recall what you've read in Unit Five.

China was one of the largest **recipients of foreign direct investment** in 2003. And in 2004, foreign multinationals are again expected to target the country.

In 2003, China attracted 58 billion US dollars in foreign direct investment. And **the capital injection** from multinationals increased by 15 percent during the period, making them the most important source of investment. **Mergers and acquisitions** involving foreign companies and domestic enterprises have given these foreign players the possibility of **establishing a presence** in fields as diverse as finance, automobiles, tourism, and telecommunications.

The multinationals see China as an attractive international investment opportunity because of its stable political environment, **sustained** economic growth and sound business infrastructure.

China's Ministry of Commerce has posted the performance of the top 30 **chain store enterprises** in 2003. The results show that the chain stores have maintained their steady growth.

The **revenue** of the 30 chain stores reached 270 billion yuan in 2003, up 29 percent over the previous year. Despite the impact of SARS, nine of the firms **achieved a revenue** of over 10 billion yuan. The total number of stores hit 10 thousand, **a year-on-year increase** of 35 percent. The daily household goods supermarkets are the dominant type of chain stores, with their revenue **accounting for** 56 percent of the total. In addition, the large chain stores are **enlarging their scale** by mergers and acquisitions.

China's state-owned assets supervisory commission announced on Friday its preliminary plans for **restructuring key state-owned enterprises** in the country's northeastern region. The long-awaited paper named the most urgent problems in the industrial sector, and **identified** the regions advantages in its drive for **rejuvenation**.

The number of key state-owned enterprises in northeast China **accounts for** less than ten percent of the country's total, but the **aggregated assets** of the regional sector account for more than half of the country's total.

The State-owned Assets Supervision and Administration Commission, or SASAC, said the state will give financial and policy support to the northeast and **reinforce** its advantages in certain industries like petroleum, auto manufacturing and steel.

Key enterprises of the region include the Daqing Oil Field, Anshan Iron and Steel (Group) Company and the No. One Auto Manufacturing Company. These key enterprises will become a **major driver** in the reform of the local economy.

A riot of color has invaded **markets and exhibitions** in Guangzhou, Wuhan and Sanya as **spring flowers bloom** in the balmy/mild weather.

Hundreds of thousands of tulips are on display at the Guangzhou International Tulip Exhibition. 28 **rare varieties** of tulips, coming from as far as Holland, are on show. Most of these flowers are being seen in China for the first time.

It has become **a custom** in Guangzhou to take flowers home for the Spring Festival. Tens of thousands of local residents have been **flocking to the city's flower markets** each day during the holiday. Apart from traditional blooms, **exotic flowers** from Holland and Africa are especially popular with **market-goers** this holiday season.

Central China's Wuhan city also **heralded/predicted** an early spring as a variety of beautiful flowers brought seasonal joy to the city. Locals enjoyed **a sensory** overload as blooms turned their town into **a kaleidoscope of fragrant color**.

As if this sea of flowers were not enough, the city of Sanya on South China's Hainan Island has welcomed **a horde of visitors** eager to satiate/satisfy appetites for color with the seabed's splendid corals.

Not far to the north, the mountains of Guangdong Province have attracted many visitors as the area's famous plum blossoms **come into bloom**. An unexpected snowfall added to the beauty of the scene.

Meanwhile, in the north of China, an exhibition of **spring blossoms** in Tianjin featured more than 300 pots of **gorgeous flowers**, with forsythia and Japanese quince as the main attractions. Artificial snow added to the fun.

In north China's Jilin Province, Mount Changbai presented **a breathtaking scene**, celebrating the beauty of winter and calling in the spring.

More and more people are becoming keen on the idea of spending their holidays out and about. But signing up for a tour means being **bundled onto** a crowded coach and herded around various **over-visited** scenic spots. And the idea of **hauling a backpack** over hill and dale rarely appeals to any but the young and adventurous. For China's emerging upper-middle class, private cars mean that **dream destinations** are within reach.

During the Spring Festival, the number of tourists driving private cars

amounted to thirty percent of the total figure of those who did not stay at home for the holidays. According to statistics, up to 60 percent of tourists from Shenzhen, Guangzhou and Shanghai drove their own private cars to **holiday destinations**.

Traditional hot spots at this time of year include Southwest China's Guilin city and China's answer to Hawaii — the Pacific island of Hainan. But with their own wheels and the open road before them, many car owners **gave** the more conventional hot spots **a miss** and explored **less-visited** areas.

Some holidaymakers from the northernmost Chinese province of Heilongjiang even drove as far as **the steaming tropical island** of Hainan. The local government of Hainan has organized activities such as "island tours" to develop this new trend.

China would **keep its currency stable** this year, and the yuan would remain **pegged** to the dollar, said the National Bureau of Statistic (NBS) spokesman at the end of the press conference held by the NBS yesterday in Beijing.

Chief economist and spokesman for the NBS said the RMB needs to **remain stable**, as stability is beneficial both to Asia and the rest of the world. He added that there were no plans to adjust exchange rates.

The remarks have **quelled any expectations** raised from a report by the China Business Post published in December. The report said China's central bank was quietly moving ahead with a plan to **peg** the yuan to **a basket of 10 currencies,** instead of just to the US dollar.

China's central bank says there are **no specific plans or timetable** to reform the country's foreign exchange system.

A bank spokesperson **denies a weekend report** that the value of the Chinese yuan will be raised by 5 percent in March. China Business Post reported on February 7, that the yuan will be **revalued** next month. The central bank, or the People's Bank of China, says that such plans just aren't true.

In a bid to further **boost** the development of **the telecom sector**, China's Ministry of Information Industry is likely to **relax its control** over telecom fees this year. This is revealed by sources close to the ministry. Analysts say the move is expected to make a big impact on the domestic telecom market, which has already seen fierce competition partly **triggered** by price wars.

By the end of last year, the number of **mobile subscribers** reached 270 million in China, making it the largest mobile telecom market in the world. However, there have been almost no changes in the telecom fees over the past years. If the ministry **relaxes its controls**, price cuts will be one of the most competitive ways for **telecom operators** to attract customers.

However, sources say that **relaxed control** is no indication that the country is likely to adopt **one-way charge** for mobile telecommunications, because of investors' **sensitivity**. It may take more time to put this **on the agenda**.

The network inter-connection among telecom operators is another problem, especially the linking of **mobile and fixed-line networks**. The ministry is also trying to work out new uniform service and fee policies for the sector.

China has stepped up reforms of its banking system to meet the demand of the increasingly competitive worldwide market. The obligation to the World Trade Organization to open its **banking sector** to foreign competition by 2006 has put new urgency into the campaign.

And in some comparatively developed rural areas, the banking sectors are **piloting a new form of bank**, the rural joint-stock commercial bank.

In a city in eastern Jiangsu Province, seven banks have chosen to set up their offices along this street, which is less than 100 meters long. Some 20 domestic or overseas banks are currently providing their services in the city. Among them, the ones growing most rapidly are those rural commercial banks reorganized from former **rural credit cooperation**.

The Zhangjiagang Rural Commercial Bank is one of them. Its deposits have almost doubled, compared to the figure two years ago when it was **a rural credit cooperation**. That means an increase of some 4 billion yuan in two years, or about 480 million US dollars. And its bad debt only accounts for 2 percent of its total assets.

The bank is **rooted** in the countryside and has a clear understanding of the development of the rural economy.

Localized and market-oriented, these banks often blossom across the countryside, and this brings them some **unique advantages** in attracting local residents and small-and medium-sized enterprises.

Rural commercial banks are **timely and efficient**. They can guarantee our capital when needed. Dozens of rural commercial banks have been approved by the China Banking Regulatory Commission and are expected to be set up nationwide in the following two years. Plans to **absorb** foreign capital into these banks have also been discussed.

————⋘◉⋙————

The China Banking Regulatory Commission (CBRC) on February 8 announced **a probe into bank loans** in fast-growing sectors like steel and cement in the latest move to prevent the nation's economy from **overheating**.

The move followed a conference by the State Council, or cabinet, earlier this month, which, analysts say, responded directly for the first time to **a months-old debate** among economists if **excessive investment** exists in some industries.

The conference decided to **harness the excessive investments** in the three sectors of steel, aluminum and cement, where the government believes a recent capacity expansion has far outstripped demand, and low efficiency and serious pollution have become **protrusive problems**.

The purpose of the CBRC probe, the commission said on February 8, is to get **a better picture of bank loans** flowing into the steel, aluminum, cement, real estate and automobile sectors and see if banks have done their jobs in **delivering funding support** to agriculture, credit consumption as well as small- and medium-sized enterprises.

All state-owned commercial banks, joint-stock banks and county-level rural **credit cooperatives** are required to **submit self-appraisal reports** to the CBRC by the end of February. The commission will hold its own inspections into financial institutions in March and April.

Signs of **overheating** raised concerns among many economists and government officials as early as the first half of last year, while others feared **constrictive measures** would backfire by **derailing** the rapid economic growth that is key to generating new jobs for workers laid off from the state sector.

China's economy grew by 9.1 percent last year despite the SARS (severe acute respiratory syndrome) **outbreak**, the fastest pace since 1997 when the Asian financial crisis struck.

In a report to the State Council at the end of last year, the State Development and Reform Commission (SDRC) proposed measures to prevent further **investment excesses** in steel, cement and aluminum.

The rapid **capacity expansion** in recent years, with thousands of new plants **mushrooming** mostly in the northern and eastern parts of the country, has **distorted industrial structures**.

But the expansion has benefited manufacturers in those sectors, although analysts say the **robust growth** in profits is hardly sustainable. Profits at the nation's 39 major metallurgical firms **jumped** by 93 percent last year on a year-on-year basis, official statistics indicated last week.

Sources said the State Council would soon send investigators to key regions to ensure that corrective measures are **implemented**. The investigators are mainly from the SDRC, land resources and environmental

68

authorities as well as the People's Bank of China, the central bank.

The **environmental and land resources** authorities are reportedly **drafting stricter rules** on approving new steel, aluminum and cement projects. In the middle of last year, the central bank made the nation's first governmental effort to prevent **economic overheating,** imposing stricter lending rules on **real estate** to prevent **excessive investment.**

A few months later, it announced its first **hike** in bank reserve requirements in recent years in an effort to slow down rapid monetary growth, a move that **prompted worries** that this measure would **undermine the momentum** of the nation's economic growth.

Before the government moved, commercial banks had already **revised their lending policies** in an effort to **steer clear of the investment bubble.** Among them, the Minsheng Banking Corporation issued stricter rules on lending to steel firms at the end of last year after its quantitative analysis on the sector detected signs of **overheating.**

<hr />

China will continue to reform its **financial sector**, but the process will be smoother this year. He was speaking Tuesday at a national conference on financial work in Beijing.

Representatives from the country's **banking, securities and insurance sectors** mapped out overall **guidelines** for this year's financial work. Chinese Premier said that the financial sector should play a bigger role in the country's **macroeconomic development** in 2004. He concluded that reform should continue actively this year, but that the process should be smoother.

The Premier spoke of **challenges** the country's financial sector faces such as reform of state-owned banks and financial institutions, rural credit cooperatives and **non-performing loans**.

Details of the reforms **in the banking and securities sector** have not been made public but both the Security Regulatory Commission and Banking Regulatory Commission say a series of reform policies are ready to be carried out later this year.

Meanwhile, **the insurance sector** announced it would speed up its development in 2004 by reforming state-owned insurance companies and further opening up to foreign ownership.

The China Insurance Regulatory Commission says **insurance premium income** for 2003 jumped by 27 percent on a year-on-year basis to some 47 billion US dollars. **Life premiums** came in at 36 billion dollars, up 32 percent from a year before. And **property premiums** stood at around 11 billion dollars, an increase of 12 percent over the previous year. The insurance industry's assets now stand at about 120 billion dollars. By the end of last year, two of China's biggest insurance companies, People's Insurance Company of China and China Life Insurance Company had managed to **get listed** in Hong Kong and the US.

The rapid growth of 2003 has led some to suggest that China's economy may be **overheating**.

Director of China Center for Insurance and Social Security Research of Peking University said, "I think China's economy is still on a good path...although some areas are overheating, **the overall picture** is good."

As China **marks** its third year of WTO membership, financial reform is expected to deepen as part of the country's **overall economic reform**.

———— ✦ ————

China's insurance companies may soon be allowed to directly **trade stocks** and possibly **issue subordinated bonds** to boost their capital base. Chairman of the China Insurance Regulatory Commission made the announcement at an **on-going** national conference on insurance in China.

A decision earlier this month by China's State Council supported the idea of insurance companies entering the capital market directly. Both insurers, who have long been trading through **securities funds**, and stock investors, have warmly welcomed the decision.

The CIRC Chairman says the commission, **under the precondition** of containing risks, will be quick to **draft rules** that allow insurance funds to directly invest in the capital market in various ways. The Chairman made the remarks at an annual conference on February 10.

Chinese insurance companies have long been lobbying regulators for more investment freedom to **enhance returns**, a key factor in ensuring their ability to **pay claims**.

Largely due to policy restrictions, they held 52 percent of their investments in bank deposits at the end of last year. The total amount stood at some 874 billion yuan, or 105 billion US dollars. Interest rates are at a decade low in China.

The Commission Chairman also noted other key issues of insurance reforms, one of the most important being **specialization** of insurance companies. In order to increase the competitiveness of the **insurance industry**, China will approve some insurance companies to **specialize in** certain business segments, such as endowment/donations, health, property and unemployment insurance.

———◦◦◦———

The China Insurance Regulatory Commission, **watchdog** of the Chinese insurance industry, held a press conference this morning. The Chairman said the Chinese insurance industry has made **considerable achievements** in the past decade.

He said the insurance sector has **witnessed** fast and steady growth in recent years. With continuing efforts to reform and open up the industry, the entire market has been greatly improved. In 2003, **the premium income** of the insurance sector reached more than 388 billion yuan, or around 47 billion US dollars. This is a 27 percent increase over last year. The total assets of the industry are 913 billion yuan, or about 111 billion US dollars, an increase of 42 percent. Improving **the social security system** for farmers is an important task.

Government attaches great importance to **social security** for farmers. We encourage insurance companies to develop more products **with a low premium** that farmers can afford. In 2004, we will choose two to three places for a trial. At the same time, the government is trying to work out related insurance policies to better protect farmers' interests.

The government is now considering **the time schedule** and other details for allowing insurance companies to invest in the stock market. **Risk control** is a precondition.

The chairman also **outlined the main tasks** of the commission for 2004. They include continuing reform of the industry; establishing a multi-layer market structure and setting up more market players; allowing more overseas companies to enter the domestic market; and improving supervision of the industry.

The State Council in China has **released** a new policy on promoting the stability and development of the country's capital market. The announcement has **generated wide interest** in the financial community.

Entitled, "Opinions on ways to encourage reform, opening-up and stable development of capital market", the nine-point strategy **outlines the guiding principles and tasks** in order to promote the development of the capital market. It also aims to improve related policies on the sector. The State Council has emphasized in the document the importance of a strong capital market in bringing greater efficiency in resource allocation in the economy.

Deputy General Manager of Dept. of R & D, Southwest Securities Co., Ltd, said, "This is the first time the State Council has issued a policy concerning the development of the capital market since 1992. This shows the government attaches great importance to the issue. The new document **touches upon many aspects** including policy and regulation, market structure, investment products and **market players**."

It could be described as objective and strategic, and lays the foundation for the **sustainable** development of the whole market.

While stressing the need for **raising the quality and transparency** of listed companies, the document points out that new products should be developed to meet market demand. The document also says that a multi-layered capital market, including **a corporate bond market** and a growth enterprises market, is needed to expand the channels for various companies to raise funds. In addition, mutual funds and **pension funds** should be granted more freedom to play an active part in the stock markets. Also, **brokerages** meeting the standards could raise capital through **equity and debt markets.**

Outlines for capital market development include improving the quality of **listed companies**, **diversifying** investment products, establishing a multi-layered market, setting up more institutional investors and encouraging brokerages to raise funds through securities market

Currently, the key to the development of the capital market lies in **addressing two issues**: one is the improvement in **returns on investment** in the capital market; the other is the state-owned shares. The document mentions the two problems and puts them **on top of the agenda**. But, we expect more detailed and specific plans to follow. Otherwise, the goal of a healthy and prosperous capital market will be hard to achieve.

In the strategy, the State Council has vowed to solve the problem of **non-tradable shares** actively and prudently, while urging the protection of investors' interests. Meanwhile, the country will continue its efforts to open up its capital markets to overseas investors, and honor its commitments to the World Trade Organization concerning the securities sector.

Unit Seven
Education and Employment
in China (I)

导　读

　　建构主义理论认为，世界是客观存在的，由于每个人的知识、经验和信念不同，每个人都有对世界独特的看法。知识并非是主体对客观现实被动的镜面式的反映，而是一个主动的建构过程。学习不是简单的行为主义的 S - R (刺激-反映)过程，而是新旧经验之间的双向的相互作用过程，即通过同化(assimilation)和顺应(accommodation)两种途径来建构个人意义的过程。同化是指学习者将外在信息纳入已有的认知结构，以丰富和加强已有的思维倾向和行为模式。顺应是指学习者原有的认知结构与新的外在信息产生冲突，而引发原有认知结构的调整和变化，从而建立新的认知结构的过程。同化是认知结构的量变，而顺应则是认知结构的质变。学习就是一个同化、顺应、再同化、再顺应的循环往复的过程。顺应要以同化为前提，同化和顺应的统一就是知识建构的具体机制。因此，学习不仅是对新知识的理解和记忆，而且包含着对新知识的分析和批判，从而形成自己的思想观点；学习不仅是新知识经验的获得，同时也是对既有知识经验的改造或重组。

　　在建构过程中主体已有的认知结构发挥了特别重要的作用，在认知客观世界的过程中认知结构是不断发展的。学习者对知识的接受不仅以自己的知识经验为背景，对新知识进行分析、检验和批判，而且要对原有的知识进行再加工和再创造。

因此，建构主义的学习观认为，学习是一个积极主动的建构过程，学习者是信息加工的主体，知识意义的主动建构者。教学必须以学生为中心，教师的作用并非直接向学生传授、灌输知识，而是帮助、促进学生去主动建构所学知识的意义。学习者建构知识的过程是双向性的，一方面，他们通过提取已有知识(阅读心理学家把读者已有的关于世界的知识称为"图式")建构当前事物的意义，以超越所给的信息;另一方面，根据具体实例的差异性而重构记忆中的先验知识。教材所提供的知识不是教师传授的内容，而是学生主动建构意义的对象。

建构主义认为，学习者原有的经验或知识结构是建构新知识的基础。维果斯基(L. Vygotsky)的"最近发展区"理论和克拉申(Krashen)的"i+1"假说都印证了这一点。因此，外语教师在提供丰富的语料的同时，还应该根据实际情况设置切合学习者认知发展水平并略高于学习者现有水平的学习任务。

依据建构主义的观点，阅读是读者充分利用已有知识，建立和同化语篇意义的心理过程，强调了能动性和已有知识在阅读过程中的作用。同化、顺应，再同化、再顺应的过程需要大量"类同"的预料的不断强化。所有这些特征和心理过程要求在"重复性"较强的中国媒体英语中得到充分的体现和满足。本单元和下一单元选取了与中国学生求学、就业等生活密切相关的语篇为语料，与学生背景知识相吻合，是学生非常关切的"热点话题"，符合读者心理意义建构和交际的需要。

Key Points

1. College and university students are well-informed of China's education, and they have experienced the whole journey of education from kindergarten to college. So read the following passages and exchange your experience with your counterparts.

2. Word cluster will mainly concern higher education, Project of Hope, and employment.

3. Note the essential issues concerning education in China and

consider the counter-measures.

The Chinese Ministry of Education will **launch the second round of its plan** to support educational development in relatively poor western areas in September. Under the plan, **educational institutions** in better-developed eastern areas will send teachers or **donate money**, books or computers to those in western regions, or provide skill training for teachers in western areas.

"The **backward educational system** in poor western areas is **a major hindrance** to local economic and social development, and we will continue to organize educational institutions in eastern areas to help schools and universities in the western regions," said an official with the ministry's Department for Basic Education, quoted by Friday's *China Daily*. The plan, **highly regarded** by the Chinese government, has proven successful since the first round was launched in 1992.

The ministry's statistics show that in the last decade, Beijing, Shanghai and 10 other eastern cities or provinces sent 973 teachers and donated more than 78 million yuan ($9.4 million) as well as many books and computers to the Tibet Autonomous Region and other western provinces or autonomous regions. Such **assistance** has played an important role in ensuring students in poor western regions continue to receive an education.

Since September 1st and the beginning of the new school term, new textbooks have been handed out to over 10 million primary and middle school students throughout China. This is part of an **ongoing curriculum reform project**, which focuses on **de-emphasizing traditional boundaries** between subjects and increases the number of comprehensive courses.

The basic curriculum for primary and middle school students has been **redesigned** to provide **an integrated course** of study throughout the nine years of compulsory **schooling.** Courses are now divided into two groups — **single-subject and comprehensive** courses. Students will

76

focus on comprehensive courses in primary school. In middle school, the focus will broaden to include more single-subject courses along with the comprehensive ones. The subjects of physics, chemistry and biology, for example, have been **integrated into** a comprehensive course simply called, "science". History and geography have been grouped into, "society".

This kind of **integration** of courses brings the primary and middle school curriculum into closer alignment with earlier reforms in the College Entrance Exam, known as "3+X". Teachers report that the new curriculum has already brought about positive changes in their students' learning.

An English teacher of No. 11 Middle School of Beijing said, "The students have shown more **initiative**. A teacher needs only to guide the students to explore the subject actively, to make them do the bulk of the work." Educators say the new textbooks are **designed** to give students more chances to use the knowledge they've learned and more room for them to manage their own time.

The **curriculum reform** started last September in 38 **pilot areas**. 400-thousand primary and middle school students got the new textbooks. This autumn, around 20 percent of cities and counties nationwide have joined the reforms and over 10 million students now have **access to** the new textbooks. It is estimated that these reforms will involve 35 percent of the country next year and will spread throughout the whole country within two to three years.

New Trends in Shanghai Graduates' Hunt for Jobs

In 2000, 47,000 college students graduated in Shanghai. These included 27,000 **bacca laureates**, 6,500 **postgraduates** and 12,800 **training school students**. Seventy-nine percent of them signed job agreements with employers, including 95 percent of postgraduates, 85 percent of the baccalaureates and 59 percent of the training school students. The graduates of well-known universities got better jobs than the previous year, and more than 90 percent **benefited from their universities'**

reputation.

The hiring situation of graduates in 2000 **revealed new trends**: More students decided to continue to study in **postgraduate programs** or in foreign countries. Thirty-three to 50 percent of graduates from well-known universities took the **postgraduate enrollment examination**. In the end, at least 20 percent of the graduates got in. Some of those who failed this year began to prepare for the next examination. Half of the training school graduates **devoted** themselves **to** preparing for the entrance examination for universities. Most of them gave up job opportunities for this.

Studying abroad once more is popular. In Shanghai, five percent of graduates from famous universities decided to study abroad or were preparing for it. One hundred and sixty-two graduates from Fudan University and nearly 90 from Shanghai Jiaotong University have gone studying abroad after graduation. From each of the **ordinary universities**, 10 graduates intended to continue to study in foreign countries. More **postgraduates** applied to work or study abroad, especially those in the famous universities. The number of Shanghai graduates who will **study abroad** is expected to rise to 2,000, including 120 students from Fudan University and nearly 80 students from Shanghai Jiaotong University.

Some students started their own companies. This year, graduates began to focus on **founding their own companies**. Postgraduate degree-holders from Fudan University and Shanghai Jiaotong University, in particular, desired to **found their own companies**. About 50 students **launched** their own companies and 30 already made their own business plans. Many other students look forward to having their own companies.

More students joined **non-public enterprises** on their own initiative. The number of students who joined non-public enterprises **on their own initiative** increased greatly. According to statistics, about eight percent of students chose non-public enterprises. In recent years, graduates didn't care whether their workplace was **State-owned or non-public**, but focused on working conditions, salaries and welfare. Since more non-public firms are devoted to the IT industry, postgraduates are also **flowing to these enterprises.**

Jinzhou Railway No.1 Middle School in Liaoning Province **delivers poverty aid** and clothes to 25 students from **impoverished** families. The year 2000 saw more work to help poor students at post-secondary institutions based in Shanghai. About 17 million yuan in **government subsidies** and funds raised by colleges and universities were delivered to poor students **in the form of grants.**

Students studying in Shanghai's **institutions of higher learning** and **vocational schools** totaled 232,300 last year. Among them, 43,100 students or 18.58 percent of the total were from families with a per-capita monthly income of less than 400 yuan; 29,900 or 12.48 percent were from families with a per-capita monthly income below 280 yuan. The number of poor students increased by about 5,000 over 1999.

The **appropriation and use of poverty aid** in Shanghai's colleges and universities in 2000 were more standardized than in the previous year. In 30 percent of the colleges and universities, 10 percent of **tuition fees** were set aside for a **poverty aid** fund. The **earmarking** of aid funds was also guaranteed in other schools. Part-time work and part-time study program offices were established in **departments of student affairs**, and specialized staff were put in charge of financial aid in 98 percent of the schools.

At present, there are 90 **newspaper stands**, 38 copy centers and four **student-staff supermarkets** in the 132 part-time work and part-time study program bases in Shanghai's institutions of higher learning. A total of 41,190 students participated in the program in Shanghai, **resulting in a profit** of 29.89 million yuan.

The work of granting loans to poor college and university student has also made great progress. Last year, the Shanghai branches of the Industrial and Commercial Bank of China, the China Construction Bank and the Agricultural Bank of China and the Pudong Development Bank **held consultations** in dozens of colleges, universities and vocational colleges, handled **loan-granting procedures**, and approved loans of more than 310 million yuan. To date, 76.02 million yuan, which is 35 times more than that in 1999, have been delivered. Altogether, 26,144 students have been granted aid loans.

Chinese Middle and Grammar School Textbooks Most Difficult in the World

Deputy Director of the Basic Education Department under the Ministry of Education compared the Chinese and foreign education systems recently. Current Chinese science textbooks **at the middle and grammar school levels** are the most difficult in the world, and their **narrowly focused** content is hard to understand. Chinese math textbooks generally are two grades higher than those in foreign countries and they contain much **less human** content than European and American ones.

The difficulty of the textbooks and the pressure of exams are **taking a toll on** students. The Ministry of Education has surveyed more than 10,000 students, and most of them said they disliked school. Seventy percent of schoolmasters and teachers thought that what the schools do best is teaching basic knowledge and skills. But more than 90 percent of students said they don't have enough sleep and **lack free time for hobbies**. They gradually become **examination machines**. The survey said textbooks stress only basic knowledge and **neglect the students' personalities**, values and normal development. During the educational process, students just receive knowledge, and only in their first few years can they do some creative homework.

It is claimed that the present basic education system fails to meet the needs of both the society and students, and that the government will reform textbooks and **upgrade the quality** of the teaching staff.

Chinese college students suffering **financial difficulties and problems** in continuing their studies are to get support from the Central Government. From September 1st, the State Council will release about 200 million renminbi, some 25 million US dollars, a year to provide scholarships.

The **scholarship** is the first of its kind to be provided by the Central Government. It's aimed at outstanding college students as well as students of professional and technical schools **in such dire straits** that they're facing difficulties in continuing to study. Students who get excellent results in college enrollment exams may apply for the scholarship. Apart from their **outstanding performance** in their **academic work**, the applicants are required to be **morally upright**. The scholarship is divided into two grades. In the first, ten thousand students will get 6,000 renminbi a year each. The second awards thirty-five thousand students 4,000 renminbi a year.

Chinese Vice-Minister of Education said, "This scholarship is another big move taken by the Central Government to develop education. It will guarantee poor students can finish their studies without any worries about money."

Students from teacher training, agricultural, **water conservation**, petroleum and geological universities will be the **favorites**. Those who get the assistance will also get their tuition fees **waived** for the year they're successful in winning the scholarship.

Middle school graduates are getting ready to **head for the ivory towers**. But before that, they have to think about their financial situation. In order to ensure that none of them drop out of school due to lack of money, provincial education departments as well as institutions of higher learning are busy **perfecting** the student loan system.

It has long been the goal of the education departments to help students stay in school. East China's Jiangsu Province was the first one to **make changes** for the students' convenience. Since last year, students in

Jiangsu can apply for loans from **local credit cooperatives** in their hometown instead of the cities where universities are. In this way, they can go through all the application procedures and then enter school without worries. On the other hand, this can greatly help banks, which are always **congested** at the beginning of a new semester. Other provinces, including Zhejiang, Henan and Liaoning have **followed suit** this year.

To further **simplify the application and ratification process**, new measures have been taken in many areas. In the past, one university could only cooperate with one bank. But now, banks have to compete to **sign a contract** with the same school. The competition often helps to enlarge the amount of the loan. Shanghai went one step further in **putting the program on line**.

By the end of June this year, over 760 institutions of higher learning had started the student loan project. Banks in China have **ratified** a total of 350,000 applications. Three billion yuan, or over 350 million US dollars, had been **channeled into the program**.

For hundreds of millions of children in China, the arrival of September means the start of a new school year. More teenagers in cities and towns have entered high schools **thanks to** extra education funds **earmarked for expanding enrollments**. But in the vast rural areas, education authorities still need to work to ensure that after the summer no kids have **dropped out of school**. According to China's Ministry of Education, the number of senior high school students has reached more than 13 million, the highest in history. Most of these are fortunate urban teenagers.

The undergraduate **recruitment expansion** practised for five years may **come to a halt** this year at universities that are governed by the Beijing Municipality. An official from the Beijing Municipal Education Commission said that such a policy change is under consideration.

If the policy is changed, the **municipality-owned** universities will no longer expand **recruitment** until the Beijing Olympic Games in 2008, according to a press officer with the commission. He admitted that the number of university graduates is higher than the amount of jobs and that is **attributed to** the policy change in consideration.

Other cities in the country may follow Beijing's example. Beijing **accommodates** more universities than any other cities in the country. Over 900,000 students are now studying at Beijing-based universities, both public and private. **Privately owned colleges** will not be affected by the halt of recruitment. These are more **market-oriented** than **state-run** ones.

Postgraduate and higher vocational education will be priorities for further development, depending on market demand. Private universities are encouraged to continue expanding recruitment. Universities involved are only municipality-owned, **excluding** those directly **under the leadership of** the Ministry of Education, such as Peking University and Tsinghua University.

The details of the change are expected to be released in April. Due to **an excessive supply** of graduates in Shanghai, both **job offers** to university graduates and graduates' expectation for salaries declined, the *Shanghai-based News Morning Post* reported.

At a major job fair that was held last weekend in Shanghai, most **attendees** that will achieve bachelor's degree in summer said they have lowered their monthly **salary expectations** to about 1,500 yuan (US$180). In the past, university graduates in big cities like Shanghai and Beijing usually expected their salaries to be around 3,000 yuan (US$360). During **website fever** in 2000, computer technology graduates saw the price reach 5,000 yuan (US$604) to 6,000 yuan (US$725).

At yesterday's fair, a fresh graduate student from Shanghai surburbs offered **monthly salary expectation** of only 800 yuan (US$97) for a post as a secretary for a real estate service company. Attending companies said that the current salary expectations of university students are reasonable since graduates have **outnumbered the jobs available.**

It is also emphasized that companies will consider **enhancing** their salaries if university graduates **excel at** their jobs after they work at their positions for a period of time. Some companies are **hesitant** to hire university students who offer too low salary expectation as they may **quit** after finding another job with better pay.

Graduates across China have begun **trying their luck** in the job market after the Spring Festival Holidays. The **job seekers** do not want to **miss any opportunity** in this competitive season of **job-hunting**.

In Beijing, the "Spring Human Resources Job Fair" has attracted many **ambitious job seekers** over the years. Some 9-hundred enterprises offering about 15 thousand jobs participated in the gathering.

A large number of college graduates, eager to enter the job market, attended Hubei's first job fair after the Spring Festival. Crowds of graduates **dropped off their resumes at recruiter stands**, hoping to find a good job in the right company. Those running the job fair say high-tech enterprises, especially those related to software, telecommunications and medicine, have been the **favorites of job seekers** this year.

At least a hundred enterprises took part in today's job fair. And local companies, as well as **recruiters** from other metropolises have all brought more opportunities to the **job hunters**.

In Guangdong Province, the government held a series of job fairs for graduates, aiming to **match** enterprises **with appropriate recruits**. And organizers at a job fair say about 250 companies have **posted job information**, and over 3-thousand jobs have been **advertised**, for some 5, 000 college graduates. But they say the competition among job seekers is still **fierce,** despite the large number of **posted jobs**.

Unit Eight
Education and Employment in China (II)

Key Points

1. This is a unit to consolidate your knowledge of China's education, graduates' job-hunting and assistance to poverty-stricken students.
2. Familiarize yourselves with words and expressions in your own context of education.

College students in Beijing are spending their weekend **in search of employment**. Four big **job fairs** opened in the capital today, with thousands of **vacancies**. Most **positions** require years of relevant work experience, but most of the job-seekers won't graduate until June.

Three of the four job fairs are those with at least a master's degree or special skills. The fourth and biggest fair is being held at Beijing's China International Exhibition Center. It's attracted more than one thousand firms across the country, including **big names** like China Petroleum and Hai'er. But their offerings for college graduates are limited.

A college student said, "I found that college graduates like me have less chance here than people with relevant **work experience**. But I still want to try."

Nearly three million students will graduate from universities and colleges across China this year, an increase of about one-third over last year. The increased competition means the class of 2004 has to work harder to **land a job**. For fairs like these, it's an employer's market.

The ongoing **CCTV Cup English Speaking Contest** has entered the second day of its finals. Seven college students from the Chinese mainland and Macao SAR spoke about their **vision of the future**. A CCTV reporter went to the CCTV studio on Friday and reports on the new look of this year's contest.

A review of day one's competition helped the new contestants to warm up and won **understanding smiles** from both the audience and the judges.

The 2003 CCTV Cup English Speaking Contest proved even **tougher** than previous events, as a variety of competition forms were used. Each contestant has to **deliver a two-minute prepared speech**, which only accounts for 15 percent of his or her final score. Another 15 percent goes to their answer to two questions, one from **a question master** and another from **the live studio audience**.

A question master of the Contest told the reporter that usually he based his questions on contestants' speeches.

A bigger challenge comes when each contestant has 30 seconds to prepare for **a one-minute impromptu** based on **a randomly picked topic**. And they have to defend their opinions in a **heated debate** with a group of four. Often it seemed as if they were being pushed into a corner, but their **cunning defense** and unexpected verbal fight back won over even the debating team.

As the **judging panel** was busy scoring, two commentators gave THEIR encouragement to the contestants by further discussing their **impromptu topics** and commenting on their performance. A professor, who already has 20 years' experience with English teaching in China, says she was **impressed** to see so many non-English majors express themselves freely in a foreign language.

Today's highest score went to a contestant from Tianjin University of Finance and Economics, who also **ranks first** in the competition to date.

And the audience chose the participant from Sichuan University as their **favorite**.

Senior students in colleges are currently facing **two major challenges:** passing their final exams to get their **graduation diploma,** and getting a good job. But some of them are finding out that the latter task is much harder than they ever **dreamed** it would be.

Every period of one's life has its own challenge, and finding a job is now the major challenge facing graduates. The challenge is becoming **a serious problem**. After two months of **hunting for a job**, a senior still has nothing to show for it.

"I started **e-mailing my resume** to companies 2 months ago, but received no feedback. The job-seeking competition is fierce now."

But he will not be the only worried person of the 2.8 million Chinese graduates next year. Some experts predict that 750,000 of them may not find work next July. It seems the **expanded college enrollment** since 1999 is an explanation for **the employment crisis**. But the most important factor seems to be that despite the fact there are enough **vacancies,** most graduates aim only for **high positions** with high salaries in the big cities.

A **recruiter** from Hubei Province said, "The graduates should consider their profession first in their **job-seeking process**. Our company is in a remote area where most of them don't want to go. So I don't expect a good result from today's job fair."

But some other experts **take an optimistic view** of the situation. They argue that government statistics of low employment among graduates are not comprehensive. Considering China's rapid economic growth and new policies drawn up by the Chinese government, they believe most of the graduates will find work next year.

An officer of Beijing Bureau of Personnel said, "Our policies help graduates use more ways to get jobs. We encourage graduates to work **in rural and western areas**, as they are needed there. Also, we've held a series of job fairs for graduates with enterprises which need the graduates. So I think most of them can get work."

The Chinese government stopped **the practice of assigning jobs** to college graduates almost 10 years ago. Before then, graduates didn't have to worry about being unemployed. But now, they have to **adjust their attitudes** toward job-hunting and **face up to** new challenges by themselves.

Facing the current situation, today's graduates are trying a number of **routes** towards **self advancement**. Some are choosing higher education at home while others are **opting for** study abroad. Others are trying their luck on the job market. But whatever their choices may be, each graduate will sooner or later face the challenge of finding a job.

The increasing number of college graduates in China has prompted the country's Ministry of Personnel to **launch a nationwide** "College Graduates' Employment Service Week" **to help graduates find jobs**. Nearly 5,500 enterprises and work units, as well as more than 100 web sites, are taking part in the activity.

Starting from today (Monday), the Week will provide free services, including job fairs and **on-line job hunting services**, for **soon-to-be** graduates. Cities around China are holding **simultaneous job fairs.**

Statistics show that China will see 2.8 million college graduates this year, a sharp 30 percent increase over the same period last year. The Ministry of Personnel is expected to hold a total of 90 job fairs across the country during the week, and **secure employment** for over 75% of graduates.

The **Online Job Hunting Service** for university graduates is now into its fifth day. About 3,200 companies have **posted job information online**, and more than 40,000 jobs have been **advertised** for graduates. Eighty web sites are available for job seekers to **browse.**

This is the first time that online job hunting has been available in China and many university graduates are **putting their resumes online** to increase their opportunities of finding a job. According to the people **in charge**, the service has attracted more **advantageous graduates**, and 51 percent of the participants have the bachelor degrees or higher. The job seekers have expressed their satisfaction about the service.

"Online job services give us more opportunities to display our talent through the Internet. This service provides as much information as possible, and it's really convenient," said a master graduate of Foreign Language Institute of Peking University.

China National Talent Web is the **sponsor** of this online service. It has organized 3,200 companies and 80 web sites, including Beijing Talent Web, the major participant, to join the online job hunting service.

The Education Ministry says about four million students have entered universities and colleges in the autumn term. With poorer students getting greater **assistance** from the government and schools, no student has had to **drop out for economic reasons**.

Of the 4 million freshmen, about 20 percent of them registered under **straitened economic conditions**. Schools and the government have worked together to **facilitate access to** higher education for those students, providing them with **subsidies** for transport, tuition and living costs.

A freshman in Lanzhou University said,"Without help from government and schools, it would have been impossible for me to come here to study."

Another freshman from Northwest Teachers University said, "I had very little money when I arrived at the school. But officials in the university **accepted me without hesitation**. They arranged for me to study and live like all the others."

The Education Ministry says about 100 thousand students from the poorest families have had their **tuition fees** paid for. Schools have **put aside** about 200 million yuan, or 15 million US dollars, for **assistance**. Loans from government **total** about 5 billion yuan, or 600 million US dollars.

The Chinese have a long tradition of **respect for teachers and valuing education.** A complete teachers' training framework was **put in place** when the modern normal university system was introduced into China 100 years ago.

They are the students of today. They will be the teachers of tomorrow. The students and faculty members of Central China Normal University are gathered in the newly-built stadium to **mark the centennial anniversary** of the school and also the 100-year-history of modern teachers education in China.

President of Central China Normal University said, "The school is **a cradle** for teachers in Central China. Most of our graduates work in the field of education, especially basic school education."

The **predecessor** of the current school was the Boone Memorial School, founded by William Boone in 1903 as an Anglican **boarding school** for teacher training. Over the past century, the school has trained over 160,000 students to teach in schools all over China. **Thanks to** the national policy of **revitalizing the country** through an emphasis on education, science and technology, normal universities in China have **witnessed** rapid development over the past years. There are now over 1,000 of them in the country. However, due to the imbalances of economic development nationwide, many **underdeveloped areas** in China still lack good teachers.

Member of French Academy of Science Marianne Bastid said, "The problem is that salaries of teachers are not paid, the central government is supposed to give the money, but sometimes the money is **appropriated** by the local government for other needs."

Although, in China, students at normal universities have had **the privilege** of free tuition and guaranteed jobs when they graduate, the low income of teachers has high school graduates reluctant to attend teachers' school. The CCNU is **hosting a university presidents forum**, bringing in educators from around the world to discuss the best ways of encouraging and training teachers to meet China's needs in the 21st century.

As teachers' incomes and welfare provisions are still far from satisfactory, China faces a big challenge. It must take action to **nurture more qualified and dedicated teachers**, the people who will form **the backbone of a healthy education framework** right across the country.

———————— ❈◆❈ ————————

Beijing's municipal government is trying to raise the standard of its workforce by encouraging more post-graduates to **join the ranks of** the local public service. In the past, the authority's Development Planning Committee **took on** 10 people with Ph.D degrees but that number now stands at 15. Today (Sunday) the committee began interviewing applicants for this intake.

The interview part of the **civil service exam** tests two things — the applicant's **psychological approach** as well as their ability to **think logically.** The interview lasts just half an hour and the applicants have to demonstrate that they have the ability to **organize, coordinate**, use language and solve practical problems.

Thirty-seven of the initial 126 applicants made it through to today's **interview stage**. The successful jobseekers will work with the committee in a range of areas including **public administration and finance.** The committee's director is pleased with the quality of the **candidates**.

Director of Beijing Development Planning Committee said, "Most of these applicants have **high qualifications**. I hope the committee can make use of their talents. A number of central government departments and Beijing's rural governments also want to take some of them on."

The committee will select the final 15, based on the **candidates'** area of study, work experience, and the results of the interview. By the end of this year, the committee will also go in search of **prospective recruits** who have a master's degree and some work experience.

———————— ❈◆❈ ————————

The latest research of the United Nations Educational, Scientific and Cultural Organization, known as UNESCO, suggests that students from

China, Japan and the Republic of Korea have the **best academic record** in the world. The research also **recognizes the quality** of China's elementary education.

According to the UNESCO report, high school students in the three Asian countries have the best **academic record** in some sciences, including mathematics, physics, chemistry, biology and geology. Students on the Chinese mainland and Hong Kong also display **advanced reading ability**. The report indicates that whether students get **good marks** depends heavily on the national education system.

At the elementary school level, China has the most difficult courses in some sciences, and the depth of understanding among China's primary school students is **two grades higher** than that of other countries. Meanwhile, Chinese primary and middle school students have relatively good study foundations but most lack experience of **practical applications**.

Even though the Taiwan authorities still refuse **to recognize China's mainland academic qualifications,** more students from the island are **looking to the mainland** for an education. A record number of 200 students from Taiwan have been accepted by a dozen universities in Beijing for this autumn term.

The students were welcomed to Beijing on Saturday and their presence brings the number of Taiwan students in the Chinese capital to 1,000. Some of the most **popular courses** for the group are business, traditional Chinese medicine, law and philosophy.

A freshman from Taiwan, studying Traditional Chinese Medicine in Peking University, said, "I am very interested in traditional Chinese medicine. This university is one of the most **prestigious** in this field and I can learn a lot here."

Another freshman from Taiwan of People's University of China said, "Beijing is attractive because of its **long-standing history and civilization.** Beijing is the capital and **presents culture** from across the whole country."

Taiwan's economy has been suffering a little of late and some students say they **opted for** study on the mainland mainly for career reasons. The mainland's rapid economic growth offers hope for better employment prospects. Mainland universities have been open to students from Taiwan since 1984.

--------❖❖❖--------

The **gap** between rural and urban education in China is widening, and "vigorous measures" must be taken to improve rural education standards, a Chinese government document says.

China's State Council issued the full text of its decision to strengthen rural education Saturday, which explicitly **defines rural education** as the focus of national education policy.

"Rural education serves as the foundation, **the driving force** and an important factor that influences the overall building of **a well-off society** in an all-round way," says the official paper, published after the closing of a national conference on rural education **convened** by the State Council, which ended Friday.

Well-developed rural education will help modernize China's agriculture through raising the **expertise** of China's 800 million farmers, helping **redundant rural laborers** become valuable human resources for China's industrialization and urbanization.

It calls for fulfilling the "two basic targets" of universal nine-year **compulsory education** and **eradication of illiteracy** among young and middle-aged people in the less-developed western regions in five years.

The decision **directs the state to divert** central funding to rural education. New **poverty relief** funds from the central and regional governments will be used to support educational causes in poor rural areas.

It also calls for promoting adult education among farmers to improve efficiency of agriculture and farmers' incomes. More than 100 million farmers will receive education in practical technique each year and more than 20 million farmers will receive **orientation courses** to prepare them for urban life and **non-agricultural business**.

The central and regional governments **share responsibilities** for meeting basic requirements of compulsory education in rural areas. Overall, county-level governments **bear the main duties** for the administration of compulsory education.

County governments are expected **to raise their capabilities** to meet expenses for compulsory education through increased central funding. New educational **allocations** will mainly go to the rural areas.

The paper says a mechanism will be established to ensure that children of poor rural families can go to school. By 2007, children of poor families will all have **access to** free textbooks, **subsidies** for **lodging expenses** and be **exempt from** miscellaneous expenses.

The document calls for public **donations** to education and says the donations will be fully tax **deductible**.

It also calls for improving **the proficiency** of rural school teachers and better educational facilities through building a lifelong educational system for teachers and implementing **a distance education project** in rural primary and high schools.

The decision has **set a target** of equipping all rural primary high schools with computer classrooms and all rural primary schools with **satellite educational program** receiving facilities and educational CDs and players in five years.

The *People's Daily*, China's leading newspaper, **hailed the decision** as a major move to improve rural education in **its editorial** to be published Sunday. It says this is the first time the State Council has ever held a meeting to specially discuss ways to improve rural education since the People's Republic of China was founded in 1949.

———— ❧ ⬥⬥⬥ ❧ ————

People living in **a poverty-stricken** mountainous area in Shaanxi Province have found a way to **integrate** the local school with the village, offering much needed farming skills and techniques. What sorts of education reforms has the village **gone through** in order to achieve its increased living standard?

When we step into the supermarkets and are often **dazzled** by the variety and quantity of food and vegetables, it may never cross our mind that there are still people suffering from **destitution** and struggling **on the verge of poverty**. But there are indeed such people, especially those living in mountainous areas of China, who don't have much contact with the outside world, and who are desperately trying to **set out on the road of prosperity.**

The Qianyuanzhuang Experience has helped many farmers **escape** from poverty, but **self-sufficient** production will never really lead the farmers towards prosperity. Qianyuanzhuang and other similar villages in China still have a long way to go in practising modern and **market-oriented farming.**

A village in a prefecture of Shaanxi Province suffers from **barren land and lack of** natural resources. It is a well-known **poverty-stricken** village in this not so **well-to-do** area. The yearly per capita income of the village in 1983 was merely 83 yuan, far less than the average income of the surrounding villages. For years, there was only one small path in the village leading to the outside.

Some villagers don't even have steamed corn bread; bran has to be added when they make them. The place is so poor that it cannot even support its people.

According to once a village official and headmaster of the village school, in 1987, 638 people from 138 **households** in the village lived on about 160 hectares of land **scattered** on the mountain slopes. There are four mountains, three big **ditches** and 42 mountain **ridges**—poor natural surroundings. Farmers here are hardworking; they go to work in the fields at sunrise and go back home at sunset, but barely have any harvest.

Barren land, together with a lack of knowledge, made it impossible for farmers to harvest **bumper yields**. For years, hard work has brought the

95

local people hardly enough to eat.

Why are they poor? The core of the problem is **the lack of talent**. From 1972 to 1982, there were 120 junior and senior school graduates, but almost all went outside, with only 7 left in the village. Why should so many of them leave? Because it was too poor here, and they wanted to leave. They didn't think how to change the situation here. Thus it became **a vicious circle**: the poorer the place was, the more people were leaving; and with no talent, the place became even poorer. So what could be done to make these people stay? This is the problem we are trying to resolve.

In 1987, the village began to change their thinking and set out on the road to solve the **dilemma of poverty and brain-drain** in the village. Over 10 years have passed; the village has changed a lot in that time. Another village teacher planted grapes in her field, altogether 200 plants. She said she **benefited** a lot from planting grapes.

The village teacher told the reporter that he earned 4,500 yuan every year. In summer, it is all **green with bunches of grapes** here. This field yields 1,500 kilograms of grapes. Starting from 1989, I have gained over 60,000 yuan from this piece of land, **affording college education** for my three children.

Now, houses like this in the village are common. There has been **a sea change** here, totally different from the past. In 2002, the **per capita income** in the village was over 2,000 yuan; many people built new houses. And the villagers raised money to build a road leading to the county. It has become more convenient for them to contact the outside world.

In the village, the most **eye-catching** construction is the teaching building of the village school. This is the only junior high school in the neighborhood. Villagers hope that their children can help the village **shake off poverty** after they have gained knowledge. But many years had passed, the village was still poor, lacking talents that could teach them **agricultural know-how**.

The former headmaster said, "a survey shows that **of the peer group** in the whole prefecture, only 5 percent of the students could enter more advanced schools. That's to say, the other 95 percent would have to stay on the farmland, but what about these people?"

In a local education director's view in 1987, education in the countryside should **cultivate talent** for agriculture. The education mode is **test-oriented**, and the key is to help students **further** their learning in advanced schools. It didn't pay attention to those who cannot enter higher schools. That's why students are not prepared to stay at home. ... And after they returned home upon graduation, they are not psychologically prepared to engage in farming; neither do they have the technical know-how to do so. In a nutshell, they neither love farming nor are capable of farming."

What should be done to cultivate talents the countryside really needs? In 1987, the village **launched an educational reform program** under the guidance of the headmaster. They were resolved to first and foremost equip the students with farming skills.

In order for the students to know more about basic farming skills, students in primary and junior high schools are all offered relevant courses. And the students may choose different subjects according to their own interests. There are courses on planting, mulching, date tree **trimming**, **grafting**, pig and chicken raising, motor and auto car repairing, etc. Students all feel that the courses are useful.

A student said, "We may teach our parents at home or we can make money in the future."

"If I cannot get a place in senior high school, I can use my knowledge of tree planting to **earn a living**." Another student said.

The former headmaster said, "We thought it over carefully at the beginning. In primary schools, for example, we add only the most basic skills in the five-year education. And in order not to affect this goal, we have stretched the usually three-year junior high **schooling** to four years. But we still use the textbooks for three-year students. Why should we add one more year, you may wonder. We **inserted** this additional year evenly over the three-year courses, and finish them in four years. In the extra time, we offer technical courses that are practical for local farmers. There are two **lifelines** in our school: one is to prepare students for higher schools, the other is to **assume the responsibility** of teaching some technical skills to those who cannot enter high schools, in order not to affect their future development. In this way, they will be able to make their own living with their skills when they **step into society**."

To ensure the two lifelines, teachers in the village school have to give at least one course in technical skills in addition to cultural courses. Some of the students can enter **a higher school,** but some can't. Take me for an example. I couldn't enter a higher school, but I learned some practical skills and I'm still able to make a living in society.

In the past ten or more years, the school has sent over 300 students to **senior high schools** and prepared the same number of farming experts for the village and the neighborhood. The education reform has achieved preliminary effects. What then has the village done for those with **no scientific knowledge** and who still live in poverty?

Another villager told the reporter that he didn't dare raise pigs in the past, because he didn't know what to do if the pigs were ill.

The former headmaster told the reporter, "These are the people engaging in farming. If we don't offer them **adult education** and teach them skills, the younger ones are unable to catch up immediately. It was a gradual process. At the start, we divided them into different classes according to their schooling. We had popular, primary and intermediate classes. Another way is to divide the classes according to different subjects. For example, some villagers raised goats and we taught them how to raise goats better; and if they happened to raise pigs, we would teach them accordingly. The training is **well targeted** and the villagers are more interested and active in learning. The third way is **to install a satellite ground reception system** so that every household has access to cable TV. We make use of advanced science and technology to **popularize knowledge** in villagers' homes. We broadcast videos brought from outside and farmers can get educated when they sit at home with food bowls in their hands."

The village school not only helps provide the talents the village desperately needs, but also helps the villagers **shake off poverty**. For the school to play a greater role, it incorporates support from the local officials. The late party secretary of the village led the local people to set up teaching buildings, offered free farmland to the school for experiment, and **launched an overall reform plan** to **integrate** farming into education.

The **underlying purpose** of integrating the village and the school was to **readjust** the external relationships of education, namely the relationship between the village and the school. Before the **pilot reform**, officials in the village wouldn't go to the school to solve problems they met in agricultural production. And the school concentrated on teaching only and had no relation with the farmers, agriculture or the village.

In line with the plan of integrating farming and education, beginning in 1987, the headmaster of the school also took an important post in the village and therefore took part in the village's decision-making.

With this cross-post holding system, we established a village education commission, the most **grassroots** and smallest education commission across China. The major task of the commission is to work over the development layout of both the village and the school. The village **retained** the teachers to form **a think tank** for the village. Each village, however small it is, has a school, and in each school, there is at least one teacher. And this teacher is sure to have more learning than the villagers. He or she acts as a consultant for the village's future development. If there are more teachers, they will form a think tank.

In the village, teaching is the most **respectable profession**. Teachers should not only give **cultural courses**, but also come up with ideas for villagers to **relieve poverty** and become **welloff**. Farmers can really learn about **the power of knowledge** from these teachers.

Unit Nine
Cross-straits Relation

导 读

现代语言学的一个重要特征就是以联系的观点来研究语言，从系统的角度分析词汇项的语义关联性。比如结构主义语义学认为某些词与另一些词之间是有联系的，相互间存在一种含蓄的语义关系。这种含蓄的语义关系表现在上下义关系、反义关系和相对关系三个方面。就语言而言，有些词是概括性的(general)，表示类概念，语义学上称为上义词；而有些词是具体性的(specific)，表示种概念，这类词称为下义词。这种关系表现在语篇中，上义词通常出现在总结概括句或主题句中，而下义词通常出现在具体描述句或例证句中;同样反义关系和相对关系则出现于对比和比较性的语篇中。语篇通过这种关系构成了文脉和意脉的连贯和一致。因此，通过词汇语义上的相互关系，可以形成语篇的宏观和微观结构框架或语义网络。

本单元选取了以"台湾问题"为主的焦点语篇，反映两岸的政治、经济、文化及军事上的合作与斗争关系。语言词汇主要涉及两岸经济文化的交流、台独与反台独以及中国政府的对台政策和外交等主题。

Key Points

1. Taiwan is an integral part of China. However, the Taiwan authority, headed by Chen Shuibian, is conspiring to separate it from China. So the cross-straits relation is of great concern both at home and

abroad.

2. Group words and expressions concerning the Taiwan affairs.

The Chinese central government has **drawn up new measures** to facilitate communication between the mainland and Taiwan. The measures were announced at a press conference held by the Taiwan Affairs Office of the State Council on Wednesday. The spokesman for the Taiwan Affairs Office **took questions** from reporters after the announcement.

The Deputy Director-General of the Bureau of Exit and Entry Administration **released** the new measures adopted by the Public Security Ministry aimed at enhancing cross-strait communication. The new measures include **simplifying travel procedures** for crossing the Taiwan Straits and making Taiwan residents' stay in the mainland easier and more convenient.

In the followup Q&A session, reporters focused on **the upcoming election** in Taiwan. The spokesman **reaffirmed** the Chinese government's **stance** on the issue.

The central government's stance on the Taiwan regional election is clear. We won't **get involved**. We don't care who the winner is. All we care about is the new leader's policy on the **reunification of China.** He also commented on the Taiwan leader's policy of "establishing a structure of peace". The spokesman pointed out that both sides had to obey the "One China Principle," which the leader has never **acknowledged** during his nearly 4 years in office. His ambitions for Taiwan Independence were clear.

"On the one hand, the leader continues to **provoke the mainland** with his **separatist words and actions**, and on the other, he is announcing his plan to establish a structure of peace. He is **a cheater**. He wants to **deceive and mislead** the Taiwan people."

Asked about Taiwan spies being caught on the mainland, the spokeman said the Taiwan Authorities have **intensified their espionage activities** on the mainland, which will severely **jeopardize** relations across the Taiwan Straits. He didn't release details about the meeting between the Director of the State Council's Taiwan Affairs Office and US Under-Secretary, but said the two have exchanged opinions on the Taiwan issue. The mainland would continue to push forward exchanges **on all aspects** in order to realize peaceful reunification.

Travel has just become easier for Chinese crossing the Taiwan Straits. The popular **direct ferry service** linking southeast China's coastal city Xiamen and Jinmen island in the Taiwan region has increased the number of runs. Starting from today (Tuesday), people from both sides can take the service every day.

It's **a scene** familiar to many Taiwan businesspeople waiting for the early morning ferry. And from now on, this new ship will take them home and back across the strait every day, with six other ships already **in the service** for three years. One Taiwan businesswoman told CCTV, "This convenient service has saved us a lot of time." A Taiwan resident said, "With the daily ferry service, my son can come back home every week."

"There used to be no ferry service on Saturday. If I wanted to go home, I had to take a day off on Friday, which is a lot of trouble. Now the service is available every day, so I can go home on weekends."

To reduce **check-in and check-out time** at the border check points, Xiamen now has separate channels for arrivals and departures. Ticket service has also been **upgraded** to include **on-line booking.** During the three-week Spring Festival travel peak, the Xiamen-Jinmen ferry service managed to take more than 20,000 people back and forth in more than 230 runs.

Chinese police and **state security authorities** have **cracked a Taiwanese spy ring** gathering information on the mainland missile bases and naval installations, a Taiwan newspaper said Friday.

Taiwan's "defense minister" **declined** to comment on the report, saying it doesn't comment on **intelligence work** for security reasons.

The mass-circulation *United Daily News* quoted **unnamed** "reliable sources" as saying that the Chinese mainland had arrested three people **spying** for Taiwan's military intelligence bureau.

One of the men, spy ring chief Col., was working for a technology firm in the east Chinese city of Nanjing while collecting information on the military bases.

However, in a second story, the newspaper appeared to **cast some doubt** on its main report. The daily quoted his wife as saying her husband had retired from the military last year and had called her from Japan earlier this week to say he would return to Taiwan soon.

Taiwan's "defense minister" told reporters that he would not comment on the reports. "To protect the security of such people, we do not make any comment at all, and we hope our **compatriots** can support us (on this) ."

Taiwan's other news media also reported the spy ring, saying the spies detained have been handed over to **judicial departments** for **prosecution**.

———————————✦━━━◆━━━✦———————————

The Chinese government firmly opposes the so-called Taiwan Relations Act of the United States, said Chinese Foreign Ministry spokesman in Beijing Tuesday.

The US government had **repeatedly reiterated** its **adherence** to the one-China policy and commitment to the three Sino-US joint communiques since the two countries established diplomatic ties. US President George W. Bush said the United States opposed "Taiwan independence" and Taiwan's attempts to **unilaterally** change the **status quo**.

China urged the US government to keep its promises, and firmly continue its opposition to "Taiwan independence" and any attempt by Taiwan to **use a referendum to this end**, so as to ensure the healthy, stable and smooth development of Sino-US relation.

US Secretary of State has for the first time **clarified** his opposition to Taiwan's referendum. Powell was speaking at a hearing of the House of International Relations Committee on Wednesday. The Bush administration does not **see a need for Taiwan's referendum** and opposes actions to change the status quo.

Neither Taiwan nor the mainland should take **unilateral action** to change the current situation. He stressed that they must **work out ways** to solve their different views and interests together. The Bush administration has made it clear to Taiwan that it is **committed to** the one-China policy. Sino-US ties are the best in thirty years and he expects more progress in the future.

The Chinese government has warned Taiwan authorities to immediately stop **separatist crimes** through advocating a "referendum", and not to **cheat and fool** the people of Taiwan.

An official with the State Council's Taiwan Affairs Office **sent the warnings** from Beijing on Monday. He was commenting on the Taiwan leader's **separatist activity** seeking "Taiwan independence" through a referendum on a new "constitution".

Taiwan authorities, **under the pretext** of local people's interests, recently **scraped** together all sorts of "Taiwan independence" **separatist forces** and carried out "Taiwan independence" separatist activities.

They attempted to prepare a legal basis for future "**referenda**" on "Taiwan independence", he said. The attempt is a very dangerous **separatist move**, an **overt challenge** against the one-China principle. And it is damaging to mainland-Taiwan relations, **a menace** to peace and stability across the Taiwan Straits and Asia-Pacific area, as well as a severe **provocation** to 1.3 billion Chinese people, including Taiwan compatriots.

The Taiwan leader has gone back on his five no's policy promise. They were: no declaration of "Taiwan independence", no **incorporation** of the "two states" remarks into Taiwan's so-called "constitution", no change of Taiwan's formal name, no referendum on "Taiwan independence", and no question of **abolishing** the National Unification Council or the National Unification Guidelines during his **tenure**.

The official said that the activity has revealed his true **separatist attempt**. The leader has fooled the Taiwan compatriots and international opinion by saying that his separatist activity has nothing to do with his promise, but his **fraud** will not succeed.

The Chinese mainland respects the **wishes** of Taiwan compatriots to be masters of their own affairs, but firmly opposes **separatism** through a so-called "referendum" on "constitutional" and "independence" issues. The **risky move** has completely **breached** the fundamental interests of Taiwan compatriots.

The official stressed that there is only one China, and Taiwan is an **inalienable part** of the sacred territory of China. He noted that the Chinese people and government have **a clear and decisive stance** about safeguarding **national sovereignty and territorial integrity**. Anyone attempting to **separate** Taiwan from China will be punished severely by the 1.3 billion Chinese people, including Taiwan compatriots.

China will not tolerate any move aimed at separating Taiwan from the motherland and will **defend the integrity of China's sovereignty** at all cost. This warning was made by a spokesman for the State Council's Taiwan Affairs Office on Wednesday. It was made as the "legislative yuan" of Taiwan votes on the introduction of a new constitution through referendum. The move could provide a legal basis for the island's independence.

Looking at Taiwan leader's recent **provocative moves** for a timetable for a new constitution through referendum, the spokesman said China is strongly opposed to any attempt to move the island toward independence and will defend **China's integrity** at all cost.

Spokesman of State Council's Taiwan Affairs Office said, "We will try with our utmost effort and sincerity to realize the reunification of the motherland through peaceful means. But the leader's recent **provocation** is a serious challenge to the one-China principle and severely affects cross-straits relations. This is against the fundamental interests of Taiwan people and could lead the island to disaster. Chinese Premier Wen Jiabao made the **stand** very clearly last Friday when he said the Chinese government will defend the national sovereignty at all cost."

This is the most important and **sensitive issue** in current Sino-US relations and will be **high on the agenda** between Chinese Premier and US leaders during his upcoming visit to the United States.

The spokesman called on the US to **stick to** the one-China principle and not to send **ambiguous messages** to the separatist forces in Taiwan.

"We hope the US will truly stick to the one-China principle and the three joint communiques between the two sides. In particular, the US should not send **wrong signals** to the separatist forces on the island. It will not be helpful to cross-strait relations, Sino-US relations, nor the reunification of China."

Just last Tuesday, US Deputy Secretary of State said the Bush administration will **deploy** sufficient forces in the Asia-Pacific area and provide Taiwan with "sufficient defense articles for self-defense".

On the issue of **direct flights** across the strait, the spokesman stressed the government's position of "**direct, two-way, and mutually beneficial**" flights. Under this principle, discussions may soon start between civil aviation organizations across the strait.

A Chinese official warned on Wednesday the Chinese mainland would not **tolerate** continued bid by Taiwan's leader toward independence, and any attempt to **split** China would **bring disaster** to the people of Taiwan.

A spokesman of the Taiwan Affairs Office of the State Council said if Taiwan authorities continue to go down along the road of "Taiwan Independence", and push for "Taiwan Independence", it would definitely harm the fundamental interests of the general public in Taiwan and bring disasters to the people of Taiwan.

"We would in no way **remain idle** on that matter," the spokesman told a regular press conference when asked to comment on the remarks of " **'Taiwan Independence'** means war".

The Taiwan island authority is to vote on the so-called "law on referendum" on Thursday afternoon. This could allow for referendums on **highly sensitive issues**. Representatives from Jinmen and Mazu, as well as overseas Chinese in the United States, Austria, and Thailand have **unanimously** condemned the event.

Looking at Taiwan leader's recent **provocative moves** for a timetable for a new constitution through referendum, a representative from Jinmen said it will be harmful for the Taiwan compatriots.

A representative from Mazu has also accused the leader of attempting to realize his aim for "Taiwan independence" by using tricks such as a proposed referendum and constitution, and nation-building and democracy as **excuses** to cover his **real intentions**. The Mazu representative has called on Taiwan compatriots to think carefully about the referendum, as well as its consequences.

"We are against all kinds of actions that may lead to war, including the proposed referendum and constitution."

Meanwhile, the All-China Federation of Peace and Reunification in New York has also strongly condemned the so-called "law on referendum". They say it is AGAINST **the common will** of Taiwan compatriots. They also said Taiwan's leader — in the name of "democracy" — is attempting to realize his aim of Taiwan island's independence. Overseas Chinese in Philadelphia have stressed that reunification is exclusively in the internal affairs of China, and no country has right to interfere on this issue.

They also stress that China's central government has made its utmost effort to press for the peaceful reunification of China. They added that they fully support all measures taken by the central government to safeguard the **sovereignty and territorial integrity** of China. Chinese communities in Austria and Thailand have also condemned the attempts on this issue. They have strongly reiterated that Taiwan is an inalienable part of the Chinese territory. They stressed that the peaceful reunification of the Chinese nation is **a deep-rooted belief** shared by all Chinese people, including those living overseas.

Beijing has **pledged** to respond with tougher action if Taipei passes a law allowing the island to hold a referendum, creating a legal basis for formal Taiwan independence.

Spokesman with the Taiwan Affairs Office of the State Council said yesterday the mainland strongly opposes any law containing clauses allowing **alterations to the island's name, flag, anthem and territory** by means of referendum.

"We will not hesitate to **make a much stronger response** if such a law is approved," he said during a regular press conference.

The spokesman declined to **elaborate on** what measures Beijing would take, but said "all will be known in days," as the law is expected to be passed today or tomorrow. However, he did refer to a government white paper issued in 2000, "One-China Principle and the Taiwan Issue," to demonstrate Beijing's determination to **curb any scheme** to **divide** China.

The document says, "If a grave turn of events occurs leading to the separation of Taiwan from China **in any name**... then the Chinese Government will be forced to **adopt all drastic measures possible**, including the use of force, to safeguard China's sovereignty and territorial integrity and **fulfill the great cause of reunification**."

In an interview with the Washington Post on Friday, Chinese Premier said Beijing will "pay any price" to **block** Taiwan independence.

The latest warning comes as Taiwan's "legislative yuan", or the top legislature, is meeting to work on **the passage of the referendum law**.

The session opened yesterday and is due to end tomorrow.

A draft law presented by the pro-independence Democratic Progressive Party, led by Taiwan leader, has proposed to hold referendums on the island's formal independence.

For Beijing, which considers Taiwan an inalienable part of China, **the legislative procedure** is considered as a move to create legal grounds to **split** the island from China.

The spokesman accused the leader of taking advantage of the legislation to serve his **separatist attempt** to establish the "republic of Taiwan".

"We have long been supporting the wish of Taiwan compatriots to be their own masters and pursue democracy. But if the leader **obstinately** sticks to **a wrong course** and takes further steps towards independence, it will inevitably hurt the fundamental interests of the Taiwan public and bring disaster to Taiwanese people."

At the press conference, the spokesman also warned that **heightened tension** in cross-Straits ties could "temporarily and partially" affect bilateral economic and trade exchanges. We hope the situation will never happen or at least will not last long.

However, he **reiterated Beijing's long-standing principle** up to now of "not letting political disputes affect and interfere with cross-Straits economic co-operation."

Despite the political **stalemate**/predicament between the mainland and Taiwan, bilateral economic relations have grown stronger over the past two decades. According to statistics from the Ministry of Commerce, Taiwanese investors have sunk up to US$100 billion on the mainland in more than 62,000 projects.

Today marks the 60th anniversary of the release of the Cairo Declaration. The document, issued by the leaders of China, the United States and Britain during World War Two, is **deemed essential** to future allied military operations against Japan. One of the most important **missions** set in the declaration was to **strip** Japan **of** all the territories that it seized by force, including Taiwan and the Penghu islands. Some Chinese international law experts say this aspect established the legal basis for China's sovereignty over Taiwan.

These experts **convened** this morning in Beijing to review the historic document. They say the significance of the declaration lies in the fact it serves as the **legal framework** for the international community to punish Japan for its **aggression**. It also demands that Japan return all the territories it has **stolen** from China **unconditionally**.

"The Cairo Declaration recognizes that Taiwan is an **inalienable** part of China's territorial sovereignty. It also explicitly asks Japan to return Taiwan and the Penghu islands to China unconditionally. This historic fact also serves as a strong **rebuff** to today's separatist activities in Taiwan region," said deputy director of Taiwan Affairs Office of State Council.

"The Cairo Declaration is not just a piece of paper. Actually, its stipulations were carried out in the late stages of World War Two. On October 25, 1945, the Chinese government **regained** Taiwan. From then on, China's sovereignty over Taiwan once again became a fact, not just something recognized by international law", said professor of Law School of Tsinghua University.

Other experts present also pointed out that over the past six decades, the **validity** of the Cairo Declaration as a document of international law has been widely acknowledged around the world. They added that efforts by some separatists in Taiwan to **invalidate** the declaration have been in vain.

Chinese Premier has said the United States should clearly state its opposition to an independent Taiwan. He's vowed China will **pay any price** to block the island's independence. The comments come ahead of his December visit to the US, Canada, Mexico and Ethiopia.

In an interview with the Washington Post on Friday, the premier says the Chinese government completely understands the desire of the Taiwan people to expand democracy, but no Chinese government will **tolerate attempts** by the Taiwan leadership to **separate** Taiwan from the Chinese territory.

The comments follow increased **separatist' rhetoric** by Taiwan leader.

Chinese Premier says Washington must be **crystal-clear** in opposing all **separatist tactics** used. He also proposes a mechanism for regular discussion to resolve US-China trade disputes.

It's China's cheap labor rather than the RMB exchange rate that contributes to the **trade imbalance**. The premier also says progress has been made in **narrowing differences** between the United States and the DPRK, and further progress is possible if both sides stick with multilateral talks in Beijing.

Unit Ten
Developing Cities in China

导　读

　　阅读过程是一个智力过程，语篇所有信息就是在这个过程中储存在记忆里的。语篇之所以能成为语篇，读者之所以能利用各种语义层面上的衔接手段解读语篇，都是因为读者有这个阅读过程的心理基础。作为衔接手段，语篇内指称关系的建立离不开读者的记忆储存，它是读者的心智体现或心理表征，因为指称在语篇内部可能会有连续的指代关系，这时指称已经不是语篇内部原先的具体所指，而是读者心理表征中的指称，即读者记忆中建立的上下文相互联系的指称链或语义链。

　　这种心理表征有两种情形：一种是有关真实世界的心理表征；另一种是由特定语篇产生的心理表征。在一定程度上两者是不可分离的，因为读者对语篇的理解不会脱离其对真实世界的认识。读者的心理表征包括语篇本身的信息和读者处理语篇信息时所依赖的世界知识。世界知识是共享的，是读者与语篇或作者沟通的基础。读者对真实世界的知识越丰富，越有利于读者对语篇的理解和记忆。

　　语篇指称照应的确立既不能限于语篇本身，又不能脱离语篇。由语篇和真实世界在读者心智上所产生的心理表征是确立和理解语篇照应关系的关键所在。国外媒体英语篇章由于其特定的文化背景和价值取向，语篇的内外照应及语言体现形式成为中国英语学习者和读者的难点。而中国迅速发展的英文媒体语篇恰好弥补了这一点，因此，对于中高级语言学习者具有较强的可读性。

本单元选取了丰富的有关中国主要城市发展的英文媒体语篇。读者可以充分利用自己所掌握的有关这些城市的知识，预测和学习相关的篇章和语言知识。建立 cities or metropolis → its geographic and cultural properties → significant projects → activities involved → policies and blueprint for development 等相关的城市发展语义框架和语言词汇语义链。

Key Points

1. This unit will provide readers with techniques to report news about cities in China.
2. Resort to your knowledge of Chinese cities and describe a city familiar to you.
3. Group words and expressions concerned with the city life.

It may be seven years away, but China's **economic hub** Shanghai is already **gearing up** to host the 2010 World Expo. The city is **sponsoring** a forum on the event on Thursday to learn from the experiences of other expo cities. Shanghai's Vice-Mayor says he's confident the city will hold a successful expo in 2010. **Creativity** will be key to the success of the event and the preparation plans and work will open to the public.

Besides the central government's financial support, Shanghai welcomes overseas and private investment in the event. The Vice-Mayor says the forum is **an opportunity for China to exchange ideas** with the other former hosts of the event. Organizers are looking for the best ways to **attract the interest and investments** from the business sector. More than 230 participants from previous World Expo cities will attend the forum.

On Wednesday, the Shanghai Municipality and the International Exhibition Bureau said Shanghai will **host similar forums** each year until the 2010 World Expo.

───────────── ❧ ❦ ❧ ─────────────

Shanghai has drawn up **preliminary plans** for financing and investment for the Shanghai World Expo in 2010. The funds will come mainly from government investments, bank loans and company sponsorships. The city has also started **recruiting professionals** from around the world for the event.

It is estimated that the Shanghai Expo will require a total of 25 billion yuan, or three billion US dollars, for **the acquisition of land** and construction of facilities. Shanghai has established **a land reserve center** and a special company to seek financing and carry out investment.

Deputy Director of Shanghai World Expo Affairs Coordination Bureau said, "Input from the Government as well as State assets and capital will no doubt **constitute** an important part of the investment. However, concrete projects will be run openly in line with market rules."

In addition to the financing and investment plan, Shanghai Expo organizers have started **recruiting management and technical professionals** worldwide. The 50 senior and medium level positions **involve** development strategy research, financing and investment, project management, legal counsel and Expo promotion. They are also **soliciting** an emblem, anthem and slogan for the event.

China's two economic **powerhouses** are combining forces to make greater progress. Shanghai and Hong Kong have set down an outline of future economic and trade cooperation that aims for **win-win** development that should affect all of China.

Meeting the press in Hong Kong on Monday, Chief Executive of the HK SAR and Shanghai Mayor **unveiled** the achievements of the first HK-Shanghai Economic and Trade Cooperation Conference.

After **in-depth talks** between officials from the two sides, an agreement was signed to generate further cooperation **in the areas of** investment, trade, financial services, education, health care and the exchange of talents.

During the press conference, Shanghai Mayor said that Shanghai and

Hong Kong are facing a rare opportunity for more cooperation which is expected to push ahead with the new round of development in the two cities. He promised that the municipal government will do more work to promote the bilateral cooperation.

Shanghai has been experiencing rapid economic growth and **looked to** Hong Kong to provide the city with needed skills and experience. On the other hand, Shanghai's **consumer market potential** offered many opportunities for Hong Kong businessmen.

Commenting on the competition issues, the CEO said **healthy and orderly competition** would be good for the development of both cities, adding that Hong Kong and Shanghai have much space for win-win cooperation.

The Shanghai delegation arrived Sunday for a three-day visit to Hong Kong.

Shanghai is **casting an international net** to fill management and financial **positions** at the Shanghai World Expo Bureau which is responsible for organizing the 2010 Expo. The first 50 positions were opened up on Wednesday, the first anniversary of Shanghai's successful bid for the world expo.

The **job vacancies** are in the areas of development strategy research, financing and investment, project management, legal work and Expo promotion. Applicants can send their **supporting documents** direct to the Shanghai World Expo Bureau or apply through international human resource organizations.

The organizers are also **looking for creative ideas, for an emblem, an anthem and a slogan** for the event. They also revealed the location and design of the 400 hectare Expo site at a press conference on Wednesday.

Beijing's municipal government is trying to raise the standard of its workforce by encouraging more post-graduates to join the ranks of the local **public service**. In the past, the authority's development planning committee **took on** 10 people with Ph.D. degrees but that number now stands at 15. Sunday the committee began interviewing applicants for this intake.

The interview part of **the civil service** exam tests two things — the applicant's psychological approach as well as their ability to think logically. The interview lasts just half an hour and the applicants have to demonstrate that they have the ability to organize, coordinate, use language and solve practical problems.

Thirty-seven of the initial 126 applicants made it through to today's **interview stage**. The successful **jobseekers** will work with the committee in a range of areas including public administration and finance. The committee's director is pleased with the quality of the **candidates**.

"Most of these applicants have **high qualifications**. I hope the committee can make use of their talents. A number of central government departments and Beijing's rural governments also want to take some of them on," said Director of Beijing Development Planning Committee.

The committee will select the final 15 based on the candidates' area of study, work experience, and the results of the interview. By the end of this year, the committee will also go in search of **prospective recruits** who have a master's degree as well as some work experience.

A ceremony marking the official opening of **the fifth ring road** was held on Saturday. After three years of construction, the fifth ring road, the first **express beltway** around Beijing, is now open to traffic.

The beltway is nearly 100 kilometers long and allows traffic to travel at speeds of up to 100 kilometers per hour. To build the road took three years and an investment of around 13.6 billion yuan, some 1.7 billion US dollars. It connects 10 districts **on the outskirts** of Beijing and links eight other key highways.

The completion of the road is expected to **alleviate** the capital's **strained traffic** as well as **propel the growth of** surrounding areas. The ring road is also the first infrastructure project to be finished ahead of Beijing's 2008 Olympics.

It will be the key beltway providing access to downtown Beijing for the 2 million people living in this area. For the benefit of nearby residents, facilities have been set up to reduce road noise, a 100-meter wide green belt will also be built on each side of the road.

Officials say more **inner city roads** will be built to **optimize the current traffic layout**, featuring more roads going from east to west.

The words "central business district" are **on the lips of town planners** across China. Beijing's CBD is 4 square kilometers big and has **witnessed** fast growth over the last decade. A business festival that hopes to explore ways for further developing CBD's opens in Beijing on Thursday. It aims to promote the district as an international center of financial services.

Beijing's **unique position** as the nation's economic policy-making center **lends itself privileges** in the setting up of a CBD. This four square kilometers of the northeast part of the city has **established itself as a hub** for multinationals.

Already more than one fifth of the world's 500 largest companies are present in the four square kilometer area in Chaoyang District. It also contains more than half of Beijing's best hotels. This gives the area all the elements to qualify **as** the CBD of Beijing.

The district chief is **optimistic** that the area can become an international center for financial services. The Chief of Chaoyang District, Beijing, said, "Beijing has already gained an advantage to turn itself into a center for financial services. The city already has **major multinational corps**, who are aware of Beijing's **potential influence** on the domestic market. The fact that the city will open itself to the foreign banking industry next year will offer further opportunities for development."

Some believe that there is still a way to go before **the vision** can be realized. The nation's financial **decision making bodies** still fall outside the CBD area and the district's ability to **amass capital** is yet to develop. There are also issues like infrastructure buildings and transportation to consider. Local officials are turning to Manhattan to see if they can learn from the experience of others.

Manhattan Borough President said, " Transportation is always extremely important to move the workforce around to support the business. Then there needs to be a capable work force to perform the work to **fulfill the needs of** the community. One needs to be open for ideas and encourage investment from all across the spectrum, as long as it is **compatible with** people's needs. "

Local authorities have **mapped out** new plans to speed up infrastructure building, improve the environment and transportation facilities. They've also been trying to **create a platform** for international businesses to **explore investment opportunities** in the CBD area. And the response has been warm.

CEO of Clubs International Inc. said, "The most important is the people — if you can talk to the people there, they care and work hard. You have such wonderful people here, and they care. The people and infrastructure in Beijing are marvellous. The CEOs are **inspired** and want to come back. "

It usually takes about 10 to 20 years to build a CBD, during which time governments need to **face up to** issues ranging from financing to management. The smooth handling of these problems will allow Beijing, already China's political and cultural center, to **pinch a third title** from Shanghai, that of China's business center.

———⟨◆⟩———

Even though Beijing has become a modern **metropolis** that makes many an eye **turn green with envy,** the capital's city planners have decided that they must draw the line somewhere. They've decided that Beijing will retain its **original outline**, shaped by its past as the walled Ming and Qing dynasties' capital.

A bird's-eye view of the old Beijing looks like an upside-down capital letter "T". A template/mould has been **blurred** in recent times by **the sprawl of urban construction**. According to the latest "Regulations of Beijing Construction Projects and Designs", the capital will **maintain its original shape,** by building a 30-meter wide green belt along the old city walls. Modern construction within the second ring road will be seriously limited and any architecture **damaging the old city image** will not be allowed.

———————————<<<>>>———————————

World Carnival has proved to be extremely popular in Shanghai since it first opened in the Chinese metropolis on June 27, so much that organizers are planning another round this autumn. So far, more than 600,000 visitors have taken rides at the world's largest **touring fairground**.

Since opening about two weeks ago, the carnival has been attracting more than 40,000 visitors daily. Surprisingly for the organizers, more adventurous rides such as G-Force and MegaDrop have been favored by visitors **consisting mainly of** young females.

The summer carnival will end on July 27, but staff will stay in Shanghai to prepare for an autumn carnival in September and October.

———————————<<<>>>———————————

A two-day international conference aimed at **revitalizing** Asian tourism has concluded in Hong Kong. 48 countries and regions attending the meeting issued a joint declaration on Tuesday, agreeing to strengthen cooperation so as to attract more tourists to Asia.

The joint declaration was **unanimously adopted** at the Minister's Round-Table Meeting on Tuesday. The declaration defines the roles of governments and industry in revitalizing Asian tourism.

First, to achieve sustainable development for the tourism industry, governments and international organizations must **reinforce** their coordination and supervision system by expanding their contacts and building their industry network.

Secondly, governments must cooperate with each other in providing travel advice, services and conveniences for travelers. Thirdly, governments and **private sectors** must have broader cooperation in tourism planning and management. Fourthly, governments must also cooperate with **the community and media** to provide accurate and timely safety information for the tourist's destination.

One of the representatives from the World Tourism Organization says governments must **further** their cooperation and overall planning to deal with any possible crises in the future.

Professionals from the Chinese mainland will find it easier to work in Hong Kong **under a new scheme** starting Tuesday. Hong Kong officials say the new policy will further **facilitate communication** between the mainland and Hong Kong and benefit the SAR's economic development.

The new scheme aims to attract more **top professionals** from the mainland, help develop Hong Kong's economy and promote the economic communication between the mainland and Hong Kong. This new plan, with no **sectorial restrictions** or quotas, opens the door wider to **candidates** who possess the necessary **academic qualifications**, professional skills and experience.

However, under the new scheme, prospective employers must prove to the Immigration Department that they are unable to find suitable candidates in Hong Kong. In this way, mainland applicants will not be **competing for jobs with locals**. Instead, bringing **qualified personnel** from the mainland should raise Hong Kong's competitiveness in the international market.

An official of Immigration Department, HK SAR, said, "We hope this scheme will attract more mainland professionals and will help generate greater economic activity and in turn bring more employment opportunities in the Hong Kong SAR."

The new plan has **attracted great attention** in HK. So far, the immigration department has received ten applications which must be made by the prospective employer in Hong Kong. The Immigration Department will **process applications** within four weeks.

According to a survey, this kind of policy has introduced 597 professionals from the Chinese mainland, bringing considerable economic revenue to Hong Kong.

———————————————

From December of this year, a national examination on translation will be held on trial in China. **The setup of this new system** is regarded as a very important step towards a further regularization of the **professional translation market**.

At a joint press conference held by the Chinese Ministry of Personnel and the Foreign Press Bureau of China, an expert commission for this **institutionalized examination** was formed. The commission consists of over 40 **seasoned/experienced experts**, all of whom enjoy high reputation in China's translation field. Compared with the previous system which applied only to a few professional translators, this new system incorporates all people who have the qualifications to be a good translator or interpreter.

With **a professional certificate** issued to every qualified candidate, there will be a national standard for any institution or enterprise to evaluate the level of their translators. It's obvious that the establishment of this system will be **a propelling force** to stimulate the national competition in the field of translation, while encouraging more young people to improve their **English proficiency**. The scale of the examination is expected to expand nationwide next year.

———————————————

Shanghai now is attracting more and more Chinese professionals and academics from overseas, with visions of new prosperity in their home country. But some are hesitant, especially those with young children who know little about their parents' **land of birth**. The city's education authority has **launched a concerted effort** to ease parental worries about the language difficulties and culture shock that their children may face when they leave the West for Shanghai.

20 years ago, a young man went to the United States to pursue a Ph.D degree. He moved back to Shanghai last year and is now **a principal engineer** at an international telecommunications company here. But his wife, his 11-year-old son and 6-year-old daughter are still in America. Ever since he returned, he has been busy looking for schools for his children. The search has proven difficult.

My children grew up in the US, and have a different language and cultural background than local kids here. They won't be able to catch up with others in local schools, as they are used to a much more **relaxed learning system.**

The Shanghai Personnel Bureau reports that more than 32,000 people have come back to the city after years of overseas education and work experience. The number accounts for 1/5 of the nation's total, and continues to rise. Some 70% of these people are in their mid-30s to 40s, and have schoolage children.

An official of Shanghai Personnel Bureau said, "Finding a good school for their children is a big concern for **overseas returnees**. In some cases, it has become THE factor that holds back parents from returning."

Currently, there are two types of schools in Shanghai that attempt to meet the demands. There are 19 foreign-owned, western-style schools, which primarily **serve the needs of** children with foreign passports. There are also 71 local schools with international divisions for foreign kids and children of **overseas returnees**.

And just recently, two local private schools dedicated one class each as test units for kids of overseas returnees, with English-speaking local teachers in charge. Interviews are under way for admission to the fall semester. Yet, despite the increasing number of such schools, problems remain.

Foreign-owned schools are too expensive and it's hard for the kids to learn the Chinese language and culture there. Local schools with bilingual classroom settings are more **affordable**. But I doubt whether my kids can **acquire substantial English writing skills** in order to attend a good US college later on.

With Shanghai's rapid economic and social development, even more overseas Chinese will be considering a return to their homeland. And while problems for their children concerning language and culture may make them **hesitate** now, authorities are hopeful that **ongoing improvements** in the educational system will convince more of China's sons and daughters to bring their talents back home.

——————✦————✦——————

Shanghai is on its way to becoming the third largest container port in the world. The port is the largest in the Chinese mainland, handling more than 10 million standard containers so far this year. Port authorities say **the handling capacity** for 2003 is expected to **exceed** 11 million to record an increase of two million over 2002.

Shanghai Port launched its first container shipping route in 1978, and its handling capacity has been on a sharp rise ever since. In 1994, handling capacity **topped** one million containers, and the figure **doubled** in 1996. During the past decade, annual handling capacity has been growing at an average rate of 30 percent.

Shanghai Port has developed 15 international shipping routes, and has more than 1,400 cargo ships **depart for** foreign and other Chinese ports every month. The port is now building more docks for container ships, **targeting** an expected handling capacity of 25.4 million in 2020.

——————✦————✦——————

An International Auto Fair has opened in Changchun, better known as "motor-city" in China. Tuesday was the first day of the event, and the 50th birthday of China's auto industry.

The weeklong **auto fair** in Changchun is the first world-class **exhibition** to be held in China, since the country was removed from the list of SARS affected countries three weeks ago. Organizers remain on high alert against any possible virus, but participants seem to feel at ease. **Exhibitors** have managed in different ways to **impress** visitors **with** their products and mission statements.

A concept car produced by the German Audi Company is probably the most **eyecatching** car at the expo. The car is the most expensive one ever shown at a China auto fair. Priced around 30 million euros, the concept car is reported to be **environmentally clean**. Audi reps say it has been publicly displayed only once in North America before.

World-renowned car-manufacturers usually **spare no expense** and carefully design their displays to **present their images**. The biggest international **exhibitor**, the German Volkswagen Corporation, has put some two million US dollars into its display. To ensure that everything is authentic European, the company had all the building materials transported in from the continent.

Sales & marketing manager of Volkswagen AG said, "China is important for us. I think everybody knows we have a production here in China. This year, we hope to produce 300,000 cars here in Changchun. And it's also the 50th anniversary of FAW. Lots of our board members from Volkswagen will **attend this exhibition**."

Despite the price of many cars on display being way beyond the reach of an average Chinese, **auto fans** are grasping this opportunity to admire some **world-class autos**. According to an international car-manufacturer, one out of two people has a car in North America and Europe. But in China, the auto ownership rate is only 1 in 200. Therefore, international auto producers are introducing their **state-of-the-art auto culture** to China as **a prelude** to entering a market with **massive sales potential**.

Even though many of the Chinese here might not be ready to buy these world-class cars now, they definitely are dreaming about doing so in

124

the future. International auto manufacturers are aiming to **tap into** this vast market of potential car buyers. With China's rising economy, the cars of their **dreams** may soon become **the cars of their tomorrow**.

Tuesday is the 50th birthday of China's First Automotive Works Group as well as the country's modern car industry. In China's northeastern city of Changchun, people have been marking the milestone by looking to the future. This is a moment to be remembered in China's auto history, marking half a century of independent motor manufacturing in China.

For the First Automotive Works Group, Tuesday also **marks the start of their ambition** to become a world class auto giant. Unlike 50 years ago, when China was proud to have made its own truck, the group now **incorporates** international cooperation as a long-term strategy.

President of the works group said, "As **an indispensable part** of China's economy, the auto industry should be open to the world. Modern enterprises need to cooperate with other countries if they want to develop. To some extent, international cooperation can promote the independent development of our country's auto industry."

The First Automotive Works Group is **the cradle of** China's native auto industry. It saw the birth of the first truly Chinese-made sedan and truck. From a few thousand Chinese cars and trucks a couple of decades ago, the group has today **evolved into a conglomerate** with joint-ventures that have produced several million automobiles. Generations of workers from the factory are helping the Chinese realize **the dream of** owning their own car.

Automobiles are a source of great pride for these workers, especially for those who **witnessed** the whole history of the group.

A retired worker from the group said, "When I worked here 50 years ago, the factory was surrounded by **patches of grassland**. Through several decades of our efforts, it's transformed into a big group with international **expertise**. Now I'm glad to see the group has linked its fate to

125

China's progress into a more **affluent society**."

The evolution of China's first automobile company reflects the general picture of the country's auto history as a whole. The industry was once a small sector listed in the general machinery manufacturing area. But today the auto sector has become the fifth **pillar industry** among all the **industrial chains**. Auto production volume has also **surpassed** France to make China the world's fourth largest motor manufacturer after the US, Japan and Germany.

To mark the 50th birthday of China's automobile industry, a weeklong celebration will be centered around a grand auto fair that opens on Tuesday. More than 1,000 Chinese and international car-makers will display their latest models here in Changchun. It is reported that this **auto fair** will be the largest that China has ever held.

One of the characteristics of **the ongoing auto fair** held in China's northeastern city of Changchun is its distinctive cultural focus. In addition to the auto exhibition, a series of cultural events aim **to stimulate a driving appetite** among ordinary people. With the fall of the gavel, a Lincoln sedan once used in a popular TV series has a new owner. That's just one small vignette/episode promoting auto culture at the weeklong auto fair.

Years ago, auto culture may have sounded foreign to most Chinese people. Cars were regarded as **unaffordable luxuries.** But with the ever-expanding car market, auto culture is being accepted, and even appreciated by more and more people in China. A stamp exhibition tells the history of the auto industry. It presents **a step-by-step overview of the progress** in auto design and manufacture over the past century. Other auto-related stamps, such as ones dealing with pollution control, highways, and bridges are also on display. The role that automobiles play in national defense, farming and industrial production **illustrates** just how essential these machines have become.

China's auto market is vast and largely **untapped**. But only until people all across China accept the idea that they too can have their own cars will they not be uninterested or think of themselves as spectators. The auto industry understands that for this growing car culture **to flourish**, they will have to put the common people in the drivers' seat of their own dreams.

Unit Eleven
Significant Projects

导　读

现代认知心理学认为，知识是个体通过与其环境相互作用后获得的信息及其组织。储存于个体内的是个体的知识，储存于个体之外的是人类的知识。因此，个体的知识可以分为两类：陈述性知识 (declarative knowledge) 和程序性知识 (procedural knowledge)。

命题是知识和信息加工的基本单元，一个命题相当于一个观念，许多句子表达一个观念，仅含一个命题。有些句子表达了多个观念，含有较多的命题。陈述性知识是以命题或命题网络来表征的。命题并非语言学意义上的单词和句子，单词和句子只是观念的形式外壳，而命题则是观念内核，人的学习应该主要针对命题。命题是意义、思想和观念的单元，若干个彼此联系的命题可组成命题网络。人脑中的知识是通过与其他知识建立某种关系而储存的，只有通过一定的网络系统储存的知识才能被有效地提取和利用。

程序性知识是以产生式系统来表征的，产生式指条件与动作的联结，即在某一条件下会产生某一动作的规则，它由条件项"如果"与动作项"那么"构成。人脑之所以能进行计算、推理和解决问题，是由于人通过学习，头脑中储存了一系列以"如果—那么"形式表征的规则，这种规则称之为产生式。

阅读的过程是个体储存知识相互作用的过程。在媒体英语阅读的过程当中，读者既要具备与新闻事件相关的背景知识，激活和调用有关新闻事件语篇的陈述性知识，以解读和建立相应的命题网络。同时，又要依据程序性知识，逐步预测新闻事件发展的顺序，以产生式规则逐步形成新闻语篇的篇章阅读和写作操作技能。

本单元选取了有关中国在建或已完成的重大工程的新闻语篇。读者必须熟悉诸如水电、交通、环境、能源、扶贫等工程的基本概况，即相关的工程类的陈述性知识，问题性预测篇章的基本内容和相关的语言表达项。通过问题性和预测性的阅读，不断熟悉和建立此类语篇的篇章结构或命题网络，内化相关的"语义场"词汇群，从而掌握此类语篇的操作性阅读和写作的产生式技能。

Key Points

1. The following passages will concern the major projects well-known in China.

2. Through reading these reports, you will learn how to introduce various projects in an appropriate way.

After two-and-a-half-year's construction, the Longtan Hydro-electric Power Station, the key project in the development of the western regions, has entered the **damming phase** on Thursday.

Located in Tian'e County of Guangxi Zhuang Autonomous Region **on the upper reaches** of the Hong Shui River, the Longtan Station will be the second largest station in China after the Three Gorges Dam Project on the Yangtze River **in terms of power generating capacity**. The 24.3 billion yuan Longtan Station, believed to be the sixth biggest in the world, will provide much-needed clean energy for China's developing province of Guangdong. The station, which will also **facilitate flood control** in south China, is listed among 10 **landmarks projects** for China's ambitious program to develop the southwestern region.

One of the most **flood-prone rivers** in China, the Huaihe River, might soon prove less wild. Damming was completed Sunday **at a juncture** in its middle reaches in eastern Anhui Province. This makes way for **a massive water control project**.

The Linhuaigang Flood Control Project is one of the 19 key parts of the Huaihe River management **blueprint**. It's the river's biggest water control project. Total investment is estimated to be about 2.3 billion yuan, or over 270 million US dollars.

This initial damming demonstrates China's entered a new stage in **harnessing** the Huaihe River. Covering the provinces of Henan and Anhui, the Linhuaigang Project will aid flood control in the middle reaches of the Huaihe River upon completion in 2005.

According to deputy director of Huaihe Water Conservancy Committee, "The water runs fast in the Huaihe River's upper reaches, but slows down in the middle. So, **flood prevention** in the middle is the key to harnessing the river."

The planned reservoir is expected to enable the region to **withstand extremely heavy flooding.** The project is designed to protect more than 666,000 hectares of farmland and 6 million local residents.

The 1,000-kilometer Huaihe is the third longest river in China, **notorious throughout history for frequent floods.** The area now produces some 18 percent of the country's food grain and 15 percent of its coal.

China's Ministry of Railways says the government is planning to invest in **upgrading** the railway network in northeast China. The ministry says the network needs to improve in line with the region's **economic revival**.

The ministry has **allocated** 400 million yuan, about 50 million US dollars, to the Inner Mongolian city of Manzhouli on the border with Russia. It has also allocated 320 million yuan, or 40 million US dollars, for upgrades at Suifenhe in Heilongjiang, also on the border with Russia.

The aim is to **double the capacity** of these two ports by the year 2008. On major **trunk lines** in the region, the government wants to increase train traffic speed and capacity.

It also plans to build container handling **terminals** in Harbin, Shenyang and Dalian.

———&———

The transport departments of Shanghai Municipality, Jiangsu and Zhejiang provinces have reached a deal to construct **a triangular highway system** that will link all of the main cities and towns on the Yangtze River Delta.

The deal will enable drivers to **traverse** the Triangle within 3 hours. There are 16 cities and dozens of towns located in the Triangle. They **comprise** what is called in China **a "city group"**. A city group is an area with a concentration of cities, and is therefore also a concentration of economic interests.

A city group's function of gathering resources into one area is significant. There are only five other city groups in the world: two in America, the New York Group and the Five-Lake Group, the Tokyo Group, the Paris Group and the Greater London Group.

———&———

Chinese Premier has been visiting **the Three Gorges reservoir area.** During the inspection tour, he called for sustained efforts to develop the local economy.

The Premier spent three days in the area over the weekend. He visited the new **residential areas** for people **re-settled** from the reservoir area. There, he urged local officials to do more to create jobs and **boost income for the newly arrived migrants.** The reservoir area should take advantage of its rich natural resources and strong labor force to promote tourism, animal husbandry and farming. Government departments involved should also step up efforts to protect the environment and control pollution, as well as ensure the quality of the reservoir project.

———&———

A new phase of construction is to begin on China's gigantic **South-**

North water diversion project. The State Council's commission is to present a draft provision on long-term fund raising and management to the Council for approval.

To ensure the project proceeds according to plan, the State Council is expected to approve the **funding blueprint** by the end of the year. Meanwhile, engineers and workers are to begin the construction of the Beijing-Shijiazhuang **emergency waterway** along **the central route** in November. The route will carry water from the Danjiangkou reservoir in Hubei all the way to Beijing.

Along **the eastern route** which links the Yangtze River to the eastern Huanghuai Plateau and the northern port city Tianjin, work on the Hanzhuang Canal and Nansi Lake, as well as other anti-pollution facilities, will begin in December. Officials have **expressed optimism** in **keeping construction on track.**

Construction Commission official of South-North water diversion project said, "As last December marked the beginning of the whole project, this new phase will **get it into full swing**. So the project is well on target to get water flowing along the eastern route by 2007 and the central route by 2010."

Officials say planning for facilities to protect the surrounding environment is expected to finish on time.

The 3,345 meter Yangbajing No. One **tunnel**, the last and longest on the Qinghai-Tibet railway, was completed on Sunday morning. Its completion links up of all of the seven tunnels along the rail route. The tunnel is 4,264 meters above sea level, and 80 kilometers from Lhasa — capital city of the Tibet Autonomous Region. Started on November 1, 2001, it is the longest tunnel built in China so high above sea level. The 1,118 kilometer Qinghai-Tibet railway will extend from Golmud City in Qinghai Province in northwest China to Lhasa in Tibet. **To date**, construction of the railway has cost 12.3 billion yuan.

132

A high-speed railway route between Shanghai and Beijing is the focus of the China Railway Construction Summit currently underway in Hangzhou, capital of east China's Zhejiang Province. The construction plan details how the railway will adopt new **track technology** at a cost of nearly 16 billion US dollars.

The rights to build the 13-hundred-kilometer high-speed railway route are being **chased** by multinational **construction giants** from Germany, Japan and France. Germany has proposed the use of maglev — or **magnetic levitation technology** — that will cost as much as 48 billion US dollars. Japanese and French companies, meanwhile, support the traditional — though very high-speed — wheel-on-track technology that will come in at about one-third of the cost of Germany's maglev. China's railway authority says the railway line will be built by a Chinese company, while overseas firms will provide the rolling stock.

———————————

Chinese Premier on Monday described as vital achievements the filling of Three Gorges reservoir and the successful trial navigation of **the ship lock**.

In his written comments, the premier attributed these achievements to the hard work of the builders of the Three Gorges dam project, the contributions made by the people **relocated** from the **submerged reservoir areas**, and the support of people from all walks of life across the country.

The new Three Gorges dam on the Yangtze River opened to shipping on Monday as two passenger ships and five **freight vessels** passed through the lock in two hours and 35 minutes, concluding at 11:55 a.m.

Director of the Three Gorges Navigation Bureau announced later **the maiden trial navigation** via the permanent ship lock, which began at 9 a.m. Beijing Time, was a great success.

The trial navigation will last for about a year as engineers **fine-tune and test** the lock. The success of the maiden trial navigation signified the

resumption of shipping on the Yangtze River after its **suspension** of 67 straight days for the dam project.

A Vice Premier **launched** the trial navigation at the dam site. Addressing to a ceremony attended by nearly 1,000 construction workers at the dam site, he said the Three Gorges dam project had begun to **pay off** after a decade of construction.

The Vice Premier called on engineers working for the dam project to do a good job in preparing for **trial operation** of the first group of power generating units at the dam.

It was critical to step up efforts to **formulate regulations** on management of the project to ensure the safe and stable operation of the relevant facilities, and to prevent **geological disasters** and water pollution in reservoir areas.

The **two-way five-step** lock, the largest in the world, was built entirely by Chinese engineers after solving a number of **unprecedented technical difficulties**.

The lock, completed after about a decade of **strenuous work** at a cost of some 6.2 billion yuan （about 750 million US dollars）, **features** a two-way lifting facility for the 113-meter drop between the upstream and downstream separated by the **gigantic dam**.

With the permanent ship lock in operation, ships will be able to pass through the dam in about two and a half hours via the 6.44-kilometer **dock** on the northern bank of the Yangtze.

The lock has 24 **lock gates**, each weighing 867 tons, which were built entirely by China's two **flagship shipyards** located in the capital city of central Hubei Province, and in Shanghai, east China.

Previous **trial operations and tests** have shown that the gates and relevant opening and closing mechanisms **comply with** the sophisticated international standards. The metallic structures and electronic equipment of the lock gates were made and **installed** by 16 large Chinese enterprises

134

from 14 provinces and municipalities.

Scheduled for completion in 2009, the Three Gorges project will start to pay dividends this year, playing a vital role in flood control, hydro-power generation, navigation, water diversion and environmental protection.

———————— ❖❖❖ ————————

A vital section of China's long-awaited **West-East gas pipeline project** has been successfully built. On Friday, the nearly 2,000 meter span traversing the Yangtze River in east China's Nanjing City was completed.

The construction of the "shield-driven" section of the pipeline had been difficult due to the **complicated rock conditions** along both banks of the river. Increased **water pressure** during the flood season has also added to the **complexity of the project**. Chinese experts used innovative measures and new equipment to solve the various problems. The West-East natural gas **transmission pipeline** has been designed to supply billions of cubic meters of natural gas each year. The natural gas will be **transferred** to the country's east from China's northwest through a pipeline some 4,200 kilometers long.

The West-East gas pipeline project is expected to go into operation on a trial basis from October 1, with **commercial operations** starting next January.

———————— ❖❖❖ ————————

The eastern section of the West-East gas pipeline trial operation has been completed successfully. Gas from Shaanxi Province' Jingbian County is being transported by pipeline to Shanghai's Baihezhen. Trial operation began on October 1, as a **prelude** to commercial operation of the pipeline **slated**/paved for January 1, 2004.

After **the final technical evaluation**, the natural gas from Shaanxi Province has successfully arrived at its destination — Shanghai. After three days, gas will begin to pump into Zhengzhou of China's central Henan Province.

Deputy GM of Easten Section of China West-East Pipeline Co. said,

"We are planning to store around 50 million cubic meters of natural gas by the end of this month. Once we have signed contracts with customers and gas users, we can supply natural gas to customers immediately."

Shaanxi has an estimated 1.1 trillion cubic meters of natural gas reserves. It will supply many central and eastern provinces with energy for years to come.

According to PetroChina's plan, Jingbian county in Shaanxi Province will supply natural gas via the pipeline to Shanghai before being replaced by Xinjiang's Tarim basin as the gas source. In the beginning of 2005, the Tarim basin will be **directly supplying natural gas to** eastern regions.

China's National Development and Reform Commission has given an update on the progress of **major construction projects** around the country. Officials said work on the Three Gorges Project, the West-East electricity transmission system, and the Qinghai-Tibet Railway was all going smoothly.

The Three Gorges Project is the world's biggest **power generating system**. It is beginning to recuperate/regain its costs, after a decade of construction. The first two of 26 power generators **went into operation** in July, a month **ahead of schedule**. By the end of August, China had put over 90 billion yuan, or more than 10 billion US dollars into the project. By the end of this year, it is expected to be generating 6 billion kilowatt hours of power.

The southern part of China's West-to-East electricity transmission project was completed in June. The southern line **spans** over 1,000 kilometers, and runs from Guizhou to Guangdong, helping meet power needs in the Pearl River Delta.

The construction of the Qinghai-Tibet Railway is **in full swing**, two years after the project began. Investment for September exceeded 40 million yuan, or nearly 5 million US dollars. Once it's finished in 2007, the 1,100-kilometer Qinghai-Tibet Railway will be the world's longest **high-**

altitude railway.

The National Development and Reform Commission said government policy has guaranteed these projects' investment needs.

———————————

The first power generator of China's Three Gorges Project, the largest of its kind in the world, was connected to **power grid** to begin generating electricity at 01:31 a.m. on Thursday morning, 20 days ahead of schedule.

Vice general manager of the China Yangtze River Three Gorges Project Development Corporation said the **generating unit**, known as the No. 2 unit, will supply 12.9 million kwh per day to the Central China and East China power grids. The unit will have to pass a 30-day **trial operation** period under the observation of engineers before beginning commercial production in mid-August.

The 7,700-ton unit, built by **a consortium**/multinational **comprised of** Hewitt, Siemens and General Electrics, has a generating capacity of 700,000 kw.

The **integration** into the two Chinese power grids followed a successful 72-hour **trial period** on July 7. The first attempted trial operation on July 1 failed as it lasted about 68 hours, falling short of the 72 hours required. The failure of a sensor in **a water purification system** providing cooling water for the unit **triggered the shutdown** of the operation. The second trial operation began on July 4.

The generating unit has been turned over to the Three Gorges Hydraulic Power Plant, which will **assume its operational management.** A total of 26 generating units will be **installed** before the project is completed in 2009.

Launched in 1993, the Three Gorges Project will begin to pay dividends later this year, playing an important role in flood control, power generation, navigation, water diversion and environmental protection.

———————————

Work has started on the construction of the Shenzhen-Hong Kong west bridge. When it's finished, it will be the very first link connecting the two commercial centers across the sea.

At 11 o'clock on Thursday morning, Vice Premier and Hong Kong Chief Executive **signaled the official start** to the project.

The bridge is **budgeted** to cost over 12.5 billion yuan. That's about 1.6 billion US dollars. It's due to be finished by the year 2005. The project can help underline the economic relationship between the Chinese mainland and Hong Kong. He also hopes the two sides will strengthen cooperation on even **bigger scale projects**.

The CEO thanked the central government for its support for Hong Kong. The mainland's rapid economic development has encouraged the Hong Kong people. Further cooperation can **stimulate** Hong Kong's economic development.

Crossing a distance of about 180 kilometers, 50 million cubic meters of water is flowing into the Guanting Reservoir about 100 kilometers northwest of central Beijing from the Cetian Reservoir in neighboring Shanxi Province. Officials from the Ministry of Water Resources say there is an important part of **the overall plan** to guarantee **balance of water supply and demand** in Beijing by the year 2008.

On Thursday, a ceremony was held at Beijing's Guanting Reservoir to **mark the occasion**. The water **released** from Cetian Reservoir five days ago is flowing in at a rate of 30 cubic meters per second. According to the overall plan, **upstream areas** will feed water to Beijing at a certain fixed volume every year. By 2005, Beijing's capacity will increase by 410 million cubic meters.

Director-General of Water Resources Bureau and Ministry of Water Resources said, "The overall plan has a total investment of 22 billion yuan. The central government invested 7 billion, among which only 1 billion is for Beijing. The other 6 billion were all given to upstream areas as compensation."

The water will mostly be used for industrial and urban **environmental purposes**. It also creates an opportunity for **ecological restoration** along the dried-up river banks. With the much-needed fresh water, Guanting Reservoir, one of Beijing's two main water sources, will meet the standards for drinking water source by 2005.

The shortage of water in Beijing mainly comes from **the pressure of growing urban population,** and economic and social development. To solve the problem, it seems we need not only government projects like this, but also **active participation** in water conservation from all citizens.

Chinese officials are to **beef up campaigns** to rescue the 30 million people who still **languish**/wither below **the poverty line.**

Despite the great achievements made by the nation in social and economic development, **destitution/poverty** is still one of the biggest challenges facing China in the 21st century.

This is the road to Sanjiao — one of the poorest villages in China. For generations, villagers here have been living in the remote areas, some have never walked out of their mountainous hometown. Sanjiao has some 2,000 villagers, most of whom are the ethnic Miao **minorities**. Local officials told us that **the average income** in the village per year is around 400 yuan, or some 50 US dollars per person — much lower than the government's poverty line.

A villager said, "If the government provided more funds, we can make a better living. We have little farmland, and the whole family income can hardly support the lives of two children and parents." Like this family, some 90 percent of Chinese people in **abject poverty** live in rural areas. They are often **cut off from** the medical care and educational facilities.

Their region is suffered from many **unfavorable factors** for economic progress, mainly as little flat land **to cultivate**, poor natural conditions, and a lack of basic infrastructure. **To wipe out poverty** is among the government's functions, but providing **relief money** alone cannot solve the problem.

A party official of Liangwan County, Yunnan Province, said, "The failure of **the poverty relief work** in the past should be mainly **attributed to** the wrong belief that it is simply a matter of giving money. In fact, farmers used the money to buy food and drinks, and have remained to be poor. **Poverty alleviation** should be emphasized on self-help, and economic development." He said the short-cut to **get rid of poverty** is to relocate these poor people to other areas, providing them with funds and other resources. But few want to leave, and give up their traditional way of living.

However, the **relocation project** is undergoing. At Sanjiao, the local government has **allocated** some two million yuan in the past two years to build new houses, in place of better conditions. And some poor farmers have already got richer after relocation.

Head of Sanjiao village said, "We have persuaded some 200 villagers to relocate, and hope these people will bring more others in the village to follow them. This will help reduce the burden of the poverty relief project in the village."

Since the mid 1980s, the Chinese government started to carry out poverty alleviation project. Most funds have gone to China's interior provinces, and rural **poverty-stricken areas**. If the poverty relief project had been an easy thing, it would have happened already.

With China's development, there has been **a widening gap** between the rich and the poor. In the vast countryside, especially, the mountainous remote areas, just like Sanjiao, farmers' lives are still difficult. **Eradicating poverty** is still the challenging task for the Chinese government.

As for China, it still has a lot of hard work to do to enable people in poor areas to live a comfortable and well-off life.

Unit Twelve
Natural and Negligent Disasters (I)

导　读

　　长时记忆是保存知识的仓库，它包括一般性知识和个人经验。Tulving (1972)称前者为语义记忆，后者为情节记忆。语义记忆指有关词语、概念、符号和物体等有组织的知识；包括技能性的信息（如电脑操作、开车、打篮球）、空间知识（办公室的布局）、社会技能（交际会话的策略、自我介绍的礼仪规则）。语义记忆的信息与特定的时间和地点没有关系，相对稳定，是概念性知识。正如 Wyer. Jr. (1989)所述，语义记忆包括名词概念、属性概念、动作概念和命题分子。

　　情节记忆保存个人的具体经验，具有特定的地点和时间性，属动态记忆，因人而异。如最近一次看游泳，今天上午上什么课。这些情景记忆经常更新。此外，情景记忆也包含一些放在语义记忆中的概念（如教师），但这两种记忆中的表征存在一些基本差异。语义记忆中的"教师"局限于一些主观上规定的教师特征；而在情景记忆中的"教师"虽然也包括上述主观上规定的特征，但却不仅限于此。它还包括了一些教师的客观特征，如名字、个人与教师交往的经验、一些教师的典型形象和行为等。

　　本单元及下一单元选取了大量有关自然灾害的新闻报道，其主题是"灾害·对人和物导致伤害"，如有关台风的报道从不同方面描述主命题"台风typhoon"及其附带命题"暴雨、泥石流 landslides"给各种命题（the Republic of Korea, people, roads, town, property, houses, transportation）造成"伤害命题（death, damage）"，关系项基

141

本都是"导致"或更具体的"伤害"性词汇，如 lash, kill, leave…dead, miss, bury, wash away, trigger, hit, disrupt 等。主题、分主题、相关的命题网络通过连贯的句子构成概念"灾害"衔接的图式语篇。

依据长时记忆的知识特征，通过阅读此类语篇，我们首先获得语义知识——灾害的特征集合，如此语篇中，typhoon lashed the Republic of Korea; left people dead and missing; ravage the sports facilities; washed away roads; triggered landslides; disrupt transportation; dump heavy rain; kill and bury people and houses; 命题的关系项同属导致另一命题（受事）人和财产的损坏。其次，以此推断和识别具体时间和地点发生的情景知识。要实现长时记忆的目标，必须经过三个过程：摄入、储存和检索。如前所述语篇学习不可能逐字记忆。阅读者首先需摄入的是各类相关的不同命题或意念单位，形成连贯衔接的命题网络，而后依据语义知识和情节知识，按图式"上层集合"和空位属性的特征进行储存。而检索则是回述或强化的一个过程，任何知识都需要不断的检索巩固，从而达到内化的记忆效果。

从认知心理学框架理论的角度，同样可以证明语篇认知和记忆过程中的这种图式的作用。框架（frame）是一种认知模型，是具体情景的知识和信念的表征。我们的大脑中储存了诸如河流、山川、地震、台风、暴雨和洪水等的框架知识。阅读的过程中，认知系统会调用已储存的框架知识与阅读语篇信息相匹配，以促进对新信息更好的理解和学习。

Key Points

1. First pay attention to various disasters — the subjects in this unit, and then to the structure of the passages: disaster – damage – rescue.

2. Then consider the relation between nature and human beings.

3. Lexical items co-occur in the context of different calamities caused by nature or human negligence.

For the devastating **gas explosion** at the Chuandongbei Gas Field in

142

Kai-xian County, Sichuan Province, Chinese President and Premier have **instructed** the local government to get relevant departments going all out to **rescue victims** and prevent the poisonous gas from spreading further. Extra **rescue teams and experts** have arrived at the site.

At least 191 people have been **confirmed dead** and the number of **casualties** is expected to rise. More than 290 villagers have been **hospitalized** after one of China's worst industrial accidents in recent memory, **a blowout** at a natural gas field in southwest China's Chongqing Municipality. **A well burst,** releasing a 30 meter jet of high concentration and potentially deadly sulfated hydrogen.

Some 600 soldiers, armed police and fire fighters have been **mobilized** to search for **survivors** in the mountainous areas near the gas field. The Ministry of Public Security says 41,000 people have been **evacuated** from the 28 villages hit by the blowout. Fifteen **shelter centers** have been set up and supplied with food and warm materials.

As the 20 **special teams** continue **combing** the nearby areas for survivors and **identifying** casualties, six other work teams are preparing rescue materials, vehicles and equipment for an all-out effort to **curb** the blowout.

Rescue workers and technicians are preparing to contain the bursting gas well early Friday morning. Health and work safety experts arrive at **blast site**.

The State Council's work team led by secretary general of the State Council arrived in Chongqing on Thursday night along with an investigation team **dispatched** by the State Administration of Work Safety and the Deputy Minister of the Ministry of Health of China.

Sulfurated hydrogen is one of **the toxic results** of the **devastating explosion** in Chongqing. Let's take a look at the major characteristics of the gas.

Sulfurated hydrogen is a colorless, flammable and highly toxic gas produced by decaying organic matter and certain industrial processes. It is commonly known as "sewer gas" as it smells like rotten eggs.

It is slightly heavier than air and may **accumulate** in enclosed, **poorly ventilated**, and **low-lying areas**. Prolonged exposure may result in painful dermatitis and burning eyes. **Inhalation** of high concentrations of the gas can lead to extremely rapid loss of consciousness and death.

Technicians have **contained** the gas blowout in Chongqing, but rescue work continues following Tuesday's **fatal accident** that is now known to have **claimed 198 lives**. Emergency teams are still scouring/rinse the region for possible survivors, as authorities try to identify victims.

The number of deaths from the accident has reached 198, and the number of **hospitalizations** has jumped from 290 to 431, with 17 in a critical condition. Of more than 40,000 **evacuees** around half are living with friends or relatives. The local government is housing another 20,000 in schools and public buildings.

Neighboring counties, and districts, as well as the PLA's Chongqing Garrison have sent **emergency supplies** of quilts, overcoats and food. And **anti-chemical warfare troops** from the Garrison have been stationed close to the blowout site in case of future emergencies.

On Saturday morning 80 technicians **wearing protective suits** and armed with respiratory machines closed the air prevention pipe of the leaking gas well at around 9:30 am. They've injected some 480 cubic meters of mud slurry into **the leaking well**. The weight of mud is working to **offset** the pressure of gas within the well and should prevent any more hydrogen sulphide from leaking into the air.

Soon after the cap operation was completed, about 100 medical workers began **disinfecting** eight villages nearby the gas well. They have also taken samples of plants and water to test for pollution.

Meanwhile, three victims poisoned in the gas blowout have received their first installment of compensation from a local insurance company. The Chongqing branch of the Ping'an Life Insurance Company said payouts to their 7,000-odd insurance holders in the area might reach over 100 million yuan.

The tragedy took place Tuesday morning at a natural gas field in the county of Chongqing Municipality when a well burst suddenly and released a high concentration of natural gas and sulphurated hydrogen. Investigations into the cause of the disaster are underway.

————————

More than 80 people, mostly Lebanese, have been killed in an **air crash** in the West African nation of Benin.

About 200 **passengers and crew** were on United Transit Airlines Flight 141, **bound for** Beirut from Benin's capital Cotonou. It **crashed** into sea shortly after takeoff Thursday afternoon. The plane apparently had problems **retracting its landing gear** after takeoff, hit a building at the end of the runway, exploded and landed in the sea. Dozens of bodies floated among the plane's **wreckage** about 150 meters off a Cotonou beach.

Local residents have **scrambled** into the water to **search for survivors** and recover the dead. Twenty-two survivors have been found so far. Thousands of Lebanese immigrants live and work in West African countries.

Most of the passengers on Flight 141 were believed to have been returning home for the Christmas holidays.

————————

Egyptian officials say Saturday's air crash seems to have been caused by **a technical fault**. The charter jet full of French tourists crashed into the Red Sea, killing all 148 people aboard. The Flash Airlines Flight was bound for Paris after **a stopover** in Cairo.

Searchers spent the day **circling the waters** in small boats looking for survivors, but found only bodies and **debris**.

The crash occurred amid a week of **heightened concerns** about terrorist threats to airliners that have led to increased security and canceled flights around the world.

But Egypt's Foreign Minister said the crash appeared to have been due to a technical fault on the plane. We have agreed that both countries will cooperate in **the investigation into the causes of the crash** which seems to have been due to a technical fault on the plane. The French minister for aviation will come here to help in the operation of transporting the dead bodies and **retrieving** the remains of the plane.

A French Foreign Ministry spokesman said that 133 of the people aboard were French tourists. Thirteen crew members and two tourists from other countries were also on the flight. French Deputy Foreign Minister was heading to Egypt with two Interior Ministry experts to help identify bodies.

When earthquakes, floods, droughts, plane crashes, poisoning, arson and numerous mining accidents dominate the headlines, the Chinese **feel relieved** to be kept informed very quickly about the **tragic side** of the society. And, along with the **crusading media**, people begin to follow the government's commitment to accountability. They feel that they have the right to know in time what is being done to **investigate** the accidents and the crimes behind them. Now we review some of the most **sensational tragedies**.

As people were preparing to celebrate another New Year, a natural gas blowout in Chongqing claimed 198 lives and shocked the nation. The tragedy took place at Chuandongbei gas field, when a well burst and released a high concentration of poisonous gases.

Most of the victims killed in the blowout were residents living near the explosion. **Rescuers** found 182 bodies **scattered** around the poisoned area, while 16 people died in, or on their way to, hospitals.

The blowout affected four towns near the gas field — 93,000 people.

Flooding is **an annual headache** for an enormous amount of Chinese. The Huaihe River in East China is notorious for its frequent floods and **breached its banks** again in July. The rising waters affected more than a million of the 1.6 million residents in the river valley. Nearly 10 million hectares of farmland were **submerged**, and 1.5 million hectares of crops destroyed. The rising floodwaters forced more than 700,000 people to flee their homes and most were housed in **emergency camps**. Some even had to stay in hot plastic sheds that usually served as green houses.

The efforts of local residents did not go unnoticed. Chinese Premier was the highest-ranking Chinese government official to visit the region. This year also saw a particularly large number of **earthquakes**.

On February 24th, a quake measuring 6.4 on the Richter Scale hit Bachu and Jiashi in Xinjiang Autonomous Region, northwest China. It **claimed 266 lives**. More than 100 **aftershocks** measuring higher than 3 on the Richter Scale also hit the **quake-stricken** area.

The town bore/suffered the brunt/blow of the natural disaster. The homes of thousands of Uygur farmers were **reduced to piles of rubble**. After quickly burying the dead, in line with Muslim tradition, many could still hardly **comprehend the tragedy that afflicted them**.

On July 21st, another quake of 6.2 **rocked** Dayao county in Yunnan Province, where damaged and blocked roads seriously **hampered** rescue efforts in the remote mountain areas.

China entered **a quake-active era** in 1998, with the western regions located on **the juncture** of the Indian and the Eurasian Plates. Poor communication and medical conditions in China's western regions will be one of the major challenges faced by future earthquake rescue teams.

Many disasters can be **blamed** on nature, but the hundreds of coal mining accidents that have occurred in China can only be attributed to humans. China ranks first in coal production in the world. But still, the country's **death toll** for mining disasters exceeds the total of that in all coal producing countries.

One gas explosion on March 22 in a coal mine in north China's Shanxi Province, left 62 dead. What makes people **overwhelmingly indignant** is that this coal mine was **banned** three times from continuing production due to its inadequate safety measures.

On May 14, a gas explosion **ripped through** a coal mine in Anhui Province, killing at least 86 miners who were working hundreds of metres below ground.

On November 14, another mining explosion killed 48 in Jiangxi Province. And on December 7, 20 miners died in an explosion in Yuxian County in Hebei Province.

Little can be done to stop the ferocious hand of nature. But by continuing efforts to better predict and react to natural disasters, as well as limiting the possibility of manmade ones, China will hopefully be able to enjoy a quieter time next year.

A deadly stampede at the **climax** of this year's annual **Hajj pilgrimage** in Saudi Arabia has left over 200 dead. China's News Agency says at least 244 Muslim **pilgrims** were **trampled** to death during a **stoning ritual** in the holy city of Mecca. The Saudi Hajj minister added that at least 240 were wounded.

The tragedy occurred on the last day of the Hajj pilgrimage period, after a sleepless night of prayers at the climax of the annual sacred event. The deaths occurred when 2 million pilgrims flocked to Jamarat Bridge in Mena **to throw stones** at pillars **representing the devil**. The devil stoning is regarded as the most animated and possibly most dangerous ritual of the Hajj. The pilgrims frantically **throw rocks**, shout insults or **hurl shoes** at the pillars. These acts are believed to demonstrate their deep **disdain** for the devil.

Saudi police have cordoned off/defend the area around the main pillar after the crush and urged people to cast stones from a distance. Officials say security and health authorities have started **rescue operations** and were controlling **the surge** of people to prevent further **fatalities**.

The Hajj has seen such deadly stampedes almost every year. In the worst Hajj-related disaster in 1990, 1,246 pilgrims were **crushed to death** in a pedestrian tunnel at the holy city of Mecca.

The Hajj pilgrimage is an obligation for every able-bodied Muslim at least once in a lifetime. Even if unable to go to Mecca in person, Muslims manage to experience the Hajj through the celebration of the feast of sacrifice. The **religious festival** follows the end of the Hajj pilgrimage and takes up to four days to celebrate. It **commemorates** Abraham's willingness to sacrifice his son to God. Iraqi Muslims started **festivities** at dawn on Sunday with **volleys/shooting** of gunfire in Baghdad. In Bangladesh, a three-day government holiday has been declared to mark the festival.

In Saudi Arabia's holy city of Mecca, 251 people have been **crushed to death** during the ritual stoning of the devil at the annual Muslim pilgrimage. It is the worst tragedy for seven years at the Hajj.

The Islamic Association of China said Monday night that 5 Chinese Muslim pilgrims were among those who died **in the crush** on Sunday in Mecca. A press release from the association said about 10 other Chinese pilgrims got hurt. According to the press release, over 30 Muslims from Gansu Province in northwest China were pushed to the ground by the sheer weight of the crowd.

Chinese President has instructed the Chinese embassy in Ri'yadh to offer all assistance possible to the Chinese pilgrims.

The Muslim faithful still came in their hundreds of thousands. But following Sunday's tragedy, there was a much more obvious army presence at the hajj. More troops were sent in to control the crowds after 244 people were crushed to death taking part in the devil-stoning rituals. Seven more people have since died in hospital. Most of those killed were Asians, with the biggest number of dead identified as being from Indonesia and Pakistan. The deadly crush happened when people **panicked** as they were moving along a wide **ramp/lean** on their way to take part in the "stoning of the devil". In this ritual, pilgrims **throw pebbles** at a stone pillar, to symbolize their **contempt** for the devil.

The hajj is a duty that every able-bodied Muslim is expected to, and indeed wants to perform at least once in a lifetime, if they can afford it. To keep numbers down, the Saudis set **quotas** for pilgrims from each country. It's estimated about 2 million Muslims are participating in this year's pilgrimage.

At least two people were killed and an unknown number of people were **trapped under debris** in central Turkey earlier today when a high-rise residential building **collapsed**.

There has been **no official word** on the cause of the **collapse**. But local television says a blast may have occurred in a heater in the 10-story apartment building in the central city of Konya.

Many people are believed to have been inside at the time of the explosion. At least 13 people were rescued from the **debris**. Those rescued, who were mainly from the building's top floors, are in good condition.

Critics have often complained about **shoddy construction** in Turkey and have blamed it as the cause of high death tolls in past earthquakes and other disasters.

Thirty-seven people have been killed **in a stampede** while taking part in a celebration of Lantern Festival Thursday night. The victims were **trampled to death** while watching lantern shows at a local park. At least 15 others were injured in the accident. Chinese President Hu Jintao and Premier Wen Jiabao have both asked the local government to do their best in caring for the injured, and **to conduct an investigation** into the accident.

CCTV International will closely follow the situation, and give you the updated information in our coming news broadcast.

The tragedy occurred on the traditional Lantern Festival night, when most Chinese celebrate the evening watching lantern shows. Hundreds of people were **flocking** to Miyun County's Baihe Bridge in Mihong Park, for the Lantern Exhibition. Local authorities say one lantern watcher fell on **the**

overcrowded bridge, creating **a chain reaction**. Altogether, 37 people were **trampled** to death on the bridge.

Local police quickly took control of the situation, **dispersing the crowd**. Police also cordoned off Miyun hospital, where the 15 injured were sent. The hospital, the biggest in the county, saw an unprecedented number of emergency vehicles in the **aftermath** of the accident. A doctor from another nearby hospital was among the first to come to help.

According to a doctor of Miyun Traditional Chinese Medicine Hospital, "Doctors from my hospital were asked to help our colleagues at Miyun hospital. When I arrived, the wounded had been **hospitalized** while **the fatalities** were placed in the main hall."

Families of the dead and injured were **notified,** and came to the hospital to identify their relatives. However, many of them are still at a loss as to what happened. This boy lost his mother in the stampede.

A victim's son said, "There weren't enough **security control** and people were too crowded there. I can not say more."

After the incident, Chinese President told local authorities that all measures should be taken to save the injured. Government aid should be given to the families of the dead. The Chinese President also **demanded an investigation** into the cause of the accident. But for families of the victims, the special Lantern Festival night has become ... a very silent night.

The tragedy comes at the conclusion of the traditional Chinese Spring Festival celebration. For the local people in Miyun, it has been a sad start to the New Year.

Unit Thirteen
Natural and Negligent Disasters (II)

Key Points

1. The same passages as Unit Twelve will provide you more materials on destructions caused by nature and human negligence.
2. Recall what you have read and recognize the known and unknown lexical items in the similar schema.

The glass roof of a popular swimming complex in Moscow **collapsed** under the weight of snow late on Saturday. At least 11 people **died** and 96 others were **injured**. The number of dead could rise as people may be **trapped under the rubble.** A Moscow police spokesman said it was not an act of terror. The Russian capital has been on edge since a bomb in the underground earlier this month killed 41 people.

In England, another body, whose identity remains **unconfirmed**, was found on Friday off the country's northwest coast, bringing **the death toll** of shell hunters to 19.

The number of the dead cockle pickers, who were caught by **racing tides** on Thursday night, is feared to further increase as the tide at Morecambe Bay **retreats** and **rescue operations** continue. All the victims are thought to be Chinese — 16 men and 2 women. Another 14 survivors have been rescued or have **walked to safety** and are gathered at a local community center. Chinese Deputy Consul General in Manchester, told China's *Xinhua News* Agency that none of the survivors, **bar** one female

Chinese student, have passports or any other valid documents.

Morecambe Bay is **notoriously dangerous** for its fast rising tides and quick sands.

British police have started to investigate whether the 19 **cockle pickers**, killed Thursday by fast rising tides in northern England's More-cambe Bay, were working for **a criminal gang**. They expected to make arrests within days. Meanwhile, the Chinese Consul General in Britain has visited the Bay area to help the British side deal with **the tragedy**.

British police and immigration officers from a newly established special agency are focusing the **probe** on whether there are any **criminal hands behind the tragedy**.

The police **speculate** that work-gang leaders may have organized the team of cockle pickers. They are now working to find out who employed those that were killed Thursday, and expect to make arrests if it turns out they are not legal.

Investigators believe the cockle-collecting team may have been brought to the treacherous, bitterly cold Morecambe Bay from the Liverpool area, about 64 kilometers south.

However, Lancashire Deputy Chief Constable warned against linking the cocklers with illegal gangs until there is enough evidence to do so. Assistant Chief Constable of Lancashire Constabulary said, "I don't want to go down the route of **criminalising** these people. These people are victims of a process that has put them into a situation where they are **vulnerable** and they may have been exploited. I just want to protect them, really, in that regard."

Chinese diplomats in Britain are working with the British side to deal with the incident. All of the confirmed 18 dead are thought to be Chinese who could not speak English.

Chinese Consul General said, "So the most important thing is how to cooperate to identify the drowned cocklers. And I also meet the Deputy

Chief Constable of Lancashire and also to have a wonderful talk together to help to cooperate to solve this event."

British police have found 16 survivors, 14 Chinese **nationals** and two Britons, and are continuing to question them. But, regardless of the probe's conclusion, the deaths have **sparked calls** for greater protection of migrant workers, as well as **the strict licensing** of cockle pickers in Britain.

Investigators have **retrieved** the flight **data recorder** from the Iranian plane that **crashed** as it came in to land at Sharjah in the United Arab Emirates on Tuesday. They are, at this stage, **blaming a technical problem** for the crash.

The plane crashed into a desert area between **residential complexes** close to the airport killing 43 of the 49 people on board. Information released by the United Arab Emirates said that one Chinese was among the dead.

Witnesses said the plane was "wobbling" and making "strange" engine noises before it nose **dived to the ground, overturned, split in two, and burst into flames.** Iran's Aviation Authority said the plane had asked for an emergency landing as it approached the airport. This was the sixth crash involving Iranian planes since 2000.

China's Central Meteorological Station says most parts of northern China will experience temperature drops and rainfall over the next three to four days.

Temperatures in Harbin, the capital city of northeast Helongjiang Province, have **plummeted** ten degrees over the past week. The city's highest temperature on Thursday was 14 degrees Celsius, and some areas in the province have even been **hit by frost.** East China's Shandong Province is experiencing similar cold.

More rain and winds have been forecast for the **flood-stricken** area and the temperature is also expected to drop around 8 degrees. Meteorologists predict that with all this cold air moving around up north even the

154

warmer **climes** of south China will be affected this weekend.

———————8<———————

The water level in the Huaihe River's **trunk stream** is dropping, as **the flood crest** flows downstream. Meanwhile, the largest flood crest is pushing towards Hongze Lake in east China's Jiangsu Province. With the battle against further flooding along the Huaihe River won for the time being, local authorities are **stepping up their efforts** to settle flood victims and prevent the **outbreak of disease**.

On Tuesday, the water level at Wangjiaba **hydrological station** on the mainstream of the upper Huaihe River stood at about 27 meters, still 1.1 meter above **the danger line**. But floods are **receding** steadily at 2 centimeters per hour. Local authorities have **deployed** lots of Party members to help local residents **restore their normal life.** Medical and quarantine work is underway to prevent outbreaks of disease in the flooded areas.

———————8<———————

The water level in the trunk stream of the Huaihe River in East China is still rising. To reduce the danger of any **accidental breach** in the middle and lower stream, several water flow control stations have opened their **sluices** to **divert the water**. The Huaihe River remains the toughest of China's major rivers to control.

The State Headquarters for Flood Control has decided to open the 13-channel **sluice** in Wangjiaba, the key control station in the upper and middle stream. Though the water level here is still below **the danger point**, this is to prevent a last-minute **rush downstream** where the flow is much slower and **a breach** is likely to occur.

Deputy Head of Funan County, Anhui Province, said, "The flood control system is **facing severe pressure** in both the upper and down stream. We think opening the sluice here is good for **adjusting the water level** along the entire river."

Early Friday afternoon, the water level at Qiujiahu, a control station in the upper stream, reached the highest since 1949. At 1:00pm, the water in the Huaihe River, about 10 meters higher than in **the diversion area**, began to **flush** the flood diversion area.

Though part of the water from the upper stream has been **discharged** in the upper and middle stream, continuous rainfall is raising the water level in Hongze Lake at the down stream of Huaihe. Experts **calculate** the lake will soon receive another 19 billion cubic meters of water.

With the situation in the Huaihe Valley **still grave**, the flood season for other major rivers is now approaching. Weather patterns indicate more frequent heavy rainfall in these areas in late July and early August.

———————

This **flood spill-off** area along the middle reaches of the Huaihe River has taken the largest volume of water of any area this year. Here, more than 16,000 hectares of farmland have been **submerged** to a depth of 2.5 meters. And nearly 130,000 people have been **evacuated**. Local governments are working around the clock to **disinfect the whole area**. So far, some 2.8 million US dollars worth of tents, food, and other **relief materials and medicines** have been distributed among the flood victims. In Anhui and Jiangsu provinces where the situation is the most severe, medical services are also provided by professionals 24-hours a day.

In order to deal with the new **flood crests** that are expected to arrive at the upper streams of the Huaihe River Tuesday tonight to Wednesday morning, Jiangsu is enlarging the **flood discharging capacity** of the Hongze Lake, and the flood control headquarters urged all localities along the lake to **maintain high vigilance** to safeguard the embankments.

———————

Chinese Premier has visited **flood-affected** areas in Anhui Province. During the tour of the region Saturday, he asked officials to ensure **the safety and livelihoods** of people affected by the Huaihe floods. The premier got a first-hand look at the situation at the Wangjiaba sluice gates, one of the most important **flood control barriers** on the river.

The Premier is the highest ranking Chinese government official to visit the region since **torrential rain inundated**/submerge the Huaihe River nearly two weeks ago.

The gates are one of the river's key water control mechanisms. They link the waterway's upper and middle reaches and stretch across two provinces. The gates were raised for the second time within a week early on Friday to **ease pressure** from dangerously high water levels.

For nearly two days, **a torrent of** more than 13 hundred cubic meters has poured into the storage area each second. That's brought water levels down at the rate of a centimeter an hour.

The efforts of local residents have not gone unnoticed. The premier expressed his high regard for the affected workers and thanked them for **shoring up** the main **dykes** along the river.

The premier assured **the sufferers** that their safety and livelihoods would be guaranteed. He urged local officials to do everything possible to ensure the safety, health and property of those affected.

Almost half of the Mengwa area's **storage capacity** has been used, **inundating** 12 thousand hectares of land. Twenty thousand people have been **displaced** and been forced to find shelter in camps.

<hr>

The situation on the Huaihe River in East China's Anhui Province is set to **worsen**, with more torrential rains forecast in the area in the next three days. Local authorities are **pooling their efforts** to fight against a possible disaster.

In Huaihe Flood Control Headquarters, after analyzing the latest data, experts have predicted a wave of **thundershowers** over the river within the next three days, increasing the likelihood of worse floods.

The **dams** on the Huaihe River have been flooded because of the high water levels in the past days. More **downpours** will make the situation even worse. The local authorities have **evacuated** more than 220,000 people along the river to safer places and stepped up their efforts to check the dams.

Meanwhile, Hongze Lake on the lower reaches of the Huaihe River in Jiangsu Province saw the biggest **crest** from the mainstream at noon on Tuesday. The water level reached 13.89 meters, 39 centimeters above the danger line. However, **prompt flood discharging** has kept the situation stable.

In other parts of China, thunderstorms **hit many regions** on Monday and Tuesday. The provinces of Shandong, Jiangsu and Henan suffered torrential rains. Some areas **sustained heavy losses** with farmlands flooded or damaged by **hail storms.**

China is stepping up efforts to **rein in the floods** that have spread to more provinces across the country. Over a third of China's reservoirs are now threatened by floods and no letup/pause or stop in the torrential rain is **in sight**.

On Friday, the Central Meteorological Station **issued a warning** that more heavy rains are expected in many parts of eastern and central China in coming days. The warning comes a day after authorities said the safety of some 30,000 of the country's 86,000 reservoirs were threatened by floods, despite billions of yuan spent in recent years to maintain them.

Top Chinese leaders including President and Premier have called on flood control officials to give top priority to protecting people's lives and to do everything they can to prevent outbreak of disease.

More military personnel have been **thrown into the fight** to strengthen dykes along the Yangzte River and Huaihe River since the country entered the annual flooding season late last month. Many of the evacuated residents in **affected regions** are living in **makeshift shelters**, as a massive relief effort has **swung into action** to provide food and medicine.

Tropical storm "Koni," the eighth to approach China this year, is moving closer to the southern Chinese island province of Hainan. According to the Central Meteorological Station or CMS, the storm will **hit** the coastal areas of Hainan late this afternoon (Monday). Meanwhile, the CMS warns that the seventh and **worse typhoon** "Imbudo" which has so far remained far away from China's coast would hit the country's coastal areas in three days.

The CMS said in **an emergency warning** that by 08:00 am Monday, **the eye of the storm** Koni had moved to the South China Sea waters, 160 kilometers southeast of Wanning City of Hainan. The storm, with force 11 winds near the **epicenter**, is expected to hit the coast of Hainan late this afternoon. But meteorologists say that the seventh typhoon Imbudo, still coming, will be more **devastating** than Koni.

A meteorologist of Central Meteorological Station said, "Typhoon Koni will be less devastating than Imbudo. Koni with force 10-11 winds, will mainly **bring rainstorms** to the majority parts of Hainan and won't last long. However, Imbudo with force 12 winds will hit coastal areas in south China in three days and will be more devastating."

In addition to the typhoons, the meteorologists are warning of **heavy rains** in the next three days in Anhui, Jiangsu, Henan and Shandong provinces, some of which are already suffering from floods.

───────◈◆◈───────

An eight-story building in Shanghai has **collapsed** after a pedestrian tunnel being built for a new subway station **caved in** beneath it. The incident happened in the city's Bund district near the riverfront. Nobody was injured.

According to a city government spokesman, the tunnel caved in on Tuesday morning. Part of a nearby building, housing an audio-video wholesale market, collapsed after it had been **evacuated**. About 100 people were also evacuated from two apartment buildings.

The tunnel is part of the subway system's new No. 4 Line. It links Shanghai's older western section with the new Pudong financial district across the Huangpu River that cuts through the city center. The cause of the cave-in is **under investigation**.

———————⟨⟩———————

Four days after the devastating **landslide** in Zigui, Hubei Province, local authorities are continuing to look for survivors and working to prevent further losses. Meanwhile, they have to **contend with**/handle the danger of more possible landslides in the coming days.

The confirmed death toll has risen to 14, and another ten are still missing. More than 1,200 affected villagers are somehow **recovering from the shock** and their necessities have been promptly provided by local authorities.

But now they face a new threat. The nearby river was blocked by the landslide. If the **accumulating water soaks** the mountainside even more, it will bring the risk of more landslides. To cope with this danger, the local authority has mapped out a plan to **drain the blocked water**.

Residents living in the surrounding districts have all been evacuated.

———————⟨⟩———————

The huge landslide in Central China's Hubei Province has cut off a local river and caused the rising of the water level. Part of the hillside has been **submerged** for a long time and new landslides are likely.

Rescue work was forced to stop due to the danger. On Tuesday morning local residents pulled back to a safe place and authorities sent in boats to search for survivors and bodies. Twelve people were reported dead and 12 others missing. The landslide was about 1,200 meters long, 1,000 meters wide and 20 meters thick. It occurred early on Sunday morning in Qianjiangping Village.

Heavy rain has been causing smaller **landslips** and threats of big **landslides** in the hills around the village for several days.

———————⟨⟩———————

Two people are dead and 49 others missing in the wake of **a slide of mud and rocks** which hit a mountainous village in Danba County, in southwest China's Sichuan Province, on Friday night.

160

Army soldiers have rescued all the 71 people **trapped in the disaster site** to safety. Huge rocks and a thick layer of mud and other **debris** have made the search for the missing very difficult. If the currently missing people are **confirmed** dead, the mudslide will have **claimed more lives** than any other similar disaster in the nation's history.

The missing were said to have been participating in a village campfire party in honor of four tourists from East China's Shanghai City.

———— ✦✦ ————

Hurricane Claudette **ripped through** the Texas Gulf Coast on Tuesday before weakening as it moved inland. But no serious injuries were reported.

Hurricane Claudette **toppled** trees, **tore off** roofs, **flooded** homes and **knocked down** power lines along the Texas coast. It was moving toward the west-northwest at about 19 kilometers per hour after its broad eye crossed the coast in the morning.

Residents in **low-lying areas** had been urged to evacuate. The storm is the third to be named in the 2003 Atlantic hurricane season. It **languished** in the Gulf of Mexico as a tropical storm for several days.

———— ✦✦ ————

Though typhoon Imbudo has weakened to **a tropical low pressure storm**, it has left heavy damages **in its wake** in south China. Residents in the region have begun the recovery process in **the aftermath of the typhoon**.

People in many cities in south China's Guangdong and Hainan provinces are rushing to repair **damaged** dykes, reservoirs and houses. Thousands of soldiers and public facilities workers have been battling for two days to evacuate those **stranded** in the floods and winds. By Friday, navigation and airline services between Hainan island and Guangdong had resumed.

———— ✦✦ ————

The head of the US North American Electric Reliability Council (NERC) said Saturday that the **massive power outage** that hit part of the United

States and Canada on Thursday apparently started in Ohio.

It was "fairly certain at this time that the **disturbance** started in Ohio", the Council's president said in a telephone news conference, the CNN reported on its web site.

The Council was founded after the **outage/loss** in New York in 1965 and is a **nonprofit** organization sponsored by the electric industry.

------------ ✦ ------------

Two explosions in a firework plant killed at least four people and wounded 15 in Miaoli County in northwest Taiwan on Sunday evening. More than 10 people are missing.

The first explosion, in a workshop, caused explosions 30 minutes later in the **storage area**, **shattering** glass in windows and doors of neighboring houses. A TV reporter and two firefighters are among the wounded.

Firefighters, police and army troops now have the fire under control. The reason for the explosion is still unknown, but this is the third explosion to take place in this particular firework plant over the past ten years. Apparently workers were doing **extra shifts** to meet orders for the coming Spring Festival. Over the past 15 years or so, 150 people have been killed and 185 wounded in 67 firework factory **explosions** in China.

Unit Fourteen
Environmental Protection(I)

导　读

representation 一词在心理学中被译为表征。对表征有两个方面的理解：一方面，表征是独立于学习主体的外部信息结构形式；另一方面，表征是指反映外部信息的学习主体的认知结构。人们把前者称为外部表征，把后者称为内部表征。外部表征是信息的外部表现形式，它以文字材料、图表材料等符号来代表具体的事物或事件，被记录在纸上或其他的媒体上，来表示现实生活中的各种事件以及它们之间的相互关系，这种表征往往是根据客观事物的客观逻辑关系进行信息组织的。但是，人们在表征外部信息时并不是完全按照外部所表征的形式进行的，必须以个人的心理结构形式对外部信息进行重新表征才能理解外部事物以及它们之间的相互关系，这就是内部表征。

心理表征是知识理解和掌握的重要环节。学习各种各样的知识，首先最重要的是理解外部呈现的材料，理解的过程实际上就是用自己独特的方式重新组织这些材料，使材料中的各种关键信息以一种相互联系的逻辑结构联系在一起，从而形成一个有意义的整体。这实际上就是知识的表征过程。

在阅读新闻语篇的过程当中，读者需要对语篇的信息依据心理表征规律进行重新组织。把"倒金字塔"结构以顺叙的方式重新组织，从而使记叙的事件联系成一个整体，与现实事件顺序相吻合。读者只有重新组织知识，才能真正地理解语篇信息，掌握相关知识。如果对所读语篇不能重组，而是原封不动地背下来，那叫囫囵吞枣。这样不仅增加记忆的负担，而且有碍知识的创造性运用。因此，没有心理表征就没有知识的理解。此外，心理表征具有过滤信息的功能。读者对阅读语篇进行某种表征之后，就会对后来的信息进行过滤，把与原有表征相关的信息保留下来，而把那些与原有表征无关的信息过滤掉。

本单元选取了丰富的有关 "Environment and Its Protection" 方面的新闻语篇。读者可以通过阅读，获得有关 Environmental Protection 的知识表征，建立 environment → problems and issues → causes → impacts → countermeasures 这样的语篇图式知识结构及相应的词汇群。

Key Points

1. Environmental protection frequently highlights current newspapers, magazines, internet pages and other media sources. And of course, it is also the usual topic of students' papers and classroom discussions.

2. The reports hereafter will help improve your participation in talks about environment-friendly projects and actions with rich lexical items and hotspots concerned with environmental pollution and countermeasures to be taken.

Geological experts warn Shanghai is rapidly losing its **waterfront** and if efforts to protect beaches aren't made soon, the coastline along the Yangtze River will **shrink** to half its size in 20 years. The city now has about 386 square kilometres of **beachlands** scattered mainly along Nanhui, Chongming, Hengsha Island, Jiuduansha outside Pudong Airport and Jinshan Island.

"The beaches cannot just be **exploited** by man's feet but must be **preserved for nature**. They are very important to balance the biological environment," said secretary general of Shanghai Geological Society.

His group has just finished a research project on the evolution and potential of beach resources in Shanghai suburbs, and has found **disturbing evidence** of potential erosion problems facing the area.

To the **densely-populated** Shanghai, beaches are the only source available for the city to expand territorially.

According to Shanghai's general urban construction and land-use plans, by 2010, the city will **reclaim** more than 400 square kilometres of land from **alluvial/deposit beaches.**

However, as the sand carried down from the upper and middle reaches of the river decreases, there will be no new beaches formed and existing beaches likely to **wash away**.

Affected by construction at the massive Three Gorges dam project, the South-North water transfer project and forestation work in the upper and middle reaches of the Yangtze River, the **sand content** in the water is facing gradual reduction.

The secretary said if the sand drops below 250 million tons a year, while sea level continues to rise, the city will lose 89 square kilometres of **coastline** annually within two decades. "Instead of continually **exploiting the coast**, the government should protect the sand to preserve the remaining beaches, and adjust its **land reclaiming plans** to reduce the pressure upon the coasts."

———————————

Chinese Vice-Premier told a major forum in Beijing on Saturday that China would continue to cooperate with **the international community** on environmental protection. The Vice-Premier was speaking at the final session of the three-day annual meeting of the China Council for International Cooperation on Environment and Development, or CCICED.

China would continue to aim for **cost-effective industrialization**. This means the efficient use of resources, including human resources, and effective pollution controls. He also called on developed countries to **take more responsibility** for environmental protection. China set up the CCICED in 1992. Its task is to strengthen cooperation and exchanges between China and the international community on environmental and developmental issues.

———————————————

China must take stronger measures to **protect its environment** as a land stretch of 23 million mu (1.5 million hectares) in northeast China is reported to have turned into desert, said a forestry official Thursday.

Director of the State Forestry Administration told **a seminar** on forestry here that the current **desertification speed** is about 300,000 mu a year in northeast China's provinces and part of Inner Mongolia Autonomous Region.

The soil erosion area has expanded to 270 million mu in the region, and in Dahinggan Mountains, the erosion area grew up 59 percent in 2001 from 1986.

As an important wood resource base, northeast China now faces such **serious ecological problems** that the forestry resource is drying up, noting 70 percent of annual timber output comes from the younger forest. The current tree fall is far beyond the forest growth in the area, efforts called for to restructure the local **forestry industry**.

———————————————

The rare Tibetan antelope is a target for poachers/illegal hunter hoping to get their hands on the animal's fine wool. As a result, the animal has suffered **a major decline**. But there is hope that it can be reversed. Authorities responsible for the Kekexili **nature reserve** in China's northwestern Qinghai Province have set up a center to **care for** injured or lost antelopes.

These two residents, a Tibetan antelope and a Mongolia gazelle, have been at the reserve for several months. When they were first picked up by the local police, the so-called "Guards of the Antelope," they had serious bullet wounds in the legs. They have since almost **recovered**, and their next lesson is to learn to live **in the wild** on their own.

———————————————

One official says more centers like these will be set up in the future.

China is facing **severe challenges** in preventing an environmental disaster. Soil erosion, excessive development of water resources, and pollution are all **major problems** for the future.

The country's environment is being **degraded** both in its ability to function and its capacity to **withstand natural disasters**, according to a director of the Natural and Ecological Protection Department of the Environmental Protection Administration.

Some 90 per cent of the country's grasslands are degraded, according to the department, while **desertification rates** have almost doubled since the early 1980s, and now stand at over 3,400 square kilometres a year.

China also lost more than 5 billion tonnes of soil and 2.6 million hectares of **arable land** in the past half century. Total losses caused by this exceed 10 billion yuan. Meanwhile, **utilization rates** of the country's water resources are worryingly high. Use of the Yellow River stands at 62 per cent, while the Haihe River's rate is as high as 90 per cent. These figures greatly **surpass** the international warning line of 30-40 per cent.

As a result of such usage, **the ecology and environment** along the rivers is being **damaged,** according to Minister of Water Resources. And, it's not just the rivers that are suffering. A sharp **reduction in biodiversity** is another challenge facing the country.

Some 189 plant and animal species in China are among the world's 740 most endangered, according to the United Nations Convention on International Trade in Endangered Species.

Part of the reason for this is **the introduction of foreign species**, now found in most of China's nature reserves. Over 70 per cent of the country's wild paddies/rice have **suffered destruction** due to them. Environmental officials **blamed** China's rapid economic growth over the past two decades for **the environment's problems**.

———————&⊂⊃&———————

Hundreds of red-beaked gulls are **taking refuge** in Cuihu Park in Kunming, capital of Southwest China's Yunnan Province, November 19,

2003. Since the beginning of the month, large **flocks** of the birds have **migrated** to Kunming from the extremely cold Siberia, adding to the beautiful **charm and colour** of the city.

The Chinese government will invest 70 billion yuan, or about 8 billion US dollars, into six new forestry projects. Officials say it will improve **the ecological situation** in the country.

At an international symposium on the sustainable development of Chinese forestry on Sunday, the Director of Chinese State Forestry Administration, said the new projects will cover 97 percent of cities and regions in China, and the planned forest area will be over 7 million hectares.

It is estimated the completion of the six forestry projects will bring to 1,800 the total number of **nature reserves** in the country, covering about 17 percent of the territory. **Forest cover** holds **the water table** and land together, and the new reserves are expected to help **mitigate/alleviate environmental degradation**.

China will implement **an ecological compensation policy** in certain parts of the country, in a bid to promote environmental protection.

The new policy measures **the environmental cost** of a given activity, and then charges the user if the impact is a **negative** one, for example, a polluting industry. If **the impact** is **positive**, planting trees, for example, the contributor will be paid.

Vice director of China's State Environmental Protection Administration said a series of regulations related to the environmental protection funds is underway. Ecological compensation is a measure used by most of the countries in the world, and Chinese Forestry has already **put it into practice.**

China and the European Union are to set up **a dialogue mechanism** allowing both sides to coordinate efforts in **global environmental issues**. A document to set up the mechanism was signed between China's Minister of Environmental Protection and visiting EU Commissioner for the Environment on Wednesday. It is the first time an EU environment commissioner has visited China.

The establishment of such **coordination mechanism** between China and the EU is a priority for both sides that was confirmed during the recent EU-China Summit. Such a structured dialogue will allow both parties to **coordinate efforts** in issues including **bio-diversity conservation**, climate change, and **ozone layer protection**. It will also provide a forum for China and the EU to share experience in dealing with similar challenges.

China and the EU already enjoy active cooperation in the field of environmental protection. The European Union has **earmarked** 55 million euros for projects in China, the largest of which was launched in northeastern China's Liaoning Province.

The project involves 37 million euros from the EU and 11.5 million euros from China over a five year period. It aims to help the **heavily industrialized** province to **restructure** its environmental planning and management, and covers such areas as waste water management and clean production. The province was also the first stop for the Commisioner's visit, before coming to Beijing.

During her stay in the capital, the Commisioner will also visit a "Green School" and give a speech on European environment policy.

Protecting the environment and promoting **sustainable development** is one of the three key areas of cooperation between China and the EU. Margot Walstrom's visit is part of the process to **further** this cooperation, as both sides feel strongly about their duties to **address** global environmental challenges.

————— ⸙⟨⬧⟩⸙ —————

The latest report from the Chinese State Forestry Administration shows that while most eastern provinces are **benefiting from forestation**, the west still suffers from half-hearted efforts.

The report says more than 25 percent of the territory of 11 eastern provinces and municipalities are now **forested**. But in the west, **forest**

coverage averages only 9 percent, and in the worst case, only a little above three percent. Nevertheless, the eastern provinces do have worries. Just like their **counterparts** in the west, they suffer from an unsatisfactory structuring of their forest resources. Too many of the new trees are hardly bigger than **seedling size** while the areas of mature natural and primitive forests are **dwindling**/decline, causing severe soil erosion especially in the west.

———————————✧◈✧———————————

A working meeting on preventing pollution in China's main **river basins** has opened in Beijing, and Vice Premier says **pollution prevention** in the main water basins must be emphasized more than ever. Conference organizers said that **deterioration** of water quality in the areas concerned has been **halted**, but more work still needs to be done.

In his speech, he said the planned projects must be started as early as possible, and **pollutant discharges** strictly contained. He stressed that pace of construction of urban environmental infrastructure needs to be **accelerated**.

The Vice Premier also stressed the need for **desulphurization** in thermal power plants, rural pollution prevention and environmental industries. The Vice Premier urged officials in central and local governments to work harder to achieve **the environmental goals** set by the 10th-Five-Year-Plan.

Environment officials at the conference told reporters that by the end of 2005, 123.4 billion yuan will have been invested in the main water basins for over 1,500 **pollution treatment projects,** including **urban sewage treatment systems** and comprehensive treatment in the water basins. In the last four years, 490 billion yuan has been used for environmental protection nationwide. **Discharges** of carbon dioxide, smoke and industrial dust have markedly decreased.

Officials say although achievements have been made in the past few years, there is still a long way to go to meet the demands **laid out** in the

10th-Five-Year Plan.

A new environmental protection law is **in the pipeline.** The new legislation is expected to **impose much bigger penalties on** companies and individuals not living up to the letter of the environmental law.

Everyday, several tons of polluted water are **discharged** from a paper making plant in Wuhan, Hubei Province. **The pollutants** are poured directly into the upper reaches of the Yangzte River, one of the country's most important waterways and sources of drinking water.

It's not the first time this plant has been investigated and ordered to **fix the problem**. But the situation has only **worsened**. So why is this happening?

"We did **fine** the company for discharging pollutants. That's all we have the power to do. We also required them to **upgrade their facilities** to properly process these pollutants, but we can do nothing if they don't do it," said director of Hubei's Environmental Inspection Team.

Under existing regulations, the environmental protection administration can impose a maximum fine of 100,000 yuan — much less than the 80,000 yuan it costs the plants each day to deal with their pollutants. That's why many factories are more willing to pay the fine rather than do anything to stop the pollution. Environment officials say there is an urgent need to **revise the current regulations** and introduce much **heavier penalties**.

" Under the new law, punishment for any action to pollute the environment will be much heavier. Violators will not only have to **pay a huge fine**, but also will be treated like criminals. The new law will also state that officials in environmental protection authorities at different levels will be sued if they are found to have **neglected their responsibilities**," said the director of Law and Regulation Department of State Environmental Protection Administration of China.

The environmental protection administration is expected to have more administrative power under the new law.

171

Another major **obstacle** in coping with pollution is local **protectionism**. The issue has been **tackled** in Wednesday's national meeting on environmental protection attended by officials from the local and provincial levels. For the first time, the State Council is insisting that environment protection will be an important factor in their jobs.

"Protectionism exists in many places in China. The local government only pays attention to the short-term economic development by **sacrificing** the environment. Now the State Council's decision to **factor** environmental protection **into** the local officials' **administrative performance** will be very effective," said a deputy director of Pollution Control Dept. of State Environment Protection Administration of China.

The new environmental protection law is expected to **come into effect** within three years.

Between 1998 to 2002, China spent 490 billion yuan on environmental protection. By 2005, another 190 billion yuan will be put into the sector, especially to **combat water pollution**.

China has vowed to **crack down on** polluting companies nationwide. A three-year campaign started today, aiming to carry out **a thorough inspection** and **shut down** all companies that illegally **discharge pollutants**.

Everyday, several tons of polluted water was **discharged** from this paper making plant in Wuhan, Hubei Province. The pollutants are directly poured into the upper reaches of the Yangzte River, one of the most important waterways and sources of drinking water in China. A 57-year-old fisherman, said the pollution **caused a great threat** to the health of local residents. "We used to get our drinking water directly from the river, but now we have to go much further to get it. There is no fish at all here now. They are all dead."

It is not the first time that this plant has been investigated and ordered to **solve the problem**. However, the situation has become even worse. So what is the reason behind this? The local environmental protection

172

authorities say it is a complicated situation.

Director of Environment Inspection Team of Hubei Province said, "We did fine the company for their discharge of pollutants. That's all we have the power to do. We also required them to **upgrade their facilities** to properly process these pollutants, but we can do nothing if they do not do that."

According to the current regulations, the environmental protection administration can give a maximum fine of 100,000 yuan, however, the daily cost for plants to deal with their pollutants is close to 80,000 yuan. That's why many plants are more willing to pay the fine than doing anything in real earnest to stop pollution. This is not **an isolated case** in China, as there are thousands of such polluting factories **scattered** around the country. They all carry out the same practice and local environmental protection authorities **share the same problem**. Things will hopefully change soon as the new round of inspections start with more **efficient measures and stricter rules**.

A vice director of Environmental Protection Administration of China said, "I think it is very important that different government departments are joining efforts to deal with the problem. Before, many problems were **unsolved** due to inefficient cooperation between government authorities. With this joint effort, I believe many problems can be resolved."

The environmental protection administration also pointed out that local protectionism had **created great obstacles** in coping with pollution. So more efforts should be made by governments at all levels to **ensure a proper implementation** of the environment protection law and regulations.

An initial fund of 650,000 US dollars has been established for **the protection of endangered plants** in China's Three Gorges area.

The Three Gorges Dam project has had a big impact on the local ecological environment, which used to be **home for many rare plants**. So the government is planning to create a botanical garden where the endangered plants can be protected in **a simulated environment**.

More than half of the fund has been provided by the central government. The rest of the money has come from the local governments. When it's completed, the reserve will be home to more than 20 of China's most **endangered species** affected by the dam project.

A long-term national **wetland protection program** has been initiated by the Chinese government to mark the 8th World Wetland Day on Monday. The program defines guidelines, targets, key projects and major measures to be carried out over the next thirty years.

Under the plan, China will establish more than 700 **wetland reserves** and **rehabilitate the ecosystems** in nearly 1.5 million hectares of wetland by the year 2030. Wetlands are often referred to as the earth's kidneys. They play an important role in water conservation as well as the prevention of **soil erosion** and flooding. China has the largest area of wetlands in Asia, covering about 65 million hectares.

China will host its first International Expo of **environmentally friendly** cars, or **eco-cars**, in February in the southern island province of Hainan.

The expo will attract domestic and international automobile producers who want to show their latest eco cars along with new motoring technology that **minimizes environmental impact**. Nearly a hundred world auto giants, including Volkswagon, GM, Toyota and Honda, have been invited to participate.

Environment protection is now **a priority** for China's auto industry. China has already applied the Europe I gas emission standards, and Beijing has just **taken the lead** by stepping up to Europe II. By 2008 the country will adopt Europe III, which means that the introduction of eco-cars will be the number one priority for China's auto industry over the next few years.

Unit Fifteen
Environmental Protection (II)

Key Points

1. This is the continued part of Unit Fourteen concerning countermeasures to environmental protection.
2. Review the lexical items in the context of environment- friendly projects.

Forestry authorities are planning to establish another 17 **nature reserves** in China's largest **forest zone** over the next 16 years, bringing the total number to 29. Twelve reserves have already been created in the Da Hinggan Ling mountains, north China's Inner Mongolia Autonomous Region, over the past seven years.

They include one state-level reserve, named Hanma, for the protection of **virgin coniferous forests,** along with other seven reserves at provincial or ministry level to protect forestry and wetland **eco-systems and wild animal resources**, as well as four at lower levels. The local forestry department expects the reserves to cover 2.38 million hectares by 2020.

Covering 400,000 square kilometers, the Da Hinggan Ling mountains **extend through** Inner Mongolia Autonomous Region and Heilongjiang Province in northeast China. More than 400 types of animals and about 1,000 types of plants have been recorded in the zone.

The section of the Da Hinggan Ling mountains in the north of Inner Mongolia, covering 10.66 million hectares, is one of the main **virgin forest zones** owned by the state.

China's largest **wetland museum**, Huanghekou Wetland Museum, in Dongying City, east China's Shandong Province, has opened to visitors. Covering 7,856 square meters and with an investment of six million yuan (722,892 US dollars), the museum lies in the Yellow River Delta National Nature Reserve, which **boasts** one of the 13 most important wetlands in the world under the protection of the United Nations Environment Program (UNEP).

"The museum will collect and exhibit **rare wetland resources**, and become a research center for experts and institutions both at home and abroad and an educational base for students and environmentalists," said director of the local environmental protection bureau.

The nature reserve covering an area of 153,000 hectares is the largest **delta nature reserve** in China and an important **transfer station** and **habitat for birds** from northeast Asia and around the western Pacific.

With the most complete, widest and youngest **wetland ecosystem** in a warm temperature zone in China, the reserve **boasts** five wetland types including shrub wetland, meadow wetland, swamp wetland, river wetland and shore wetland.

It has 393 known species of plants and 1,542 species of animal. Among them, 58 animals such as the red-crowned crane, erne and China merganser are **under state protection.** The reserve is also one of the most important **habitats** for the endangered black-beaked gull.

Air Quality Test Centers and Sewage Treatment Plants under China's State Environmental Protection Administration used to be seen only by specialized experts. But now tourists are **getting in on the act** too, as these are the latest stops on the Beijing tourist trail. Along with the capital's new **eco-buses** hitting the road, David Rathbun looks at how Beijing is providing **a green and warm welcome** for visitors.

In the suburbs of Beijing, tourists were getting a good look at the newly established farmers' residence, Terrestrial Heat Teaching Centre, modern Greenhouse and Spring Fishing Entertainment Club. At present, some travel agencies in Beijing present more than ten new **tourist trips** under the name of "New Beijing — One Day Tour". In the past, Beijing's tourist programmes mainly focused on foreign tourists and customers from outside Beijing, but now they are trying to attract citizens from within the capital. They have **formulated the new programme** to help Beijingers get to know their improved and thus cleaner hometown. The Jinyuchi Renovation Project and Xiaotangshan Modern Agriculture Hi-tech Garden all have begun to **greet ordinary visitors**. The opening of these units closely relate to ordinary people's lives and are proving popular due to this everyday **appeal**.

There is more good news for Beijingers and tourists alike. Two new environment-friendly tour buses will soon **hit the road**. The newly developed **double-decker tour bus** is 18-meters long and four meters high and comes equipped with air-conditioning and **ergonomic/ environment-specific chairs**. This "City Cruiser" is the longest passenger bus in China. With a maximum capacity of 200, the bus will be used for **commuter transportation** in Beijing starting this May. More than three thousand such environment-friendly tour buses have been **phased into use** since 1999. **The advent** of these clean buses will improve Beijing's air quality.

April 1st is a special day, because it **marks the start** of the Yangtze River's annual three-month **fishing ban**. It's hoped the measure will help protect some of the river's **marine life** that is now faced with **extinction**.

The Yangtze River winds its way through the central part of China from the west of the country to the east. It's contributed greatly to the development of Chinese **civilization**. From ancient times until the present day it has supported the human life and the farmland that surrounds it. It's also one of China's major **shipping routes**. But the **over-exploitation** of the Yangtze, and a lack of protection for the resources in it, has led to **the**

gradual destruction of its marine life.

Hilsa herring of the Yangtze River used to reach an annual output of over 1,500 tons in the 1970s, but this **breed of fish** has now almost completely disappeared here. Ao Xie, a special breed of crab which live around the mouth of the Yangtze River, **face the same fate**. In 1981, the annual output of these crabs was 72 tons, by the 1990's the number had been reduced to only 2 tons.

Now let's have a look at the major fresh water fish. The output of black carps, silver carps, and grass carps is only one tenth of what it was twenty years ago. Even **rare species** under state-level protection have been affected. White-flag dolphins, Chinese paddlefish and mullet, continue to decrease in number.

The Yangtze River has played a very important role in China's **fresh water fishing industry**, which used to provide more than 60% of the country's total output of fresh water seafood. The **deterioration** of the fishing resources in the Yangtze River is clearly not only having a negative economic impact, but an ecological one. Experts say, if **emergency measures** are not taken, the local ecology could be **irreparably damaged.**

According to the experts, there are several reasons that have led to this situation, among them pollution, construction of water conservation facilities, extension of farmlands, and increased traffic on the river. But the main **culprit** (a person guilty or believed to be guilty of crime) for the **serious depletion** in the number of fish is **over-fishing**. Many of the fish are **migratory ones**. During the breeding season from February to June, the fish migrate long distances to the upper reaches to **multiply**. But before the fishing ban was introduced, it had become difficult for them to get past the fishing nets and reach their **breeding places**.

After detailed investigation and discussion, the central government finally decided that from April 1st to June 30th every year, **a fishing ban would be imposed**. At the end of March this year, communities along the river were informed of the new law and police patrols were set up along the river to make sure **the ban was enforced**. On April 1st, police reported that all fishing boats had been docked at the banks.

April used to be the **peak season** for fishing, so undoubtedly the new fishing ban will **affect** the annual income of the locals. In Nanjing alone there are nearly 400 registered fishing boats and over 1,500 fishermen. To compensate for the losses of **the fishing community**, the government has offered a monthly **subsidy** of more than 200 yuan, roughly 25 US dollars to each fisherman. Those who depend on fishing for a living, say they understand why the ban has been put in place, and hope it will lead to **a better harvest** in the future.

Fresh water fish from the Yangtze River can no longer be seen now at the Nanjing fish market. It's **a good indication** of the success of the ban, but how long it will take for the resources of the Yangtze to be restored to **an acceptable condition**, only time can tell.

Whether the Three Gorges Project on the Yangtze River will have **a negative ecological and environmental impact** has been a widely **shared concern** ever since the grand project started four years ago. The Government, also concerned about possible effects the project could have, has taken active measures to protect the ecology and environment of the area.

Last year, to ensure healthy ecological development in the region, the Government **drafted a plan** on the treatment of water pollution in the Three Gorges area. In addition, it also intensified environmental protection in the massive **resettlement project**, which involves moving the people of several cities in the Three Gorges to new locations. By 1999, about 14 million yuan in resettlement funds had been poured into eight enviro- nmental protection projects in the area.

One of these projects was **the relocation** of Zigui County in Hubei Province. The local government took active measures to ensure that the new town would be environment-friendly. The Government has **readjusted** the industrial structure to reduce the ratio of heavily polluting industries and **banned** the construction of any project that might cause **environmental hazards** at scenic spots or sources of drinking water. As a result, the water quality of the river that flows through the new town has improved quite a bit.

All of these measures have had a positive impact. According to a report released by the State Environmental Protection Administration, the Three Gorges Project, which has entered its second phase of construction, has not had any serious impact on the environment so far.

The report was based on **the updated monitoring results** on the ecological and environmental conditions at the Three Gorges. Since the project was **launched**, an ecological and environmental monitoring network has been in operation, keeping a day-to-day record of the ecological and environmental changes in the region. The report shows that: there has been healthy and rapid social and economic development at the Three Gorges; there is no **abnormality** in human health; the ecological conditions remain unchanged, with **an abundance of plants**, some recovered fishing resources and **well-protected rare fishes** such as the Chinese sturgeon and white-fin dolphin; industrial pollution has been **alleviated**/mitigated; and the quality of the water has remained unchanged.

However, the results of the monitoring also indicate that human activities at the Three Gorges have caused some **ecological and environmental problems**: a few rare fishes and birds now have become short-term visitors; forest area is decreasing and **the erosion problem** is becoming serious; **geological disasters** such as **landslides** occur more frequently; pollution has been caused by ships and garbage dumping; and sewage systems in urban areas along the river are undeveloped, with most of the sewage water and garbage **dumped** directly into or along the river.

The following are the major ecological and environmental statistics obtained from the monitoring conducted last year at the Three Gorges.

Ecological Conditions

*Climate. The climate at the Three Gorges in 1999 was **basically**

180

normal. There was no serious flooding or drought, though there were heavy rains that caused flooding in the summer and abnormally cold weather in the spring and fall in some areas. Following the **devastating floods** in the summer of 1998, there were **droughts** in the fall in most parts of the region. The drought continued into early 1999, causing **crop failure** in some areas.

*Land plants. There is a total of 6,388 species of higher plants in the area, 188 of which are under key State protection and 57 of which are **rare and near extinction**. There are more than 8,000 ancient trees, 29 of which will be **submerged** in water after the dam is completed.

*Land animals. Animals and birds **close to extinction** include mandarin ducks and golden monkeys. It has not yet been determined how the mandarin ducks will fare/survive after the construction of the reservoir because their living environment will have changed quite a bit.

*Fishing resources and environment. The fishing output in 1999 in the area was 3,612 tons, down 67.16 percent from 1998. A test of the water quality on the river shows that the fishing waters were polluted to some extent, with the copper and petroleum content exceeding **set limits**.

*Rare animals near extinction. In 1999, some 107 species of fish were found in the area, 18 of them having just been recorded and 24 of them living only in the Yangtze. Between 1997 and 1999, a total of 31 species of fish **indigenous** to the Yangtze were discovered. In 1999, **concentrated spawning** of Chinese sturgeons occurred twice in the area, on a scale slightly larger than that in 1998. From 1997 to 1999, 33 white-fin dolphins and 7,489 river dolphins were found. No poaching of the white sturgeon was reported in 1999.

*Agricultural ecology. A survey conducted in the 19 counties and 199 townships in the area last year showed that the coverage of **cultivated land** was decreasing, with the farmland recording a high multi-crop index. Monitoring results indicate that the farmland in the area was not polluted.

*Geological disasters. Last year, 450 geological disasters, including

landslides and mud-rock flows, occurred, causing 500 million yuan of economic losses.

Emission of Pollutants

*Major sources of industrial pollution. In 1999, Chongqing **discharged** 902.2 million tons of industrial waste water, 82.89 percent of which was treated, with 66.38 percent reaching the national standard for discharged waste water. The top three **polluting industries** were the chemical, food, tobacco and beverage processing, and ferrous metal smelting and forging industries.

Monitoring of 124 main sources of industrial pollution in the area showed that the **pollutants** mainly came from downtown Chongqing, Jiangjin City, Changshou County, Fuling District and Wanzhou District, which contributed to 93.9 percent of the **industrial waste water** that flowed into the Yangtze. The 124 sources discharged 244 million tons of waste water in 1999, chiefly containing COD, ammonia nitrogen and phosperus. Compared with the previous year, the waste water discharge in the Three Gorges area increased by 117 million tons.

*Urban sewage water. There are 66 **outlets** of urban sewage water that flow directly into the Yangtze River. The annual **sewage water discharge** there is estimated to be 323 million tons, most of which comes from downtown Chongqing, Wanzhou District and Fuling District. The main pollutants were BOD, COD and ammonia nitrogen. The monitoring conducted in 1999 at the 10 typical sewage water outlets found that the amount of the discharge was within the normal range.

*Industrial solid waste and domestic waste. In 1999, industries in Chongqing produced 15.11 million tons of solid waste, which included 518,100 tons of hazard waste, 578,100 tons of dregs and 169,600 tons of soot. Each year the city also produces 2.19 million tons of domestic waste and dumps about 21.7 million tons of waste on the river bank.

*Pesticide and chemical fertilizer pollution. A total of 132,200 tons of fertilizer were used in the area, averaging 526.87 kg per hectare, lower than that in 1998. The quality of the soil improved to some extent, with a slowing of nitrogen and potassium loss.

*Pollution caused by vessels. Last year, 808 vessels at the Three Gorges were monitored and another 8,755 vessels were surveyed for the discharge of sewage water. Results showed that the vessels **discharged** 779,000 tons of sewage water into the Three Gorges, only 74.1 percent of which was treated. Among the 147.14 tons of **discharged pollutants**, 57.8 percent were petroleum pollutants, **representing** a 48 percent increase over the previous year. While most of the pollution was caused by passenger ships in 1998, cargo ships contributed to most of the pollution last year. Twenty pollution accidents caused by vessels occurred there in 1999, discharging 11.8 tons of diesel oil and 100 tons of **polluted water**, and **dumping** 20 bags of garbage into the Three Gorges section of the Yangtze. Though the number of pollution accidents was not as many as that in 1998, the impact was more serious.

Quality of the Environment

Twelve monitoring surveys were conducted in 1999 at the river sections of 10 major cities. The results indicate that, in general, the quality of the water was fine, but slightly worse than in 1998. There are 12 major industrial waste water outlets and 66 urban sewage water outlets at the Three Gorges. The monitoring results show that some sections of the river along the outlets are heavily polluted. Compared with 1998, however, the area of polluted water has been reduced by 1.43 km.

In the next 10 years, the number of China's **nature reserves** will increase to 1,800. By then they will cover 155 million hectares, 16.1 percent of the country's area. The result will be an **all-inclusive** natural protection network with formal regulations.

In accordance with the General Plan on the Protection of Wild Animals and Plants and the Construction of Nature Reserves issued by the State Forestry Bureau, and the western development strategy, in the next 10

183

years China will build a group of reserves in western areas with **varied wildlife** but fragile ecological environment. By 2010, the number of nature reserves will increase from 1,276 to 1,800, and a plan to protect, recover and develop wetlands sustainably will be implemented. Thirty-two demonstration sites will be launched to promote the protection of wetlands. Other key **wildlife rescue projects** include building 32 wild animal and plant monitoring centers.

By the end of 2000, 1,276 reserves had been established, covering 123 million hectares or 10.6 percent of the area of China. These reserves protect most of **the rare and endangered wild species** and their **habitats**. The reserves also protect about 20 million hectares of primeval forest and 12 million hectares of wetlands. Among them, 19 reserves, including the Changbaishan Reserve and the Shennongjia Reserve, were **registered** with the International Human and Ecological Circle Protection Network. Seven were listed in the International **Wetlands Protocol** and another three will be included in the East Asia-Australia Bird Migration Network. The reserves in China have made great efforts to protect wildlife and global **biological diversity**.

The final phase of the World Summit on **Sustainable Development** in Johannesburg has brought together more than a hundred heads of state-and-government or their representatives. UN Secretary-General urged rich countries to take the lead in getting rid of **unsustainable practices** and protecting the global environment. **On the sidelines** of the summit, Chinese Premier met with British Prime Minister and Italian Prime Minister. Earth Summit aims for sustainable development.

Addressing the world leaders, Kofi Annan said that the most important target to achieve at this summit is responsibility — responsibility for each other, especially for the poor, the **vulnerable**, and the oppressed, as well as responsibility for the future, for our children and for their children. He noted that **conservation of the environment** may be expensive, but the cost of failure to protect it is far greater. He stressed the importance of **integrating civil society and business** into government efforts to realize sustainable development.

South African President called on world leaders to **set concrete goals** to reduce poverty and to protect the environment to build a better world for the future. He called on every country to **act in unity** to ensure that there is a practical and visible global development process that **eradicates poverty** and advances the human condition.

During his meeting with the British Prime Minister, Chinese Premier said China values developing friendly relations with Britain. He noted this year marks the 30th anniversary of the establishment of ambassadorial-level diplomatic ties between China and Britain, and the fifth anniversary of Hong Kong's return to China. High-level exchanges between the two countries have been frequent in recent years. He said as permanent members of the UN Security Council, both China and Britain should increase exchanges and consultations on major world issues. China wants to push all-around bilateral cooperative relations to a new high. Bilateral trade volume **surpassed** ten billion US dollars in 2001.

During his meeting with the Italian Prime Minister, the Chinese premier said China values the Italian role played in the European Union and **the international arena**. China and Italy have **shared identical views** and common interests on a number of international issues and he is pleased with the good momentum of the development of bilateral ties. China and Italy have made considerable headway in cooperation on environmental protection, citing the Sino-Italian environmental project launched during the Earth Summit as an example of the two countries' partnership.

Chinese Premier warned Tuesday **environmental degradation** worldwide has gone on **unreversed** after 10 years of the Rio De Janeiro Earth Summit. "While such **long-standing problems** as poverty, hunger, waste of resources and ecological destruction remain unresolved, abnormal climatic changes, fresh water shortage, spread of HIV/AIDS and other new **threats** have **cropped up**. As economic globalization presses on, the gap between the North and South, as well as the digital divide, keeps on widening.""What **merits our particular attention** is that terrorist activities, regional conflicts, trans-border crimes, rampant drug trafficking and other threats to peace and security remains quite serious."

The ongoing summit is expected to focus on **building a commitment** at the highest levels of government and society to better implement Agenda 21, adopted 10 years ago in Rio, as the roadmap for achieving sustainable development.

———————◄◇►———————

Black-necked cranes are seen in a nature reserve located in the Lhasa River valley in Lhasa, capital of southwest China's Tibet Autonomous Region, Dec. 13, 2003. Black-necked cranes are the only cranes known to live on plateaus. There are some 5,000 black-necked cranes in the world and most of them spend the winter and breed in Tibet, which has therefore strengthened the protection of the rare bird.

———————◄◇►———————

The Chinese premier told world leaders that the **pressure and challenge** facing the international community are evidently on the increase, rather than decrease. **Fulfilling the objectives** of sustainable development as set by Agenda 21, is still a long and **arduous journey**. Sustainable development is a crucial and pressing task facing all countries in the world.

Meanwhile, according to delegates to the summit, governments have reached agreement on **renewable** energy sources. The text calls on all countries to "substantially increase" the **global share** of renewable energy but fails to set any target percentages or dates. The agreement is a crucial step on the way to developing **a common position** for a final overall declaration which delegates hope to sign at the end of the summit on Wednesday.

186

The European Union had been pushing for the share of **renewables** in global energy use to be raised from 14 percent to 15 percent by 2010, but the United States and other oil-producing nations have opposed this.

Unit Sixteen
Prevention and Combat of
Epidemic Disease (I)

导　读

　　词是语义的基本单位。词义的表征，主要指概念的表征，这在认知心理学中是一个重要的研究领域。有关概念的表征，心理学家和人工智能专家曾提出多种模型，其中较典型的有层次网络模型、激活扩散模型和原型模型等。

　　语义网络模型认为，任何词的意义都以与其他词的关系而定，储藏在语义结构中的词是由复杂关系的节点连接起来的，每一个节点代表一个词或一个概念，它们构成一个系统。系统具有层次性，一些节点与其他节点处于同一水平层次上，但它们又处于一些节点之下，以及另外一些节点之上。这些节点所代表的概念按照这种逻辑的上下级关系组织起来，构成一个有层次的网络系统。如：

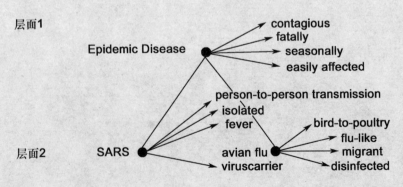

图中圆点为节点，代表一个概念，每个概念都有与其相应的特征。层次网络理论按照认知的经济原则对概念的特征进行相应的分级储存。在每一级概念的层面上，只储存该级概念独有的特征，而同一级的各概念所具有的共同特征则储存于上一级概念的层面上。在这个模型中，概念按上下级关系组成网络，因此每个概念和特征都在网络中有其特定的位置，一个概念的意义或内涵要由该概念与其他概念和特征的关系来决定。

激活扩散模型也是一个网络模型，它认为词汇是以网络关系的形式表征的，但其组织不具有严格的层次性，而是以语义联系或语义相似性将概念组织起来的。相互关联的各个节点之间的距离既决定于结构特征，如从属关系等，也决定于功能上的因素，如典型性、各个节点联系的频率等。各个下位词与上位词之间的距离也不一定相等。

原型理论(prototype theory)认为词义不是以一组特征的形式表征的，词或概念是以原型的方式存储于人的头脑之中的，人们只有掌握了一个词或概念的原型，这个词或概念才能被达到。同属于一个概念的各个成员的典型性各不相同。典型性最强的为原型，处于范畴的中心位置，我们用它来鉴别其他成员。其他成员按其与原型的相似程度处于从典型到最不典型的某个位置上，和原型差别最大即最不典型的成员处于这个概念和其他概念的边界上，最不能代表这个概念。

此外，对于大脑词库的语义结构，语言学家从语义联系的类型分析的角度进行研究。认为处于同一语义场中的词似乎是储存在一起的。语义场中，语义联系最为强烈的是并列关系（如 salt 和 pepper, butterfly 和 moth, 以及 right 和 left, hot 和 cold 等反义或相对关系）和搭配关系（如 salt water, butterfly net 等）。可互相转换的近义词（starved 和 hungry, chase 和 pursue 等）之间的联系也很强烈，当上位词是使用频率高的词项并且所涉及词语都源自同一语义场时，词语上下义关系（如 bird 和 robin, thrush 等）的联系也较紧密，而不同语义场中词语的联系则相对较弱。

从这些理论研究可以看出，词汇的记忆是以意义上相互联系的概念形式储存的。相关的概念形成复杂的语义网络，相互之间可以激活和调用。因此，语言学习意味着建构概念网络表征，而不是识记孤立的词汇项。

　　本单元语篇主要与"epidemic disease"相关。2003 年和 2004 年我们经历了非典（SARS）和禽流感（bird flu 或 avian flu）的袭扰，因此，这些语篇为读者提供了大量的实用性语料。

Key Points

1. The subject in this part concerns epidemic disease like SARS and bird or avian flu which hit Southeast Asian countries and other regions. Read the reports and you'll be familiarized with expressions on epidemic disease and its prevention.
2. Run through the passages and figure out the definition, combat, and considerations of epidemic diseases.

Chinese researchers have **turned a corner** in the race to **develop a vaccine** for severe acute respiratory syndrome or SARS. There's been **a breakthrough** with significant results in animal testing. The discovery was made by China's top vaccine researchers and immuno-therapists at the National SARS Prevention and Treatment Central Command. They've been working on developing a SARS vaccine for the last six months.

Officials at the State Food and Drug Administration said **pre-clinical studies** have been completed. **Animal testing** shows the potential vaccines are able to fight off the SARS virus without poisonous **side effects**. An official of the State Food and Drug Administration of China said, "Chinese researchers first made the discovery, and it's also the first successful research on **vaccine development**. The World Health Organization called the **outcome** of our studies 'heartening'."

These potential vaccines will be ready to test in **human trials** next month. Volunteers will be selected in Beijing and Guangzhou to try them. But whether a SARS vaccine will be available in time, should an epidemic

reoccur, remains to be seen.

The World Health Organization has welcomed China's achievements in developing a SARS vaccine. But, it has **cautioned** that many **hurdles** still remain before a safe and effective vaccine can be produced.

A senior official from the Beijing WHO Office said the vaccine is only one element of bringing SARS **under control**. The WHO hopes scientists in countries around the world will share their SARS research information. China announced Monday all 55 of the vaccines had met standards required for **testing on humans**.

It was only waiting for authorization from the State Food and Drug Administration to begin **clinical tests,** possibly before the end of December. The vaccine's **pre-clinical tests** on monkeys have so far shown no serious **side effects**.

The Chinese government has stepped up measures to prevent any **recurrence** of the SARS **epidemic** which hit China earlier this year. Vice Minister of Health says even if the disease **reappears**, it will not spread as severely as in the first **outbreak**.

The official said currently there are no SARS cases on the mainland. He said authorities at all levels have **put in place** stringent programs to **combat** SARS. And, he said a regional monitoring and reporting system has been established to make sure the ministry is informed quickly, if any sign of the disease **re-emerges**. The official said throughout the health system, training for the prevention and treatment of SARS has been carried out.

The onset of winter means **ideal conditions** for the spread of flu. With a possible **re-emergence** of SARS added to the mix, the medical community and the public are doing all they can to **stave off** another epidemic. Experts say SARS and flu have many differences, and to cope with the task, people should be aware of them.

Medical experts say the major difference between SARS and flu is that SARS has some **symptoms** of pneumonia, while flu just shows symptoms of outer respiratory **infection**. Experts warn that medical workers should **take note of** those differences and **prescribe** the correct **remedies** for the disease.

The United Nations is warning that the global AIDS epidemic shows no sign of **abating/declining.** There have been more deaths and **infections** this year than ever before. The UN issued the **warning message** on Tuesday, one week ahead of the World's AIDS Day on December 1.

UN AIDS, the United Nations agency responsible for the **global fight** against AIDS, said in this year alone, 5 million people worldwide have become **infected with** HIV and 3 million have died. It estimates that 40 million people are living with HIV, including 2.5 million children under the age of 15. Sub-Saharan Africa is the most **severely affected** region.

There was some positive news in the report, with several countries making progress in **combating** the spread of the disease. Uganda was considered one success story, marking its 12th **consecutive** year of reduced HIV infections.

Today is World AIDS Day. The official figure in China shows 840,000 people here are **infected** with HIV/AIDS. This is up about 20 percent over last year. Most of those infected are under 40 years old. Experts are warning the Chinese government to take **tougher measures** to curb the rapid spread of the disease, especially among the younger generation.

Saturday night the young fever at a disco in Kunming, capital city of southern Yunnan Province. China's opening up has given the young more freedom than their parents' generation. Today, they can **experiment with** clothes, ideas, and behavior.

But this new freedom has brought new dangers. Siri Tellier, the Chair of UN **theme group** on HIV/AIDS in China said, "I do have the understanding of young people more curious, more seeking knowledge and idealistic than the old people. So it's important that they know AIDS exists, and know how you get it."

AIDS had long been regarded as **a foreign disease**. It's only in recent years that the government has begun to **come to terms with** the true extent of the country's AIDS problem. Latest government figures show reported cases of HIV/AIDS are just under one million. But experts say the real number could be much higher.

Most of **the infected** are drug addicts and prostitutes in provinces like Yunnan, which borders South Asia's **drug-producing Golden Triangle**. Yunnan had China's first reported AIDS case and still has the largest number of infections in the country. And with AIDS spreading across the nation, China is moving to educate its people, the young in particular.

The Chief of Health Section, UNICEF Office for China said, "Young people on the one hand, the most at risk, because half of new infections are young. But on the other hand, they are most influential. It's better to catch people when they are **forming their behaviors**, than to change their behaviors later."

A class in one of Beijing's vocational schools teaches the students about AIDS, and how **to avoid** it. The program was arranged by UNICEF (United Nations International Children's Emergency Fund) and the school. A seventeen-year old from the Beijing Oriental Vocational School, along with most of his classmates, is hearing about condoms for the very first time. They've had almost no formal **sex education**, so the class is quite **an eye-opener.**

A student said, "Today I've learned something about safe sex and condoms. I think it's useful in helping me protect myself against HIV/AIDS, as well as other **sexually transmitted diseases**, in the future." And a teacher said the government textbook on AIDS prevention doesn't go far enough. It only speaks **in generalities**, discouraging pre-marital sex and irresponsible behavior. It fails to even mention safe sex.

The seriousness of the situation is forcing Chinese to **re-examine** their attitudes towards AIDS. But there aren't many specific measures focusing on the most **vulnerable group**. The younger generation faces an uncertain future.

Experts point out that as young people become increasingly aware of the danger of AIDS, and understand the consequences of NOT adopting safe sex practices ... China, the world's most **populous** country,will have its BEST chance to prevent AIDS ... in EPIDEMIC proportions.

Treatment for SARS has been **under the microscope** in Beijing. Combined **therapy** of Traditional Chinese Medicine, or TCM, and western medicine has been declared safe. WHO officials announced their evaluation Friday in Beijing after review during a three-day **seminar**.

The three-day seminar brought together dozens of medical experts from China and the World Health Organization. They've concluded the **integrated treatment** of SARS using TCM and western medicine is safe. Experts have also recognized **potential benefits** of traditional Chinese medicine. But this does not mean the WHO recommends using TCM to treat SARS.

Dr. Simon Nicolas Mardel, World Health Organization, said, "There is no specific treatment that WHO can recommend for SARS. The treatment by western medicine has powerful **side effect** against this background, the study suggests that TCM do not have serious side effect. What we cannot say is that it can be used routinely. But we do see potential benefits of TCM."

During the SARS epidemic, nearly sixty percent of the more than 5,300 cases on the Chinese mainland were treated with **a combined therapy** of traditional Chinese medicine and western medicine. And thousands of medical workers and millions of ordinary people used traditional

Chinese herbs as **a preventative**. But Dr. Mardel was clear about the best way to guard against a possible return of SARS.

Dr. Simon Nicolas Mardel also said, "I want to conclude and remind that no matter how effective a preventative measure might be, SARS is spreading by health facility. So the most important task is to put **extreme strict control measure** rather than using drugs..."

Follow-up research on long-term effects of the combined therapy continues. Medical experts have yet to develop an effective treatment for SARS.

Quality control and **quarantine measures** are becoming more and more closely **associated with** ordinary Chinese people's everyday life. As China's State Administration of Quality Supervision, Inspection and Quarantine defined at this morning's news conference, the nation will endeavor to transform "Made-in-China" products **an synonym** for high quality and **market competency**.

Effective quarantine measures at China's major entry ports have **shielded** the country **from** the further **encroachment** of the SARS epidemic. Deputy Director of the Administration said that in the event of emergencies such as the outbreak of SARS, quarantine departments will work hard to **safeguard** the people's health.

"At the onset of the SARS epidemic, we installed **ultra-red** temperature **monitoring apparatus** at checkpoints of every entry port. Everyone entering or leaving the country was required to fill out **a health declaration**. In addition, we divided special passages for tourists and promptly sent people exhibiting SARS — like symptoms for further medical observation."

Not only this, the director added the administration also **executed a nationwide inspection** on the quality of products related to SARS prevention. Those cheating people with fakes have been severely punished. He stressed a stepped up quality monitoring system is in the making, to keep people's everyday life away from the threat of low quality products. Together with

the law enforcement departments, the administration has been endeavoring to **track down** illegal cases in major industrial sectors. On the other hand, he noted the administration will provide better service for the nation's exporting companies, especially those aiming at overseas market expansion with quality products.

To ensure the quality of exported goods, we put every process of the manufacturing **under strict monitoring**, including material screening and transportation. A more clearly defined classifying management system will soon be adopted at local quarantine and inspection departments, to help expand the exports.

In line with the international practice, the administration will introduce series of higher quality criteria into the quality control of all Chinese products, especially in the food processing sector. The director pointed out that everyday essentials like rice, flour, and vinegar should improve their quality to get further market entry. As the initial step, the **market entry system** will be introduced for the processing of meat, dairy, drinks and 10 other varieties of food. Moreover, the administration also urges all overseas companies to better understand China's quarantine law and other relevant quality regulations, to enter China's market.

The administration also reminds all consumers of noting **a special "QS" label** attached to qualified products when they go shopping. That's the food safety mark issued by the Chinese government.

HIV affects many people, but is particularly **prevalent** among people who are of a productive age. Analysts estimate that well over 42 million people in the world are living with HIV and AIDS, most of whom are **in their peak years** of economic productivity.

On Thursday, the International Labor Organization launched a manual to promote its code of practice on HIV/AIDS in China to help the government, workers and employers cope with the epidemic in the workplace.

What are the **legal and ethical issues** that face working people with

HIV? and how should businesses maintain their economic edge while coping with HIV-infected workers? To give answers to these questions, the International Labor Organization launched a code of practice on HIV/AIDS on Thursday in Beijing, aiming to provide some guidance to both employers and employees on how to cope with the **worldwide epidemic**.

The code has been used by the United Nations as **a framework** for its own personnel policy. UN Secretary General Kofi Annan welcomed it as a **system-wide** instrument in the fight against AIDS. The Chinese version of the manual has been published to help the Chinese government, workers and employers to **take the fight** against HIV into the workplace.

According to the National Center for AIDS control and prevention, China has seen a 20 percent increase of HIV cases over the last year. Analysts predict that the number may hit 10 million by 2010, which **poses a big threat** to Chinese society.

Health Insurance Official of National Labor and Social Security Ministry said, "HIV/AIDS is a disease that has **a big impact** on human beings. If it is not controlled, it will do great damage to China's productive force. China will cooperate with international organizations to deal with the problem."

Due to **a lack of knowledge** about the disease, many employers have **harbored** negative attitudes about working with a person who has HIV. Through **proactive policies** as well as prevention and education programs, the international labor organization aims to equip people with the tools to protect both the workforce and business development.

———————————<<<◇>>>———————————

With the coming of winter, many people in China are concerned about a possible **comeback** of SARS. Beijing is **on high alert** after a laboratory researcher from Taiwan was confirmed to have **contracted** the deadly virus. All municipal **entry-exit inspection** and quarantine departments and hospitals in Beijing have strengthened SARS prevention and monitoring measures.

Earlier in the week, **temperature screening systems** were **re-activated** at Beijing's capital airport and railway stations. Health officials say all the hospitals in the city have initiated clinical procedures to **detect any signs** of SARS as early as possible and prevent the spread of the disease.

The new equipment includes a system introduced from the United States which can rule out fever cases caused by flu or pneumonia.

A Beijing health official said, "Beijing's **state of readiness** is very different now to that of Spring this year. We are well prepared to prevent and control the SARS epidemic."

Meanwhile, The Chinese Ministry of Science and Technology announced that China has had no **lab-related** SARS cases. The Ministry has issued two provisional measures on SARS virus research, banning **disqualified** labs, **unauthorized** researchers, **unproven** research activities, unauthorized virus preservation, and specimen **smuggling**.

Scientists think a new **variant** of the SARS coronavirus may have **infected** the suspected SARS patient in Guangdong Province. This is the result of the latest tests by medical agencies in Guangdong, but it has not been **confirmed** by the World Health Organisation which will announce its final results next week.

Medical experts in Guangdong said the coronavirus sample, collected from the patient, is a new **variation** of SARS. An academician from the Chinese Academy of Engineering said, "In a series of **sample tests**, we have discovered an S gene in the coronavirus. It presents **a gene sequence** different from those that have already been discovered. We are sure it is a new variation, not a polluted sample."

Over the past few days, a team of medical experts from the WHO and Chinese Ministry of Health have been working together to **achieve the diagnosis**. Samples have been sent to other major SARS labs around the world. Two labs in Hong Kong are expected to release their test results early next week. The suspected SARS patient is recovering and those who have been in contact with him have shown no SARS symptoms. The flu-like virus was declared under control in July last year, after more than 300 people died of the disease on the Chinese mainland.

The World Health Organization has said that China is still **a safe place** to travel to, despite the recent confirmation of a SARS case in Guangdong. At a press conference held in Beijing on Monday evening, WHO officials said they believe this single case does not **constitute an immediate public-health risk**.

Experts from the WHO said the Guangdong case is the only one they have seen in China so far. They confirmed the patient appears to be on the way to **recovery** and there has been no further **transmission** of the disease. As this case does not **pose an immediate threat** to public health, a WHO team member who had visited Guangdong and been involved in the investigation there noted it was perfectly safe to travel to the province. But the WHO officials noted that there were **unanswered questions** about SARS. Though they were unsure about the origin of the virus, one expert offered 3 possibilities.

Compared with the SARS outbreak early last year, the WHO said China is now **in a much stronger position** to deal with the deadly disease. Meanwhile, the WHO welcomed the decision by the Guangdong government to try and **minimize contact** between humans and the animals thought to be carrying the SARS virus.

Unit Seventeen
Prevention and Combat of
Epidemic Disease(II)

Key Points

1. Just as SARS spread last spring, the bird flu is continuously attacking southeast Asian countries and rural places in China. Across the country, the central and local government and people are going all out to combat the disease. Read the reports and recall what we experienced in reading and fighting against the SARS last year.

2. Compare the passages with Unit Sixteen and find out the linguistic points in stories of epidemic disease.

In **an exclusive interview** with China Central Television, a SARS team leader for the World Health Organization's China office said she has **received a report** from the Chinese Health Ministry on the suspected SARS case in Guangdong. The WHO is now **awaiting the outcome** of tests that are still underway.

She said reports showed that the SARS case in Guangdong was discovered, **isolated** and reported promptly, and other **preventative measures**, including **contact tracing**, were also carried out. "The government is doing all the **precautionary measures**...The measures has put into place." The SARS prevention system in China was working, and because of this the epidemic could be **kept under control.** Hall added, "The government has spent a huge commitment... So the system is working."

The WHO official said a large SARS **outbreak** in China was not likely. She also said she was encouraged by the **information sharing** and close working relationship that had developed between the world health body and the Chinese Health Ministry.

A team from the World Health Organization is continuing to help Chinese experts conduct tests and **track down** people who may have had contact with a man suspected of having SARS. They toured the area on the outskirts of Guangzhou where the man comes from, and spoke to locals to **figure out** how he might have been exposed.

This **residential block** is the key target of the investigation. Medical detectives visited the patient's home and a nearby drugstore where the 32-year-old television producer bought medicine before he was **hospitalized** nearly two weeks ago.

More than 80 people who had contact with him have been **quarantined**, but none have shown symptoms. Doctors say the patient's temperature has been at normal levels for a week.Director of Guangzhou Institute of Respiratory Diseases said, "We didn't discover the SARS virus in samples of respiratory test paper, stool, serum and plasma taken from the patient."

———————§━◁◆▷━§———————

For now, investigators are mulling/studying where to send samples abroad for further examination to confirm or **refute the presence** of SARS. The flu-like illness was declared under control by the government in July after more than three hundred people died of the disease on the Chinese mainland.

———————§━◁◆▷━§———————

Hong Kong, a close neighbour of Guangdong Province where the suspected SARS case was confirmed, has **stepped up its surveillance and monitoring system** to prevent **a resurgence** of the disease.

At a press conference on SARS prevention, one health official said any possible SARS cases will be reported as early as possible to control its spread in Hong Kong. The government will strengthen its communication with Mainland authorities and urge private doctors and hospitals to report any pneumonia cases where patients had visited Guangdong 10 days **prior to** falling ill. He also required quick tests on **samples of** all pneumonia cases that develop in the community. Other measures include stepping up checks at **border control points** and increasing publicity on SARS prevention measures.

Hospital Authority Chief Executive said he now requires all patients visiting clinics to have their temperatures checked. He also asked all staff and visitors in the hospital area to wear masks and for visitors to wash their hands before leaving the **wards**.

The **precautionary measures** at immigration control points have also been strengthened. Referring to the Philippino woman suspected of **contracting** SARS after returning from Hong Kong, the WHO had been contacted and that the government was following the situation closely.

———————

The Ministry of Health says China has already taken numerous measures to **contain** bird flu. Inspection teams have been sent to **affected areas** to help prevent the virus from spreading to humans.

According to Vice Minister of Health, **emergency measures** have been carried out in affected areas of China. The cities and villages have already been educated on how to prevent the spread of the bird flu virus.

The bird flu virus can't **stand heat**. And if it is heated to 100 degrees Celsius, it will be killed. And it's also very **vulnerable to** sunshine, dryness and normal **disinfectant**. Therefore, people should be relatively safe if they stay away from **infected birds**.

Up till now, there is no scientific proof that the virus is **transmitted** among humans. According to the latest measures, local governments will report to the Ministry of Health when they suspect a bird flu case.

———————

Other efforts to **contain** the deadly bird flu disease are also underway, following the confirmation of previously suspected cases in one autonomous region and two provinces, and reports of new suspected cases in three other regions.

The latest areas thought to be affected by bird flu include Shanghai Municipality, East China's Anhui Province and South China's Guangdong Province, increasing bird **flu-stricken** areas on the Chinese mainland to six.

Government departments have issued **tight controls** to prevent further spread of the deadly disease. The State Administration for Industry and Commerce has asked local authorities of the affected areas to **close their markets** for live poultry and related products in order to **block their entry or exit**.

The State Administration of Quality Supervision, Inspection and Quarantine has **banned** exports of poultry and related products from the Guangxi Zhuang Autonomous Region, Hunan and Hubei provinces. It has also temporarily **halted exports** from Shanghai, Anhui and Guandong to other **localities** including Hong Kong and Macao.

Meanwhile, the Ministry of Commerce has set up a team to **oversee** the supply of meat products across the nation. The team is responsible for coordinating between different localities to ensure a plentiful supply of pork, beef and lamb.

Beijing has **suspended bird trading**, and closed all bird markets in its latest measure to **combat** the deadly bird flu that is spreading in the country.

On Feb.5, the Beijing Municipal Forestry Bureau suspended **imports and exports** of wild birds and their related products, as well as the transportation of wild birds. To restrict possible channels of infection, the related departments have also strengthened measures to **crack down on illegal fowl trading** activities, sending inspection teams to bird markets around the capital.

Official sources say the **forestry** bureau, as well as industrial and commercial departments will be examining the implementation of the **vaccination and disinfection** of birds in zoos and breeding areas. They will also be **keeping a close eye on** underground trading and hunting activities.

———————————8———————————

In Beijing, the municipal government held a press conference on Friday, **centering on** its work to keep bird flu out of the capital. Officials say strict measures have been taken to prevent the disease from entering the city. However, officials say prevention is not the only priority for the government. Economic development is also essential.

Deputy director of the Beijing Health Bureau says the municipal government has formed **contingency/emrgency plans** and taken a series of **concrete measures** to cope with the challenge. Having learnt the lessons of last year's SARS epidemic, Beijing has established a system of monitoring, quarantine and reporting. So far, no cases have been reported in Beijing, but the possibility remains.

Deputy director of Beijing Health Bureau said, "Our preventive measures have been implemented promptly and comprehensively. But some factors like **migrating** birds may still spread the disease. We've prepared for that, and are confident we can deal with it."

The official said poultry products on sale in Beijing are safe. The government has **launched comprehensive inspections of** the whole production process: from breeding, slaughtering and freezing, to the point of sale. The inspectors say consumers should only buy poultry products from **authorized markets.**

According to an inspector, "All poultry products which have passed inspections will carry a label. Consumers can be confident of products carrying this mark."

Another focus is on the source of the poultry products. Beijing has strengthened its **check-points** on roads, railways and ports. All vehicles carrying raw poultry materials must be **sterilized**, and undergo full inspections of their **permits** and cargoes. Any freight truck which does not pass these inspections will be **barred** from entering Beijing.

Prevention is **the top priority** for many officials now, but for the government, there is more work to do. The Acting Mayor of Beijing said the bird flu prevention and control work is very important, but at the same time, increasing agricultural production and farmers' incomes must not be neglected.

In Beijing, twelve **monitoring centers** have been established to prevent the possible **transmission** of the disease by **migratory birds**. The deadly disease affects both birds and humans, and the Ministry of Health has taken other **precautionary measures** to prevent human infection.

The return of spring will bring thousands of birds back to Beijing. Every year, 30,000 return from their winter grounds in southern China, where there's been an outbreak of bird flu.

Twelve monitoring centers have been set up in the capital in places where migratory birds gather. Workers will **disinfect** bird habitats and **file daily reports**. They will **log three observations** a day, noting the number of birds and their health condition. Any sign of bird flu will be immediately reported.

Humans are also **at risk**. Following the bird flu **outbreak** in east China provinces of Zhejiang and Jiangxi and central China's Hunan Province, the Ministry of Health sent a team of experts for inspection and guidance on **preventing human infection**.

Director of China Disease Prevention & Control Center said, "We've found some problems in preventing human infection. We must strengthen **surveillance** on all flu cases, as bird flu symptoms are the same as other types of flu. And in many places, there's over **disinfection**. Scientific disease prevention and control procedures should be followed."

The battle to contain bird flu in China has entered **a critical phase**. So far, 14 provinces and regions have confirmed outbreaks of the disease.

———————❖◀◀◆▶▶❖———————

Taiwan will **cull**/pick out an additional 230,000 poultry after **a milder strain of** the **avian flu** was detected at eight more farms across the island.

A Taiwan agricultural official said on Feb.5 that the **infections** that began in central Taiwan are now being reported as far north as the outskirts of Taipei and into the southern counties. Experts believe the virus was brought by **migratory birds,** whose **habitats** are not far from the eight affected farms. Authorities have acted immediately to **prevent** the virus **from** spreading. Taiwan has destroyed about 100,000 poultry, after an outbreak of the H5N2 **strain** of bird flu virus was detected in mid-January.

———————❖◀◀◆▶▶❖———————

Countries and regions in Asia are taking further measures to contain the spread of the bird **flu epidemic**. More birds are being **culled**/picked, even in Singapore where no bird flu cases have yet been found.

The Indonesian government **issued a regulation** on poultry **extermination** on Sunday. It says that farmers who work with the government to **slaughter** their birds will receive financial compensation while those who fail to cooperate could face a two-year prison term.

Also on Sunday, the Singaporean agricultural department announced **the shutting down** of chicken farms on an outlaying island, where birds could not be protected from the virus if cases **erupted**. The 250 healthy chickens on the farms are to be **culled**. The move aims at preventing the spread of the disease to Singapore via wild birds. The owners of the farms accepted **the closures** and received **financial compensation** from the government.

Elsewhere in the Malaysian state of Sabah, a total ban has been **imposed** on the import of chicken and **chicken parts** from infected countries.

The bird flu **epidemic** has so far been found in nine Asian countries and a region.

206

The World Health Organization says **human-to-human transmission** of bird flu is a possible explanation for two deaths in Vietnam, in what could be a first in Asia's latest **bird flu crisis**. Scientists had believed and health officials hoped that the disease could only be **contracted** through exposure to **infected birds** or **droppings**.

But the deaths of two Vietnamese sisters late last month challenged the theory. The sisters are part of **a cluster of four cases** of respiratory illness in the northern province of Thai Binh. The cluster included the two sisters, their brother and his wife. The brother died shortly before his sisters were admitted to hospital. In an apparent bid to **play down concerns** about humans passing the disease onto each other, the WHO **cautioned** there was no evidence of efficient human-to-human transmission of H5N1 in Vietnam or elsewhere.

———————

The World Health Organization has announced the possible first case of bird virus human transmission did not **alter** the organization's overall **state of alert** against the disease.

The United Nations health agency believes at least two Vietnamese, one of whom died last month, may have **caught the virus** from another member of their family rather than directly from poultry.

But the head of WHO's Global Influenza Program said **person-to-person** transmission should come as no surprise, because it had occurred in limited numbers in apparently similar **avian flu outbreaks** in Hong Kong in 1997. And there has been to date no significant further human-to-human transmission.

———————

The **genetic sequencing** analysis of viruses taken from two Vietnamese sisters showed that there are no possibilities of person-to-person transmission of bird flu, according to the World Health Organization (WHO).

"WHO has today received the results from a study of virus **isolated**

207

from a 23-year-old woman who is part of a family cluster in Vietnam **under investigation** as the first possible instance of human-to-human transmission. Virus genetic material from this woman, as for the other case in this cluster, is **of avian origin** and contains no human influenza genes," it announced on its website on Thursday.

Earlier, the organization announced a similar testing result for other case **in the cluster**, 30-year-old sister of the 23-year-old woman.

The findings indicate that H5N1 has not changed to a form easily **transmitted** from one person to another, it said, adding that "no illness has been reported in other family members, in the local community, or in health workers **involved in care of** these patients."

However, spokesman of WHO in Vietnam, told Xinhua on Thursday that, "The results are encouraging, but unfortunately, they are still not **the conclusive proof** we need to fully **discount the possibility** of human-to-human transmission of the H5N1 virus."

A representative of WHO in the country, **echoed his statement** by saying that the results did not **exclude** a very limited person-to-person transmission of H5N1.

The cluster involves a 31-year-old man, his two sisters, and his 28-year-old wife in Vietnam's northern Thai Binh Province. A school teacher, died on Jan. 12 in the Hospital of Tropical Diseases in the capital city of Hanoi.

After having a temperature on Jan. 6, he was admitted to the Thai Binh Hospital which said he had showed **symptoms** of flu for three days. On Jan. 9, provincial doctors decided to **transfer** him to Hanoi. In the city, he was cared by many people, including two of his younger sisters, his newly-wedded wife, and his mother-in-law.

One day after his death, his sisters were **hospitalized**, although his wife had no symptoms of flu. Then, the wife was **discharged from hospital**, but both of the two sisters died on Jan. 23. The two sisters were confirmed to have **contracted** H5N1. Meanwhile, no samples of his brother were available for testing since his body was cremated/burned.

With more **avian flu** reports **cropping up** in China, the nation is faced with great challenges in preventing further spread of the disease. The Chinese government has, however, promised an **aggressive effort** towards **containing the epidemic**. During his inspection of the affected areas, Chinese Premier Wen Jiabao sent a message to local people that, although **a tough job**, the government will step up its efforts to deal with the disease.

The deadly **avian influenza** has fast spread throughout China. The Chinese Premier toured parts of the central Hubei and eastern Anhui provinces affected by the flu and promised compensation for farmers. Central authorities have issued **strict guidelines** to try and control further spread. All **poultry** found within five kilometers of affected sites must be **vaccinated**. And all birds, even the vaccinated ones, found within THREE kilometers of affected sites, must be culled.

Chinese Premier said, "Even if fowl have been vaccinated, they still have to be **slaughtered**. I hope people can understand that."

With regard to the **reported outbreak** of the bird blu in 10 provinces and municipalities around the country, the Premier said while preventing human infection is very important, attention must also be paid to protecting **the poultry industry**. To help cope with the disease, the State Council has established National Bird Flu Prevention Headquarters to coordinate prevention measures. Chinese analysts have so far not found evidence to **link the Chinese outbreaks**.

A **veterinary specialist** with National Animal Husbandry and Veterinary Service said, "The epidemic is still developing. I think the major reason of the outbreak is **a lack of adequate raising conditions** for poultry, and the temperature. Some birds' immune systems have failed to **resist** virus attacks, but these cases do not seem connected."

Migrant birds are still suspected to have **carried the virus** to

domesticated flocks. The Chinese Ministry of Health says that so far, there have been no known human cases of infection. The Chinese government and the WHO have both repudiated/rejected claims that the virus originated in China. There are, as yet, no clear answers as to where it **originated**, nor how it develops. But China has, at least, improved mechanisms to cope with the spread of an epidemic.

Although avian flu has spread rapidly in China, last year's experience of SARS has left the authorities and people **better equipped** to cope with the new challenge.

China says the bird flu outbreak in five of its provinces has been brought under control thanks to **stringent prevention and control measures**. The news comes a day after the Ministry of Agriculture declared suspected bird flu cases in those areas.

The areas are Gansu and Shaanxi in the northwest, Anhui in the east and the central provinces of Hunan and Hubei. Local governments began **culls and compulsory quarantine measures** as soon as suspected cases were **spotted**. Samples have been sent to the National Bird Flu Reference Laboratory. No person has been reported to **contract** the disease.

Since suspected cases of the virus **surfaced** in the northern port city of Tianjin, its close neighbor, Beijing, has taken **active measures** to keep the disease at bay.

In order to prevent the chickens from getting bird flu, all the chicken farms in Beijing are **quarantined**. Only the workers and those essential to maintain the quarantine are allow to enter **the enclosure**. Beijing Huaifa Chicken Farm is an example. This **chicken farm** has more than 40,000 chickens. Its products get sent throughout the whole country. As soon as the first outbreak of the bird flu in China was announced, the farm began **implementing strict measures** to guarantee its chickens' safety. Every meal for the workers inside the farm is being taken in by a **specially-assigned** person. Before going into the farm, the deliverer is **sterilized** with ultraviolet rays. Efforts into cleaning inside and outside the farm have doubled, with stronger **disinfectant** being used.

Director of Beijing Huaifa Chicken Farm said, " The prevention measures on our farm are being **strictly implemented**. And the chickens we offer to the market are safe. We must guarantee this, because it **effects** the health of many people out there."

Yet concern remains. The director says despite the farm's **remote location**, wild migrant birds may still bring the disease.

Beside Tianjin, other 11 provinces have suspected or confirmed cases of bird flu. Beijing, Tianjin's neighbor, has strengthened its **check-points** on roads, railways and in ports. Every slaughterhouse has been inspected to confirm that the poultry products are safe. The capital has also stored four million doses of the **anti-virus vaccine** to fight the disease.

For most consumers, the greatest concern is over poultry products directly available to them. Companies like Kentucky Fried Chicken have insisted their food is safe. But not all consumers are convinced.

Kentucky Fried Chicken, the multinational **fast food giant**, announced earlier it has also taken measures to ensure the safety of its food. It is accepting only safe chickens; cooking them at a high temperature; and implementing strict cleaning measures throughout its stores. The company hopes to **woo/draw back consumers' confidence**. But some consumers are still worried about eating chicken.

Beijing Resident said to the reporter, "Because of the bird flu, I pay more attention to poultry food. I have **lessened** the amount of chicken in my meals and eat more bean products and fish."

Beijing officials say the poultry products on Beijing's markets are safe. However, bird flu appearing in Beijing **remains a possibility**. They say Beijing residents will be the first to know if the virus does enter the city and the government will do everything in it's power to guarantee residents' health.

———————❈━⬦═⬦━❈———————

The Chinese Ministry of Agriculture says so far the fast-spreading bird flu has not resulted in any **human infections** and governments at all levels have **responded to** the outbreak of the disease by implementing **prompt** quarantine and vaccination measures, said senior Chinese agriculture and health officials at a press conference this morning in Beijing.

Up to now, millions of **fowls/husbandry** have been slaughtered to cut off the **transmission of the highly contagious virus.** Building on lessons learned from the battle to **contain** SARS last year, a daily reporting system has been set up to ensure the smooth flow of sharing information. New laws and regulations on animal health are also being drafted.

China's Vice-Minister of Agriculture says 23 bird flu cases have been confirmed since the **eruption of the disease** was first reported on January 27. Up till now, nearly 50,000 sick fowls have died of the disease. Resulting from prompt preventive efforts, more than 1.2 million fowls have been **culled nationwide.** And the Vice-Minister reports that no cases of humans **contracting** the disease have been reported.

The spreading of bird flu in China is **highlighted** in three aspects. First of all, all of the affected areas are quite **remote and far apart.** Secondly, the situation in China's southern regions is more serious. Thirdly, the H5N1 virus, the chief **culprit** of the disease, is highly **contagious and deadly** to poultry. Winter and Spring are known to be **the peak season** for **communicable** diseases. And the quarantine and vaccination system for animals is still quite **inadequate** in China. That's why bird flu **containment** remains an arduous mission for China.

According to China's Animal Quarantine Law, a nationwide **emergency-response package plan** has been carried out to slaughter sick poultry and enforce vaccination on all other poultry being raised in areas within a five-kilometer radius from affected areas. Moreover, all fowl markets in a 10-kilometer radius around **problem areas** have been ordered to **suspend**

their business.

A daily reporting mechanism and four-level diagnosis program have been established to get the latest facts on the situation. The initial stage **necessitates** experts to make clinical diagnosis. In the second step, professional labs at the provincial level will examine the results and make **preliminary judgments**. Following that, the State Reference Lab will examine the virus samples and determine **the type of strain**. The final results can only be confirmed and released by the Ministry of Agriculture.

A close sharing of information with the World Health Organization and the UN Food and Agriculture Organization has been in place ever since the onset of the bird flu outbreak. The two UN agencies have sent experts to **assess and assist** China's containment. In addition, joining hands with the country's health authorities, the ministry has also endeavored to ensure the safety of the **food supply** through strict import bans on **poultry products** from affected countries.

Unit Eighteen
Science and Technology (I)

导 读

　　Krashen 区分了"习得"（acquisition）与"学得"（learning）这两种截然不同的学习方式。"习得"是调动人脑中的语言学习能力，像儿童习得母语那样，在交际的过程中理解话语意思，无意识地学会使用语言；"学得"指有意识地通过学习语言的规则和形式去获取语言知识。只有"习得"到的语言知识才导致语言的运用，"学得"的语言知识只能帮助人们有意识地检查说出来的话语是否正确。根据连接论，"学得"的规则若无足够的语言数据支持（即没有大量的语言接触），只懂得一些语法"规则"，是难以建立起概率型式的，使用起来不会流利顺畅。许多英语学习者采用的是"学得"的方式，把语言作为单纯的课本知识来学习，脱离了语言使用的环境，因此，造成只有单词和语法，却没有特定的语言交际技能。

　　"习得"语言因有语言数据和与之相关语境的支持，在大量接触和运用语言的基础上自然冒出概率型式，使用起来理应流利。但是，"学得"的知识只要是来自目的语，就应该有助于建立语言概率型式，大量的输入应该可以转换成"习得"知识。外语教学中，为了正确流畅地使用语言，应该立足于一定量的语言输入。报刊等媒体英语即现实语境的交际性语言，有利于学习者在应用中"习得"英语。

　　本单元及下一单元以中国人民飞天梦"神舟 V"的升空、美国"机遇 Opportunity"号和"勇者 Spirit"号宇宙探索、网络、知识产权等科技领域的新闻报道为背景语篇，提供大量相关的语料，以满足"习得"输入的需要。

Key Points

1. Reports on the development of science and technology often attract college students' attention. Exploration of outer space, in particular, has been of nationwide and global concern since the launch of Shenzhou V and NASA's "spirit" and "opportunity" landing on the Mar. Read the following news pieces and you'll know how to convey what you have about science and technology in varied aspects.

2. Trace the series of Shenzhou V's launch and the realization of Chinese people's flight dream, and group words and expressions concerned.

China plans to **launch a new generation of rockets** later this year. The small satellite launch vehicle, Explorer I, will use **solid fuel** to carry a scientific experimental satellite into space. The **new breed of rocket** is needed to complement the Long March group, the country's large-scale liquid-fuel **space launchers**.

Explorer I has been designed to take small and micro satellites into space. The solid-fuel rocket will be able to carry loads weighing less than 100 kilograms.

Chief commander of Explorer I Project said, "The solid fuel space launcher will help us **view disaster areas** as soon as possible — **emergencies** like fire, floods, and earthquakes."

The United States, Russia, Japan and India have already developed their own solid fuel **boosters,** with the US and Russia **leading the field.** The European Space Agency is also preparing for the creation of the solid fuel boosters.

Another chief engineer of Explorer I Project said, "Solid **propellant**

orbital launch vehicles have been developed for a long time. This is just a beginning for China, but some of our techniques, such as control and **high-speed movement**, have reached an advanced level."

The relative safety, low cost and **high thrust** of solid-fuel rockets make them an important factor in the **commercialization** of the space industry.

———❦⬤❦———

NASA's Mars **rover** "Opportunity" has **rolled off its lander** and onto the rusty soil of Mars, a week after its arrival on the Red Planet. It will carry out **a mission** to explore the planet's **geological history** and search for signs of water.

The cheers were loud at NASA's Jet Propulsion Lab in California on Saturday. Everything was going as planned. Opportunity drove onto the surface of Mars and beamed photos of its new position in the Meridiani Planum to the orbiter Odyssey. The safe **separation** from the landing device drew praise, but it was **a mineral discovery** that drew most of the cheers.

———❦⬤❦———

NASA has declared the Mars Rover Spirit **cured** after the repair of a problem with its computer's **flash memory system**. The **malfunction** had **stalled the wheeled robot** for two weeks.

Spirit was described as being in critical condition when it abruptly stopped sending science data to Earth about two weeks ago. NASA scientists had been conducting a delicate process of deleting files and **reformatting** Spirit's flash memory system. And the craft was able to resume its science work on Thursday.

Meanwhile, NASA scientists said the other rover on Mars, Opportunity, was continuing to work well. On the same day, NASA sent Opportunity on a roll across a patch of Mars, moving the rover closer to a rock outcrop that scientists want it to spend several days studying in detail. The move was Opportunity's first since rolling off its lander, on Saturday.

———❦⬤❦———

NASA's Opportunity rover sent back its first 360-degree colour

panoramic images of the surface of Mars on Monday. It has also **extended a robotic arm** that will touch the planet's surface.

Good news from NASA's Jet Propulsion Lab in Pasadena, California again. The Mission team **unveiled** the first 360-degree color **panoramic picture** sent by the Rover Opportunity on Monday.

Jeff Johnson with US Geological Society said, "I am very pleased to announce this morning that the full 360 degrees mission success panorama from pan cam has been acquired."

The photographs show **a wide expanse of red soil** and the **bumpy edge** of a crater where the craft sits. Engineers said photographs showed that all the pieces of the arm are in place. Opportunity's **robotic arm** includes several instruments that can be used to study materials found on the planet's surface. The rover has already spied a mineral called gray hematite in the soil at its landing site. **Preliminary evidence** suggests the iron-rich mineral is of a variety that forms in liquid water. The finding provides the first signs that the site was once wetter, and maybe even **hospitable to life** long ago.

Meanwhile, Engineers announced that Opportunity's twin, the Spirit rover, has been getting back to work. Engineers believe at least one and maybe both of the robots may last at least twice as long as their projected 90-day lifetimes.

One of NASA's **twin Mars rovers**, Opportunity, is getting ready to travel to **a rock formation** which may contain water.

On Wednesday, NASA scientists **released a map image** of mineral composition from the Martian surface. The image indicates the existence of **a high concentration of** hematite — a mineral that could indicate the presence of water. NASA says geologic evidence of water would support the possibility that Mars once, or still has, life.

The latest Mars rovers, Opportunity and Spirit, both have found **intriguing geological data** about the possible existence of water. But scientists remain cautious about reaching a conclusion.

———————◇———————

China's astronaut team is to start training in March for the nation's second **manned space flight** on Shenzhou VI, reported the *Beijing Youth Daily* on Monday.

The 14 astronauts have been resting since Yang Liwei, a member of the team, completed China's first manned space flight in October last year. They have done only **light physical training** and reviewed flight operations.

The training for Shenzhou VI would be mainly based on the training courses of Shenzhou V, said director in charge of selection and training of **astronauts** in China. However, some changes would be made as two astronauts were expected to fly in Shenzhou VI, the *Beijing Youth Daily* quoted him as saying.

The 14 astronauts will be divided into seven pairs according to their characteristics and cooperation. Three pairs will form a new team for China's second manned space flight and, finally one pair will fly Shenzhou VI. China has made plans to select and train new astronauts as the 14 astronauts are all over 30. The selection would be conducted in two or three years.

———————◇———————

China's success in its first manned space flight **marks the completion** of its first-step task and conditions are now mature for the second step of the nation's manned space program, a person in charge of the project said on January 29.

The successful first manned space flight, which **embodies the country's achievements** in the space program in 11 years, is a **historic breakthrough**, as displayed in the following facts.

A whole research and testing system of manned spaceship has been established, which laid foundation for the sustainable development of China's manned space program.

218

Striding development with high starting point and high performance has been realized; the general project plan is correct and technological requirements rational; plans for **sub-systems** are correct and performance of these systems could reach the general technological standards; systems could work **in coordination** and following tasks are taken into consideration. All these bear in general Chinese characteristics and technological advancement.

The country has mastered the basic technologies required by manned space mission, including those in astronaut selecting and training, as well as their health and life guarantee; highly **reliable carrier rocket**; manned spaceship; manned spaceship launching; manned space flight communication and flight control; astronaut rescue in normal and urgent circumstances; effective loading and platform supporting.

The country also completed its planned **to-the-ground** observation, space experiments and other tasks, and gained **a large batch** of high-level technological results.

Feasibility study has begun for the follow-up task of the manned space program, and related departments will strive to produce high-level results according to **pre-set timetable**, the person in charge said.

———————

China has launched a campaign to **fight junk e-mails,** or "spam" , during the first half of 2004, reported the *China Police Daily* last Saturday. According to **the circular** jointly issued by the Ministries of Public Security, Education, and Information Industry, and the Information Office of the State Council, the campaign will focus on **e-mail service** providers and institutions with over 1,000 e-mail **subscribers**, including colleges, universities, institutions, and enterprises.

Statistics show that last year, about 70 million junk e-mails went to domestic e-mail boxes every day, including many which were **pornographic or reactionary**, or promoted gambling or spread computer viruses, said the *China Police Daily*. Over 80 percent of the country's e-mail boxes and over 90 percent of the e-mail servers are to have taken prevention measures against spam by the end of June.

It urged prosecution of those involved in criminal behavior such as spreading illicit/illegal material and viruses. Local publicity departments in charge of on-line news should cooperate with the departments to **fight spam** and ensure the normal operation of e-mail services during the campaign, said the circular. The circular also suggested **legislation to regulate preventative measures** and promote the sound development of Internet services in China.

The National Development and Reform Commission says that China's high-tech industry **surpassed** its expectations and **surged** ahead last year with a 30 percent growth.

The commission says the high-tech industry reached the Tenth Five Year Plan's benchmark, two years **ahead of schedule**. In 2003, China's high-tech production totaled 2.75 trillion yuan, that's a 30 percent increase. It accounted for 21 percent of the total **industrial output**. From October 2003, high-tech products have maintained a continuous trade surplus. The country's output of major high-tech products such as mobile phones, color TVs and color displays **ranks among tops** in the world. With electronic information manufacturing becoming the top sector in China's industry, **ranking third** in the world.

Microsoft says that some of the **source code**, or **software blueprint**, for its closely-guarded Windows program has been **leaked** onto the Internet. They say the leak could potentially expose its products to **hackers** and illicit copying.

Microsoft said that copies of the source code from its Windows NT and Windows 2000 operating systems were being traded over the Internet. But the company says the copies comprised only a small portion of the millions of lines of code used to create its cash cow products.

A senior analyst of Forester Research said, "It is **a big chunk** of the source code, so either the person who did this had to have access to a whole lot of the source code or someone has gotten into the systems and been in places where they shouldn't have been, those are basically the two options."

Source code is the **intellectual property** and **lifeblood** of any software company, since it is the basic language used to create software programs. Microsoft has only shared its source code with close partners and carefully chosen organizations. But these relationships always exist with legal agreements threatening **litigation**/prosecution if any of the code is leaked. The leaked code appears to have **originated from** an unidentified software developer with access to Microsoft's code. One major risk resulting from source code being exposed to the public, is the possibility that hackers can then use this information to break into computers running Windows NT or Windows 2000, and destroy or steal data. The other risk, potentially even more damaging, could come from others using the code as a base for developing software that competes with Windows. Microsoft said that it was working with the Federal Bureau of Investigation and legal authorities to **track the origin** of the source code leak.

China has started **the first phase** of its lunar probe program with funding of 1.4 billion yuan (about170 million US dollars), as preparations got underway for a satellite to **orbit the moon** by 2007, a senior program official said here Friday.

Deputy director of the China National Space Administration, said the satellite program, part of the country's **ambitious three-stage lunar project**, would be followed by the landing of an unmanned vehicle on the Moon in the second stage by 2010 and collecting samples of lunar soil with an **unmanned vehicle** by 2020. The last two stages were still **under review** by scientists before official approval.

The satellite would obtain **three-dimensional images** of the lunar surface, analyze the content of useful elements and materials, and **probe the depth** of the lunar soil and the space environment between the Earth and the Moon.

On Dec. 31, 2003, China would use its mature space technology and facilities in the first phase, using a Long March III A carrier rocket to launch the satellite.

He described the satellite project as an important step toward China's exploration of deeper space, and the Moon would provide **a good platform** from which to explore. The lunar program is also known as the **Chang'e Program**, referring to a goddess who reached the Moon in an ancient Chinese fairy tale.

———————

The China High Tech Fair opened Sunday morning in Shenzhen. The fair is fast becoming a regional focus for **highlighting** the latest in state-of-the-art technology. Vice Premier Wu Yi opened the fair. Over 10,000 high-tech projects are on display from 42 countries, including the United States, Canada, and countries from Europe.

Vice Premier congratulated organizers on the strength of the exhibits, and said the Shenzhen fair can only get bigger and better in the future.

Ahead of China's first **manned space flight**, Chinese aviation and space technology is on **prominent display**. There are also **niche exhibitions** of information, biology, new materials and agricultural technology.

Almost thirty multinational companies have stands at the fair. And for the first time, major stock exchanges from New York, Tokyo, London, and Hong Kong are displaying their state-of-the-art financial systems.

Another highlight is the exhibition by some 300 Chinese students returning from study abroad, displaying projects they hope to develop at home. And, for the first time, Taiwan has sent a delegation to the Fair.

———————

The rapid development of the Internet can play an important role in social, economic and cultural progress, including that in China. But, the medium also has its **problems**. One notable issue, according to some experts, is **copyright infringement** online, the on-going annual Internet Forum in Beijing is handling this problem.

The Internet can enrich its users' social and cultural lives with its fast speed, easy access, and low cost. But at the same time, the Internet can be **a haven** for certain types of crime, such as **copyright piracy**.

Today, the number of China's **netizens** has surpassed Japan to make it the number two nation in terms of users, right after the United States. Protecting online copyright is a problem worldwide, no less so in China than in other countries. Beijing first issued regulations in 2001, to try to deal with **Internet piracy**. But **fuzzy wording** in the regulation, and the rapid growth of the medium, made it difficult to **police and enforce**. Another problem experts see is the legacy of the past. Deputy director of National Copyright Administration of China said, "Copyright awareness amongst China's Internet service **operators and netizens** is quite **shallow**. This relates to the general social environment of China, where the economy and law are still in the **initial stage** of socialist development. It's not easy to **shake off** 40 years of China's planned economy."

Experts agree that the quality of a web site depends on its content. But without copyright protection, writers may be unwilling to put their work online. So copyright protection directly impacts the development of the web. According to analysts, WTO membership has improved copyright protection in China. But the very nature of the web also poses problems.

A Research Fellow with China Academy of Social Sciences said, "The Internet is characterized by **the global transmission of information**. This makes it more difficult to protect copyright in the **virtual world**, than in the real world. But this does not mean there is no solution to the problem. China has taken measures to **protect online copyright**. However, they haven't been as effective as first **envisaged**."

Some developed countries have established comprehensive laws to protect online intellectual property rights. For instance, the United States has the Digital Millennium Copyright Act. Experts believe China can learn from examples such as this.

———❧———

Researchers at the Fouping nature reserve in Northwest China's Shaanxi Province have discovered a series of 12 caves key to the reproduction of pandas in the region. This is the first time **a concentrated area** of wild panda reproduction has been discovered in China.

The **complex** was discovered about 1,900 meters above sea level in the central area of Qinling. In the same reserve, this baby panda was born three weeks ago. In May 2003, researchers shot these pictures of the panda's parents **mating**. Experts say pandas usually expand their natural **domain** to about two square kilometers from the caves where they mate. The discovery of the twelve caves is good news as it shows that a lot panda **breeding activity** may be taking place here.

———❧———

Chinese scientists have made a breakthrough in **hybrid rice** research that could **revolutionize** thousands of years of rice growing practice.

Researchers in east China's Jiangxi Province say they have developed a new hybrid rice based on a gene combination of **conventional rice** and a wild rice **native to** the province's Dongxiang region, known for its ability to endure cold weather.

Nicknamed "automatic rice" by researchers, the hybrid rice can **survive the freezing winter** and germinate/sprout the following spring, freeing farmers from the annual ritual of sowing. At its third-year end, the new breed can still yield over 6,000 kilograms each hectare. Although that represents a 750 kilogram drop from the first-year output, the quality **remains stable** over the three year period.

Scientists declared the **trial program** a success and say they plan to promote the new breed in wider areas.

Chinese scientists started a comprehensive scientific **exploration of a lakebed** on Thursday to find out why it went dry. Luobupo Lake in Xinjiang Uygur Autonomous Region used to be the largest in northwest China before it became **barren**.

The mission hopes to reveal how the lake dried up as well as offer **an insight into local and global changes** in climate. An exploration team from the Chinese Academy of Science will spend the next 15 days covering 1,600 kilometers around the lake area. They will **drill for rock samples** in the center of the lakebed to analyze what may have caused changes to the environment. It is the first time by a Chinese scientific team to carry out such an experiment in **the lifeless zone** of the area.

China plans to launch **its third generation communications satellite**, the Dong Fang Hong IV, in 2005. The satellite, better known as DFH4, meets China's need for a large capacity and long-term geo-synchronous communications and broadcast satellite.

The DFH4 is a state-of-the-art satellite. It has 50 **transponders** and has **a life span** of 15 years. Following the launch of the DFH4, China also plans to **put into orbit** a similar satellite for public communications' use.

The new satellites **mark a new era** in China's space technology, greatly improving the country's communication, broadcast and information capabilities. China's first and second generation communications satellites were launched in 1984 and 1997.

Unit Nineteen
Science and Technology (II)

Key Points

1. Through reading the following reports, you will trace the successful launch of Shenzhou V, and share the happiness of Chinese people across China and the whole world.

2. Recall what you kept in mind about last year's exciting moments and find the English expressions you need.

China will use its most advanced rocket, the Long March CZ-2 F, to **launch its maiden manned spacecraft mission**. Commander-in-chief of the rocket system for China's manned space flight program, says that the rocket is the longest and heaviest one that China has ever developed.

It measures 58.3 meters in length, with **a takeoff payload** of nearly 500 tons. With the application of 55 new technologies, including **fault detection** and **escape systems**, the rocket has reached advanced international levels in all the technical indices. The Long March **series of rockets** has so far successfully **sent** four unmanned Shenzhou spaceships **into orbit**.

━━━━━◆◁━▷◆━━━━━

At about 9:30 a.m. Wednesday, the first **earth-to-space dialogue** was conducted between Doctor Li on the ground and astronaut Yang Liwei **on board** Shenzhou V, according to the Command and Control Center in Beijing.

"I feel good and my conditions are normal." Yang told the doctor about his body temperature and blood pressure.

According to plan, there will be several earth-to-space dialogues during the space flight. And medical workers on the ground will be able to **acquire real-time information** about conditions of the astronaut traveling in the space at the moment.

———————

The **launch** of Shenzhou V, China's first manned spacecraft, has been successful as the spacecraft has entered precisely **the preset orbit**, an official in charge of the country's manned space-flight program announced Wednesday morning.

Yang Liwei, 38, became the first Chinese national to enter **outer space**, and China, the third country to **conduct manned space-flight** after the former Soviet Union and the United States.

"The spacecraft and the carrier rocket separated at around 9:10 a.m. (Beijing Time), and the spacecraft entered its preset orbit precisely. The launch is a success."

The Shenzhou V, **atop** a China-made Long March II F launch vehicle, **lifted off** from the Jiuquan Satellite Launch Center in northwest China at 9 a.m. Wednesday.

———————

China's first astronaut, 38, was **hurled into outer space** by Shenzhou V spacecraft at 9 a.m. Wednesday from Jiuquan Satellite Launch Center in northwest China's Gansu Province.

Amidst **deafening roars**, the Shenzhou V manned spacecraft was **lifted** into the sky by a Long March-II-F carrier rocket. Both the spacecraft and the carrier rocket were designed and built by China independently.

Director-general of China's manned space program, announced success of the launch about ten minutes after **the blast-off**, when the spacecraft entered its preset orbit **with precision**.

This, China's maiden manned space flight is scheduled to last 21 hours. Success of its launch means that China has become the third country capable of sending people into outer space, following the United States and Russia.

"Today, our **long-held manned space flight dream** has finally come true," said vice director-general of China's manned space program.

The Chinese people's space dream could be **traced to a fairy tale** that has been told since ancient time, about a woman of **surpassing beauty** flying to the moon after taking some magic medicine, where she stays as the **Moon Goddess**.

Back in the 14th century, a Chinese attempted to send himself into sky by lighting 47 gunpowder-packed bamboo tubes tied to his chair. Although he got killed in this **bold attempt**, The Chinese has since been widely regarded as the world's first person using rockets as **a flight vehicle**.

Thirty-three years ago, Hu Shixiang pressed **the rocket blast-off button** to send China's first man-made satellite into space. China's **space exploration** activities had since started.

Five years later, with the successful landing of the country's first **recoverable satellite,** China turned out to be the third nation in the world having acquired the space vehicle recovery technology. "This laid a solid foundation for China's manned space flight program", said chief designer of China's manned space program.

"The successful launch of Shenzhou V proves that China's space technology has advanced from the **research phase** into the **application phase**," said director-general and chief designer of the space application system under China's manned space program.

Since China officially launched its manned space program in 1992, its experts have **resolved** a range of technical problems with the astronaut system, space application system, spacecraft system, rocket system and **launch pad** system.

Between 1999 and 2002, China successfully launched four **experimental and unmanned spacecraft**, paving the way for this manned flight. The Jiuquan Satellite Launch Center, located at the **juncture area** of the

Badain Jardan Desert and the Gobi Desert in northwest China's Gansu Province, is the country's largest **spaceport** from which all the previous four spacecraft were launched.

The astronaut is expected to land somewhere on the grassland in the central part of Inner Mongolia Autonomous Region, North China, after **orbiting** the Earth 14 times.

Before being selected as the member of China's first batch of would-be astronauts, Yang, a native of Suizhong County, northeast China's Liaoning Province, is **a veteran fighter pilot** of the People's Liberation Army (PLA) air force whose flight experience reached 1,350 hours.

In 1998, Yang and 13 other PLA fighter pilots were selected from 1,500 **candidates** to form the country's first team of would-be astronauts.

Director-general of the astronaut system under China's manned space program noted that all would-be astronauts have become capable of working and living in space after receiving tough physical, psychological and technical training in the past five years.

The manned space program's **ultimate goal** for China was to explore outer space and make a good use of the rich resources of space. Human civilization is moving forward step by step with **mankind's domain** expanding gradually from land to ocean, to sky and finally to outer space, and outer space exploration has turned out to be an important **driving force** for mankind's economic and social development.

At 6:28 a.m. Beijing time, China's first **taikonaut** successfully **touched down** in the **designated landing place** in the Inner Mongolia Autonomous Region.

The search team has found the **re-entry capsule** of Shenzhou V.The main landing place covers an area of some 2,000 square meters. Officials say that **search team** is equipped with the capacity for medical research and **emergency aid**. At 6:07 a.m. Beijing time, the research helicopter received **radio signals** from the Shenzhou V at the landing area in the

Inner Mongolia Autonomous Region. The **chute** of the spacecraft opened a little earlier. Five helicopters and 14 special vehicles **approached** the landing site. China's first manned spacecraft had entered the country's **territorial air space**, according to a monitoring station at Hotan in the Xinjiang Uygur Autonomous Region in northwest China. On a large screen in the Beijing Aerospace Command and Control Center, the curve indicating real-time movement of the spaceship showed the spacecraft was flying over China's territory.

After four unmanned launches, China's first manned spacecraft, the Shenzhou V, is finally in space.

China launched four unmanned craft in the Shenzhou-series, all between November 1999 and December 2002. The four unmanned flights laid the technological foundations for the next step, to put a man in space on the Shenzhou V.

The Shenzhou V was **carried aloft** by a Long March 2F rocket. These rockets are **a work horse** of the Chinese satellite program. The Long March 2F is a stable and reliable system, with a range of **fallback and safety devices**. If any one of 310 automatic safety checks indicates a problem, the system would **shut down and abort the mission**.

The Shenzhou V itself has **four sections** — an orbital module, a re-entry capsule, and primary and secondary propulsion units. The orbital module also has its own propulsion system, solar power, and control systems, allowing **autonomous flight** in case of emergency.

The **solar panels** on the orbital module look like a pair of wings. They supply most of the power needed for the spacecraft to fly when it is **in orbit**. The solar panels can also be **rotated** to obtain maximum **solar reflection**, regardless of the angle the spacecraft has to the sun.

The orbital module and the re-entry capsule can both hold crew. The **crew compartment** in the re-entry module can hold up to three crew. But only one taikonaut is needed to pilot the Shenzhou V this time.

230

The re-entry module is the astronaut's home during his stay in space. It's the "living room" and "bedroom" rolled into one. Engineers have built 123 **fail safe devices** into the Shenzhou V, to cope with every kind of **malfunction imaginable**. The spacecraft is also equipped with remote monitoring and control, and two-way visual and audio transmission facilities. This allows the taikonaut to stay in contact with ground control, and also give ground control the ability to take over **piloting the mission** if necessary.

Every component and system on the Shenzhou V has been inspected and tested to ensure the spacecraft functions perfectly. The tests included mechanical, structural, electrical, thermal vacuum, and noise and vibration tests. The **interior** of the capsule has also been checked for air pressure, humidity, temperature and noise levels to make sure they were **within acceptable ranges** for the pilot.

A range of safety measure are in place to protect the taikonaut. The seats have been specially designed to **minimize discomfort,** even during the stress of take-off and re-entry. Should any **malfunctions** occur once the spacecraft has achieved orbit, then the taikonaut can take over and manually **pilot the ship**. The re-entry system also enables the craft to return automatically to the designated landing area in case of emergency.

The Shenzhou V weighs almost 8 tonnes (7940kg). And it's almost 9 meters long (8860mm). It has about 700 hardware and over 70 software systems to make it fly, keep it **aloft**, and bring it home.

In some ways China **sowed the seeds of invention** for carrier rockets when it developed gunpowder and fireworks. From these very beginnings the nation is now joining **the elite** of the space race. Though they are crucial to space technology, the development of carrier rockets was not always straight forward and it has taken a long way to **get these projects off the ground.**

China decided to develop its own satellites in the Second Plenary

Session of the 8th CPC Central Committee on May 17, 1958. Though the carrier rocket development project had got **the green light**, it did not have any support from other countries, so in 1965 a special committee of top Chinese scientists was **charged with the task** of researching rocket technology.

In the winter of 1968, China lunched its first carrier rocket, the "Long March I," carrying a payload of two Dongfanghong 1 satellites. Unlike its first and second generation **predecessors**, the third generation Long March I rocket was **powered** by solid, not liquid, fuel. The successful launch of China's first satellite **marked a new era** in the country's space exploration: China had become the fifth country in the world with the capacity to launch its own satellites with a self-made rocket.

On November 5, 1974 China launched its first large scale liquid fueled carrier rocket, but unfortunately it was destroyed 20 seconds after launch due to an electrical failure. A year later, the "Long March II" was successfully launched with China's first **recoverable satellite on board**, making China the third country after US and the former Soviet Union with the capacity to **retrieve** satellites and **space probes**.

Later, China researched and made improvements to a series of Long March rockets such as Long March versions 2-C, 2-D, 2-E, and 3...all the way to the the Long March's 4-A and 4-B. By then China had successfully launched 14 Long March rockets, having sent satellites of **a variety of sizes and functions** into planned orbits.

In the early 1990's, Long March rockets started **blasting off** for international commercial launches. Though at first, the carrier encountered **setbacks** with several launch failures. On February 15, 1996, a Long March 3-B carrier rocket fell to the ground 22 seconds after launch. It was the most significant failure China ever had in launching international commercial satellites. However, normal service was soon **resumed** and a Long March 3-A and a Long March 3 successfully blasted off in 1997. To date, China has had 22 commercial launches, delivering 27 foreign satellites into their **designed orbits** without any incident.

In preparation for its manned space program, China sent its first spacecraft Shenzhou I into orbit on November 12, 1999 using the new and improved Long March 2-F rocket, **making China the third country**, after the former Soviet Union and the US, which had the capacity to launch manned spaceships. Until September this year, Long March rockets have been successfully launched 64 times out of 70, a 90 percent success rate.

China is now starting a carrier rocket project that hopes to build a new generation of rockets, characterized by **non-poisonous, non-polluting materials,** low costs and high reliability.

———————————

The space craft Shenzhou V will carry flower, plant and vegetable seeds from Taiwan into space.

Experts from the Chinese Academy of Agricultural Sciences say Taiwan researchers **responded** warmly towards the motherland's offer to send Taiwan seeds into space aboard the capsule. They collected and sent **varieties of seeds** from the island, including those of green peppers and tomatoes. After the spacecraft finishes its mission, the seeds will be sent back to Taiwan to help scientists there **probe the possibilities** of raising plants in outer-space. China started its space breeding program in 1987 and has been sending seeds and **seedlings** aboard rockets many times since, approving the farming of more than 50 types of seeds that are **descended** from those **irradiated in space**.

———————————

After **a tiring day** in Space, China's first taikonaut touched down safely this morning in the Inner Mongolia Autonomous Region. Three hours later, Yang Liwei flew back to Beijing where he got a rapturous/pleasant or cheerful welcome from his proud countrymen and women.

After hours on a military plane, China's first astronaut landed at the Xijiao Military Airport in western Beijing. Greeting him were the commander of the Shenzhou mission, General and his **entourage**.

233

Yang and the ground staff drove back tens of thousands of people lined up the street to welcome the hero back. At the Aerospace City in northwest Beijing, he was treated **with a fanfare of drum and gong playing**, as well as dances and smiles. His comrades, who watched him complete the **unprecedented national feat** in space, were the most excited by his return.

Director of Beijing Space Command and Control Center said, "I was very excited seeing Yang Liwei walk out of the spacecraft in very good physical and mental condition. Excitement is the best way to **describe my first impression**. At the same time, I felt tired. because all the people here in the center have worked hard for nearly eight years. We feel proud of our job as it **fulfills a dream of our nation**."

Yang Liwei is **a national hero** today. As the first Chinese man in space, he becomes an **overnight celebrity**. And if tens of millions of people already see him as **symbol** of China's latest achievement, that number can only grow in the future.

———————————————

The European Space Agency (ESA) on Wednesday **congratulated** China for successfully putting an astronaut into orbit aboard the Shenzhou V spacecraft **in a historic mission**.

"China becomes the third country to send human beings into space", demonstrating the reliability of its aerospace technology.

"This mission could open up to a new era of wider cooperation in the world space community," said ESA Director General in a statement. "We **extend our warmest congratulations** to the People's Republic of China on this outstanding achievement. ESA and China already have a long-standing record of cooperation that began in 1980 with an agreement to **facilitate** the exchange of scientific information."

The cooperation agreement with the Chinese Academy of Science related to the launch of ESA Cluster satellites was signed in 1993, and another agreement between EAS and China in the Double Star project was signed in 2001.

The way has been paved not only for **reciprocal exchanges** between scientists, but also for the establishment of broad cooperation between ESA and the Chinese government.

ESA and China will soon **materialize** space cooperation for peaceful purposes covering the areas of space science, Earth observation, environmental monitoring, meteorology, telecommunications and **satellite navigation**, microgravity research and human resource development and training.

———⟨⟨⟨⊙⟩⟩⟩———

South Africa Wednesday **congratulated** China **on** the launch of its first manned spacecraft, **terming it as** an encouragement to the African nation and all other developing countries.

Spokesman for the Department of Arts, Culture, Science and Technology told Xinhua that South Africans are proud to associate themselves with the success of the People's Republic of China's first manned space launch and hope to **participate in** future **commercial advantages** this may hold.

Director of Emerging Market Focus and an expert in Chinese-African relations said, "Space is no longer the monopoly of the developed world. It is good to see that a country **representing** the developing world can achieve such a success."

Few South Africans were aware of the fact that a Chinese space **tracking ship** was docked alongside Cape Town's Table Bay harbor. It has until now been **a tightly held secret**. However, it is **interpreted as** a sign of cooperation with the Chinese space program and there is hope that it could help open the doors for future commercial cooperation.

The launch has made China only the third nation to achieve a manned space flight after the United States and the former Soviet Union — **a prize** for which the Chinese government invested 11 years of planning and many resources.

It is a prize to be shared by all developing nations among which China counts itself — and more specifically for South Africa and Africa as whole.

South Africans are aware that there have been some discussions between China and members of the University of Stellenbosch satellite division of the faculty of sciences, and there will now be **renewed hope** of further cooperation, especially in the field of **commercial applications**.

China has already achieved a lot with the use of its Long March rocket launch vehicle to develop commercial satellite applications.This could be **adapted** for use such as **optimal exploitation** of agriculture in South Africa and Africa as a whole. It opens the door to **new avenues** of cooperation between developing countries **in the realm of space**.

The University of Stellenbosch has developed a successful **microsatellite division** and has done research for countries such as Malaysia and Saudi Arabia.

———— 8 ⟨⟨◆⟩⟩ 8 ————

US space agency NASA has **added its voice** to congratulations being sent to Chinese mission controllers following the launch of China's first astronaut Wednesday.

Applauding the successful launch, NASA Administrator said in a statement that 38-year-old Yang Liwei's flight into space was "an important achievement in the history of human exploration." "The Chinese people have **a long and distinguished history** of exploration. NASA **wishes** China a continued safe human space flight program."

Although Wednesday's launch makes China only the third nation after Russia and the United States to have put a man into space, the Chinese achievement comes at a difficult time for NASA.

Following **the loss of the shuttle** Columbia in February, the US manned space program is **grounded** with no clear indication yet as to when it will resume.

Officials have said they expect to **resume flights** next year, but the earliest date thought likely for a return to flight is not until September 2004.

Without its remaining three shuttles in operation, NASA is having to rely on Russian space launches to **ferry crew replacements and supplies** to the orbiting International Space Station.

It has no other operational vehicle capable of carrying humans into orbit and the success of the Chinese launch is likely to **spur efforts** to develop a shuttle successor.

———————————&◁◆▷&———————————

United Nations Secretary-General Kofi Annan Wednesday **extended his warm congratulations** to China on its successful launch of a manned spacecraft.

"The secretary-general extends his warm congratulations to the People's Republic of China on its first (manned) mission into space, and hopes for the safe and **successful completion** of this **maiden voyage**," UN spokesman, on behalf of Annan, read a statement at the noon briefing on Wednesday.

———————————&◁◆▷&———————————

The Central Committee of the Communist Party of China, the State Council and the Central Military Commission have sent **a message of greetings** on the success of Shenzhou V, calling it "a new milestone in China's **space undertakings**."

The message was read by Chinese Premier Wen Jiabao at the Beijing Space Command and Control Center, shortly after China's first manned space flight was **declared a complete success**.

The message called the space flight of Shenzhou V a "great accomplishment", an accomplishment great enough to **go down in Chinese history**. Jiang Zemin, Chairman of the Central Military Commission, has **hailed the success as** "one more proof to the will and capability of the Chinese people to **surmount the peak of** world science and technology." He said that this is in a telephone call to the most senior official in charge of the country's **piloted** space flight program.

———————————&◁◆▷&———————————

A leading official in charge of China's manned space program said after the success of its first human spaceflight the country would **launch its lunar and deep space probe** programs and space lab and space station projects.

Deputy chief commander of China's Manned Space Program said China would **strive for breakthroughs** in space rendezvous/venue **and docking technology** for launching a space lab and eventually a manned space station.

A manned space station will enable China to carry out **large-scale scientific experiments** and applications in space, with the plan for manned space program approved by the Chinese authorities in 1992.

As general manager of China Aerospace Science and Technology Corp (CAST), the Commander said the space plans are necessary for China to **exploit space resources** for peaceful purposes. Space-based infrastructure, including the planned space lab and station, will serve as a **platform** for deep space probe.

The CAST, manufacturer of China's spacecraft and launch vehicles, will plan for the development of space lab and its launch vehicle and technology for space rendezvous and docking.

Director of the Science and Technology Commission of China Academy of Launch Vehicle Technology with CAST, told Xinhua the academy has started **developing a more powerful launch vehicle** capable of sending large satellites, lunar probe devices and other space probe facilities into space in the coming 30 years and more.

China Academy of Space Technology, China's leading satellite and spacecraft developer, announced earlier this year it had **designed a lunar probe program** and made breakthroughs in key technology.

———————⋆⟨⟨⟨◆⟩⟩⟩⋆———————

Hundreds of people **gathered** on Saturday afternoon in Hong Kong's Grand Stadium to welcome China's first astronaut. He was accompanied by **a delegation** of the first Chinese manned space mission.

A People's Liberation Army Guard of Honor offered **a solemn start** to a spectacular ceremony. Hong Kong's Chief Secretary **extended a very warm welcome** to Yang Liwei, highly praising the success of his space mission. The Head of the visiting delegation **returned his sincere gratitude** for the **hospitality** of the Hong Kong people. And then the **showbiz** began. The space hero joined forces with action movie superstar for **a musical duet**.

Earlier on Saturday, Yang was present at the opening of a four-day exhibition featuring the Shenzhou V **re-entry capsule**, the spacecraft's **landing parachute**, Yang Liwei's space suit and models of various rockets and spacecraft.

Right now, China is planning, working with other countries, to launch eight satellites including **a multi-mission satellite** which is expected to be sent into space within five years.

The new satellites will form a satellite "constellation/cluster", and together form the world's first satellite program working to **serve disaster relief and environmental protection**. The China National Space Administration says the new program will, **as a matter of priority**, provide services for the Asia Pacific region, and nations in the region have agreed to **team up with** China to develop the new space mission.

warm welcome to Yang Liwei, highly praising the success of his space

Unit Twenty
World Focus and Anti-terrorism

导　读

　　二语习得理论的五个假说中，"输入(input hypothesis)假说"可以说是其中最重要的一个。克拉申（Krashen）的输入假说认为：语言习得是通过接收大量可理解输入而产生的。即学习者首先接触大量易懂的实际语言，通过上下文和情景去理解其意思。这样，寓于交际语言中的句子结构就自然学会了。Krashen 认为感受性语言行为如听和阅读在语言学习过程中起主导作用，只要提供足够数量的可理解语言输入，其他语言技巧的提高和语法知识的获得就会随之产生。而所谓可理解输入(comprehensible input)指总体语言难度不超过学习者的学习能力(即能被学习者所理解)，但又包含略高于学习者现有语言能力的语言结构。"其模式为 i+1，其中 i 为学习者现有水平，+1 部分是语言信息中包含的新的语言成分和语言形式"。

　　"输入假说"的重要理论依据是"语言学习沉默期"，即习得者没有足够的能力说话的那段时间。在这一阶段，习得者如"幼儿期"一样，往往只听不说，对可理解语言输入进行加工整理，积累语言能力。经过一段时间的内在消化后，下意识地习得了输入的语言。成人学习第二语言同样需要积累和消化，才能逐步培养第二语言的能力，并能够使用这种能力表达自己的思想。

　　作为输入理论的发展，Swain 于 1986 年提出了"可理解输出假说"。Swain 指出成功的二语习得者既需要接触大量可理解输入，又要产出可理解输出。他认为在某种条件下，输出可以促进二语的习得，其方式不同于输入，但都可以增强输入对二语习得的作用。输出在二语学习过程中有以下三个重要功能：

（1）注意功能。输出能引起学习者对语言问题的注意，使学习者意识到自己语言体系中的部分语言问题，进而触发对现有语言知识的巩固和获得新的语言知识的过程。学习者在表达过程中，注意到问题之后，会更加注意寻找后续输入中的有关语言特征，从而产出修正后的输出，也就能不断提高语言产出的准确性。因此，输出不仅使学习者注意到他们中介语的缺陷，而且还激活了有助于二语习得的内在认知过程，从而促进语言习得。

（2）假设检验功能。二语习得要求学习者对目标语不断做出假设并对此假设不断进行修正。而输出正是一种对目标语潜在假设进行检验的手段。学习者在扩展他们的"中介语"以达到交际需求时，就必须通过输出来尝试新的语言结构形式，以形成新的假设并检验其假设的可行与否。

（3）元语言功能。即学习者所具有的关于语言"知识"的总和，是他们通过反思和语言分析所得到的关于语言形式、结构及语言系统方面的知识。当学习者反思目标语用法时，输出即起着元语言功能作用，输出能使他们控制和内化语言知识。因此，输入与输出是习得语言不可或缺的过程。

媒体报刊英语由于其独特的快捷、现实和普遍性特征，符合语言习得输入和输出的需要。本单元提供了全球关注的"anti-terror, post-Iraq war, global economy, Korea's nuke issue and mid-east peace progress"等热点新闻，事件报道频率高，延续性和反复性较强，因此，读者接受输入的机会也多，而且日常交谈的话题，更易于激活和交际应用式的输出。

Key Points

1. This unit will provide us with news reports upon world affairs such as post-Iraq war, terrorism and anti-terrorism, world economy, North Korea's nuclear issue, mid-east peace.

2. Spot the highlights you're interested in and learn what you need in

exchanging your viewpoints on conflicts in the Middle East, say, the US-led Alliance's occupation of Iraq, and etc.

New **security concerns** have **prompted** British Airways and Air France to announce the **cancellation** of seven flights to and from the United States.

British Airways **canceled** four flights between Heathrow Airport and Washington on Sunday and Monday and one from Heathrow to Miami on Sunday. Air France canceled two Paris-to-Washington flights. The cancellations came a day after US officials said new intelligence indicated these trans-Atlantic flights could be **terrorist targets.**

A suicide **car bombing** has killed at least 50 people and wounded dozens of others at a police station in a town some 50 kilometers south of Baghdad.

Hospital sources in the town say the **death toll** is expected to rise as many victims are in **serious or critical conditions.** Local police say a driver who **detonated/triggered the explosives** as his vehicle passed by the station on Tuesday morning **executed the blast**. Dozens of **would-be recruits** were lined up there to apply for jobs. US troops **sealed off** the area around the police station following the explosion. The US coalition authorities in Baghdad say no US or other **coalition forces** were killed or injured in the attack.

At least six people have been killed and several others wounded when two blasts **ripped through** a crowded Palestinian **residential area** in Baghdad. Two other **separate attacks** on Saturday left nine Iraqis and three US soldiers dead. The attacks **highlight** security concerns **on the eve of** the major Muslim festival.

Iraqi police and US soldiers **surrounded a section** of the Baladiyyat district in east Baghdad shortly after the blasts **rocked** the area. **Bursts of**

gunfire were heard.

Soldiers and policemen **at the scene** gave conflicting accounts of the blast, attributing it alternately to mortar fire and rockets.

The dead and the wounded were taken to a Baghdad's hospital.

The blasts came after a suicide car bombing at a police station in northern city of Mosul killed nine, and **a roadside bomb attack** on a US convoy resulted in three **combat deaths** near the oil fields of Kirkuk.

Saturday's attacks occurred a day before the start of the four-day Feast of Sacrifice.

Attacks on police, politicians and other Iraqis who work with the US-led coalition have been increasing. **Insurgents** are trying to **undermine support** for the US occupation authority and frighten the population into avoiding contact with the foreign administration.

――――――§――――――

An explosion **went off** just moments ago in a major **metro station** near downtown Moscow, and seven people has died so far. Russia's Interfax news agency reports that several people have been **injured.**

Emergency officials said the explosion occurred in the second carriage of a train as it left the station. They added that the explosion left the tunnel filled with smoke.

――――――§――――――

The **death toll** from the explosion that occurred aboard **a subway train** during the morning **rush hour** of Friday in the Russian capital rose to about 40.

The explosion killed about 40 and injured about 100 others, Interfax news agency reported, citing city **emergency service** sources.

Officials with the Federal Security Service (FSB) believed that the blast, in the second wagon of the train **heading for** the station in southeast downtown Moscow from a station near the city center, was probably caused by **a suicide bomber**.

Law enforcement agencies quoted **eyewitness** as saying that an explosive device filled with shrapnel was detonated by a female **suicide terrorist** in the carriage at around 8:40 a.m. Moscow time.

The explosion, said to be **equivalent** to over 1 kg. of TNT, caused an extensive fire and badly damaged the carriage with reportedly some 100 passengers on board. Some 700 passengers aboard the train have been **lifted to the ground**.

The fire has now been put out. The coach was so badly **damaged** that it is impossible for **rescuers** to **haul it out** from the site of the blast.

The train's staff reported the first data on the explosion but communications with them was lost. Rescuers and some 130 emergency buses are **evacuating stranded passengers**. Traffic on the subway line where the blast occurred has been **suspended**. At least 50 **ambulances** were outside the entrance to the station. Moscow hospitals were **put on alert**.

The Interior Ministry has **reinforced** security measures in Moscow's metro system to prevent new **terrorist acts**.

———————

Russian President Vladimir Putin has accused Chechen **separatist** leader of being responsible for the metro explosion that left at least 39 passengers dead, and injured more than 100 on Friday morning. But a spokesman for the **fugitive** (runaway) leader has condemned the explosion, as well as denied involvement in what he called, a "**bloody provocation**".

The suspected **suicide bomb** ripped through a packed Moscow underground train in the early rush-hour, killing at least 39 passengers and injuring more than 100. Police **attributed** the blast, which **blew out** windows and started a fire, **to** a suicide bomber. They said it was caused by five kilograms of **explosives**.

Spokesman of Moscow Interior Ministry Department said, " The explosive device most likely was with a male or female suicide bomber."

President Putin accused the Chechen separatist leader of being **behind the explosion. He reaffirmed** that Russia would never negotiate with terrorists, but destroy them.

244

Putin said, "The international principle of **fighting against terror**, which is accepted by everyone, is the **unconditional rejection** of any kind of dialogue with terrorists, because any contact with bandits and terrorists encourages them to **commit new, bloodier crimes**. Russia has never done it before and will never do it in the future. Russia doesn't negotiate with terrorists, it destroys them."

The attack, if confirmed to be by Chenchen suicide bombers, would be the worst of its kind in Moscow since July 2003, when two women **blew themselves up** at an open-air music festival, killing 14 other people.

The Chinese Embassy in Russia has stated that no Chinese citizens have so far been found among the metro **blast casualties**. The **disrupted line** had resumed operations by Friday evening.

———— ✽ ❦ ✽ ————

The Asia-Pacific ministerial meeting on **counter terrorism** has concluded on Thursday. Participants at the meeting in Bali **reached consensus** that more cooperation is needed among the countries to prevent and **combat terrorism**.

During the two-day meeting, delegates from 25 countries agreed to **explore new ways** of enhancing counter-terrorism collaboration among countries. They also encouraged more effective cooperation among law enforcement agencies in the region.

The **co-chairs** of the conference, Indonesian Foreign Minister and his Australian counterpart, issued a statement on Thursday. The ministers agreed to work towards developing more effective **information sharing** arrangements within the region to fight terrorists.

The statement covered 17 items and suggestions in **fighting terrorist activities**. To ensure the implementation of the above **recommendations**, the ministers agreed on the establishment of two ad hoc/special working groups of senior legal officials from around the region, to follow up on the **recommended actions**.

After the close of the meeting, a **transnational crime center** was established in Indonesia's capital of Jakarta. Run jointly by Indonesia and Australia, it will offer **anti-terror training**, as well as be an information clearinghouse.

———————

South Korea's foreign minister says his **counterparts** from Asia and Latin America want to see **a resolution** of the nuclear crisis on the Korean peninsula. The minister made the comments at the end of a two-day Forum for East Asia — Latin America Cooperation near the Philippine capital of Manila.

The ministerial meeting, attended by some 34 countries, was the forum's second since its **inaugural gathering** in Chile in 2001.

He said the foreign ministers recognized that the stand off with Pyongyang **represented a serious threat.** "The ministers of the FEALAC **voiced their support** for continuing the process of the six-party talks and **reiterated** FEALAC-wide support for peace and stability on the Korean peninsula."

The first round of talks in Beijing involving the DPRK and ROK, the US, China, Russia and Japan ended in August **without a settlement**.

Attempts by China and other countries to arrange a new round of talks with Pyongyang have still being **undergone**.

———————

The Democratic Republic of Korea and the Republic of Korea **wrapped up** their four-day ministerial meeting in Seoul on Friday. They **concluded** with a six-point statement **pledging** joint efforts in talks on the nuclear issue on the Korean Peninsula later this month.

It's the 13th time that ministers of the two sides of the Korean Peninsula have sat together, but the first since the date of a new round of six-party talks was announced by the DPRK. Once an exact date and **venue** are decided, defense ministers from both sides will meet for the second time in three years. The joint statement also included a new round of reunions between families divided since the Korean War, and expedited/step up work on a joint project to build an industrial zone on the DPRK side of the border.

———※◆———

Chinese embassy sources in Israel say one Chinese person was **critically wounded** in the Thursday's suicide bombing. The Chinese Ministry of Foreign Affairs said it is deeply concerned about the **deteriorating situation** between Israel and the Palestinians.

Foreign Ministry spokeswoman said China **opposes any action** which would harm efforts towards a peaceful solution. China also urges Israel and the Palestinians to **exercise restraint** and return to **the correct track** of peaceful talks.

Meanwhile, other countries and international organizations including Russia and the United Nations all condemned Thursday's **suicide attack** and urged the Israelis and the Palestinians to **pursue** an enduring settlement of their conflict.

———※◆———

US civil administrator in Iraq, has condemned Sunday's two suicide bomb **strikes** at the offices of two Kurdish parties. In a statement read by a coalition spokesman, he also pledged the US will **bring** those responsible **to justice**. There was no immediate **claim of responsibility** for the attacks.

Coalition Spokesman said, "I wish to express my **outrage** at today's terrorist bombings in Irbil which constituted a cowardly attack both on innocent human beings as well as on the very principle of democratic **pluralism** in Iraq. I further wish to express **my deepest sympathy** to the families of those who lost their lives in today's bombings as well as to those who were injured. We **pledge** to work with the Iraqi **security forces** to find, capture and bring to justice those responsible for this horrible acts and those who aided them."

The two suicide bombers struck the offices of two US-backed Kurdish parties in **near-simultaneous attacks** as hundreds of Iraqis gathered to **celebrate** a Muslim holiday.

The latest reports include 56 killed and approximately 200 wounded. The attack is **a surprise blow** to the political leadership of the Kurdish minority, the most **pro-American** group in Iraq.

The two parties, the Kurdistan Democratic Party and its rival the Kurdish Patriotic Union of Kurdistan had **fought a long battle**. But now they **forged a common ground** under the US occupation and sought to establish an enlarged autonomous area in northern Iraq.

And a US military spokesman said one US soldier was killed and 12 others wounded when an American base was attacked by rockets in northern Iraq on Sunday. **Insurgents** were said to have fired seven rockets at the base in Balad, some 80 km north of Baghdad. Following the attack, US troops **conducted a massive search** in the area and captured 12 men and 4 women. The attack came after a pair of suicide bombings killed 56 in northern city of Irbil, and an explosion at a munitions/military supplies dump in south Iraq killed 20 earlier in the day. The attack has brought the number of US soldiers killed by **hostile fire** to 251 since May the 1st.

In the United States, UN Secretary General Kofi Annan met separately on Tuesday with US President George W. Bush and Secretary of State Colin Powell to discuss issues in Iraq. **Top of the agenda** was a US request for UN **involvement** in handover of **sovereignty** to Iraqis, made urgent by **an impending** US election. Annan announced his decision to send a team to investigate election possibilities.

Annan says the team is expected to help Iraq to **overcome obstacles** to meeting a June 30th deadline for handing over US-held power to Iraqis.

"On Iraq, I believe that the stability of Iraq is in everyone's interest. The UN does have a role to play. That's why following the meeting of 19th January, I have decided to send a team that will try and go to work with the Iraqis and finding the way forward. Everyone agrees that sovereignty should be handed over to Iraq as soon as possible," Annan said.

For now at least, the importance of a UN role in Iraq is acknowledged by the US President, who declared war on Iraq before **reaching a consensus** at the United Nations.

Bush said, "We have a lot of work to do in certain areas and right now we are focused on Iraq and I have always said the United Nations play a vital role, an important role. We have discussed ways that by working together the Iraqi people can be free, the country **stable and prosperous**, an example of democracy in the middle east."

Annan met with US Secretary of State Colin Powell ahead of his meeting at the White House. Powell took the opportunity to **defend the administration's decision** to invade Iraq, saying the US army was there because of Iraq's "intent" and its weapons-making ability.

Powell had earlier said he did not know whether he would have **recommended an invasion** of Iraq if he knew Iraq had no **stockpiles of banned weapons**.

During an interview with the Washington Post on Monday, Powell **conceded** the Bush administration's **conviction** that Saddam Hussein already had such weapons made the case for war more urgent.

He noted that the **intelligence** suggesting the existence of WMD is to be investigated by a commission Bush is setting up.

Recently the European Union's chief officials also **voiced their support** for the Geneva Initiative for peace in the Middle East and urged an early **resumption of** peace talks between Israel and Palestine. They met with major advocates of the Geneva Initiative on Monday.

European Union External Relations Commissioner and European Commission President met with Israel's Beilin and the Palestinian Rabbo, the **architects** of the Geneva peace initiative, in Belgium on Monday.

They discussed the **alternative plan** to the **US-backed roadmap** for peace in the Middle East. Both Beilin and Rabbo called for increased efforts to **engage in** the peace process.

Palestinian Negotiator said, "What we are doing today **coincides**

completely with the roadmap and all of the other initiatives by the EU and other international forces who seek to see the beginning of serious peace process in Middle East."

The Geneva plan calls for the creation of a Palestinian state that would **exist** alongside Israel, with Jerusalem as the capital of both states.

According to the plan, 25 percent of the **illegal Jewish settlements** would be incorporated by Israel, leaving the remaining 75 percent to the Palestinian state.

The Palestinians would be required to recognize Israel as **a Jewish state** and end violence against it. In return for giving up their right of return, about 3.5 million Palestinians living **in exile** would be **eligible** for compensation from Israel.

In the UK **shouting protesters** forced the British House of Commons to briefly **adjourn** a debate on Lord Hutton's report on last year's suicide of Iraq weapons expert, David Kelly. The shouting by protestors on Wednesday **interrupted** British Prime Minister Tony Blair's statement on the report, and in particular, on the Iraq war intelligence.

"Murderer!" "Whitewash!" The shouts from anti-war **demonstrators** forced Speaker Michael Martin to order the public gallery cleared, and proceedings suspended for about 10 minutes, after Blair's speech was interrupted for the fifth time.

The protestors believed the report by Lord Hutton was so favorable to the government that it can only be described as **a whitewash**.

The Hutton report cleared the government of "**sexing up**" a dossier/file on Iraqi weapons.

Before the **adjournment** Blair defended Hutton's report, which **cleared his government of allegations** that it hyped/bragged evidence in the dossier to **justify** war and mistreated adviser David Kelly before his July suicide.

Blair also continued to justify the war on Iraq.

250

"I think we did the right thing, I think the world is a safer place as a result of it, I think we are better able to **tackle weapons of mass destruction** worldwide as a result of it and I think this country and its armed forces should be proud of what we achieved," said British Prime Minister Tony Blair.

Meanwhile, five protesters dressed as Lord Hutton were arrested after they threw white paint at the gates of Downing Street. The protestors said their move was intended to **highlight** the "whitewash" of the Hutton Report.

In Britian, the country's Defence Secretary is now **under fire** about the intelligence report that led to British involvement in the Iraq war. And BBC staff are **staging street protests** over the Hutton report.

British Defence Secretary found himself Thursday at the center of yet another row over the **intelligence dossier** Prime Minister Tony Blair used to justify war against Iraq.

The latest **controversy erupted** when Blair said he did not know, when he won parliamentary backing for war in March last year, that a government claim Saddam could **deploy** such weapons within 45 minutes referred only to battlefield arms, not long-range missiles which could threaten other states.

But Hoon says that he knew, leading opposition politicians to demand why he had not told the Prime Minister.

Testifying at a heated parliamentary committee meeting, Hoon said he had not discussed the **precise intelligence** details with Blair because it had not then been a major issue.

How intelligence was handled **in the run-up to war** is now the target of an inquiry, set up by Tony Blair.

Meantime, also on Thursday, BBC employees **took to the streets** to **vent their anger** over Hutton's report that **forced the resignation** of the broadcaster's two top officials.

Staffers at BBC offices throughout Britain **rallied in support of** former

Director General and called for the BBC to **resist pressure** from government.

The resignation of Dyke and BBC Chairman Davies came after Lord Hutton **slammed standards** and management oversight/neglect at the BBC.

------◆◆◆◆------

Former chief US weapons inspector has reacted to CIA director's speech. He made the comments during **a panel discussion** at the Carnegie Endowment/donation for International Peace on Thursday. He said the CIA director's speech was further evidence of the need for a **thorough investigation** of pre-war intelligence. He said an independent investigation must examine whether intelligence was **manipulated** by politicians.

Kay said, "I heard that speech as saying you know 'we always said it was intent and it was capability and not weapons and it was those others who **consumed** our intelligence who **hardened** it.' Now if that's true, that genuinely is **disturbing** and will have to be investigated and I mean these are the reasons we need an important commission. I believe the independent commission ought to look to see whether there was **abuse** by political leaders of the data. I think that is an important question that needs to be understood."

------◆◆◆◆------

US President George W. Bush has established a **bi-partisan commission** to investigate failures in intelligence used to justify the Iraq war. It will report back in March of 2005. But US Secretary of State Colin Powell said the government will not **apologize for the alleged intelligence failures.**

Bush said, "Today, by executive order, I am creating **an independent commission**, chaired by Governor and former Senator Chuck Robb, Judge Laurence Silberman, to look at American intelligence capabilities, especially our intelligence about weapons of mass destruction."

Bush said his government is determined to ensure American intelligence is "as accurate as possible for every challenge in the future".

Bush is **scrambling** to limit the political fallout/side effects from former chief US weapons inspector's revelations that almost all the pre-war intelligence about Iraq's **alleged unconventional weapons** was wrong.

Colin Powell joined the president in **defending his government's case** against Iraq.

Powell said, "I don't think any apologies are necessary. As Director Tenet said yesterday, when he prepared the intelligence **estimate** that was presented to the American Congress in the fall of 2002, it represented a solid body of advice, a solid body of information that had been collected by analysts and other sources."

The US President gave the commission until the end of March, 2005, to report back, meaning the results of the investigation will not be known until after the November election.

————————————————

With US **election campaigns** heating up, George W. Bush's military service during the Vietnam War is once again **facing scrutiny**. The White House has **released documents** to support Bush's **assertion** that he fulfilled his duty.

The documents including annual retirement point summaries and pay records the White House says show that Bush served as a member of the Air National Guard. The records show that Bush received 56 points for service, six more than required, in each of the two years from 1972 to 1974. He was also paid for **part-time services**. Countering charges, the photocopies **payroll records** distributed are not all **legible**, the White House has promised clearer copies later this week.

————————————————

In the US, General Wesley Clark has **thrown his support** behind front-runner John Kerry's campaign to be the Democrat party's presidential candidate. The former NATO commander **dropped out** of the White House race on Wednesday after placing third behind Kerry and John Edwards in Virginia and Tennessee.

Clark **campaigned** alongside Kerry in Wisconsin on Friday and the smiling pair embraced after the four-star General gave Kerry his backing.

The **endorsement** is the latest in a wave of good news for Kerry. The Massachusetts senator has won 12 of the first 14 contests and **picked up a stampede of support** in the race to find a challenger for President George W. Bush in November. Kerry said he was proud to have Clark stand beside him.

———————————◦◦◦———————————

US President George W. Bush has defended his decision to launch war against Iraq using a **shifted rationale/basic principle**, saying ousteding Iraqi President Saddam Hussein who had the capacity to produce weapons of mass destruction.

The US president was speaking in an interview with NBC's "Meet The Press." It had been taped on Saturday in the Oval Office. Bush responded to questions regarding **claims of stockpiles of biological and chemical weapons** in Iraq that the US president had warned about, and had used to justify his decision to go to war in Iraq. He also offered **speculation** over what might have happened to the weapons his administration had claimed existed before the war.

Bush said, "They could have been destroyed during the war, Saddam and his henchmen/regime could have destroyed them as we entered into Iraq. They could be hidden, they could have been transported to another country and we'll find out."

Bush denied he led the United States into war **under false pretenses.** But he did acknowledge that some prewar intelligence was apparently inaccurate. The interview came at a time when **polls** showed that the intelligence failure had begun to **erode Bush's approval ratings**.

Democrat candidate John Kerry criticized Bush's statements on Sunday morning in Richmond.

He said, "This is **a far cry** from what the president and his administration told the American people throughout 2002."

The Massachusetts senator said Bush was, in his words, "telling the

American people stories back in 2002," regarding the extent of the threat **posed** by Saddam. Kerry also demanded a full investigation into the gathering of US intelligence, and how it was used to justify the administration's decision to **invade Iraq**.

The Russian **armed forces** have started **a massive strategic military exercises** involving strategic nuclear forces and conventional forces.

During the exercises, sea and land-based strategic missiles will be launched, but no missile launches are planned in the direction of the Atlantic Ocean. The military insists the exercises are not related to **the upcoming presidential election**, and are not intended to demonstrate the country's nuclear capability to the world.

Unit Twenty-one
Tourism in China

导　读

现代语用学和认知语言学日益关注世界知识对语篇理解的作用，提出了有关心理储存现实知识的框架(frame)、脚本(script)和图式(schema)等内涵相近的概念，认为三者作为现实世界状态、事件或行为的典型的、有层次的内在结构关系，已把大量的有关特定范畴(domain specific)的知识编入其中并整体地存入人的记忆中。在语言使用过程中，只要类似的场合一出现，它们便会被整体地激活并投入使用。

前面已谈到有关图式的概念及其意义，这里侧重讨论框架和脚本的内涵与意义。框架是嵌于信息提取网络中的信息包块(packets of information)，由人类众多普遍和熟悉的活动构成。人类大脑中储存的某种图式(schemata)或构架(framework)，相互联结，形成一个系统，并把其结构和联结关系(coherence)投射到人类经验的某些方面。也就是说，知识是以"块构"(chunk)或网络形式组合在一起的。人类大脑中储存着大量的框架，在不同情景下，可启用不同的框架。语篇阅读过程中，人们对其反映的现实信息的理解是框架所允许或规定的那种理解。交际者通过运用框架不但能把要传递的信息加以概念化并最终用语言表达出来，同时还能理解所接受到的信息。

语言使用中最常用的两种框架是"交往框架"(interaction frames)和"认知框架"(cognitive frames)。日常会话大多属于前者，在此框架中我们知道怎样恰当地打招呼、相互介绍和问候。而认

256

知框架对应的是传统语言学里的意义。如：要理解 golden week holiday 的意义，一般要激活如下背景知识：中国的"五一"和"十一"，一周的假期，人们选择出行旅游等。框架与语言表达形式的选择具有密切关系，这种选择包括对单个词、词的系列、句法范畴甚至是语音模式的定夺取舍。

"脚本"这一概念是围绕单词或被单词激活的语义信息切块(chunk)。它以本族语者内化为一种认知结构，代表的是现实世界的一小部分知识。脚本与事件的序列(sequence)和角色关系(role relations)有关。每个脚本都是由词汇节点(lexical nodes)和这些节点间的语义联系(semantic links)构成的图形(graph)。一个单词的词条(lexical entry)就是在该单词周围形成的一个范畴(domain)，而该单词是这个范畴的中心节点(central node)。语篇序列(sequences)可产生命题形式的预料(expectations)或预测(predications)。如：围绕flag-raising ceremony，可以激活 Tian'anmen Square or school，government，company square，national anthem，guards of honor，feeling of pride 等。因此，语言习得者的"框架"和"脚本"知识至关重要，习得的语言知识是相互联系的语义信息切块，是可以相互激活的范畴词群。

本单元语篇主要涉及旅游范畴的新闻，集中了假日旅游相关的交通、自然与文化名胜、风景特征、旅行感受等"框架"知识和词汇群。

Key Points

1. Every year we will enjoy two golden week holidays, long summer holidays and the Spring Festival vacation. People and students in particular, amuse themselves through travel to natural and cultural scenic attractions across the country. The following reports are a vivid account of last National Day holiday.

2. Read the passages and tell us your own story and experience during the vacation, or your plan this May Day, the weeklong celebration of the International Labour Day.

China is **celebrating** National Day. 54 years ago, former Chinese leader Mao Zedong **announced the birth** of New China. Today 250,000 people from all over the country gathered on Beijing's Tian'anmen Square to **participate in a solemn flag-raising ceremony**.

At 6:06 a.m. this morning, to the accompany of a brass band, **the guards of honor** marched out of the Tian'anmen Gate Tower. 250,000 people, from all over China, stood on the Square to watch the flag going up **with the rising sun**.

The National Day flag-raising ceremony in Beijing has become **a must** for many Chinese. And every year, **the mood of optimism** is growing as China becomes more developed and prosperous. Like the flag, China's star is also rising.

Good weather coupled with new **tourist attractions** have made day two of China's National Day holiday a record-breaking one for tourism. The number of visitors to major **scenic spots** around the country reached the highest level of the year so far. And improved services and facilities at these places **of interest** are ensuring that the increase in **visitor numbers** is being matched by an improvement in the overall visiting experience.

Traditionally popular with tourists from both home and abroad, the Three Gorges have become even more **attractive** with the construction of the world's largest hydro-electric **power complex**. This year, the dam's flood-discharge channel is open to **sightseers**, resulting in long lines waiting at the entrance from early on Thursday morning. **Throngs of** roughly the same scale also **patronized** other major destinations **dotted** around the nation. Services like free **shuttle buses** to scenic areas in these spots helps make the experience more convenient and enjoyable.

A tourist said, "If I have trouble, I can easily find a place to seek help or **file a complaint**. This is nice. I'm in a good mood."

The State Tourism Administration estimates that, on Thursday alone,

99 major scenic spots around China received a total of more than 2.7 million visitors, bringing in a revenue of 10 million US dollars. And so far, the security arrangements in place are coping well with **the dramatic increase** in visitor numbers.

During each golden week holiday period, the formidable **passenger traffic volume** at land **border checkpoints** between the mainland and Hong Kong **poses enormous challenges** to officials on both sides. But cross-border passenger flow has been unexpectedly smooth during the ongoing National Day holiday.

As always, Lo Wu checkpoint bore the **surge** of this year's massive passenger flow. The first **travel peak** appeared on October the first, when some 260,000 passengers crossed the border. Hong Kong reported over 100,000 arrivals. During rush hour, Hong Kong immigration department opened over 120 counters, substantially cutting waiting time to not more than 10 minutes for each passenger.

Yesterday alone saw some 700,000 mainland tourists **flock** to Hong Kong, 200,000 of them were independent travelers. Both numbers were **record highs**. Despite the huge volume, complaints about slow border crossing were rarely heard this year, and passengers were happy with clearance arrangements.

A Chinese mainland tourist said,"I didn't expect immigration clearance to go so smoothly. This is my first trip to Hong Kong. I had been told by others that border crossings could be **troublesome.** But from my own experience here, I think it was very smooth."

At Lok Ma Chou checkpoint, **passenger traffic** was **light** through yesterday. But transportation authorities have put on more train and **shuttle bus services** to deal with possible **traffic surges**. Hong Kong multi-departmental command center is already in place. At seaports and the airport, passenger traffic only rose slightly yesterday. The latest information shows that tourist arrivals for today are only half of yesterday figure, promising an even quicker passenger flow.

The second **travel peak** is expected to come on October 4, the Chinese traditional Chongyang Festival, which is also a public holiday in Hong Kong. Add the coming weekend, and Hong Kong people will have three days free. Many of them will surely cross the border to **revel** in the pleasures of the mainland.

With the National Day holiday fast approaching, cities and towns all over China are busy getting ready to **mark the occasion**, with **holiday decorations** being put up everywhere.

In Beijing, more than 300 parks and **tourist attractions** will open up to welcome tourists during the "Golden Week" holiday period which starts on October 1st. Some of them, like the Yuan Capital Site Park, are newly restored areas opening up to the public for the first time. Apart from these, the Zhongshan Park, the Beijing Botanical Garden, the Sculpture Park, Fragrant Hills, and many other parks are holding various activities to celebrate the holiday.

In the streets of Chongqing, Xi'an, Zhengzhou, and Changsha; in the parks of Shijiazhuang, Jilin, and Nanchang, millions of **potted flowers** are **blossoming, bursting in an array of shapes and colors.**

Meanwhile, in Hong Kong and Macao regions, people are expecting **an influx of tourists** from the mainland now that central government's facilitated individual travel policy on Hong Kong and Macao bound tours is in place.

Tourists arriving in Macao on Saturday with lucky numbers were welcomed **with a sweet surprise.** They were presented with souvenirs by the regional government's tourist officials waiting at land, ferry and airport entry-points.

A three-hour-long **tourist promotional campaign**, including lion dances, a cocktail party, Mexican folk music and dances, was held in front of the Macao Tower on Saturday afternoon. The celebration **culminated** in a luck-draw with the first prize — a luxury Mercedes worth about 125,000 US dollars — claimed by a tourist from Hong Kong.

As the week-long national holiday **draws to a close**, holiday-makers all over China are starting to **pack up their things** for their return home. And transportation authorities are beginning to **feel the pressure.**

Although there are still two days left before the week-long holiday **comes to an end**, many travellers have already set off on their journey home, to avoid **traffic congestion**.

Travel agents all over China report that flights between the **hot tourist destinations** today saw **a surge** in the number of passengers. In Chengdu, for example, a major **traffic hub** in southwest China, air traveller numbers today (Sunday) were up eight thousand more than yesterday.

Extra trains and additional carriages have been added to all major railway routes across China. Traffic volumes on the nation's major cross-boundary roads are increasing as those driving their own vehicles head home.

Golden Week has been boosting tourism, business, transportation and related sectors in China since it was **initiated** four years ago, as increasing numbers of people **seize the opportunity** to travel and more importantly, to spend during the holiday.

With the end of China's National Day Golden Week Tuesday, the passenger transport sector is **breathing a big sigh of relief** after handling **record numbers** of tourists during the past week.

More than 260 thousand people passed through Shanghai's main railway station on Tuesday, the final day of the holiday, with most of them **outbound on their way home**. But it was a different picture today, with passenger numbers over the whole railway sector significantly lower.

Road traffic was also heavy at popular **tourists spots** on the last day of the holiday. In some of the country's largest cities such as Beijing and Shanghai a lot of residents took a last opportunity for **a short trip out** to the suburbs — but fortunately there were no reports of major **traffic logjams**.

Airlines are also celebrating the Golden Week. They've been reporting 95 percent **occupancy** on all flights from Beijing to North East China. Routes from cities such as Kunming and Haikou were also reportedly operating at near maximum capacity.

Since China and the European Union **initiated a tourism agreement**, the number of countries open to Chinese tourists has increased by 12, **excluding** only Denmark, Britain and Ireland.

Although the China National Tourism Administration still needs some time to work out policies on group tours to the EU, travel agencies and airlines with flights to and from Shanghai are already preparing **anticipated business**.

According to the China International Travel Service's Shanghai Office, Finnish, Dutch, and French tourism representative offices in the city have made inquiries about jointly **operating tourist routes.** Many Chinese travel agencies are also listing European routes on their promotional plan for next year.

Zhao Dexiang, senior executive of China International Travel Service, Shanghai Office, said, "If we can get a considerable number of tourists, we can really cut costs on service. And if we can arrange close cooperation with our European partners, low prices can be worked out for the benefit of both sides."

The major factors **affecting service fees** are hotel accommodations and **air fares**. Some Chinese travel agencies are negotiating with major international hotel groups in Europe for discounts. And Finnair, Lufthansa, and the KLM Royal Dutch Airlines have indicated they will increase the number of flights from Shanghai to Europe next year. The increased competition will help **drive down prices.**

Industry insiders in China predict group tours to Europe lasting seven to 10 days will stand at 1,250-2,500 US dollars per person in the future, but travel schedules and services will see a great improvement.

Unprecedented numbers of people gathered at major **scenic spots** around China on the first day of the week-long National Day holiday, showing that more and more Chinese are able to go greater distances during their **yearly autumn trip**. Despite the sudden peak in numbers, the transportation departments have seemed able to **handle the tourist onslaught**.

Plenty of sunshine and **azure sky** are what usually delight people most on a typical autumn day. People who chose to be on the road around China certainly **acquired the largest satisfaction** in both concerns on the first day of their weeklong tour. Nationwide, 99 major scenic spots received more than 1.5 million tourists on Wednesday, a 6 percent increase over the same period of last year.

On the other hand, the nation's transportation departments seem to be **at ease** in handling the increasing traffic volume brought by **the travel surge**. Whichever way people choose to go for their holiday, there are now more choices. Extra travel trains linking major cities and travel destinations are **put into service** during the holiday period. There are also more flights starting from hub airports like Beijing, Guangzhou and Shanghai to scenic spots around the nation.

The week-long National Day holiday offers something for everybody. It's a case of different strokes for different folks. Some join the **tourist floods**, going far and wide to **explore new horizons**. Others prefer to stay at home and enjoy the **holiday night life**.

The Three Gorges Dam project is more than just a mammoth/ tremendous engineering plan. With its spectacular **flood relief scenes**, it's attracting more and more visitors. Besides Chinese visitors, many foreign travellers are becoming **fascinated with** the world's biggest dam and are coming to see it first-hand.

Moving to south China's important port city, Guangzhou, a lumber show from the US **dazzled** local visitors with exciting gimmick/skill performances. They included cutting, seesawing and climbing trees, displaying the **masterly skills** of American lumberjacks.

In the central Chinese province of Hubei, a light show in the city's historical Huanghe Tower Cultural Park is proving popular with visitors.

Along the West Lake of Hangzhou City in east China, travellers are watching **eruptive fountains** set in the lake.

In Jiangsu's provincial capital Nanjing, tens of thousands of lights **illuminated a dark** Thursday night as people gathered **in reverence** at the Confucius Temple. Some creative **neon lights** created **a romantic setting** for both young and old — the perfect excuse for a walk on a sweet autumnal night.

The Chinese capital of Beijing **witnessed a rapid resurgence/recovery** of travelling during the week-long National Day holiday. Local statistics show that over 3.7 million tourists from home and abroad visited Beijing, an increase of 10 percent over the same period last year.

Tuesday was the last day of the National Day holiday, but the number of train and bus passengers from Beijing to the northeast and Shanghai was still rising and tickets for fast trains had almost been sold out.

The **short-distance trains** from Shanghai were carrying an increasing number of passengers and additional trains to Nanjing and Hangzhou had been started to cope with the traffic.

The number of passengers for **inter-town buses** were on the decline, however short-distance buses were transporting more passengers. As for air travel, the Beijing Capital International Airport was expected to have handled some 100,000 travellers.

From October 1 to 7, that was yesterday, the number of tourists visiting 99 selected **tourism destinations** around China hit nearly 13 million, and the total **admission ticket revenue** was nearly 50 million US dollars. Those figures represent a more than 8 and almost 7 percent increase respectively over the same period last year.

In Beijing, there was **a marked increase** in the number of visitors, with some 3.8 million domestic tourists coming to the capital. And they were **in a spending mood** too, **splashing out** some 4 billion dollars. With regard to tourist satisfaction, surveys found 96 percent of those **polled/charged** were satisfied with the services they received, up one percent from last year.

The General Assembly of the World Tourism Organization opened Sunday in Beijing. The assembly is the largest in the global travel industry.

Over 100 tourism ministers and more than a thousand delegates from over than 110 member countries were at the opening ceremony in the Great Hall of the People in Beijing. They will **work on a development guideline** for global tourism during their weeklong meeting, looking at the sustainable development of tourism, **poverty alleviation** and the recovery of the world tourism industry.

It is the largest international event held in Beijing since the city was **pronounced** free of SARS in July. During his speech in the opening ceremony Chinese Premier Wen Jiabao **reviewed the current situation** for China."China suffered seriously from SARS this year but we have taken many measures to **restore the tourism industry**, which took the greatest blow. Now it is recovering fast," said the Premier.

The Secretary General of the World Tourism Organization, made a positive long-term prediction on China's tourism industry. "We believe that China will become the largest **destination country** by 2020,though it may be delayed for one year or two."

Some of the most significant news for this assembly is the World Tourism Organization's **elevation** into **a specialized agency** of the United Nations.

A carnival parade of costume display from 2,000 ethnic groups worldwide has opened the Sixth Beijing Cultural Tourism Festival. As part of the city's celebration to mark its 850th anniversary as the nation's capital, the event **added light, color and the sound of music** to the lives of thousands of people lined up along the route.

Chinese Vice Premier said, "I'd like to **avail this opportunity** to announce the opening of the Sixth Beijing International Cultural Tourism Festival."

This announcement from Chinese Vice Premier turned Ping'an Avenue **a major thoroughfare** in downtown Beijing, into **a sea of joy**. Well-known for the strings of traditional style Chinese buildings lining both of its sides, Ping'an Avenue was unusually dynamic on Sunday morning. **Lively tunes** danced through the air, and **fancily dressed performers** from around the world skipped gaily through the street. The **ethnic costume parade** is one of the most popular events on the festival program, bringing great pleasure to Beijingers, who are increasingly attracted to any foreign **novelty**. This year's parade is said to be the largest ever. Some 2,400 folk artists from 52 countries and regions use age-old ways from their own cultures to congratulate the ancient capital on its birthday. The event also **received a blessing** from the World Tourism Organization, currently holding its 15th General Assembly in Beijing.

Francesco, secretary-general of World Tourism Organization, said, "On behalf of the World Tourism Organization and the delegations attending the 15th WTO General Assembly in Beijing, I'd like to **convey my best wishes** for this exceptional festival, exceptional for Beijing, for China, and for the world tourism."

And the city is more than happy to be **the stage for dialogue** between diverse world cultures. Delivering a speech to welcome **the distinguished guests**, acting mayor of Beijing Wang Qishan promised that the municipal government will endeavor to **rejuvenate** the ancient capital and give the world the best ever Olympic Games in 2008. For city folk in Beijing, the excitement has just begun at this year's festival. Following the opening parade, concerts, photo shows, and exhibitions **featuring foreign cultures** will add **exotic flavors** to the city's golden autumnal days.

A large number of **city dwellers** decided to get away from it all this National Day Holiday by travelling to the suburbs and countryside. There, they could **escape from** traffic jams and pollution, and relax by **taking in the natural landscape** and enjoying the sunshine and fresh air.

Many Nanjingers **flocked** to the Culture Park 30 kilometers away from **the hustle and bustle of the city**. The Mongolian grassland and the yurt/tent scenery gave the southern city dwellers a taste of what it was like to live in a prairie in northern China.

Visitors could ride horses, shoot arrows or slide on boards over the grassland for fun. Some also got to milk cows. One young couple even came here to hold their wedding ceremony.

Circuses from 10 ethnic groups including the Buyi, Miao, Yao and Tujia gathered in Duyun City, Guizhou Province, to **dazzle local citizens** with an **extravaganza**/crazy performance of acrobatic displays. The **elevated stand lion dance** is a traditional game played by the Gelao ethnic group, and **depicts** the ethnic legend of the Monkey King rescuing the mother of hero Mulian. Other performances like "pulling water barrels with eye lids", and "climbing the knife-ladder" **astounded** local audiences with their **jaw-dropping stunts**.

In Sanjiang City in the Guangxi Zhuang Autonomous Region, an Ethnic Dong Culture Week called "tour to the Chengyang bridge" marked the beginning of a week-long festival to promote the local cultures. During the day, visitors were invited to catch fish in ponds with their own hands to experience the local lifestyle. As night fell, the ethnic Dong people treated their guests with their **fragrant wine and food**, and played Lusheng, a folk instrument to celebrate the dance party.

Qingdao, is certainly not a secret **summer retreat**, at least not in

China. Known for its mild weather, clear turquoise/blue water, golden sandy beaches, Qingdao attracts thousands of visitors every summer. In fact the tug of the "perfect summer" memory is so strong, many keep coming back like migrators.

Bordering Jiaozhou Bay and the yellow sea from three sides, with more than 800km long coastal line Qingdao is the biggest **icefree harbor** in Shandong Peninsula. Since been chosen as the **host-to-be** of 2008 Olympics sailing programs, Qingdao is noticeable **spurred** with extra enthusiasm and local pride.

Harbor cruises offer service city views by day or night, you can choose from a few carrier, having short and long cruise around Qingdao harbor!

Qingdao coast offers some of the best **recreational opportunities** available — swimming, fishing, boating, parasailing, boardsailing, and much more. There are six beaches within Qingdao city where you can enjoy the sun and fun!

You can easily deceive yourself into being in a mini European Union — **with such a large variety of architecture styles**. According to a typical urban legend, an Anderson fairytale looking house, known as "Princess house", in early 20th century, was built by a devoted adorer/ worshipper to a Danish princess as gift and the adorer tried to persuade her coming to live in Qingdao. Sadly the stone-hearted princess never came.

One glimpse at Qingdao 's old town still **suggests a very distinctive European feel.**

It doesn't take long until you sense the real Qingdao pace and feel here: European buildings are only like some random backdrop of today's vivid Qingdao life: Essentially, Qingdao stays **simple and Chinese to the core.**

"Bathing by the beach, eating clamps and drinking **draft beer**"are three most **enjoyable moments** in life rated by **contented** Qingdao people. But most tourists have no idea what the draft beer to go "da pi" is. These barrels can be found in front of most small **delis and shops.**

268

Many famous people in the history have traveled through Qingdao, found their **inspirations** here and even eventually stayed here. Mr. Kang Youwie, China's first real **reformist** from late 1800's, spent his late days in this house, which he called as "**heavenly pleasure garden**".

The movement he led, known as "hundred day long reform" in the history, unfortunately was extremely **short-lived,** but his idea of learning from the west, **abandoning tyrannies** of some old customs paved for coming generations.

Does his open-mindedness has anything to do with his extensive traveling around the world and exposure to the different cultures? He has even been to 31 countries including some really remote place like Sweden and Egypt, when there were no such thing as airplane! His **memoir** of his 15 year long journey was finished in this house. After years away from China, did he look at the country from this balcony with the eyes of **a time traveler**?

Yingbin lou distinguish itself from other European buildings in Qingdao with its bold colors, **graceful shape and lines.** The interior is even more **delicate and impressive.** You can't help whoa/exclaim the governor's dedication to this house. The things, from the Crystal lamps, ceramic tiles, to the furniture and even the clock, are all shipped all the way from Germany. And isn't that impressive! The clock over hundred years old, is still working perfectly!

Here is also known as "politicians' **favorite**" after the colonial time. Mao Zedong, Jeang kaishek, and many other famous politicians stayed in this **legendary place** when they spent their summer time in Qingdao.

The only catholic church has become **the landmark** of the city since it was finished in 1934. As **the sacred place and shelter** for this believers for over a half century, the church magnifies tourists to come and admire this grand example of Roman architecture in China.

The **picture-postcard** like old town does not **allure** throngs of visitors outside. This neighourhood has been **emerged** into a slightly more bohemian and artistic area. Nearby galleries and coffee houses are great places to rest your tired feet after **a stroll** around here.

When you are in need of **injection of some easy joy and laughter**, come in to the dolphine park, built in 1995. It was the first one and still one of the best in China.

It is clear that the city is trying to **convey the idea of living with art.** Key elements of the city — sea, greens and buildings are incorporated harmoniously, decorated with sculptures everywhere. This sculpture garden in East part of the new town is a perfect example: full of sculptures **inspired by human body, nature and history**, adds some real artistic and human **touch** to the grand view.

Qingdao contributes the best known Chinese beer to the world since 1903. The Qingdao Beer City is the biggest in Asia and most lively during the summer, when **International beer festival** is held here. Over 10,000 people from both home and abroad are attracted to the 10-day long festival each year.

The festival is a truly **paradise** for beer lovers with something for everyone. The selection ranges from some bitters from local brewers to some excellent cider/wine, perry and beers from European and North American lagers/drinkers.

To **cater for** the growing **influx** of visitors, many new hotels built **outdoor dinning space** with sea view. In such a beautiful setting, anything looks like delicacy! Forget sharks fin or oysters, Qingdao locals favorite razor clams, and shrimp!

Qingdao's limited nightlife creates unlimited chances for mingling. Swanky/fashionable **cocktail fans** and **proletarian beer drinkers** find themselves sharing the same space and the same **taste of music**, and equally much fun!

The most fashionable and **vibrant cosmopolitan city** of northern china — Dalian.

Located by yellow sea on Liaoning peninsula, Dalian is **a thriving coastal city** known as "the pearl of the northeast", northern China's answer to HK. **Boosting** in trade and tourism, Dalian is **the locomotive** to the economy of northeastern China.

"The city of soccer" and "the city of fashion" and "city of greens" — Dalian is known for its modern, active yet still **relaxing lifestyle**.

Pulsating/beating with buoyancy and drive, Dalian is a perfect place to **recharge some extra doze of youth and vitality** for visitors who can handle the beat.

With its 40% of the area covered by greens, Dalian is a pleasant city to **cruise around.** For first time visitor to Dalian, **strolling** around sidewalks is the simplest entertainment itself.

Neighborhoods of different characters are connected by squares and parks that are always **boiled with life.**

It seems to be easy to **spot** some pretty, tall and slim girls in Dalian than anywhere else. **Privileged with beatiful appearance,** everyone here understands it takes more than natural beauty and height to become a professional model. **Acquired grace** is more important and harder to obtain.

Most girls here attending the school are only **dreaming for the spotlight**. Many see modeling training as additional practice for obtaining **self-confidence**, which is important for any future job options.

Many girls from Dalian woman Ranger/Police were graduated from here.

No wonder these **street patrol police** and **honor guards** in time of occasions are popular targets of **tourists flashes**.

You might think it takes **diligent training** to become a woman ranger, you are half-right. At least in Dalian, physical appearance is also an important **attribute** to screen applicants. Anyone shorter than 1.7meters is out on the first round.

But something for everyone in Dalian is Soccer! Soccer is Dalian's **obsession**. Indubitably/undoubtedly, soccer is the sport of Dalian. A brace of Dalian players play on the Chinese national team and no surprise, the star defender Sun Jihai, serving British Premier Division team is also from Dalian. They are everyone's heroes here, regardless of age!

The **passion** for soccer here starts to develop early and stays on.

Trams in Dalian have **trundled** through the old town since the 1940s.They speak of a time before turbo engines, still **twining up** today's daily life.

Unit Twenty-two
Culture and Social Concerns

导　读

　　大脑词库也称心理词典(mental lexicon)，是人脑中关于词汇信息的内存，是人脑中关于词汇的存储与提取的信息集。双语心理词库是心理词库研究中一个跨语言和跨文化的领域，研究重点集中在双语词库概念与形式的表征关系上，其争论的焦点问题在于：在习得双语的人的大脑中，关于两种语言词汇知识的心理词库是独立存储的还是共享的？对于这个问题，不同的学者从不同的角度，提出了各自相应的模型，如早期的并列型、复合型和从属型，以及后来的概念调节型和词汇连接型、混合模型与非对称模型、分布式模型等。从不同层面和水平研究双语词汇的心理表征形式。

　　概念调节型（concept mediation）认为双语词汇在词名层没有直接的联系，需通过共享的概念来调节；词汇连接型（word-association）则认为双语词汇在词名层直接连接，二语词和概念的连接要经过一语词。而且，研究者发现当受试者的二语水平很低时，其双语的表征模型为词汇连接型，随着二语水平的提高，表征结构转为概念调节型。混合模型（the mixed model）认为两种语言既在词名层直接连接，也同时和概念层直接连接。在混合模型中，如果不同节点间的连接强度（link strength）或同一对节点间的不同方向的连接强度有所不同，就构成了非对称模型（the asymmetrical model）。分布式模型（distributed model），即不同类型的词共享的概念节点数不同，比如说，具体词和同源词在两种语言中的翻译对等词比抽象词和非同源词的翻译对等词共享更多的概念节。

无论何种模型，其关键在于词汇表征的存储和提取形式受不同因素的影响，如年龄、流利程度及语言词汇的类型等。从我国高校学生英语学习情况看，大多数属于词汇连接型，即二语词汇的存储和提取要依靠母语词汇。语言应用尤其是在短文写作中，具体词和同源词的应用远远高于抽象词和非同源词。如看到母语词"应用或利用"，提取的往往是 use or adopt，而 apply，utilize，accommodate，及其相应的 application，utilization，accommodation 即使认识，学生也难以提取。这是否说明学生识记的词汇过于依靠一语对等词，却没有二语词汇相应的语境、文体及隐喻概念？

中国媒体报刊英语可以把二语语言和学习者熟悉的相应"母语文化"语境协调起来，避免学生因学习方式、心理词汇表征等因素的影响而导致"语用失误"或"用词不当"。大量同语域的语料增强了二语输入的强度，有利于学生双语心理词库的不断丰富和纠正。本单元为读者提供了丰富的有关"社会关注"的语篇，反映现代科技、经济和社会的发展，给我们的观念和生活带来的问题，如"民工 migrant workers"、学生心理健康、就业压力的影响、西方文化的冲击等。

Key Points

1. The reports will present us various aspects of life and society that are changing with the advance of modern civilization.
2. Read carefully and focus on the changes of your own concern, and then present your opinions.

China's millions of young and single male migrant workers, who are **loaded with heavy daylight labor**, are being troubled by the lack of sex, probably the most urgent **private need** in their hard lives away from home.

In Beijing, the capital city of China, there are 2.245 million migrant workers, most of them being **adult or married males**. Inadequate sexual life is a common problem for them, due to economic or geographical reasons. This **cruel fact** not only has affected their normal life but also leads to physical and psychological, even **social problems.**

In order to make a living and support their families in rural areas, these **peasant-transmitted workers** can endure any sufferings, including overloaded labor, but is there a limit? According to a small-scale survey made among 40 migrant workers by *Beijing Star Daily*, 45 percent, or 18 of interviewed workers had no sex in the past six months, nine single adults have never had sex during their **urban life** since they came to Beijing.

A 33-year-old worker from Henan Province told the reporter from *Beijing Star Daily* that after work, what he thinks about most is his wife. But he cannot remember when they last spent their intimacy time. Each time he sees young lovers **strolling** in the street, he feels the terrible gnawing.

Since it is hardly for them to find a way out for their libido, most of them prefer porn movie, fantasy, dirty talks or frequent masturbations. Nearly all single male migrant workers have been to underground cinemas, some even relying on it for their spare time. Most of them often read pornographies, including books, magazines and pictures, which are regarded as "precious" for them and preserved in their bags as "**pressure-alleviating pills**".

It becomes commonplace that **envious, jealous, sour or even more complicated sentiments** emerge when they see intimate lovers in the street. Sex fantasy is more universal among these young adults. Some use peripheral way to meet their desire like **harassing women** in a crowded bus. More vehement/excited behaviors, such like rape and sexual harassment are also occasionally committed.

Several prostitutes are seen waiting for businesses on the street. The sexual services in cities provide, to some extent, possiblity to satisfy their needs, while at the same time, adds more social problems.

As for going to a prostitute, though the idea has **hit upon** many of them, it is still **beyond their financial capacity**. Being almost the lowest class in a city, they have too **little pocket money** to afford a call girl. For some young and restless, melee and skirmish (conflict and fight) become a usual way to unleash their excessive energy.

While filling a questionnaire, most of them marked the options labeled with "**depression**", "**oppression**" and "uncomfortable" terms.

"China has more than 100 million migrant workers," said a professor in sociology from Renmin University of China, "As a special group, their real **sexual lives** were still in the dark." He said that though the results from surveys of such a small scale may not be typical enough, the **concern** about migrant workers' sexual life shows the progress of the media, and the society as a whole.

They are also human beings, and they need normal sexual life, which is a basic human right that should not be **neglected**.

————❦————

In a world that **abounds with** opportunities, women say an ideal husband should **boast career development potential** and preferably a decent income, but not necessarily very high academic qualifications, a recent survey showed.

Psychologists with the **elite** Peking University have found that a man's **schooling** does not matter as much to young women as it did in the 1980s, as most women believe that a man with potential makes a better partner, regardless of his education.

A professor and his colleagues made **a comparative study** recently on classified ads put up by "lonely heart women" in *Women of China* between 1985 and 2000.

Some 73 per cent of the women who **posted ads** in 1985 said explicitly they wanted to marry men with higher education, whereas only 29 per cent said the same in 2000.

In 2000, 65 per cent of the women expected **potential partners** to be successful in their career, compared to 42 per cent in 1985. This change in expectations, according to the study, shows that high **qualifications** do not necessarily guarantee good pay and career success.

"It's natural for women to prefer men **with greater capacity and higher**

276

social status," the professor said. "From the evolutionary point of view, men with better social and economic conditions are more likely to ensure the **well-being of their offspring**."

Classified ads for lonely hearts have helped several million people **find matches** since they appeared in Chinese newspapers and magazines in 1981. Despite a drop in the number of advertisers in recent years, the professor found that more women are willing to post ads in their search for "**Mr. Right**."

Shanghai **teenagers** are more ambitious and spend more time **worrying about** their future careers than their French **peers**, who are more concerned about setting up a happy family than them, according to a recent survey.

Two magazines — **Shanghai-based** *Attraction* and French publication *Science & Vie Junior* — recently **surveyed** 3,700 Shanghai children aged 12 to 18 and 400 **youngsters** in Paris about their **ambitions** for the future. The results were published yesterday.

The survey found that most of Shanghai youngsters worry most about their **future careers** while the Paris teenagers care more about having **a stable life** and happy family. The differences are caused by the different education they receive and different social values they hold, said local sociologists.

When asked what a successful life means to you, 53 percent of the surveyed Shanghai children said it involves having **an interesting career**. But more than half of the French respondents said setting up a family is the key to success, which may be surprising to most Shanghai residents.

"In France where the **divorce rate** is always high and unhappy marriages instead of **everlasting love** are often seen due to open sexual ideas, children admire a happy marriage and a complete family", explained a humanities professor at Jiaotong University. "While in Chinese people's opinion, a successful career will bring you everything, including **fame, love**

277

and family."

The survey also suggests local youngsters **worship** billionaires while Paris children **admire** Nobel Prize winning scientists.

"The results indicate local youngsters are **eager** for quick success and **instant benefits**. They have become ambitious because our media and advertisers appeal to people to compare their **fortunes** with others", said director of the Institute for Youth Research under the Shanghai Academy of Social Sciences. "By contrast, French people don't pay much attention to wealth because their society is **a mature, well-off society**."

However, Shanghai and Paris youth have a few things in common. Nearly half of the respondents in both cities said they would establish a nature preserve to protect endangered species if they owned a 10,000-square-kilometer swatch/sample of land.

"The concept of environmental protection, only mentioned sometimes by adults, has been **well-accepted** by young people, which gives us much hope", said a sociology professor at Fudan University.

Chinese Culture Minister said Thursday that China has made great progress **in the cultural sector**. At a press conference organized by the State Council Information Office, the Minister gave an outline of China's cultural development and international exchange.

The minister said that since 2002, the ministry has been **running a project** promoting outstanding cultural works nationwide. In recent years, investment in the cultural infrastructure had reached **record levels**. Ongoing projects include the national theater, the national museum, the national library and the national **arts gallery**. The Chinese government had signed cultural cooperation agreements with 145 foreign governments. China has set up **cultural centers** in a number of countries including France, Egypt and South Korea.

He also pointed to government efforts to **preserve cultural heritage**. To date, China has had 29 sites included by the United Nations Educational, Scientific and Cultural Organization on the World Heritage list. China would take two **major approaches** to further developing the culture sector.

First, we will promote **non-profit** public **cultural undertakings**, including the establishment of more libraries and museums. Second, we will gradually transform state-owned cultural organizations into enterprises, and encourage more investment.

To meet the goals set for cultural **market access** in line with World Trade Organization commitments, the ministry was also **conducting an overhaul/check** of video game arcades, Internet cafes and entertainment clubs.

On the opening of the audio-visual market, overseas competition was good for the improvement of China's cultural sector. China would strengthen efforts to fight piracy.

Beijing saw the launch on Monday morning of **a top-class training center** dedicated to protecting and restoring **cultural relics** in China. With an investment of nearly 4 million US dollars, the Sino-Italian joint venture is the largest and most advanced institution of its kind in China.

The training center will provide courses in **the restoration of** cultural and historical relics made of porcelain, stone and metal. Trainees will also be taught how to protect **archaeological digs**.

The Italian side has provided over 1.8 million US dollars and 25 experts while China has invested nearly 1 million US dollars in funds, in addition to providing the premises and part of the training staff. The center now offers a nine-month program focused on practical skills. It aims to train **specialized personnel** for cultural relic protection and set an example for fellow institutions around China.

Director of Cultural Relics Protection & Restoration Center said, "Our training is different from that provided at other schools. A student in our training program will **take over** 1,500 hours of class, among which more than half will be spent on the field. So our stress is on the practical skills."

An Italian expert said, "The center is a result of cooperation between

Italy and China. After studying at the center, trainees will use Italian **archeological skills** to work across China. This will lay a solid foundation for long-term cooperation between Italy and China in archeological research."

China and Italy set up their first **archaeological training facility** back in 1995, in Xi'an city. Since then, 53 Italian archaeologists have worked and taught in China. In March 2000, the two countries **signed a framework agreement** for long-term cooperation, which **got into full swing** in early 2002.

------◦◄◌◌►◦------

A kissing contest planned for Valentine's Day in north China's Tianjin Municipality is **courting controversy** in a country where displays of **romantic affection** are traditionally kept private. The contest, organized by a supermarket called "Everybody is Happy", will be held on Feb. 14. The couple making the longest kiss will win 2,000 yuan (240 US dollars). The supermarket started to take contestants' registrations on Tuesday.

But the contest has **aroused love-it or hate-it responses** from customers. Most senior and middle-aged customers consider the contest inappropriate and a violation of the Chinese tradition of modesty. However, young people are more open to **the novelty of demonstrating their love publicly**.

A university student said that kissing was as common as shaking hands nowadays. "I will definitely **sign up for the contest** if I have a girlfriend," said the student, who considers kissing a common practice among couples. Sociologists said the contest would **reveal people's private lives** to the public and should be held cautiously.

Although **hotly debated**, the contest will go ahead as long as there are couples wanting to participate, said a spokesman for the supermarket.

------◦◄◌◌►◦------

THE **break-up of a relationship** can mean sleepless nights, problems concentrating, loss of **appetite**, even depression. Every person **reacts to the crisis** differently. "One cannot expect to function normally in the first phase of **a separation**," says German psychotherapist Doris Wolf, author of a book on how to deal with a break-up. "Even if you are someone who has kept your feelings under control you can **experience emotions** as never before,"says Wolf, pointing out that men and women generally react differently.

Men tend to **suppress their pain** by working, or with a new relationship, or alcohol. Women, on the other hand, sometimes **suffer from** depression, fear of the future, or guilt feelings. In contrast to men, women, however, often **have a good friend** who will listen, give comfort or advice. That, says Wolf, is important, because anger, sadness and frustration need to be expressed. A psychologist from Munich, Germany, advises people to **avoid idealizing the ex-partner**. Avoid displaying pictures of yourself and the ex, or of a favourite restaurant you visited together, or of music that you both enjoyed.

Even if you both plan to "**stay good friends**", it normally doesn't last. That's because one partner might always **nurture the hope** of restarting the relationship. The psychologist says this could stop new experiences, and **disappointment** will be the outcome.

A much more meaningful approach would be to **keep a diary** with a section on negative things. "Writing things down helps **put a distance** between you and the experience and that is important," says another psychologist, who **holds seminars** on getting through the break-up of a relationship. Creating **a separation ritual** could also be important. However, each person should find her or his own method. One person might write a letter that is never sent while another might **prefer a drawing or mental exercise** as a sort of ritual.

One way to deal with extreme anger could be to do unusual things like **throwing an egg** into the bathtub. Even cleaning up the egg mess afterwards could be helpful because a separation affects both **the soul and the body,** which is **under extreme tension**, Wolf explains. This is only reduced by exercise and cleaning is exercise. And, nutrition is extremely important during this phase.

A company's attempt to own "Valentine's Day" has **sparked some debate** in China since the application to register the name of **the romantic festival** as a trademark was made on Feb. 3, just 11 days before the festival. General manager of the applicant Leesa New Life Technology Development Co. Ltd., said the trademark "Valentine's Day" would be used on the company's shower equipment, which was designed to create **a romantic ambiance**/atmosphere in the bathroom.

If the application to the Trademark Office of the State Administration of Industry and Commerce (SAIC) succeeds, the name of the festival, said experts, could not be used as a trademark in some **commercial places** as the company applied for registration in the category of service areas, which include public bathhouses, **beauty salons** and health care units.

The registration, theoretically speaking, could be approved, experts acknowledged, since the name "Valentine's Day" does not **violate** the eight articles **prohibiting** the registration of certain trademarks in accordance with China's Trademark Law, which **forbids** the registration of names the same or similar to the nation's name, of **ethnic discrimination** or harmful for **social morals**.

SAIC's officials decline to comment on the company's move, saying the decision has not been made yet. But most people have **voiced their objection to** the trademark application.

As a popular festival in China, a noted lawyer with Beijing's Jiayuan Law Firm said the name of Valentine's Day should be regarded as **a public asset**. It would be unfair for the public and other businesses if it belonged to one company.

"If the registration succeeds", he said, "many more companies might **follow suit** to put more holidays in their pockets." It should be a holiday's name, not a trademark.

A Shanghai cinema says it will give out free condoms to its customers watching films on Valentine's Day this Saturday. The cinema, together with a department store asking people to kiss in public, is **creating controversy.**

The Broadband International Cineplex located at Shanghai Times Square said 3,000 condoms will be available at the ticket kiosk/box on Saturday and customers can help themselves. "We believe in a developed city like Shanghai that condoms are no longer **a taboo** for our customers," said an employee. "Providing condoms supports a healthy and secured sex life and can **arouse awareness** about safe sex and AIDS prevention."

While receiving **applause** from young people, many cinemas **disapprove of** the idea.

"Watching a movie is **a spiritual enjoyment** and irrelevant to condoms," an employee from the Shanghai Film Art Center said. "Saint Valentine's Day means showing **love and care** to all the people around you." The complaint is echoed by others. "China isn't so open at present. Sex is a private topic," said a 55-year-old local company clerk. "It is awkward to provide condoms in public, and it is meaningless to highlight a Western celebration."

However, sociologists said condoms do not directly lead to sex. "But when condoms are distributed in a public place like the cinema, people should consider **the reaction** of others, especially children and the elderly," said a student at Fudan University. "It is much better to distribute condoms at an AIDS prevention lecture or **a fashion party**." Meanwhile, Champs Elysees International Wedding Collection Gallery, in Xujiahui, announced yesterday that couples can win a pair of roses and tickets for a party arranged the following day at the mall, provided they **kiss passionately** in public.

The store, selling **wedding-related** items, uses the gimmick to attract more attention.

"We hope to make a kind of fanfare with the event to promote our brand to potential customers," said a store employee.

However, none of the eight interviewees said they will perform kissing in public. "I'm not interested in such activities and neither is my girlfriend," said a senior university student. "Kiss in public? **Love is not a show**," said a 25-year-old woman.

In other Valentine's Day **promotions**, the Shanghai PortmanRitz-Carlton, is offering a one night stay at the **presidential suite** for 88,888yuan (US$10,709). The hotel promises to decorate the room with 5,000 roses, among other **romantic arrangements**. "With passion and enough money, the guy **treating** his woman **to** that may just be the ideal lover of every woman," said a 26-year-old white-collar worker. "But it's **beyond our reach** in this world. I don't expect my boyfriend to waste money on roses and **fancy hotel rooms**. With that amount of money, I would prefer a car."

———————

Forbes Magazine released its first Forbes China Celebrity List on Tuesday. Houston Rockets star Yao Ming **ranked No.1** on the list.

The list looked at the income and popularity of leaders in film, sports, media, music and publishing. To be **eligible**, **listees** had to have been born and raised in the Chinese mainland. Celebrities from Hong Kong and Taiwan weren't included.

Yao led the way based on **heavy exposure in media** and **Web hits** in China; he also had the second-highest 2003 income among Mainland Chinese celebrities, at 14.6 million US dollars. Crouching Tiger, Hidden Dragon actress Zhang Ziyi ranked NO.2 in the overall list, and film star Gong Li was No.5.

———————

Authorities in Beijing are planning to carry out **renovations** on its six world cultural heritage sites this year. The Beijing Bureau of Cultural Heritage said on Sunday that it's the first time repairs on so many **heritage sites** will be carried out at the same time.

Workers will repair floors and roofs in the Temple of Heaven, a Sacrificial Altar used by previous emperors. Other sites to **undergo repairs** will include the Summer Palace, the Peking Man Site at Zhoukoudian , the Si Ma Tai section of the Great Wall, the Forbidden City and the Ming Tombs. Experts say the renovation will not affect tourists visiting the sites.

China, which feeds a fifth of the world's population on seven percent of the world's **arable land,** is facing a crisis in **food security** as economic development **eats away at** available land.

Alarm bells are again ringing in China over the food security of its 1.3 billion people as grain prices rise and food reserves drop. China expects to see at least a 40 million ton **shortfall** in grain output in 2003 with the annual harvest dropping for the 6th **straight year**. Premier Wen Jiaobao has called for increased efforts to raise farming incomes, preserve cropland, and increase grain production capacity, **signaling a renewal of concern** over grain security at the highest levels.

China's grain output has **dipped** from a record high of 512 million tons in 1998 to a ten-year low of 435 million tons in 2003. Output for this year is expected to come in at between 440 and 450 million tons, giving China **a grain shortfall** of up to 45 million tons. The shortfall is roughly equal to the annual grain production of Canada, one of the world's major grain exporters. China's total demand for grain averages between 480 million tons and 490 million tons annually, and will grow to approximately 640 million tons in 2030, when the population hits 1.6 billion, far **outstripping** its present production capacity.

An official from the Ministry of Agriculture discussed the problem with our reporter.

A counsellor of State Council of P.R. China said, "China's grain production capacity is 500 million tons a year. As of 2003, China's grain production has dropped for 4 **consecutive years**. Yet, at present our reserves are still sufficient. Annual demand for grain is between 480 and 490 million tons. Each year, 40 million tons come from the reserves which are decreasing every year. We should be okay for now, as the reserves, including the turnover/circulating grain, are enough for at least two years."

A shortfall in four consecutive years has resulted in **a sharp increase** in grain prices, forcing the country to consider importing supplies of grain. Official statistics show that recent prices for paddy rice in east China's Anhui Province reached 1050 yuan or 126.8 dollars per ton, up 80 to 120 yuan over the same period last year. In the past few months the **purchase price** for wheat in northeast China has **shot up** 32 percent, while the price of maize in Hebei and Shandong provinces has doubled, and rice prices have **gone up** by 13 percent.

Driven higher by increases in the price of grain, the cost of flour, edible oil, meat, eggs, and fodder/feedings have all gone up since October 1st in key **grain-consuming** areas, according to market data. This has **fuelled concerns** about the impact on inflation. November's consumer price index **jumped to** three per cent, its highest level in six years, largely on the back of rising food prices.

US environmentalist Lester Brown, the author of the books of Plan B and Who Will Feed China, warned last November that sudden food **price hikes** in China could be the sign of a coming world **food crisis**, brought on by global warming and increasingly scarce water supplies among major grain producers including China, United States and India. Brown said as China's population grows and living standards rise, its people will demand a more **meat-based diet**, and China will increasingly have to look to world markets to satisfy grain needs for both food and feed for **livestock.** He said that, when China turns to the world market for grain, it will need 30 to 50 million tons, more than the amount imported by anyone else in the world.

However, Brown's friend, the Chinese Counsellor, **holds a different view**.

Importing grain is equivalent to importing water and cropland. China has limited cropland. Importing grain **reduces the pressure** on domestic cropland, but excessive imports will be too **disruptive** to both domestic and world markets. At present, China's supply is more than demand. Massive importing will lead to **a price drop** on the domestic market, and the price drop will reduce farmers' incomes. It's **a chain effect**. Imports should be limited to, I believe, no more than 20 million tons a year. It won't be, as some scholars have said, that China's **self supply capability** will go down and its imports will go up to between 40 and 50 million tons. That won't happen.

Less than two months ago, China signed contracts with US businesses in Chicago totaling 1.59 billion dollars. The bulk of the purchases consisted of deals for 1.4 billion dollars worth of soybeans. The purchasing group is the second in weeks to have gone to the United States, timed around a visit to Washington by Premier Wen Jiabao. The visit is an effort to **balance bilateral trade**.

The Chinese Premier said, "We'd like to increase imports from the US, but you cannot always make Chinese eat soybeans while taking in aeroplanes."

Then, what exactly is causing the shortfall in grain output at home? According to the counsellor, **supply exceeding demand** contributes to a drop in grain prices, which in turn hurts farmers' **incentive** to grow grain. **Urbanization** and the growth of special economic zones have resulted in heavy losses of cropland, while at the same time the government is trying to **bring down stockpiles** and free up farmland for more **lucrative cash crops**. All of these have contributed to a drop in grain prices. This is likely to **trigger price rises** in food and other commodities and eventually inflation. It's a chain effect. The grain security issue has caused concern among authorities at the highest levels, who have given the issue **top priority** on the government working agenda this year. The central government said it plans to **enact legislation** to bring farmland under strict control, and to promote reform in the government's **land requisition** and management systems. Experts hope that the establishment of a standardized land management system will benefit farmers, stop the **illegal transfer of land-use rights** and effectively protect farmland and grain production.

The central government has decided to use 10-billion yuan in 2004 to **subsidize** grain production mostly at the country's 13 major grain production bases. This will be **coupled with** additional policies favorable to grain production.

A Beijing businessman has **filed an application** to trademark the Chinese name of US President George W. Bush to help market his **disposable** nappies.

The applicant filed an application with the General Administration for Industry and Commerce of China, **stating** he wants to use the **two-character phrase** "Bu Shi" as a trademark, the Beijing News reported.

"I **hit upon the idea** by chance," said the applicant. "Back in my hometown in Henan Province, the pronunciation of 'Bushi' sounds exactly like 'not wet'."

Government officials are not amused. One official from the State Trademark Bureau said the application would very likely be **rejected**, "because it may **bring about** bad social impact if a leader's name is registered as a trademark". He said it could take up to 16 months for a final decision to be made.

China's Trademark Law **bans words or patterns** that can cause "harmful effects on ethics or society" to be used as trademarks.

The authority had recently **turned down an application** by a costume company which applied to use the Chinese translation of "Lewinsky" as **a fashion brand**, referring to Monica Lewinsky who had an affair with former US president Bill Clinton.

Yuanmingyuan, the most magnificent **imperial garden** in China, has long been one of Beijing's major **tourist attractions**. But the public has so far been unable to **appreciate the garden's beauty** in its entirety, due to the destruction wrought by Anglo-French Allied Forces in 1860. A project is currently under way to **bring back the original look** of the western part of

Yuangmingyuan, which for a long time has been buried under ruins.

The first phase of the preservation program is taking place in the long **deserted western part** of the garden. **Initial efforts** are being focused on cleaning up the ruins and water system, as well as **reinforcement of the riverbanks**. In addition, work will be carried out 16 bridges in the garden to restore their original features.

Director of the Research Office of Yuangmingyuan Garden said, "We plan to spend the next couple of years trying to show people **the real charm** of the imperial garden. That should be a combination of classic ancient buildings and natural landscapes that maintain **the historic feel.**"

Originally built in 1709 during the Qing Dynasty era, the Yuanmingyuan Garden **featured typical Chinese scenery** combined with Western architecture. It was sacked during the invasion of Anglo-French Allied forces in 1860 and **reduced to ruins**. The western part, which is some 700,000 square meters in area, is expected to be opened to the public at the end of this year.

Unit Twenty-three
International Business and
Economic Cooperation

导　读

　　现代认知语义学认为词的聚合关系反映了人类认知机制对事物及本身生活经验的归类和概括。因此，表示某一类事物或某一部分生活经验的词的类聚便构成一个语义场: pink，yellow，orange，blue，violet，green，brown 等构成颜色语义场; farm，cultivate，grow，sow，plant，seed，plough 等构成农业语义场; bureau，bench，bed，wardrobe，dressing-table 等构成家具语义场。语义场中各个词项之间的语义关系是相互依赖的，某一词项的词义由与之相联系的相邻诸词决定。

　　同一语义场的词汇往往同现在与之相应的主题语篇中，构成语篇的衔接和连贯。如:

　　In western countries，farmers usually cultivate their own farms. They plough their own lands and sow seeds of various plants. In the United States and Canada，farmers mainly grow the crop of wheat while grasses grow on British farms for cattle raising.

　　因此，语义场词汇的聚合关系符合知识以概念和命题进行心理表征的规律，也符合语言交际应用的现实需要。本单元新闻语篇的词汇聚合主要集中于外贸、国际商务争端与合作等相关方面，构成外贸和经济交流与合作语义场。

Key Points

　　1. Foreign trade and economic cooperation is an inalienable part of a

country's economy. With the increase of China's comprehensive strength, China will be a major participant of global economy and WTO. Therefore, refer to your knowledge of China's foreign trade and collaboration and read these passages.

2. In reading the reports, familiarize yourselves with lexical items involved.

In southern China's **island province** of Hainan, where the annual conference of the Boao Forum for Asia, or BFA, opens on Sunday. Prominent Asian politicians, academics and entrepreneurs have been **flying into the scenic coastal town** of Boao where the meeting is being **hosted**.

Chinese Premier will **deliver a keynote speech** at the conference, in a busy schedule. Already on Saturday, he met Tajikistan's President, Singapore's Prime Minister, and other regional leaders. The premier also held talks with representatives from Chinese and international **business circles** attending the forum. Regional economic and trade cooperation, financial security, and **intra-Asian** cooperation are **top of the agenda** at the gathering. Analysts see the BFA forum as an important platform for **exploring Asian issues** and for overcoming **barriers** to greater **economic integration** in the region. Delegates will also discuss economic globalization, industrialization, and trade ties.

A **trade war is brewing** across the Atlantic and Pacific Oceans. Emboldened/encouraged by a WTO ruling on Monday, Japan, South Korea, and the European Union are demanding the US immediately **drop its duties** on imported steel. If not, they say it will face the possibility of billions of dollars **in retaliation**. A three-member WTO panel on Monday **rejected the bulk** of a US appeal against an earlier ruling that said US tariffs on imported steel violate international trade law. The decision is **final** and Washington has been given until the middle of next month to **act on the judgment**.

According to an official of EU Trade Commission, "The WTO has today (Monday) confirmed that **a protectionist measure** adopted by the US last year in March to protect their domestic steel industry is contrary to WTO rules. This means that this measure must now be **terminated**."

The European Union is threatening to **hit back** with some $2.2 billion in duties on US goods, selected for the maximum political impact, saying it could take action as early as December 6 if the duties are not **lifted**.

Other trading partners — Japan, South Korea, China, Switzerland, Norway, New Zealand and Brazil — also could **retaliate** against US exports.

Some analysts estimate total **retaliation** could reach 3.1 billion US dollars depending how damages are calculated.

The ruling handed Bush a difficult political decision **heading into** next year's presidential election and with **anti-free trade sentiment** on the rise in Congress.

An official with the Committee for Economic Development said, "If the administration decides to be **defiant** in the face of the WTO decision, then it's going to have a hard time moving the WTO trade talks forward; it's going to have a hard time **selling** the free trade zone for the Americas; it's going to have a very hard time with market opening when negotiating with our trade partners."

Some studies indicate the tariffs have cost the US a lot more than just saving American jobs and President Bush may be considering **rescinding/discarding** them at the midway point.

———— ✦◈✦ ————

Chinese President has **ruled out** any significant changes to China's exchange rate mechanism. Speaking at the APEC CEO summit on Sunday, Hu said China would maintain the Renminbi **at a reasonable and balanced level**.

The Chinese government would take further steps to **well-tune** the exchange rate mechanism as financial reforms continue. China's foreign-exchange policy **reflects the market** and is appropriate for China, **given** the country's economic and financial realities. The Chinese leader also reminded the APEC forum that China played **a stabilizing role** in the region during the 1997 Asian financial crisis, partly due to its stable Renminbi exchange rate. In a question and answer session following his address, the president said China's reform and opening up and its economic growth were **a win-win situation**, benefiting China and the world as a whole.

————————

China's top central banker has **rejected** suggestions that the fixed exchange rate is the cause of the imbalance in Sino-US trade.

In an interview with the News Agency, Governor of the People's Bank of China said the US trade deficit was primarily the result of **structural imbalances** in the US economy and **fiscal deficits**. He acknowledged a country's exchange rate is related to its **balance of payments**. But he said the country's overall trade balance rather than bilateral trade balance needed to be taken into account. In the case of China and the United States, the two countries' existing economic and trade structures meant the US would continue **to run a big trade deficit** with China.

————————

Chinese Premier says the government will reform its policy on export **tax rebates**. Speaking at a national conference on the reform of the **export rebate system** Friday, the premier **pledged** to increase **the rebate quota**. Tax rebates are common practice in international trade to increase the competitiveness of export companies.

The Premier said the export **tax refund** policy has increased the competitiveness of Chinese enterprises and expanded the country's foreign trade. However, in the past few years, the government has failed to **pay the rebates** promptly because of the rapid growth in foreign-trade business. The delayed payment of tax rebate has caused difficulties for companies and became a hidden financial burden of the central government.

As part of the reform, local governments are required to **share the**

burden of paying the increased **refunds** with the central government. In addition, the new import value-added tax and import consumption tax will be primarily used to pay the tax rebates. The Premier says the central government will pay the delayed refunds.

Government sources say that last year, the delayed payment of tax rebates reached nearly 250 billion yuan, or nearly 30 billion US dollars.

———— ⬥ ————

The US government has announced that it's decided to take what's called **safeguard measures** on three types of textile products from China. The decision will affect Chinese exports of knitted fabric, dressing **gowns** and **robes** and some **underwear**.

The US textile industry **petitioned** to the US government in July for protection, complaining the **flood** of Chinese textile products had "**disturbed the market**". China's Textile Industry Association rejects the **accusations** and is strongly opposed to the US decision. The association says the downturn in the US textile industry is not a result of China's exports, and quotas will lead to **a lose-lose situation**.

———— ⬥ ————

The United States has **scrapped** its controversial steel tariffs, **averting** an international trade war. And the European Union has welcomed the US decision.

US President George W. Bush scrapped steel tariffs on Thursday, sixteen months ahead of schedule to **avert retaliation** from Europe and Asia. The White House said Bush will, however, keep a system in place to help US steel producers by licensing and tracking steel imports to cut the risk of unexpected **surges**.

"The US steel industry wisely used the 21 months of **breathing space** we provided to **consolidate and restructure**. The industry made progress increasing productivity, lowering production cost and making America more competitive with foreign steel producers," said White House spokesman.

Bush's decision comes 11 days before the European Union was set to

slap duties on 2.2 billion US dollars of **politically sensitive** US exports, if the tariffs were not lifted. Japan was also set to **retaliate**.

EU Trade Commissioner says **the lifting** of the tariffs has ended a major **transatlantic dispute** and the European Union will now **suspend retaliatory sanctions**. The commissioner said the tariffs had allowed the US steel industry to begin restructuring, and that this could help keep world steel trade more stable. But he added the EU would continue to monitor the US system of licensing and tracking steel imports.

———————⫷⬤⫸———————

Chinese TV makers say they won't give up the American market in the wake of the **anti-dumping** ruling, made Monday on Chinese-made TV sets. The **dumping finding** was made by the US against four Chinese TV manufacturers, TCL, Sichuan Changhong Electronics, Shenzhen Konka Group and Xiamen Overseas Chinese Electronics.

An import tariff of 31.7 percent has been **imposed on** Xiamen Overseas Chinese Electronics TV sets. But the company has enough TV sets stored in the US to meet the **pre-Christmas** market demand. So the ruling by the US Commerce Department will have **little impact** on sales this year.

General Manager of Overseas Trading Co. under Xiamen OCE said, "With import duties as high as 30 percent, I think most Chinese-made TV sets are **precluded**/excluded from entering the American market. But there are still two things we can do. First, we can develop TV sets with smaller screens, under 21 inches, Secondly, we can export TV sets with LCD/liquid crystal display and PDP features. These products have not been included in anti-dumping **suits**."

TCL and KONKA are also **optimistic**, saying they will continue to expand their international markets, despite the ruling.

China is now exporting millions of TV sets to the US and a high import duty would mean that the annual 15 million production capacity of China will be wasted.

A senior researcher with the Chinese Ministry of Commerce advises Chinese TV makers to develop **higher priced** TV sets as low priced models are more likely to **provoke dumping investigations**.

The researcher added that Chinese manufacturers should also cooperate with their overseas **counterparts** in matters of production, that closer international business relationships could help avoid a lot of trade disputes. And relevant authorities here in China should establish systems to **educate and prepare** exporting companies about possible disputes, he concluded.

China's Ministry of Commerce has **dismissed the finding** as "unfair", but says it will continue to negotiate with the US side on this issue.

Fewer than 10 days ago, the US Commerce Department decided to impose import quotas on three kinds of Chinese textile products. There have also been **well-publicized cases** against Chinese companies on steel products and television. The trade disputes have **aroused wide attention**. The Import and Export Bureau of China's Ministry of Commerce says the decision does not **accord with reality**. And it's unfair treatment of Chinese businesses.

A researcher from the State Council Development Research Center said, "The US always stresses the **surging** of the US deficit in bilateral trade with China. But actually a large percentage of the trade deficit is **a transferred deficit**. It means that a lot of the products were originally created in other south east Asian countries and later **shifted** to China."

According to the Chinese Ministry of Commerce, there have been 7 American anti-dumping cases against Chinese companies this year, involving 1.6 billion US dollars. This has severely **disturbed the normal state** of Sino-US trade. Some organizations say the best thing to do now is to negotiate and try to **avoid further disputes**.

Several key US companies have just **landed contracts** with China, worth about 6 billion US dollars. The biggest deal is an agreement with GE, for 3 billion dollars' worth of their engines. The contracts are part of a move, to reduce China's trade surplus with the United States, a source of increasing concern for both countries.

US Commerce Secretary was **on hand** in Washington on Wednesday to see Boeing **ink a deal** with 5 Chinese air companies to sell 30 Boeing 737s. The contract is worth 1.7 billion US dollars.

American manufacturing giant GE has also **landed a big agreement** from China. The company has been contracted to supply **jet engines** for the regional jet program in China which is still under development. This agreement could be worth up to 3 billion dollars over 20 years. On top of that, China has **placed orders** with General Motors, Ford and Chrysler for 15,000 cars and trucks in a deal worth up to 2 billion US dollars. It means more corporate revenue and thousands of jobs for the US manufacturers who have been going through some **sluggish business** times.

Vice Minister of China's State Development & Reform Commission said, "Both sides should do its bid for the trade balance. China should import more goods to meet its domestic demand while America should **relax its restrictions** on its products sale to China, especially those of high tech products."

The two deals are expected to **even out** the trade deficit between the two countries. The US trade deficit with China **hit a record** 103 billion US dollars last year and this year's figure is on track to reach 120 billion dollars. The gap has **prompted** the US government and manufacturers to **pressure** for more balanced trade with China.

China has already made commitments to open up its markets and now the country is planning to **bolster its trade ties** with the biggest economy in the world, the United States. In return, China is expecting the US to **lift its stringent restrictions** on Chinese products.

—————&<>&—————

The huge trade deficit the United States has **run up** against China has

297

triggered disputes between the two major trade partners. Chinese economists say there is an easy way to **narrow this trade imbalance**: Ease the export restrictions.

A leading Chinese economist said China is sincere about **narrowing the trade gap** and wants to buy more from the United States. He says the latest 6-billion-dollar deals show China's good faith.

He said China is willing to increase imports from the United States, but US restrictions on certain high-tech products have prevented a freer **trade flow** and consequently, added to its own trade deficit.

Director of Chinese Association for American Studies said," The United States is a leader in **high-tech products**. But it applies a variety of export restrictions on them, and that harms Sino-US trade. Rapid economic development has created **a big demand** in China. For instance, **mega-scale nuclear power stations** and super computers. Each of these would cost billions of US dollars. Such US exports would have quickly **eased** its trade deficit."

Since the two countries **forged ties**, China-US trade has grown 40 times and China has become the United States' fastest growing overseas market. In the first eight months of this year, US exports to China grew by over 20 percent to 16.8 billion dollars. And over the past 13 years, such exports have created nearly 400,000 jobs in America.

Experts say easing restrictions would bring more profits for US businesses. Export restrictions **harm** American competitiveness on the Chinese market and works against the interests of US enterprises.

———————⋖⋗⋗———————

China's Vice Premier says that she hopes the first economic forum involving China and seven Portuguese-speaking countries will serve as **a trade" booster "**for bilateral cooperation. The forum is being held in Macao.

At a meeting with the **ministerial-level** officials who headed delegations of the Portuguese-speaking countries, the Vice Premier expressed the hope that the **participating countries** would agree upon a cooperative mechanism at the forum to **facilitate bilateral trade**. They are Angola, Brazil, Cape Verde, Guinea Bissau, Mozambique, Portugal and East Timor. Figures issued by the Ministry of Commerce show that, in the first half of this year, China imported 3.5 billion US dollars worth of goods from Portuguese-speaking countries.

———— ⁂ ————

Indonesian President said on Sunday that **the staging of** a Southeast Asian leaders' summit on the **bomb-scarred** Indonesian island of Bali was intended to demonstrate that terrorism would fail.

Her defiant/challenging speech was delivered to business leaders gathered in Bali for this week's summit of ASEAN leaders and representatives of China, Japan and South Korea.

In her speech, the president said that the selection of Bali as **the venue** for this meeting as well as for the ASEAN summit is **deliberately intended** to prove that the country is able to **maintain the rhythm of life** — including the business sector.

We would like to demonstrate that however profound the sorrow that befell us some time ago due to this **inhumane terror act**, it should not **deter** us from moving forward.

A draft of the final declaration to be issued after the summit **underscored the thrust** of preparatory talks — where **accelerating** economic integration has dominated and the issue of combating terror has hardly been raised.

Myanmar's **detention** of democracy advocate was not mentioned, but concerns among ASEAN members were likely in a final statement.

ASEAN has seemed eager to **shuffle the issue of freedom** for Suu Kyi under the carpet at this summit. Myanmar's recent decision to allow her to return home under house arrest from detention following surgery has been **seized upon** by several ASEAN members as a sign of some progress, but many international observers disagree.

———— ⁂ ————

A research academy dedicated to studies regarding the China-ASEAN

Free Trade Zone was **inaugurated** Thursday in Beijing. Former Thai Deputy Prime Minister attended the ceremony.

The Minister, who is also President of the Thai-Chinese Friendship Association, said in his speech that sincere cooperation between the two countries will bring **tangible benefits** to the two peoples. He cited the **zero tariff** for fruits in the Mekong River area starting from Oct.1, saying this is only the beginning.

The China-ASEAN Free Trade Zone Academy has two branches, one in Beijing, the other in Bangkok. The institution will play an active role in developing human resources and promoting international trade.

The head of China's largest trade promotion organization says China will send a high-level delegation to the US. They will explore ways for China to increase exports to the US. He made the remarks during a press conference on Wednesday in Beijing, **co-hosted** by the US-China Business Council. He also called on the US to **reduce its restrictions** on exports of hi-tech products to China to reduce the trade imbalance.

The US government has **implemented many trade barriers**, including export licenses to control the export of electronics, communication and space products to China. The restrictions by the US, in place due to national security concerns, have **barred** Chinese **from** purchasing such products in the US.

Chairman of China Council for the Promotion of International Trade said, "The US government has **set many barriers** in its export of hi-tech products to China. China needs these products, and China's purchase of them will help to reduce the US' trade deficit against China."

The CCPIT chairman also demanded **an objective analysis** on the US trade deficit against China. He said many US companies have production bases in China, involving exports back to the US. He says since the US companies have **shifted labor-intensive sectors** to China, the US trade deficit with China has continued to grow.

300

The US-China Business Council is a non-profit organization, established in 1973. It focuses on promoting China-US business cooperation. In its early stages, it served as a bridge for US businesses in China **in the absence of** formal diplomatic relations between the 2 countries. A delegation from the organization is currently visiting China to celebrate its 30th anniversary.

China is looking forward to closer ties with its Southeast Asian neighbors. Chinese Premier **delivered this message** as he arrived at the Indonesian **resort island** of Bali Monday for meetings with ASEAN leaders. This is the first time the Premier attended the ASEAN summit. On arriving in Bali, he went straight into talks with leaders of Indonesia, Vietnam and Myanmar.

The talks came as China and ASEAN agreed on **a special tariff-busting program** to **kick-start** their grand plan to set up the world's largest free trade area, or FTA.

Both sides have adopted **a protocol** paving the way for the implementation from the beginning of 2004 of what is being called the "early harvest program" under the FTA.

According to an agreement last year, the FTA in goods will be established by 2010 for the six original members of ASEAN — Brunei, Indonesia, Malaysia, the Philippines, Singapore and Thailand — and 2015 for the four other members.

For now, China is looking forward to closer ties with ASEAN after its **accession to** the Treaty of Amity and Cooperation in Southeast Asia this week.

Chinese diplomats say the Chinese Premier will **present initiatives** in areas including trade, public health, education, and regional security.

The creation of a new regional **economic giant** in Asia moved a step closer today with the signing of the ASEAN Concord Two. Meeting in Bali, the leaders of the Association of Southeast Asian Nations laid the foundation for a single ASEAN community by 2020. **The accord** also enables the regional group to begin building **a shared security**, social and cultural community among **member countries**.

The ASEAN Economic Community is the centerpiece of the accord. It **envisions** a single market and production base **duplicating** the European-style economic integration of the 1970s. It is aimed at the free flow of goods, services, and investment, and less restrictions on capital flows within **the bloc** by 2020.

The creation of a free trade zone is all the more significant following the failure of recent world trade talks in Cancun, Mexico. It will strengthen ASEAN's position in increasingly competitive world and regional markets. It is also aimed at **narrowing the development gap** between rich and poor members.

Chinese analysts see a number of key areas under discussion in Bali. Three major issues are **topping the agenda** at the ongoing ASEAN Summit. First, participating countries' agreement on the establishment of ASEAN Economic Community, Security Community, and Social and Cultural Community. Second, the meeting between the leaders of India and ASEAN members. And finally, the third revision of the Southeast Asia Friendly Cooperation Agreement.

The Director of Asia Pacific Institute, CASS (the Chinese Academy of Social Sciences) said, "ASEAN is also facing **challenges**. The most prominent ones are economic development and political stability. The 1997 financial crisis changed the environment for the development of ASEAN. Some countries have not **recovered** yet. And countries like Indonesia and the Philippines are not **politically stable**. Meanwhile, there is still a lot to do for ASEAN to strengthen economic cooperation and **mechanism building**."

Recent years have seen rapid development in Sino-ASEAN relations.

The economic and trade relation between the two parties **reached its peak** with the **initiation** of the Free Trade Area scheme. ASEAN is now China's 5th largest trade partner.

The fastest development of Sino-ASEAN relation was in 1998, the year after then the President Jiang Zemin's official visit. The successful **launching of the Sino-ASEAN FTA** highlights the two parties' current relations. China has signed an information and communication agreement and will **sign documents** on political cooperation at this Summit. All-round cooperation will **benefit** both sides.

As well as the Sino-ASEAN free trade zone, ASEAN is also playing an active role in discussions with Japan, the ROK, Europe, and America to set up FTAs or to push economic and trade cooperation with these developed areas.

Unit Twenty-four
Sporting Events

导　读

　　媒体在某一特定时期关注和传播的社会焦点构成"新闻丛"，如 2003 年的伊拉克战争、2004 年的战后重建、中东和平进程、2003 年的"非典"、2004 年的"禽流感"、夏季的洪水和台风等灾害、春夏高校毕业生就业等形成不同时间段的新闻丛。

　　同一新闻丛报道的主题具有一定的相关性和联系性，那么其语言风格也具有特定的相似性，尤其是在用词方面显得更加突出。同一语域的词汇反复出现，构成相关的词汇语义场。这种特征有利于语言的不断输入和强化，而学习者通过其他媒体获得的相同背景信息，也有助于学习者对语篇信息的理解和交际型输出。在不断的输入和输出过程中，内化语篇组织结构类型和语言词汇成篇知识。

　　同类新闻丛语篇、词汇和信息的不断积累，有利于学习者英文写作水平的提高。因为学习者不仅可以积累大量的现实信息资料，而且可以联系性地习得丰富的语言词汇及表达式。

　　本单元选取了有关体育方面的新闻语篇，包括登山、篮球、乒乓球、排球及大型运动项目的组织和准备等新闻。通过阅读可以掌握运动语篇的结构，以及对过程的语言描述，如比赛过程、得分纪录等。

Key Points

　　1. University students are awfully interested in such sport events as

NBA or CBA basketball, volleyball, badminton, tennis and etc. In this unit, you will read reports on diverse games across the world.

2. Through reading, you will be well-equipped with words and expressions frequently used in the context of games and contests.

After the China Amateur Mountain Climbing Team successfully **conquered** the world's highest mountain, Qomolangma, last year, they have now **reached the peak** of Aconcagua, the highest mountain in South America. It is the next step in the team's **dream of** climbing the highest mountains on all the seven continents.

The 6,964 meter-high Aconcagua Mountain in the Andes is the highest peak in South America. It is also the highest mountain in the southern and **western hemispheres**.

At four o'clock local time on Thursday, the leader of the Chinese Amateur Mountain Climbing Team, led the members **on the march** towards the peak. The first group arrived at **the summit** six hours later. The second group also reached the peak after **overcoming strong winds** during their **ascent**.

At the peak, the Chinese adventurers took in **the panoramic views** covering about 50 square kilometers.

So far, the Chinese Amateur Mountain Climbing Team has conquered five mountains on five continents. Now, Europe's highest mountain, Mt. Elbrus, and Mt. Carstensz in Oceania are the Chinese climbers' next **targets**.

———————————— >———— ————

Shanghai's **landmark** Shanghai Grand Stage will **undergo a multi-million yuan overhaul** in preparation for an NBA **preseason game** in October.

The **revamp**, including the installation of a 120-square-meter underground practice court, was required by NBA in order to **facilitate a game** between the Houston Rockets and the Sacramento Kings. The two basketball teams will also play an exibition game in Beijing.

Officials say they hope **the renovations** can be done without interrupting the routine schedule of the 29-year-old amphitheater, located one block from Xujiahui.

"It would be **in our best interest** to keep the scheduled events undisturbed while going through the proposed revamp," said an official with Shanghai East Asia Sports and Recreation Center Co. Ltd, which owns **the venue**.

The **stadium** is scheduled to host two pop concerts, a dance performance and a circus over the next two months. The official said plans for the renovation haven't been completed yet.

Shanghai Grand Stage, which was previously known as Shanghai Stadium, was completed in 1975. A renovation in 1999 reduced the stadium's capacity to 12,000 people from the original 18,000 seats, and **transformed** the area into a venue used mainly for pop concerts instead of **sporting events**.

The up-coming renovations will include **changes** to the ventilation system and the installation of more VIP boxes and a brand new press center. Officials wouldn't say exactly how much the **renewal** will cost, but did say the figure will probably run into the millions of yuan.

The renovations will also take into account the 2005 World Table Tennis Championships, which will be held at several venues including the Shanghai Grand Stage.

The preseason basketball game should be a huge event in the city as it will **star** Shanghai's biggest sports hero, Houston Rocket's center Yao Ming, who was the number one **draft pick** in the NBA last year.

———————————

With the construction for the 2008 Olympic venues about to **get under way**, China's State General Administration of Sport is now looking for specialists in the field to **lend their expertise**.

On Monday, a news conference was held by the Department **overseeing** construction of venues and training facilities.

306

The State General Administration of Sport is now responsible for the construction of 41 projects. Eight of these will be stadiums for the 2008 Olympic Games, and **the remainder** will be training facilities for **national sports teams**. Overall investment has reached some 458 million US dollars. The State General Administration of Sport has decided to **take in** a number of construction experts to help with the whole process of venue building.

Director of the SGAS Olympic Venue Department said, "We'll adopt different policies in our **recruitment**. Some of them will be full-time personnel, while others may work part-time in their specialized fields. We may invite these **part-time personnel** here to help when necessary. There are about 14 of them. One is the general engineer, and the others are experts in different fields, or **project managers**."

With these new measures, officials from the Administration hope to complete projects better and faster, to ensure a smooth Olympics in 2008.

China has **snatched its fourth diving gold medal** at the world swimming championships in the Spanish city of Barcelona.

China's defending diving champions and her partner **won gold medals** in the women's three-meter **springboard synchronized event** on Sunday at the 10th FINA World championships. In the men's ten-meter platform synchronized event, Chinese **favorites** won the bronze medal. And Australia's world champion won the gold medal in the men's 400-meter **freestyle**.

Australia's **world record holder** and defending champion **powered his way** to win the men's 400-meter freestyle event at the 10th FINA World championships on Sunday. With the victory, he becomes the first swimmer in the world to **win the event** during three **consecutive** world championships.

In the women's 400-meter freestyle, German Hannah Stockbauer won the gold medal. In the Women's **"4 times 100" meters freestyle relay,** the US team won a gold medal. In the Men's "4 times 100" meters freestyle relay, Russian Alexander Popov, three times an individual world champion, became **a relay gold medallist** for the first time when he led Russia to their first world "4 times 100" meters freestyle victory.

China's Fifth **National City Games** has opened in the southern province of Hunan, with **athletes** from Taiwan participating in the event for the first time. The 11-member delegation comprises athletes from Taipei and Tainan. The opening ceremony was held Saturday evening in the provincial capital of Changsha.

Players from seventy-nine cities and regions across the mainland will compete for over three hundred medals during **the nine-day event**. The City Games are held every four years to promote sports development in cities all over the country, and to **identify young talent** for the Chinese National Teams.

16 **stuntmen** (those with special and adventurous performance skills) are to **take a spectacular plunge** in Shanghai this afternoon. They'll **parachute** from the 345-meter Jinmao Tower, China's highest **skyscraper**.

The **breathtaking show** is to begin at 3:00 pm. All tickets were sold out days **in advance**. The parachutists are in good form and have **expressed confidence** after yesterday's successful **trial jump**. This afternoon, organizers will give them exclusive use of one of the tower's elevators and **a lounge on the balcony** at the top of the building. CCTV's 24-hour Chinese-language news channel and Shanghai TV will have **live coverage**.

Over 800 students from 20 universities around the world competed in **a dragon boat race** in Tianjin on Saturday.

There was **no shortage of replies** to the invitation to compete. Prestigious universities like Harvard and Princeton from the United States, and Australia's Sydney University all sent teams. Naturally, though **local hopes** were on the Chinese teams, like Beijing's **top-ranked** Tsinghua

University. Hong Kong and Macao also sent teams. After two hour of racing, Liaocheng University from Shandong and Tianjin's own Medical University **won first prize** in the 500-meter **sprint** for men's and women's teams respectively.

------⧗◆⧗------

Defending champion, China has **emerged as the winner** of the Asian Men's Basketball Championship in the Heilongjiang provincial capital of Harbin. China lived up to the expectations of home fans and **took home the title** over South Korea, **gaining a birth** in the 2004 Olympics.

NBA newcomer Yao Ming was no doubt the **main attraction**. Just three minutes into the first quarter, Yao began to **exert strong pressure** on South Koreans, securing the first six points. Li Nan also **turned in a superb performance** inside and contributed greatly to **the tally/score**. China dominated but South Korea **seized every opportunity** to fight back. China relied on its defense and strength to end the first half ahead 50:36. Yao Ming had 16 points and 9 **rebounds** while Li Nan **secured** 21 points.

South Koreans went into the second half with greater focus on **three-point shots**. Despite China's **stifling defense**, South Korea **narrowed the difference** to just seven points at one stage. China changed **tactics** but continued to **lose ground**.

Then Chinese veteran Fan Bin came through with some fast breaks and brilliant play. China **lifted its game** and maintained its advantage until the last minute.

The final **scoreline** was 106-96 to China.

------⧗◆⧗------

It was third time lucky for China's women **basketballers**, who defeated **visiting rivals**, the American WNBA Professional Star team, 79-74 in the Sino-US Women Basketball Challenge in Zhuzhou City.

Wednesday was **a slow day** for both teams. After China took the first two points, both teams started to play **defensive games** and were tied at 6-all in the sixth minute.

Witherspoon's **scoring** put the Americans into **a 25-19 lead** at the first quarter.

At the start of the second quarter China **lost their beat** in the face of the American's **tight defense** as they **extended their lead** to 36-26.

Then along came **Veteran** Miao Lijie, whose five **straight baskets** proved to be the turning point of the game as China **drew level**. The two teams ended the first half **locked in a 43-all draw**.

Both teams played aggressively in the third quarter and the scores were **pretty close** all the time. In the decisive fourth quarter, Chinese head coach Gong Luming sent four other veterans onto the court to **withstand the pressure**. China finished with a 79-74 victory over the visiting WNBA Professional Star team.

Four gold medals were **fought out** in the pool at the city games Tuesday night. **Triple** world champion Luo Xuejuan **beat** Qi Hui in the women's 100-meter **breaststroke competition**. Qi Hui, 200-meter world record holder, failed to deliver and was **forced into second place**.

Representing the best of a new generation of Chinese swimmers, the match-up between the two became **the highlight of** the stadium. Apparently exhausted by the semi-final of the women's 200-meter medley/mixture, Qi Hui was below her best last night and was **trailing her rival** right from the start. Led all the way and **bagged a gold** for her team Hangzhou with a time of 1 minute 7.42 seconds. Qi Hui had **to settle silver** with 1 minute 8.96 seconds.

Luo Xuejuan said, "During the 2001 world swimming championships, I said I was expecting gold in all major swimming events, including the 100-meter **breaststroke**. Today it's a dream that partly comes true. Bearing in mind that this is **the forth-straight contest** after the world championships in July, the **universiade** in August and national championships in September, the result is quite satisfactory."

In the women's 100 meter **backstroke** final, Zhan Shu gave the

Shenyang team its first swimming gold with 1 minute 1.56 seconds.

The golds for the men's 200-meter freestyle and 100 meter backstroke **went respectively to** Beijing Chaoyang's Zhang Lin and Hefei's Zhao Tao.

———————————

Steve Francis **scored 26 points** and Yao Ming 21 and 14 **rebounds** to lead the Houston Rockets to their fourth consecutive victory over the Phoenix Suns by 90-85 on Friday night. The Rockets are now in first place in the Midwest Division of the NBA.

In Jeff Van Gundy's first **season**, the Rockets have adopted their new coach's **defensive philosophy** that appears have worked through the first eight games. Houston leads the NBA in scoring defense and hasn't **conceded** more than 86 points in any of its six wins.

Yao Ming collected 21 points and 14 rebounds as the Rockets **rebounded** from Thursday's **sloppy loss** at Dallas.

Francis led the Rockets with 26 points including two baskets from behind **the three-point arc**.

Phoenix **rallied** to take a 32-31 lead early in the second quarter. With eight points from Stoudamire in the rest of the quarter, Phoenix led by as many as eight.

Stoudamire finished with 18 points and a **season-high** five blocks.

Stephon Marbury **netted a season-high 33 points** for the Suns, who finished one game in front of the Rockets for the Western Conference's **final playoff berth** last season.

A 10-2 run by Houston made it a one-point game, 54-53 with 5 minutes to play in the third period. The Rockets then completed a 7-0 run with 1 minute 11 to play in their first lead of the second half, 62-60.

But Joe Johnson's **3-pointer** gave the Suns a 65-64 lead after three quarters.

Bostjan Nachbar had **five quick points** to lift the Rockets into **a 69-69 tie** in the fourth, and a 6-0 run gave Houston a lead it would not **relinquish/**

give up.

Stephon Marbury led the Suns with 33 points, including **a jumper** with 2 minutes 40 to play to keep Phoenix within two points. But Jim Jackson's three pointer gave the Rockets an 84-75 lead. Houston went on to **close out** the Suns 90-85.

Before 1995, basketball careers were **fostered** mainly through the support of state. Now, **professional teams** are built at both state and provincial levels, raising a great number of players. Although China's competitive **sports leagues** were developing dramatically, financial support from the State could no longer be sustained, **hindering** any further improvement. Consequently, basketball became **professionalized** since 1995.

In 1995, the Chinese Basketball Association (CBA) introduced the "Home and Away" system into the league. This significantly **evoked** both basketball fans' **and media's enthusiasm**. After 8 year's of **cultivation**, the league has significantly improved with a considerable number of high-level players trained, and greatly **enhanced marketing capabilities**.

Vice President of China Basketball Management Center said, "Generally speaking, the purpose of our reform is to **discard** those traditional ways of management which **contradict** the rules of market economy. We are trying to do things as scientifically as possible. Actually, the goal is to take up more **market shares**. We'd like to attract a larger audience to basketball, and were doing so through marketing. As a result, we are increasing the basketball league's economic and social value, and we can finally find enough funds to **operate our league**."

China is **accelerating the pace of reform** in its professional sports. We introduced the idea of a free market to Chinese basketball, and we hope to develop Chinese basketball in a way that **coincides with** what other countries are doing. We want the game to be more exciting, and we want to get more attention. If we can improve our league, our national team can get much better players.

Coach of Shanghai Dongfang said, "Because of the changing system, we get more attention from our government leaders. In just 6 years, our team has **become ranked** within the top 20."

In terms of flexibility, the Shanghai Team benefits greatly from **trading players** (domestic and international), and team management. **Coached** by Li Qiuping, it took the Shanghai Dongfang six years to go from being a Division B team becoming a Division A team. Moreover, Shanghai won the CBA Finals in the 2001-2002 season. It was then that Yao Ming finished his **domestic career** and joined the NBA.

Today the CBA's marketing promises a brighter future for Chinese basketball. The NBA has already **recruited** Yao Ming and two other Chinese basketball players. Yao Ming joined the NBA through an internationally recognized procedure which, in turn, **initiated** a new stage of China-US exchange in sports.

The CBA is dedicated to producing the best basketball league in Asia. As a result of three well-known CBA centers Wang Zhizhi, Mengke Bateer and Yao Ming joining the NBA consecutively, the CBA began to **shift its focus**, adopting some of the rules of the NBA. For example in a four-quarter game, "**full-court press**"— a defensive strategy must be applied in at least one quarter. Additionally, there's **a restriction** for using more than 5 international players per regular season games and 4 for **playoffs**/finals. There are other rules are borrowed from the NBA.

The current sports clubs in China are all **cooperated** between local sports committees and various businesses. With these clubs, The Chinese Basketball Association has laid down an entire system of rules and regulations. With this new system, clubs are able to work with foreign investors, bring foreign players and coaches, and freely trade players with other clubs. The objective is to further professionalize the Chinese basketball league, and to finally **convert** the state-owned teams **into** self-managed basketball enterprises.

313

On day 9 of the 22nd Universiade in Seoul, China won another eight of the 39 gold medals **up for grabs** on Saturday. It still **tops** the Universiade medal **tally** with 36 gold medals.

Saturday was the last day for **track and field events**. Twelve gold medals were up for grabs. One went to Chinese contestants for their work in the women's **relay**. They finished first, **clocking in** at 44.9 seconds. Chinese **triple jumper** took a gold medal with a leap of 16.90 meters, the best in the men's event. In the women's 400-meter **hurdles final**, Chinese competitor finished second, with a time of 56 minutes and 10 seconds.

In the women's volleyball final, China's mainland Volleyball Team beat China's Taipei team 3 to Zero, winning another gold. And China's Women's Basketball team defeated their Italian **rivals**, 81 to 78, to **clinch the gold** in the **hoops competition**. In the women's football event, China's mainland squad beat China's Taipei team 2 to Zero.

In the gymnastics event held on Saturday afternoon, Chinese competitor **captured** the gold medal in **the floor exercise event**. His teammate finished first in finals of **the flying rings** event. Another Chinese competitor **topped the field** in the pommel horse finals, winning gold. Another two Chinese athletes were ranked in first and second place in the **high-low bars** competition.

The closing ceremony of the 22nd Universiade will be held on Sunday.

After a day's break, the 2003 Women's Volleyball World Cup resumed action in Japan on Saturday. **Taking it to the net** against South Korea, China took a straight **3-nil victory**, its sixth in the **tournament**.

The South Korean women have always been **tough opponents**. Over the past decades, they have pulled off some surprising performances in games against China. On Saturday afternoon, China fielded its two powerful **spikers** as starters. With superiority in both height and weight, the duo posed a formidable challenge to their South Korean rivals. **Smashing serves**

314

gained China six points in the first **set**.

The 16-5 lead gave the Chinese women a comfortable cushion for the second half of the first set. Zhou Suhong, Liu Yanan and Zhao Ruirui went on the offensive. They caught the South Koreans off balance and **foiled** their every attempt at defense. China held to its initiative and **wrapped up the first set**, 25-10.

South Korea gave as good as they got. In the second set, they dealt out several powerful serves and forced some openings in China's defense. Capitalizing on their opportunities, they **drew even with** China four times. But the Chinese **kept their cool**. They stuck to their plan and finally took the set 25-19. After a 25-14 third set, China **concluded the game 3-nil**, its sixth consecutive victory in the tournament. On Sunday afternoon, China will take on Argentina.

China has had its 10th **straight win** at the 2003 women's volleyball World Cup. So far China is the only **unbeaten squad** in the 12-team, **single round-robin** tournament, which concludes on Saturday.

The Chinese women moved closer on Friday to their first World Cup title in 17 years with a 26-24, 25-18, and 25-20 victory. With only one match remaining, China has virtually **secured a finish** in the top three, as well as a spot in the Athens Olympics in 2004.

Both China and Italy got off to strong starts in the first set. Italy overcame a 20-17 deficit to **tie the match** at 24-24. After China **smashed a ball home** to take a 25-24 advantage, Italy **smashed a ball out**, surrendering the opener.

The second set went more smoothly for China. The Chinese athletes took a 14-9 lead, powered by **quality attacks and a tough defense**, going on to take the set.

The Italians **put up a struggle**, taking a 19-17 lead in the third set, but the China squad scored eight of the last nine points to **clinch the victory**.

Now China is **leading the standings** with 20 points. Their closest rival is the Brazil squad, with nine wins and one loss. China will next play Japan on Saturday in their final match. And all eyes in China will be following the action.

————— ⬥⬥⬥ —————

China has beaten host Japan to take the title of the women's volleyball world cup with 11 wins and no losses. This was China's first major **world title** since they won the world championship gold medal in 1986 in Czechoslovakia.

At the end of the second set, the match might not be over, but China has already won the championship for the first time in 17 years. Brazil's 3:1 win over Italy meant that China only needed to **win two sets** in their match against Japan. A re-run of what happened 22 years ago, when China **took the title** in their last match against Japan in 1981.

Cheered on by 10,000 chanting and cheering **home fans**, the Japanese fought hard against the powerful Chinese team. However, they were unable to stop China's massive attacks, especially 1.97-meter Zhao Ruirui's **high spikes**. China proved to be just too strong for the host team, and won the first set 25-18. The second set was no different. China led the game all through to 24-18, and **championship point**. China's Wang Lina wasted no time, **grabbing the title** with a hard-driven spike. With the championship over, so was the rest of the match that produced no more **suspense**. The third set ended 25-13 to China.

Brazil took the silver medal with 10 wins against one loss, followed by the United States with 8 wins and 3 losses. The top three teams all now qualify for the 2004 Athens Olympic Games.

316

参 考 文 献

[1] 桂诗春. 试验心理语言学纲要. 长沙：湖南教育出版社，1997.

[2] 桂诗春. 新编心理语言学. 上海：上海外语教育出版社，2000.

[3] 胡壮麟. 认知隐喻学. 北京：北京大学出版社，2004.

[4] 黄国文. 语篇分析概要. 长沙：湖南教育出版社，1987.

[5] 梁宁建. 当代认知心理学. 上海：上海教育出版社，2004.

[6] 钱敏汝. 篇章语用学. 上海：上海外语教育出版社，2003.

[7] 王初明. 应用心理语言学. 长沙：湖南教育出版社，1991.

[8] 赵艳芳. 认知语言学. 上海：上海外语教育出版社，2001.

[9] David W. Carroll. *Psychology of Language*. Foreign Language Teaching and Research Press, 2000.

[10] F. Ungerer and H. J. Schmid. *An Introduction to Cognitive Linguistics*. Foreign Language Teaching and Research Press, 2001.

[11] Jean Aitchison. *The Articulate Mammal: An Introduction to Psycholinguistics*. Foreign Language Teaching and Research Press, 2000.

[12] Levison. *Pragmatics*. Foreign Language Teaching and Research Press, 2000.

[13] Michael Garman. *Psycholinguistics*. Cambridge University Press，2002.

[14] Sperber and Wilson. *Relevance: Communication and Cognition*. Foreign Language Teaching and Research Press, 2000.